APHRODITE IX

REBIRTH
VOLUME TWO

APHRODITE IX CREATED BY:
DAVID FINCH &
DAVID WOHL

TOP COW
PRODUCTIONS, INC.®

APHRODITE IX

REBIRTH VOLUME TWO

writer: MATT HAWKINS
artist: STJEPAN SEJIC
letterer: TROY PETERI

Cover art for this edition by: STJEPAN SEJIC
For San Diego Comic Con edition cover art by: MARC SILVESTRI, SUNNY GHO
& STJEPAN SEJIC
Edited by: BETSY GONIA
Book Design and Layout by: ADDISON DUKE

COMIC SHOP LOCATOR SERVICE

To find the comic
shop nearest you,
call:
1-888-COMICBOOK

888-266-4226
888-COMIC-BOOK

Want more info? Check out:
www.topcow.com
for news & exclusive
Top Cow merchandise!

For Top Cow Productions, Inc.:
Marc Silvestri - CEO
Matt Hawkins - President & COO
Betsy Gonia - Editor
Bryan Hill - Story Editor
Elena Salcedo - Operations Manager
Ryan Cady - Editorial Assistant
Vincent Valentine - Production Assistant

IMAGE COMICS, INC.
Robert Kirkman – Chief Operating Officer
Erik Larsen – Chief Financial Officer
Todd McFarlane – President
Marc Silvestri – Chief Executive Officer
Jim Valentino – Vice-President

Eric Stephenson – Publisher
Corey Murphy – Director of Sales
Jeff Boison – Director of Publishing Planning & Book Trade Sales
Jeremy Sullivan – Director of Digital Sales
Kat Salazar – Director of PR & Marketing
Emily Miller – Director of Operations
Branwyn Bigglestone – Senior Accounts Manager
Sarah Mello – Accounts Manager
Drew Gill – Art Director
Jonathan Chan – Production Manager
Meredith Wallace – Print Manager
Briah Skelly – Publicity Assistant
Randy Okamura – Marketing Production Designer
David Brothers – Branding Manager
Ally Power – Content Manager
Addison Duke – Production Artist
Vincent Kukua – Production Artist
Sasha Head – Production Artist
Tricia Ramos – Production Artist
Jeff Stang – Direct Market Sales Representative
Emilio Bautista – Digital Sales Associate
Chloe Ramos-Peterson – Administrative Assistant
IMAGECOMICS.COM

Top Cow Productions, Inc.

Aphrodite IX: Rebirth Volume 2 (New Edition).
January 2016. First printing. ISBN: 978-1-63215-760-7

The Aphrodite Protocol was initiated in an attempt to save humanity from a predicted extinction level event.

Its mission was to engineer and evolve humans into new species that could survive via technological singularity or genetic enhancement to repopulate the Earth.

Aphrodite IX was prematurely activated and enmeshed in a conflict between two of these new species.

In the East, various tribes of genetically enhanced humans collectively called the GEN live in a city called GENESIS under a theocratic monarchy.

In the West, cybernetically enhanced humans reside in the city of SPEROS in a totalitarian central party controlled state.

Initially taken in by the GEN, Aphrodite IX has now been exiled to the DESOLATE ZONE in the North.

Her real adventure is about to begin.

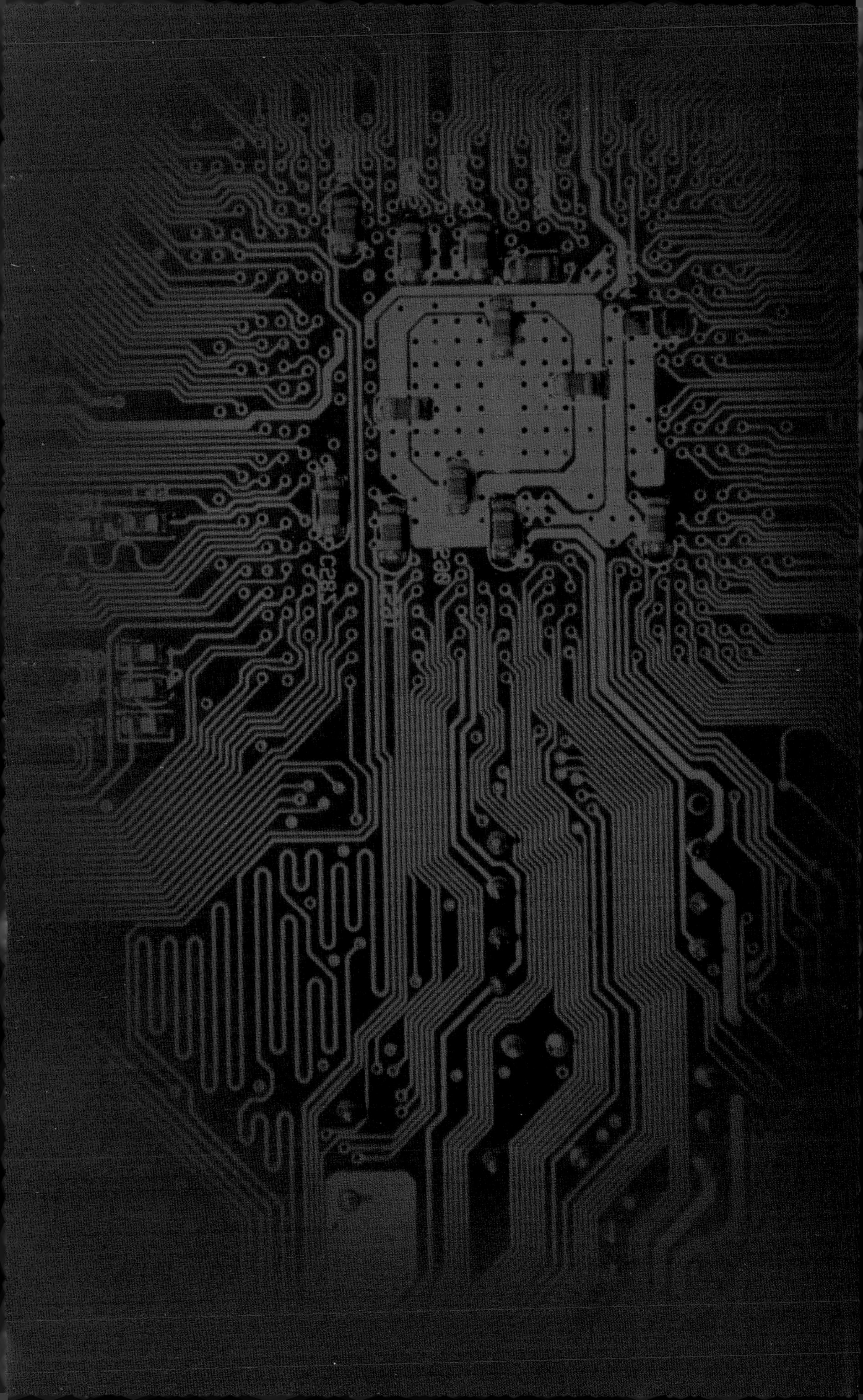

CHAPTER ONE

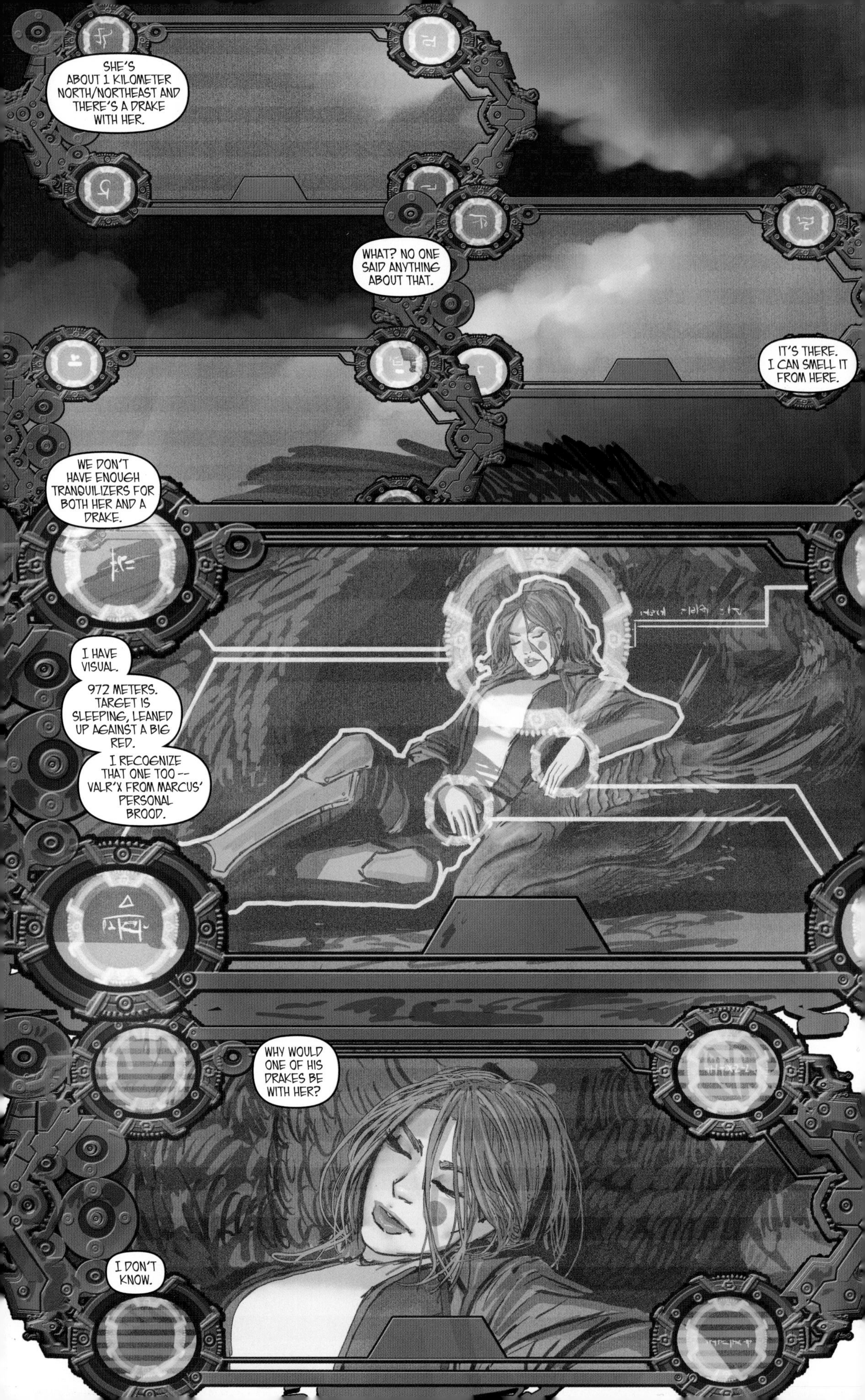
SHE'S ABOUT 1 KILOMETER NORTH/NORTHEAST AND THERE'S A DRAKE WITH HER.
WHAT? NO ONE SAID ANYTHING ABOUT THAT.
IT'S THERE. I CAN SMELL IT FROM HERE.
WE DON'T HAVE ENOUGH TRANQUILIZERS FOR BOTH HER AND A DRAKE.
I HAVE VISUAL.
972 METERS. TARGET IS SLEEPING, LEANED UP AGAINST A BIG RED.
I RECOGNIZE THAT ONE TOO -- VALR'X FROM MARCUS' PERSONAL BROOD.
WHY WOULD ONE OF HIS DRAKES BE WITH HER?
I DON'T KNOW.

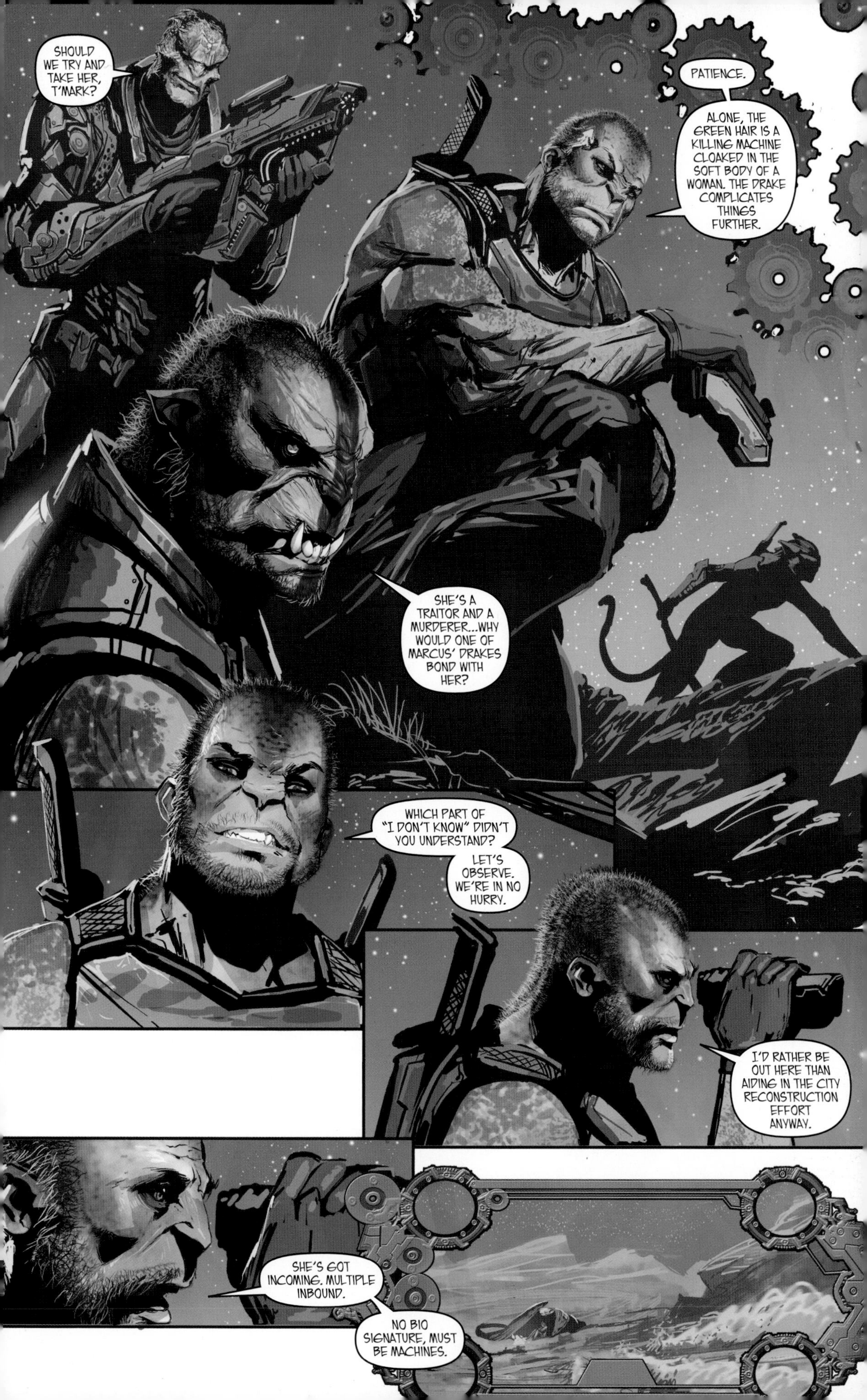
SHOULD WE TRY AND TAKE HER, T'MARK?
PATIENCE.
ALONE, THE GREEN HAIR IS A KILLING MACHINE CLOAKED IN THE SOFT BODY OF A WOMAN. THE DRAKE COMPLICATES THINGS FURTHER.
SHE'S A TRAITOR AND A MURDERER...WHY WOULD ONE OF MARCUS' DRAKES BOND WITH HER?
WHICH PART OF "I DON'T KNOW" DIDN'T YOU UNDERSTAND?
LET'S OBSERVE. WE'RE IN NO HURRY.
I'D RATHER BE OUT HERE THAN AIDING IN THE CITY RECONSTRUCTION EFFORT ANYWAY.
SHE'S GOT INCOMING. MULTIPLE INBOUND.
NO BIO SIGNATURE, MUST BE MACHINES.

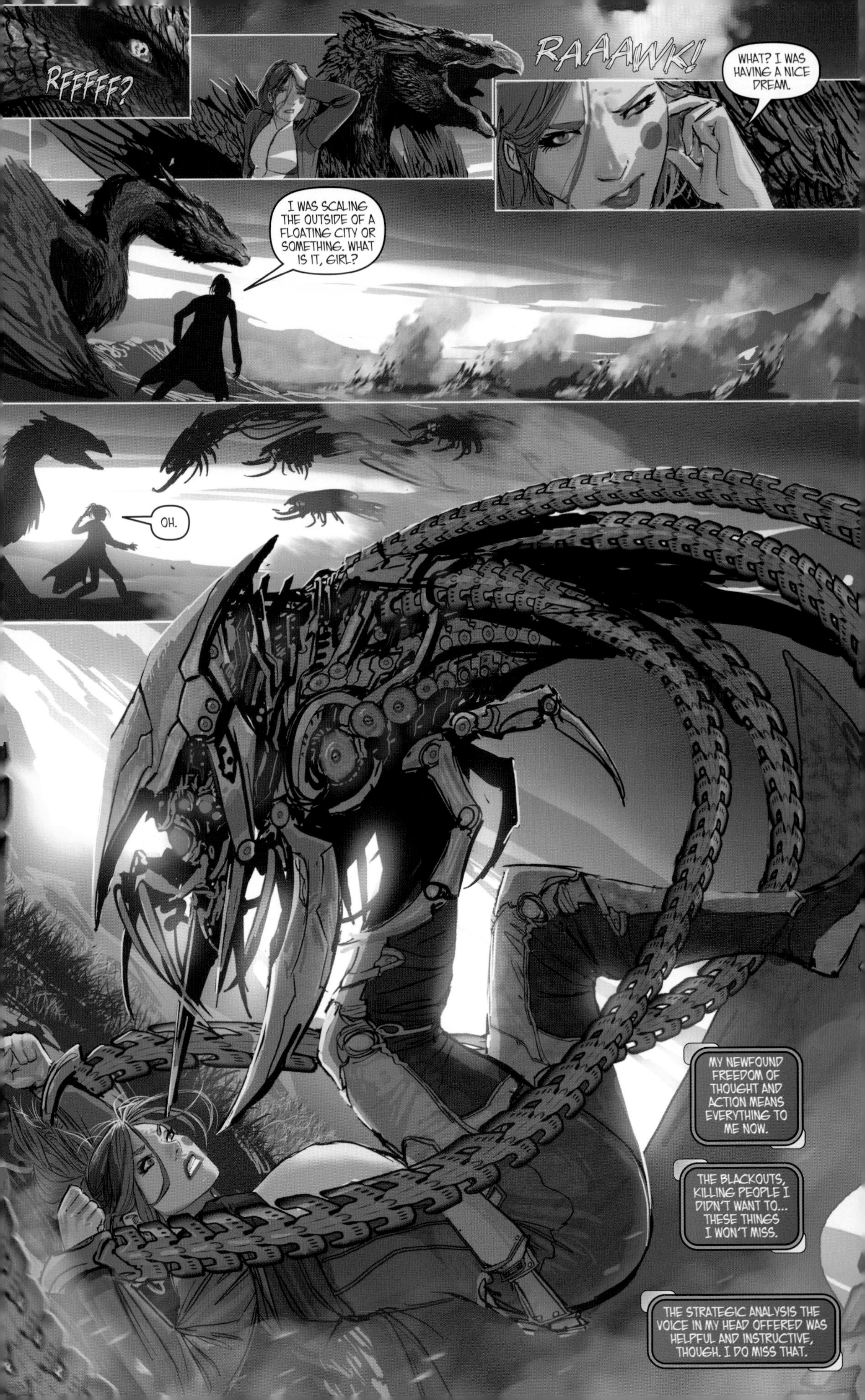
RFFFFF?
RAAAWK!
WHAT? I WAS HAVING A NICE DREAM.
I WAS SCALING THE OUTSIDE OF A FLOATING CITY OR SOMETHING. WHAT IS IT, GIRL?
OH.
MY NEWFOUND FREEDOM OF THOUGHT AND ACTION MEANS EVERYTHING TO ME NOW.
THE BLACKOUTS, KILLING PEOPLE I DIDN'T WANT TO... THESE THINGS I WON'T MISS.
THE STRATEGIC ANALYSIS THE VOICE IN MY HEAD OFFERED WAS HELPFUL AND INSTRUCTIVE, THOUGH. I DO MISS THAT.

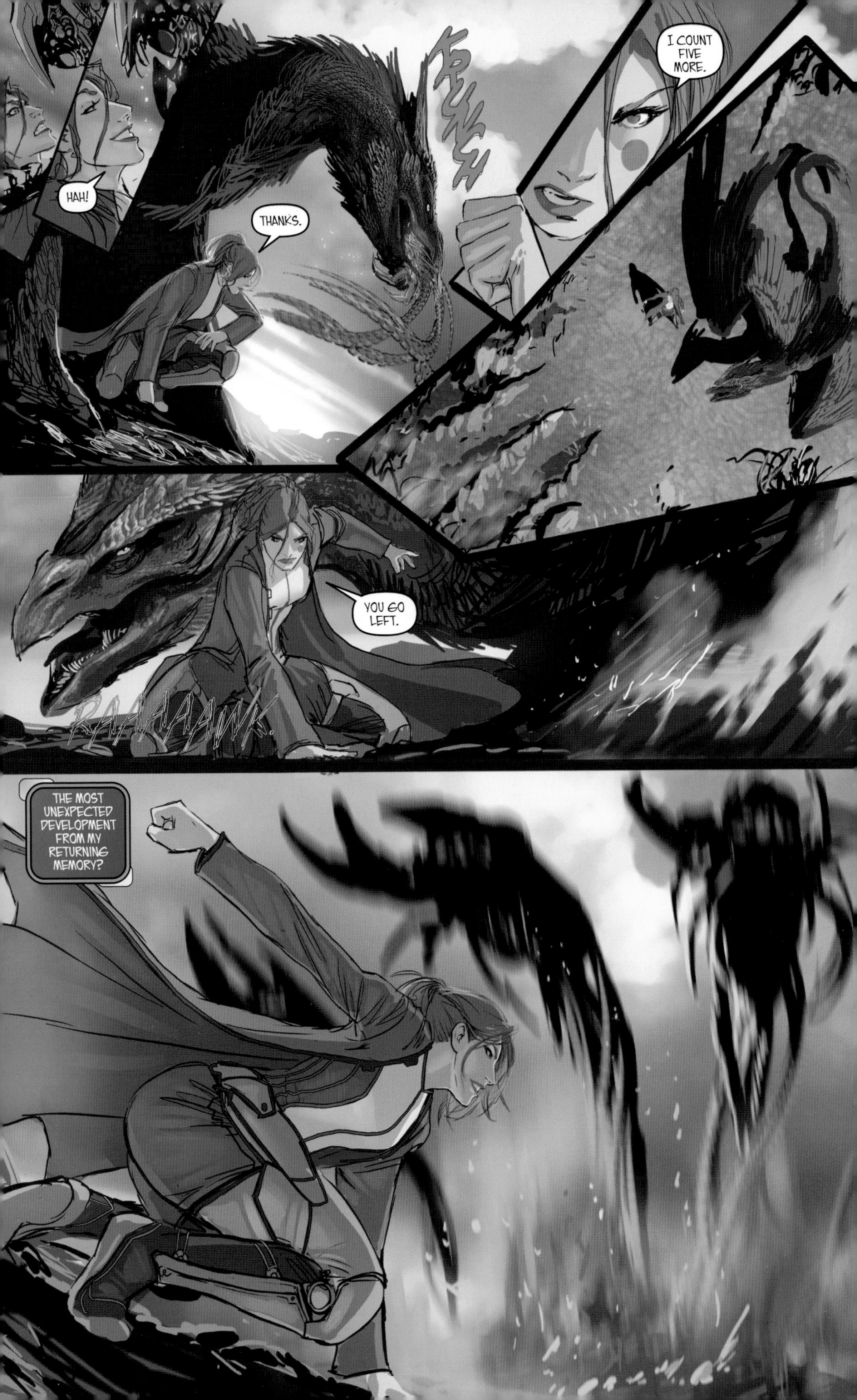
HAH!
THANKS.
CRUNCH
I COUNT FIVE MORE.
YOU GO LEFT.
RAAAAAAWK.
THE MOST UNEXPECTED DEVELOPMENT FROM MY RETURNING MEMORY?

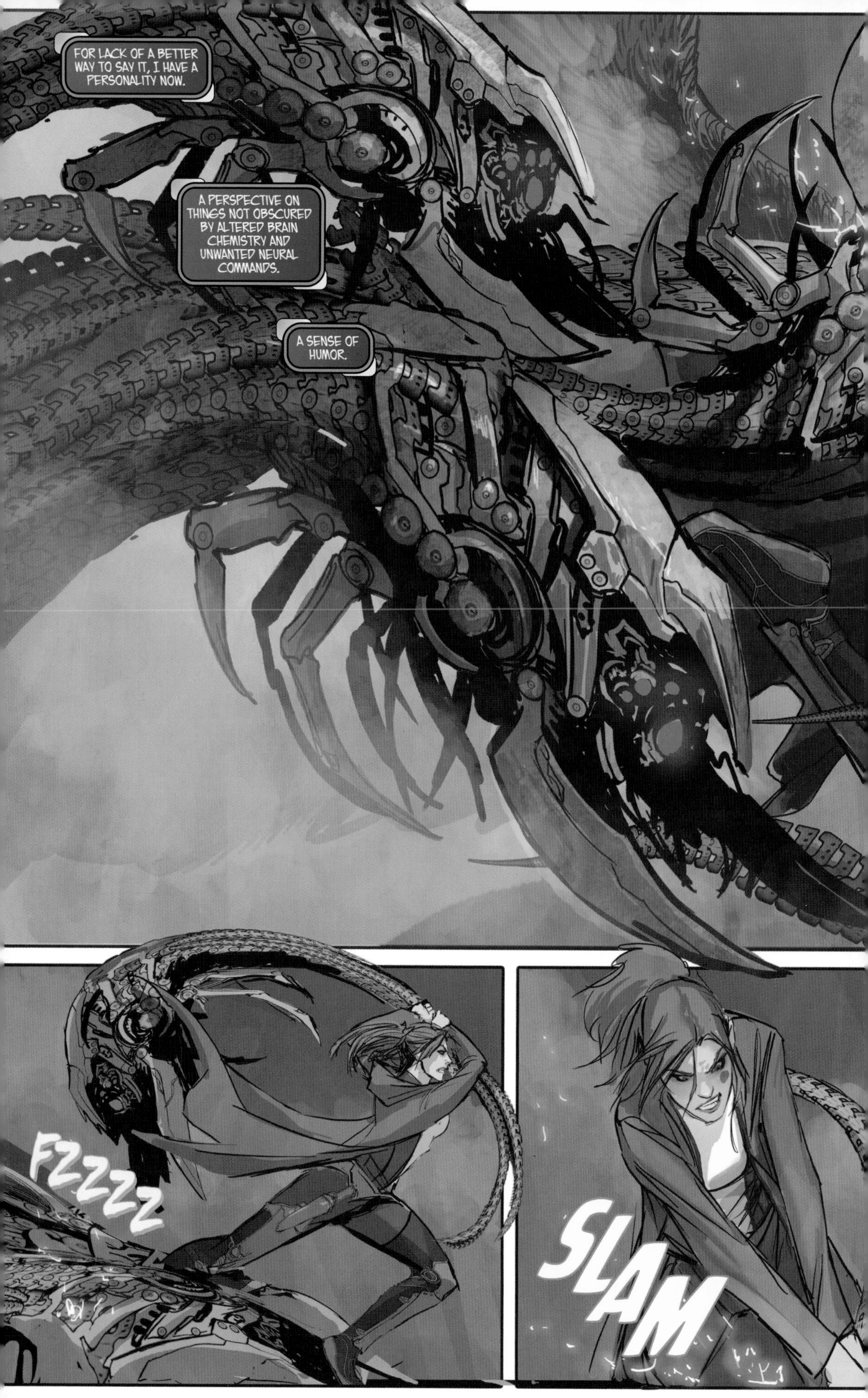
FOR LACK OF A BETTER WAY TO SAY IT, I HAVE A PERSONALITY NOW.
A PERSPECTIVE ON THINGS NOT OBSCURED BY ALTERED BRAIN CHEMISTRY AND UNWANTED NEURAL COMMANDS.
A SENSE OF HUMOR.
FZZZZ
SLAM

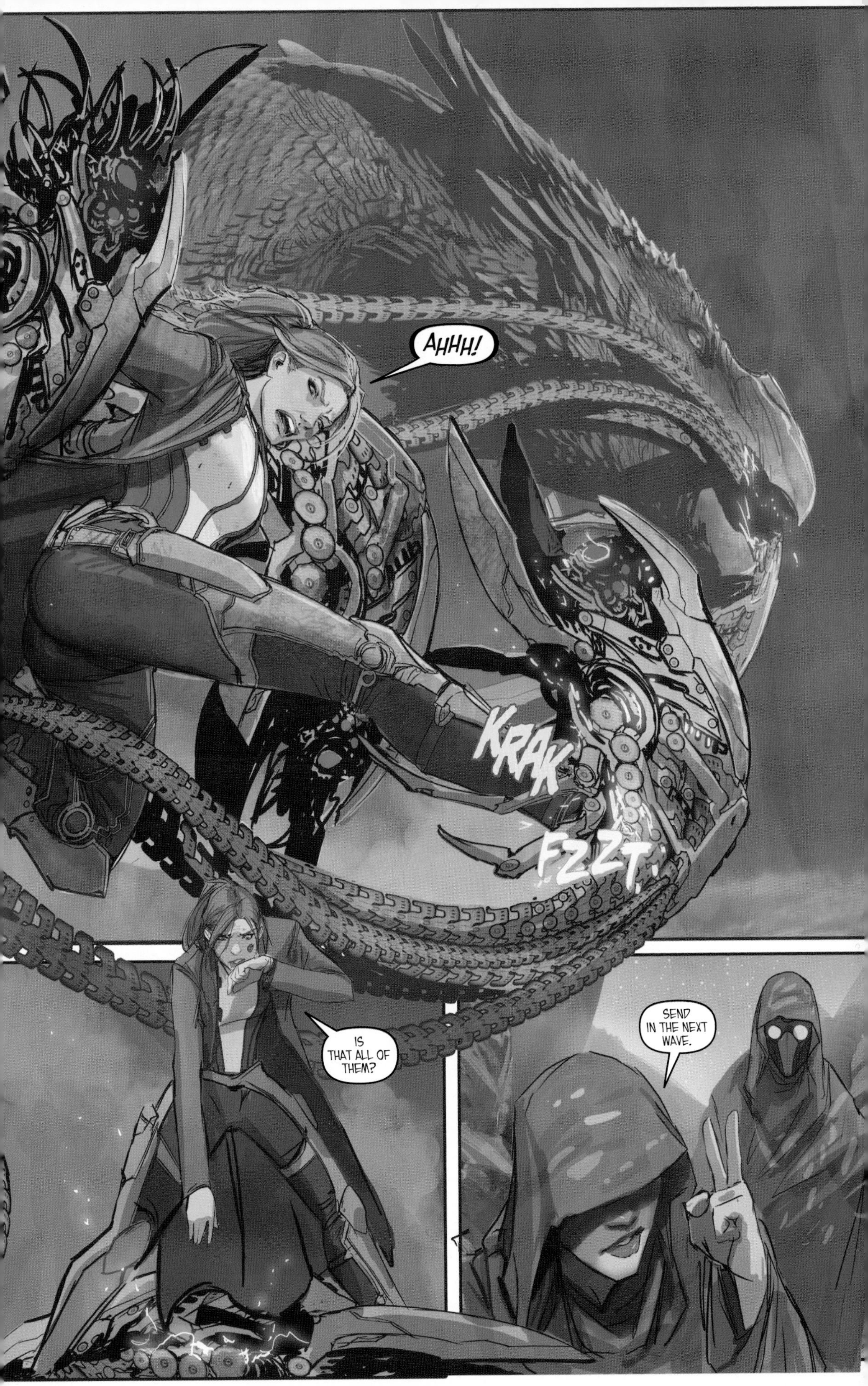
AHHH!
KRAK
FZZT
IS THAT ALL OF THEM?
SEND IN THE NEXT WAVE.

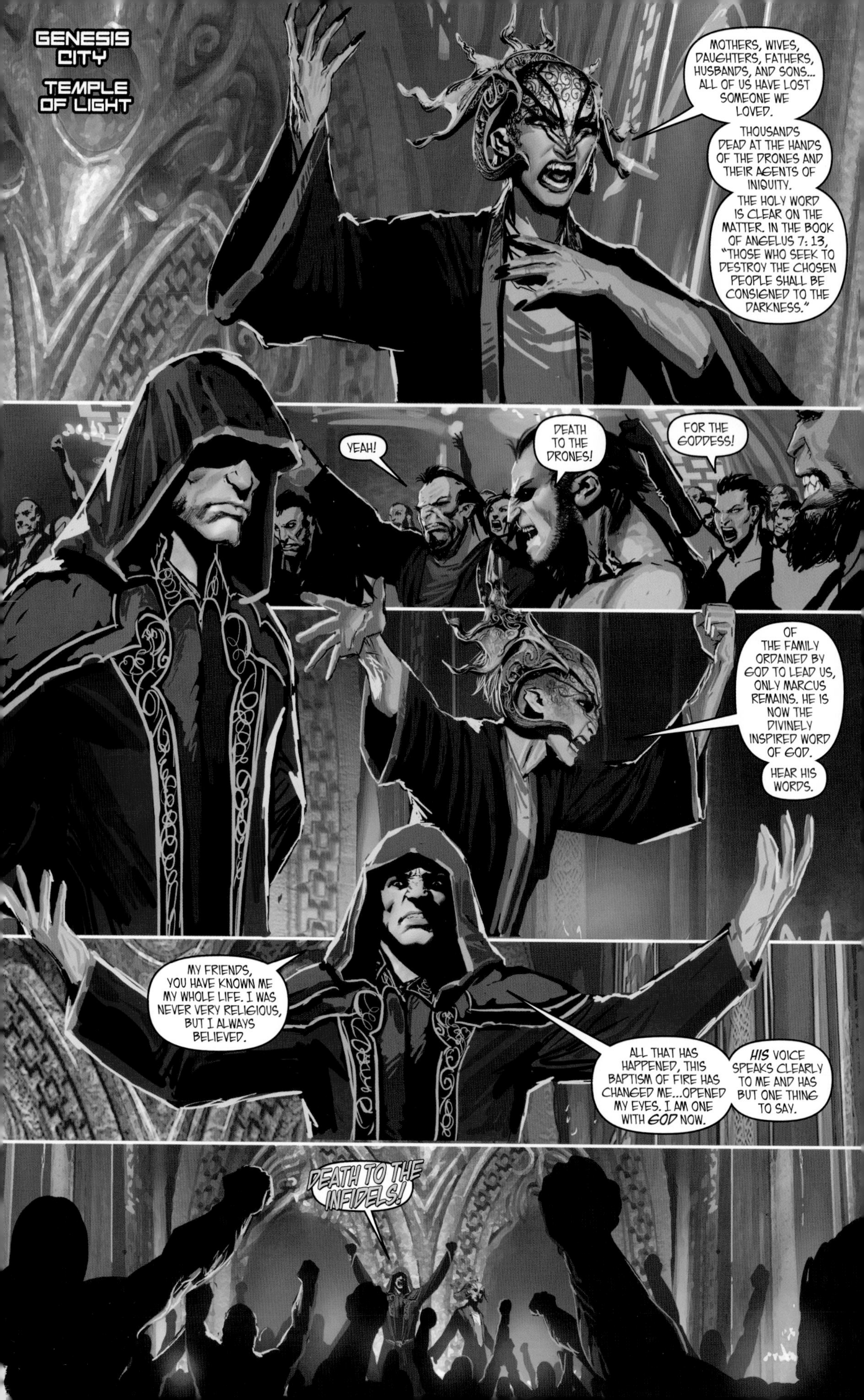
GENESIS CITY
TEMPLE OF LIGHT
MOTHERS, WIVES, DAUGHTERS, FATHERS, HUSBANDS, AND SONS... ALL OF US HAVE LOST SOMEONE WE LOVED.
THOUSANDS DEAD AT THE HANDS OF THE DRONES AND THEIR AGENTS OF INIQUITY.
THE HOLY WORD IS CLEAR ON THE MATTER. IN THE BOOK OF ANGELUS 7: 13, "THOSE WHO SEEK TO DESTROY THE CHOSEN PEOPLE SHALL BE CONSIGNED TO THE DARKNESS."
YEAH!
DEATH TO THE DRONES!
FOR THE GODDESS!
OF THE FAMILY ORDAINED BY GOD TO LEAD US, ONLY MARCUS REMAINS. HE IS NOW THE DIVINELY INSPIRED WORD OF GOD.
HEAR HIS WORDS.
MY FRIENDS, YOU HAVE KNOWN ME MY WHOLE LIFE. I WAS NEVER VERY RELIGIOUS, BUT I ALWAYS BELIEVED.
ALL THAT HAS HAPPENED, THIS BAPTISM OF FIRE HAS CHANGED ME...OPENED MY EYES. I AM ONE WITH GOD NOW.
HIS VOICE SPEAKS CLEARLY TO ME AND HAS BUT ONE THING TO SAY.
DEATH TO THE INFIDELS!

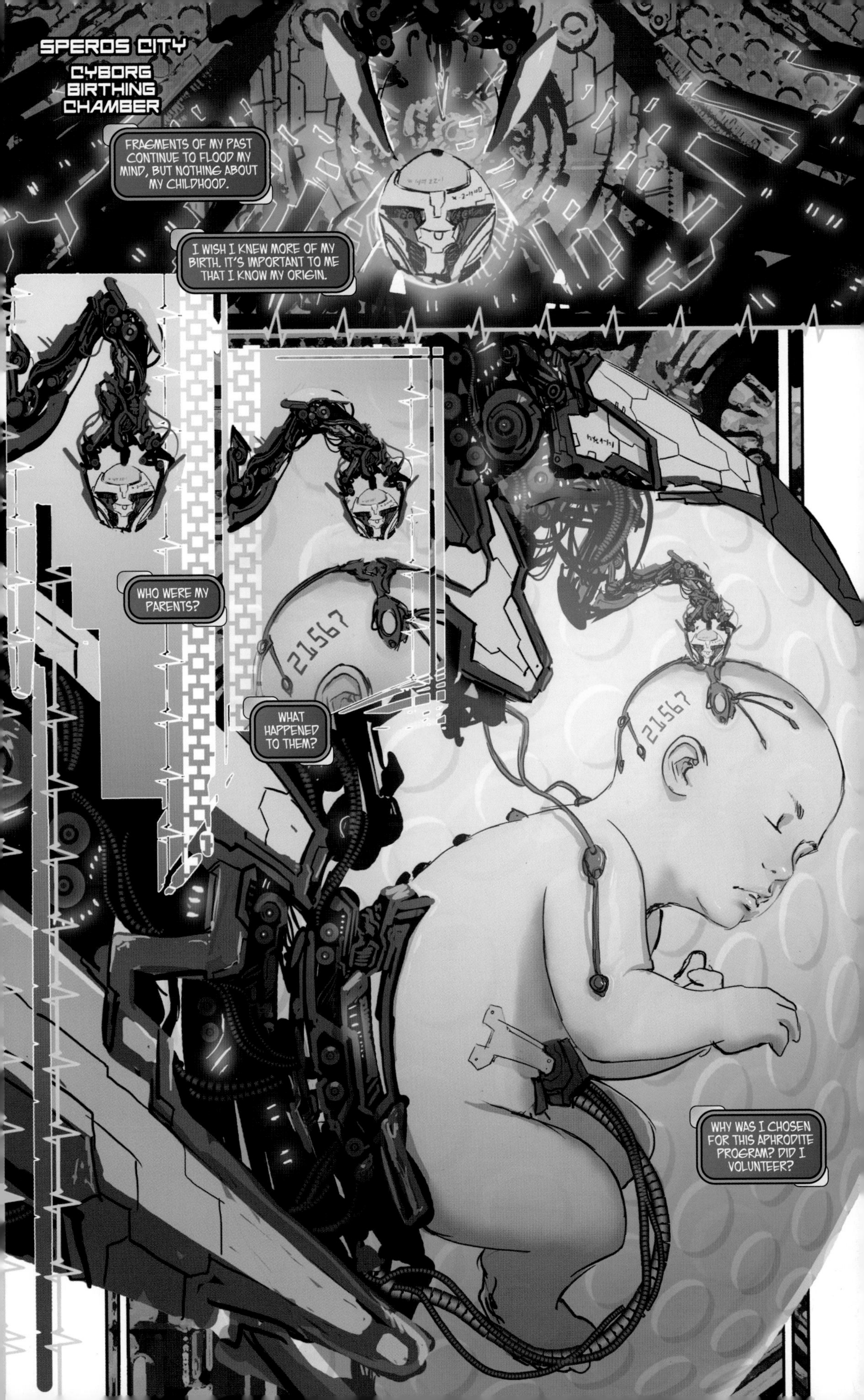
SPEROS CITY
CYBORG BIRTHING CHAMBER
FRAGMENTS OF MY PAST CONTINUE TO FLOOD MY MIND, BUT NOTHING ABOUT MY CHILDHOOD.
I WISH I KNEW MORE OF MY BIRTH. IT'S IMPORTANT TO ME THAT I KNOW MY ORIGIN.
WHO WERE MY PARENTS?
WHAT HAPPENED TO THEM?
21567
21567
WHY WAS I CHOSEN FOR THIS APHRODITE PROGRAM? DID I VOLUNTEER?

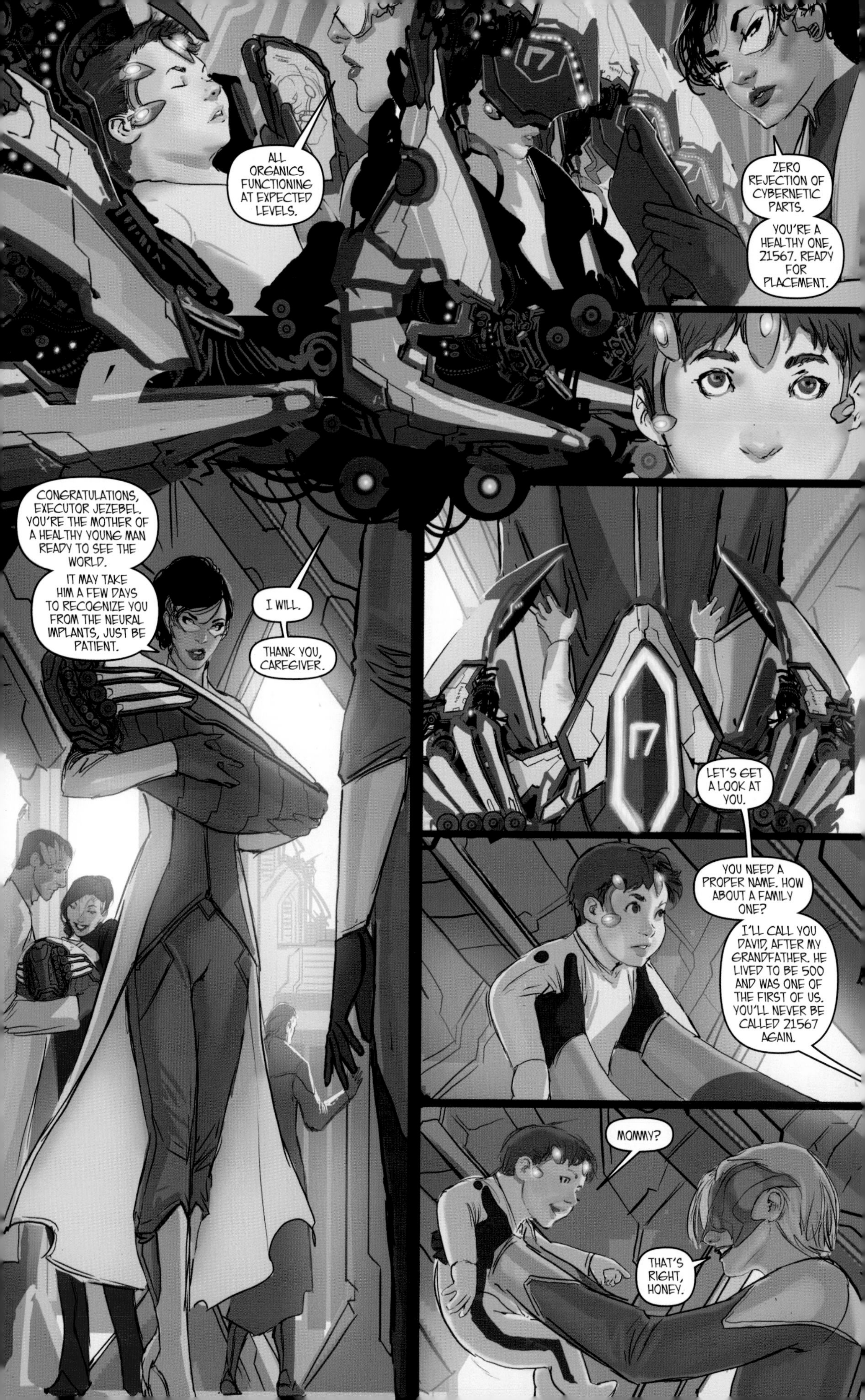
ALL ORGANICS FUNCTIONING AT EXPECTED LEVELS.
ZERO REJECTION OF CYBERNETIC PARTS.
YOU'RE A HEALTHY ONE, 21567. READY FOR PLACEMENT.
CONGRATULATIONS, EXECUTOR JEZEBEL. YOU'RE THE MOTHER OF A HEALTHY YOUNG MAN READY TO SEE THE WORLD.
IT MAY TAKE HIM A FEW DAYS TO RECOGNIZE YOU FROM THE NEURAL IMPLANTS, JUST BE PATIENT.
I WILL.
THANK YOU, CAREGIVER.
LET'S GET A LOOK AT YOU.
YOU NEED A PROPER NAME. HOW ABOUT A FAMILY ONE?
I'LL CALL YOU DAVID, AFTER MY GRANDFATHER. HE LIVED TO BE 500 AND WAS ONE OF THE FIRST OF US. YOU'LL NEVER BE CALLED 21567 AGAIN.
MOMMY?
THAT'S RIGHT, HONEY.

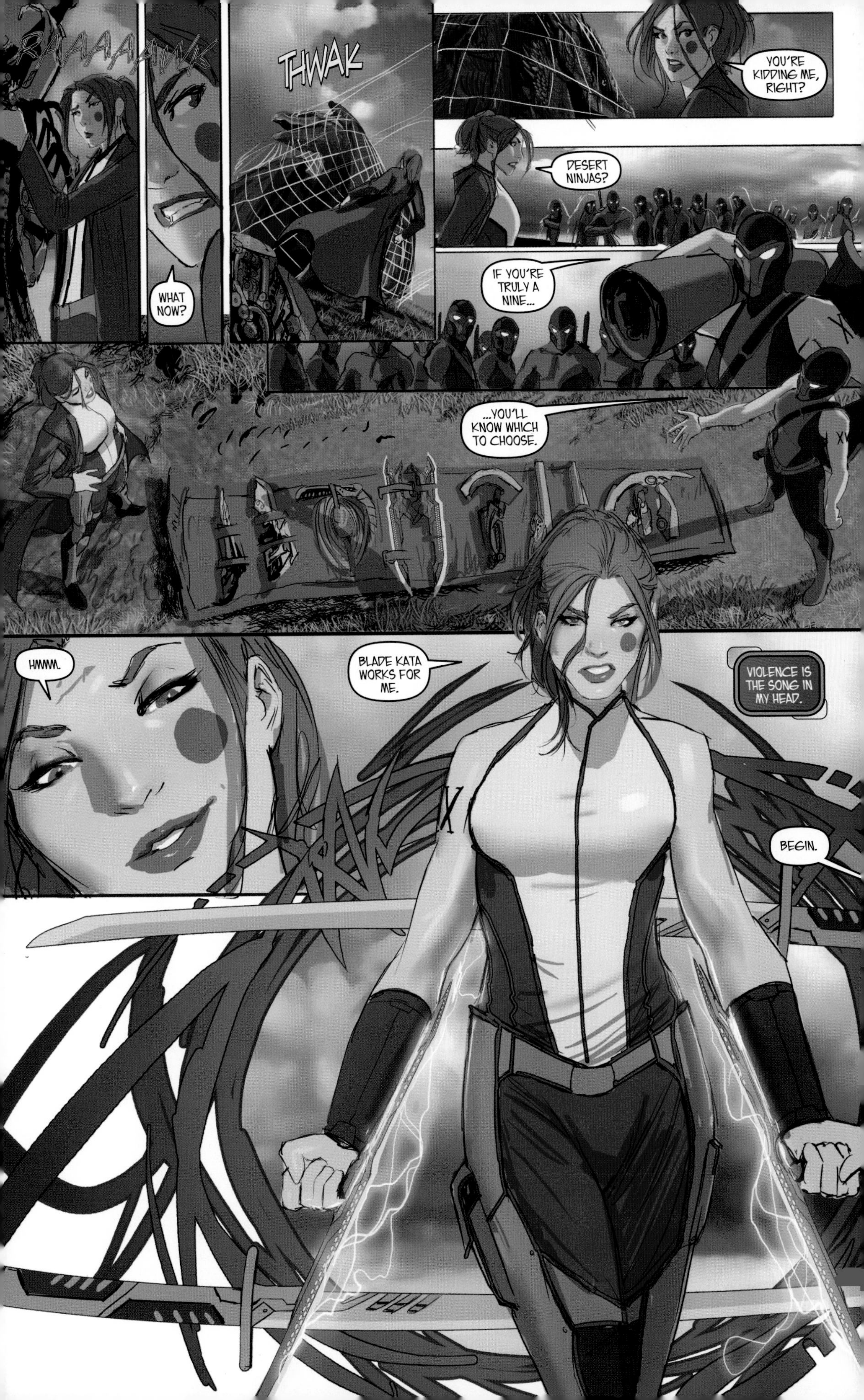
RAAAAAAWK
WHAT NOW?
THWAK
YOU'RE KIDDING ME, RIGHT?
DESERT NINJAS?
IF YOU'RE TRULY A NINE...
...YOU'LL KNOW WHICH TO CHOOSE.
HMMM.
BLADE KATA WORKS FOR ME.
VIOLENCE IS THE SONG IN MY HEAD.
BEGIN.

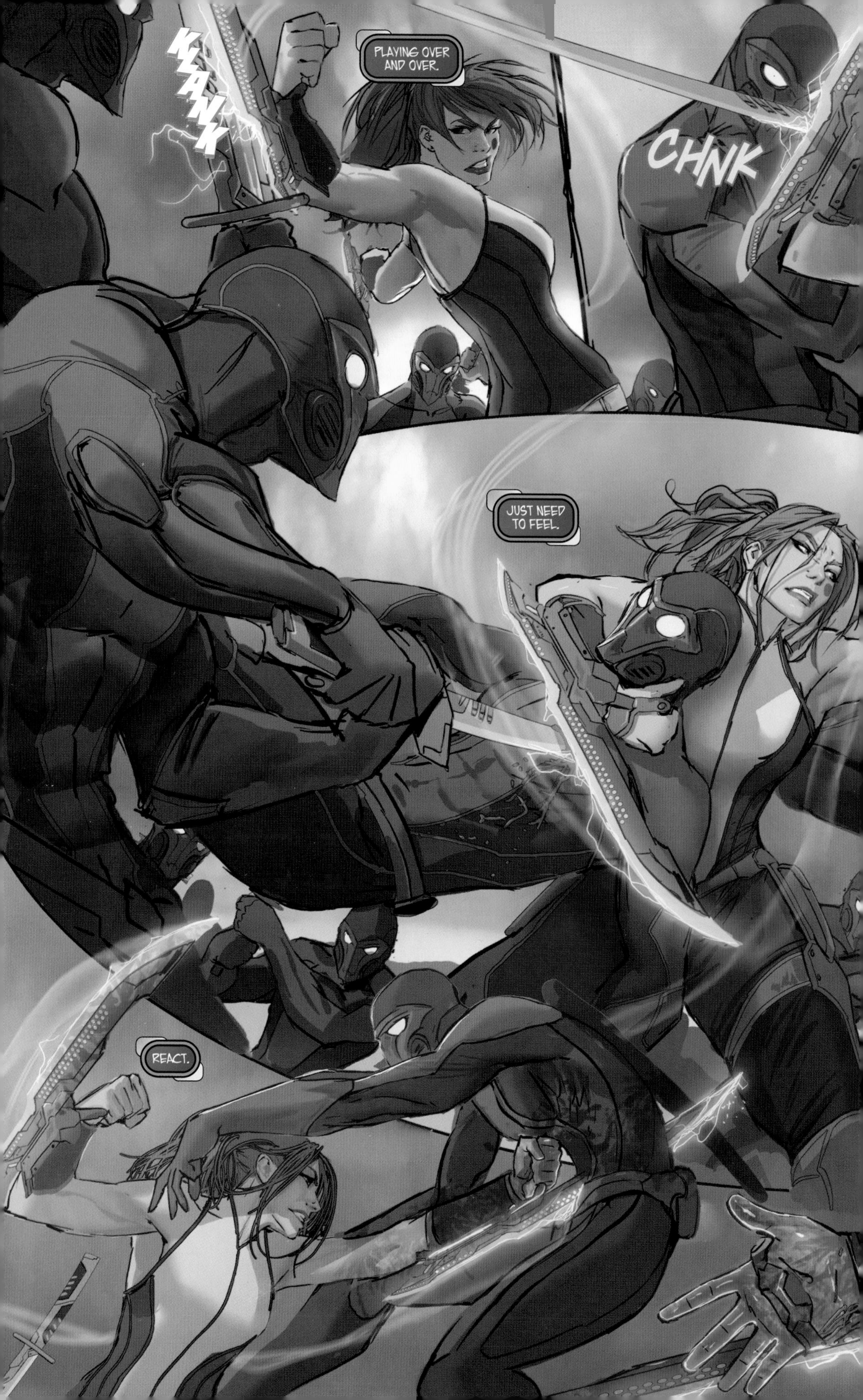
KLANK
PLAYING OVER AND OVER.
CHNK
JUST NEED TO FEEL.
REACT.

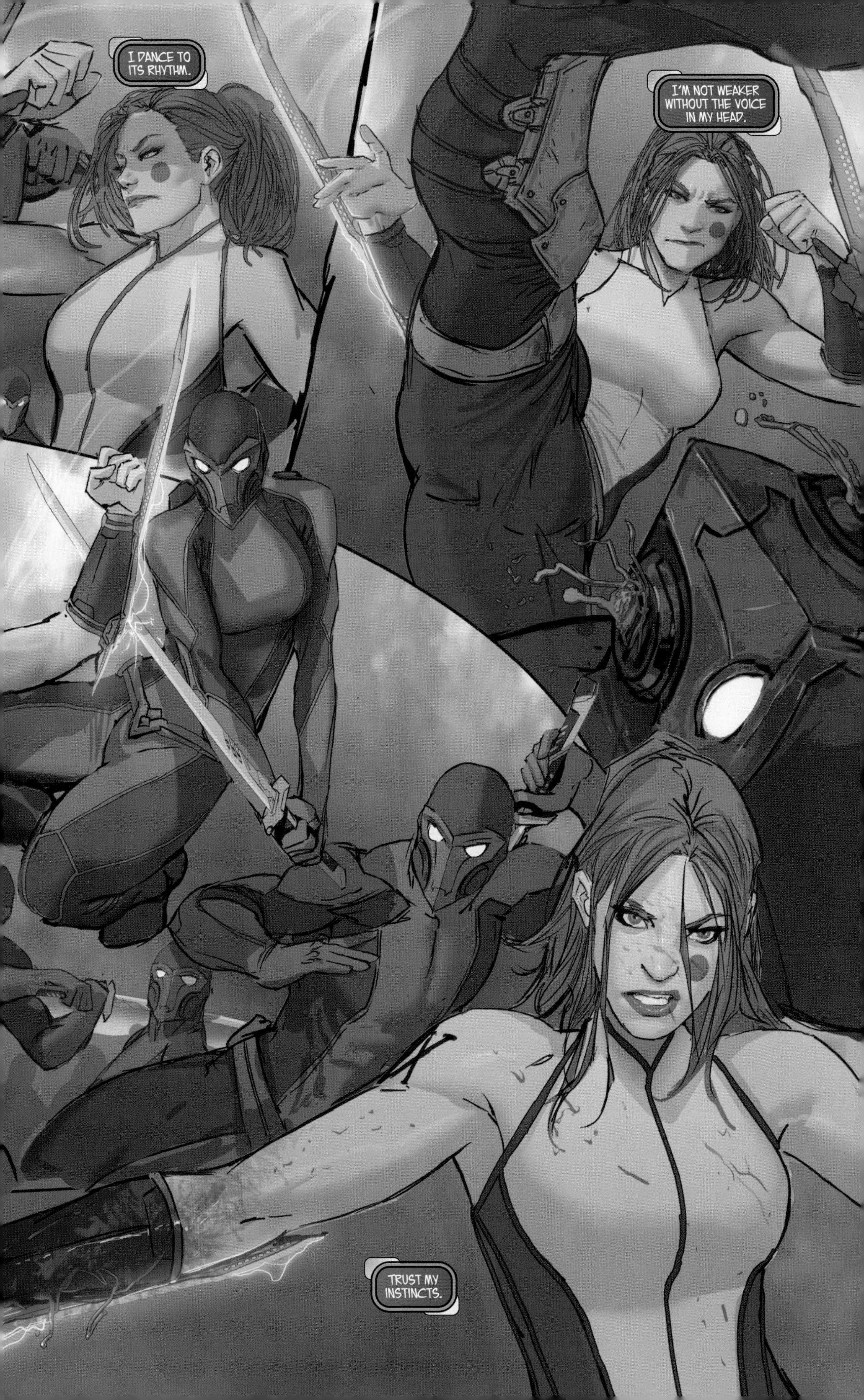
I DANCE TO
ITS RHYTHM.
I'M NOT WEAKER
WITHOUT THE VOICE
IN MY HEAD.
TRUST MY
INSTINCTS.

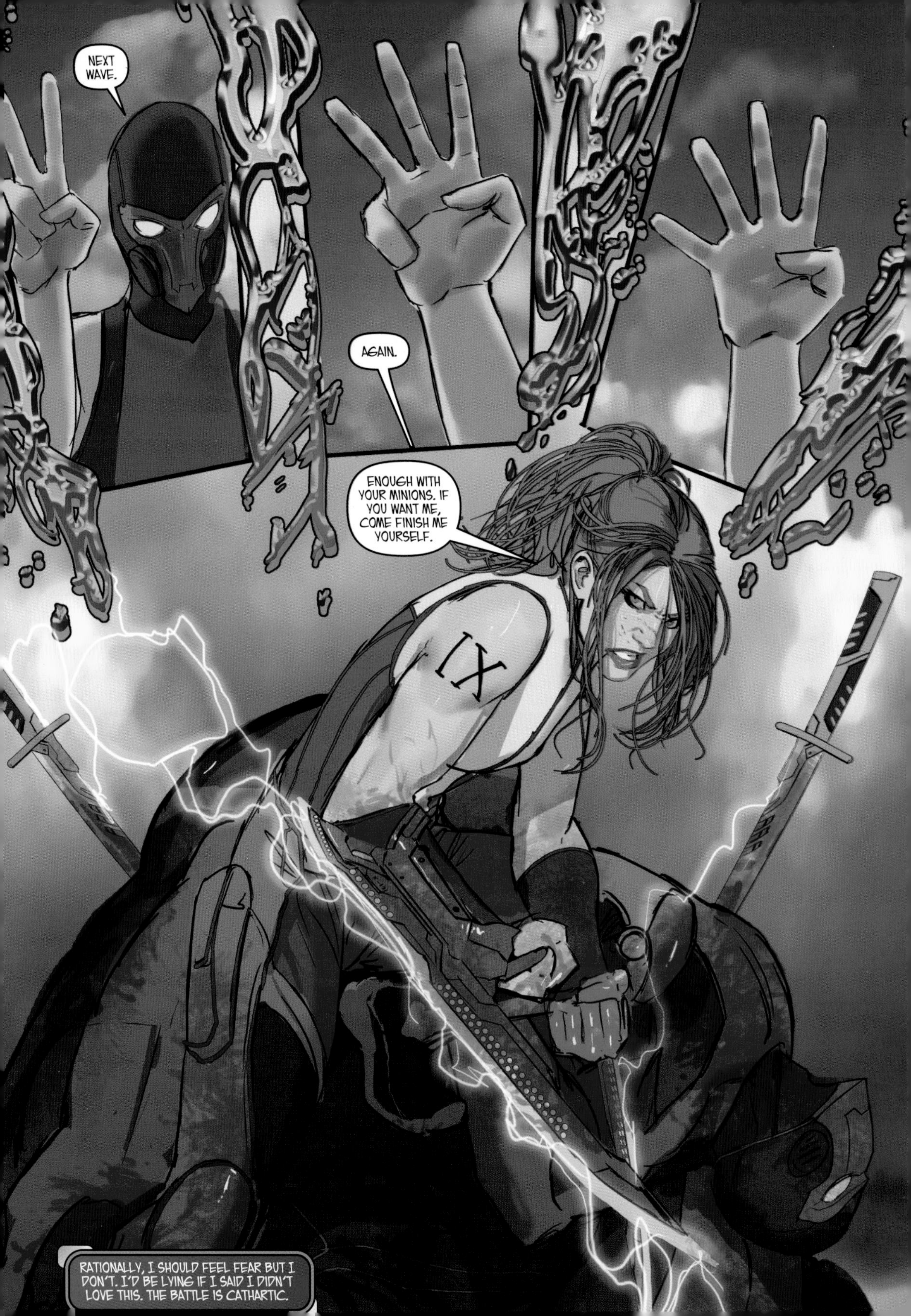
NEXT WAVE.
AGAIN.
ENOUGH WITH YOUR MINIONS. IF YOU WANT ME, COME FINISH ME YOURSELF.
RATIONALLY, I SHOULD FEEL FEAR BUT I DON'T. I'D BE LYING IF I SAID I DIDN'T LOVE THIS. THE BATTLE IS CATHARTIC.

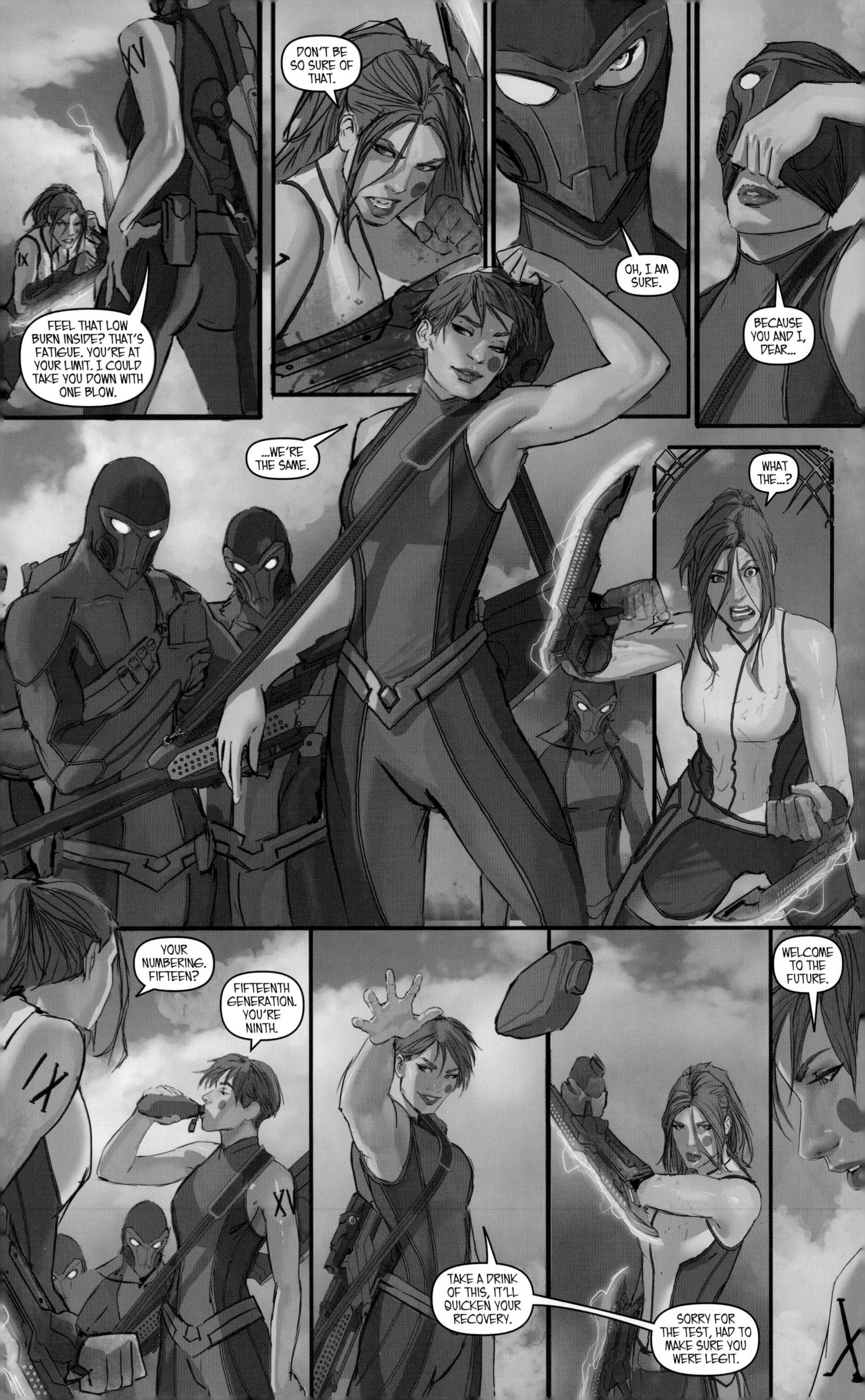
FEEL THAT LOW BURN INSIDE? THAT'S FATIGUE. YOU'RE AT YOUR LIMIT. I COULD TAKE YOU DOWN WITH ONE BLOW.
DON'T BE SO SURE OF THAT.
OH, I AM SURE.
BECAUSE YOU AND I, DEAR...
...WE'RE THE SAME.
WHAT THE...?
YOUR NUMBERING. FIFTEEN?
FIFTEENTH GENERATION. YOU'RE NINTH.
TAKE A DRINK OF THIS, IT'LL QUICKEN YOUR RECOVERY.
SORRY FOR THE TEST, HAD TO MAKE SURE YOU WERE LEGIT.
WELCOME TO THE FUTURE.

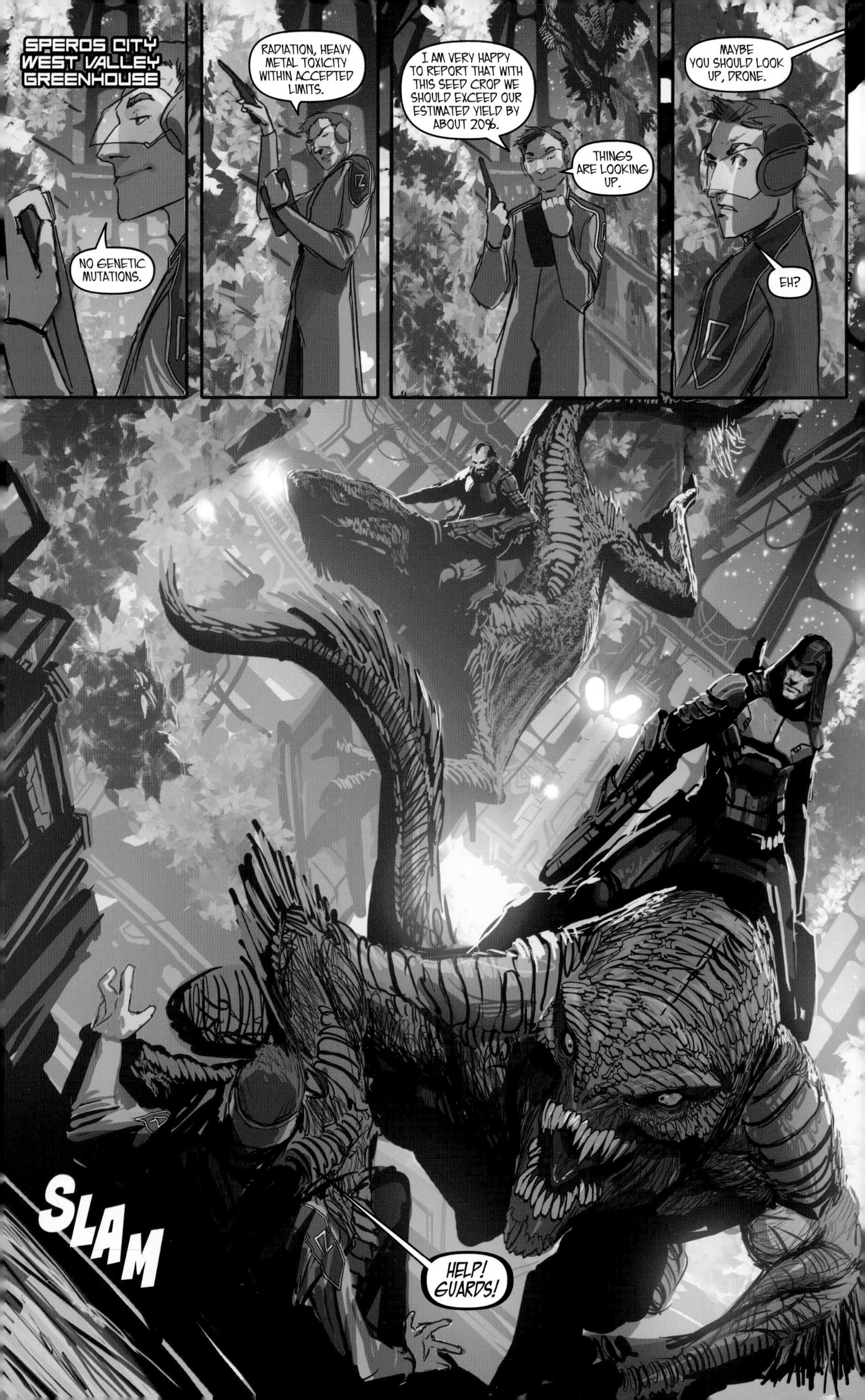

SPEROS CITY
WEST VALLEY
GREENHOUSE
NO GENETIC MUTATIONS.
RADIATION, HEAVY METAL TOXICITY WITHIN ACCEPTED LIMITS.
I AM VERY HAPPY TO REPORT THAT WITH THIS SEED CROP WE SHOULD EXCEED OUR ESTIMATED YIELD BY ABOUT 20%.
THINGS ARE LOOKING UP.
MAYBE YOU SHOULD LOOK UP, DRONE.
EH?
SLAM
HELP! GUARDS!

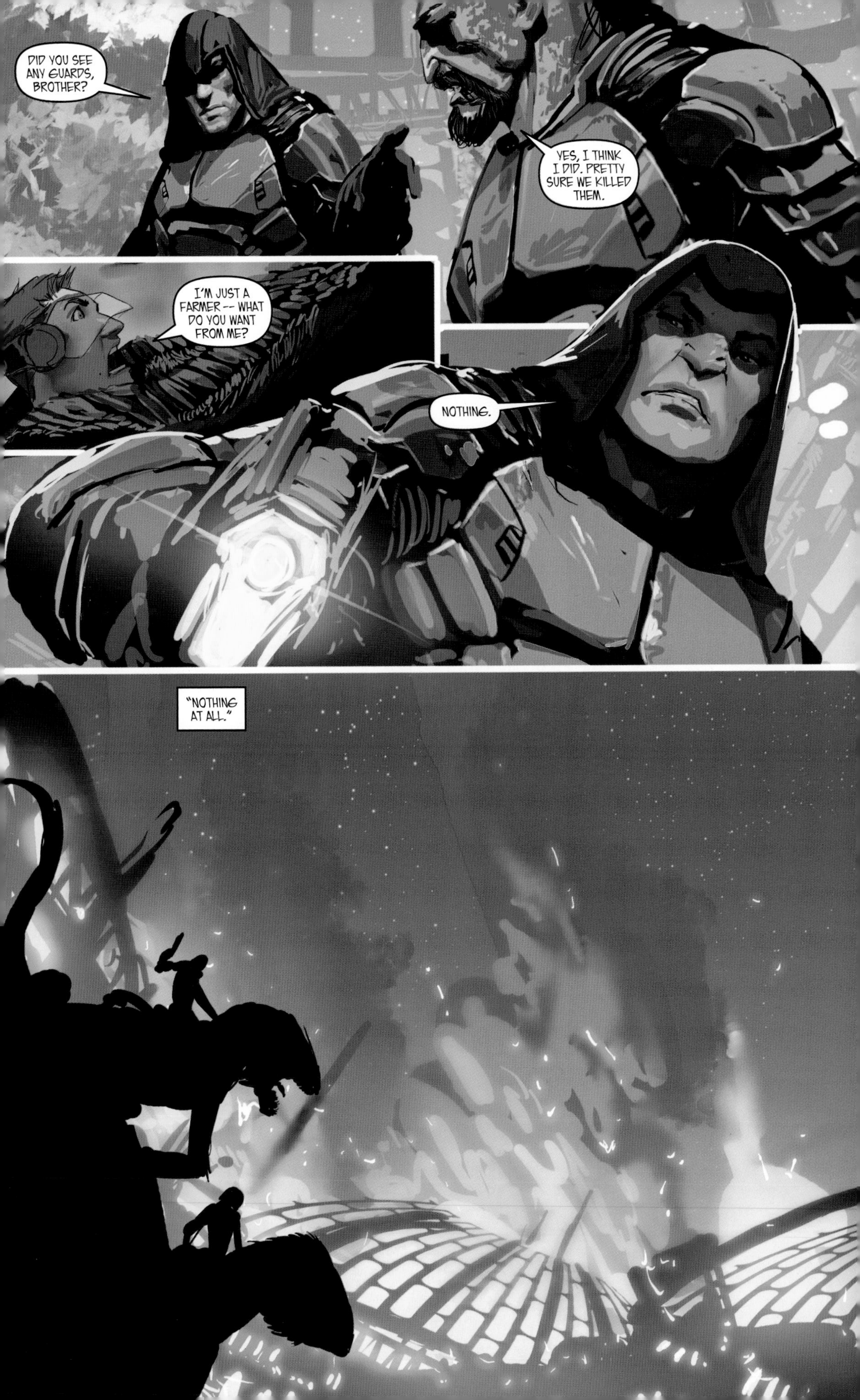
DID YOU SEE ANY GUARDS, BROTHER?
YES, I THINK I DID. PRETTY SURE WE KILLED THEM.
I'M JUST A FARMER -- WHAT DO YOU WANT FROM ME?
NOTHING.
"NOTHING AT ALL."

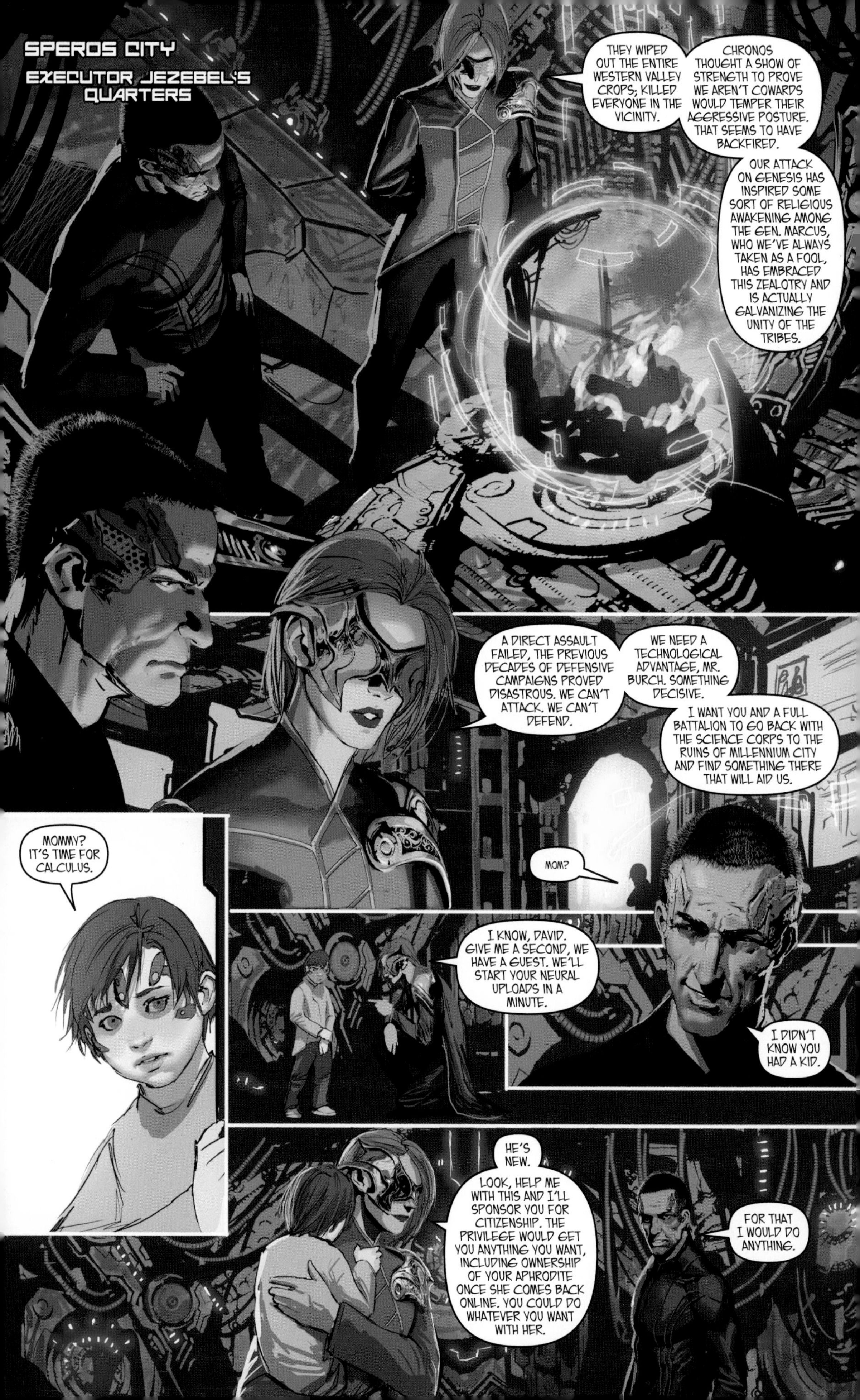
SPEROS CITY
EXECUTOR JEZEBEL'S QUARTERS
THEY WIPED OUT THE ENTIRE WESTERN VALLEY CROPS; KILLED EVERYONE IN THE VICINITY.
CHRONOS THOUGHT A SHOW OF STRENGTH TO PROVE WE AREN'T COWARDS WOULD TEMPER THEIR AGGRESSIVE POSTURE. THAT SEEMS TO HAVE BACKFIRED.
OUR ATTACK ON GENESIS HAS INSPIRED SOME SORT OF RELIGIOUS AWAKENING AMONG THE GEN. MARCUS, WHO WE'VE ALWAYS TAKEN AS A FOOL, HAS EMBRACED THIS ZEALOTRY AND IS ACTUALLY GALVANIZING THE UNITY OF THE TRIBES.
A DIRECT ASSAULT FAILED, THE PREVIOUS DECADES OF DEFENSIVE CAMPAIGNS PROVED DISASTROUS. WE CAN'T ATTACK. WE CAN'T DEFEND.
WE NEED A TECHNOLOGICAL ADVANTAGE, MR. BURCH. SOMETHING DECISIVE.
I WANT YOU AND A FULL BATTALION TO GO BACK WITH THE SCIENCE CORPS TO THE RUINS OF MILLENNIUM CITY AND FIND SOMETHING THERE THAT WILL AID US.
MOMMY? IT'S TIME FOR CALCULUS.
MOM?
I KNOW, DAVID. GIVE ME A SECOND, WE HAVE A GUEST. WE'LL START YOUR NEURAL UPLOADS IN A MINUTE.
I DIDN'T KNOW YOU HAD A KID.
HE'S NEW.
LOOK, HELP ME WITH THIS AND I'LL SPONSOR YOU FOR CITIZENSHIP. THE PRIVILEGE WOULD GET YOU ANYTHING YOU WANT, INCLUDING OWNERSHIP OF YOUR APHRODITE ONCE SHE COMES BACK ONLINE. YOU COULD DO WHATEVER YOU WANT WITH HER.
FOR THAT I WOULD DO ANYTHING.

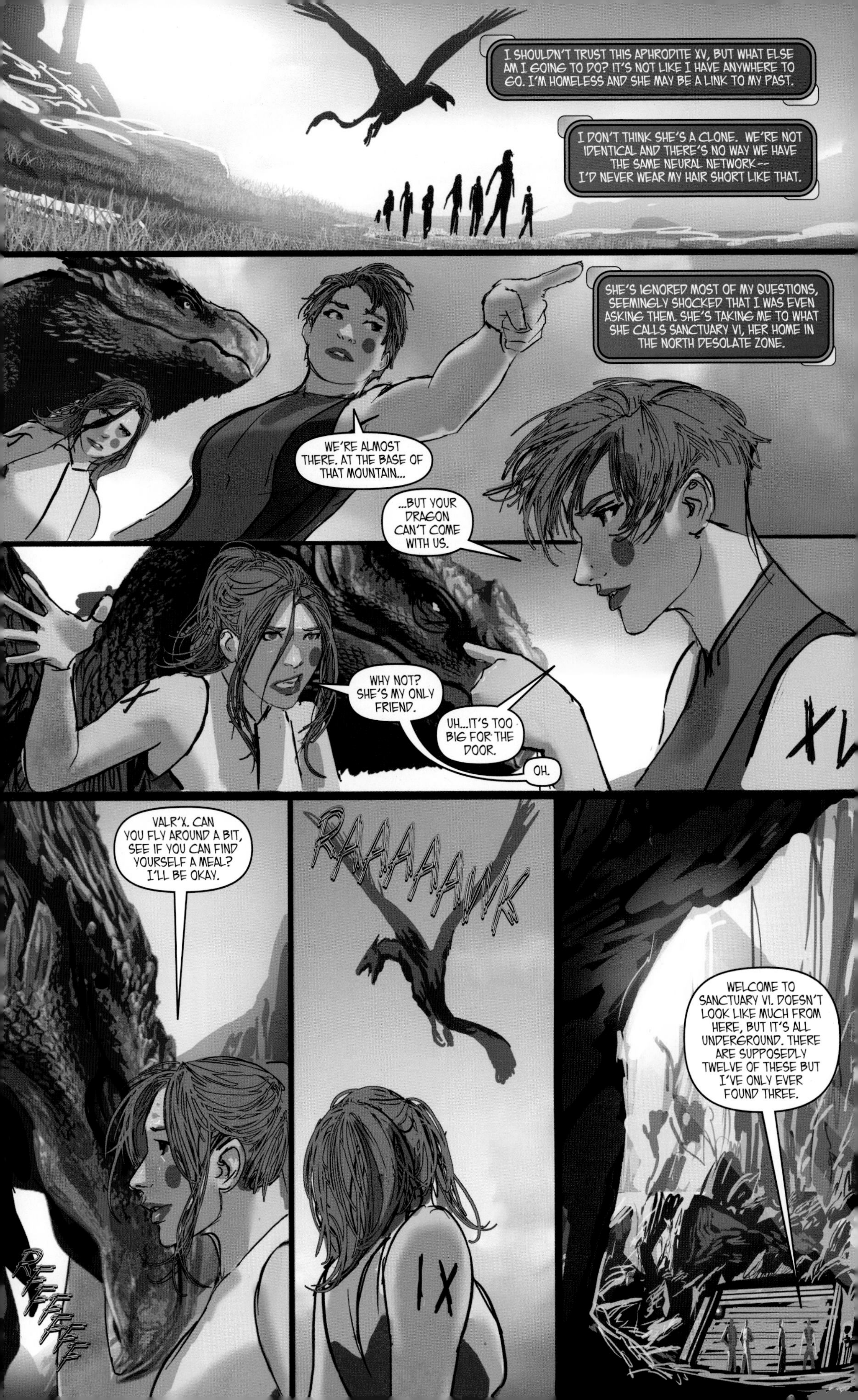
I SHOULDN'T TRUST THIS APHRODITE XV, BUT WHAT ELSE AM I GOING TO DO? IT'S NOT LIKE I HAVE ANYWHERE TO GO. I'M HOMELESS AND SHE MAY BE A LINK TO MY PAST.
I DON'T THINK SHE'S A CLONE. WE'RE NOT IDENTICAL AND THERE'S NO WAY WE HAVE THE SAME NEURAL NETWORK-- I'D NEVER WEAR MY HAIR SHORT LIKE THAT.
SHE'S IGNORED MOST OF MY QUESTIONS, SEEMINGLY SHOCKED THAT I WAS EVEN ASKING THEM. SHE'S TAKING ME TO WHAT SHE CALLS SANCTUARY VI, HER HOME IN THE NORTH DESOLATE ZONE.
WE'RE ALMOST THERE. AT THE BASE OF THAT MOUNTAIN...
...BUT YOUR DRAGON CAN'T COME WITH US.
WHY NOT? SHE'S MY ONLY FRIEND.
UH...IT'S TOO BIG FOR THE DOOR.
OH.
VALR'X. CAN YOU FLY AROUND A BIT, SEE IF YOU CAN FIND YOURSELF A MEAL? I'LL BE OKAY.
REEEEEEF
RAAAAAAWK
WELCOME TO SANCTUARY VI. DOESN'T LOOK LIKE MUCH FROM HERE, BUT IT'S ALL UNDERGROUND. THERE ARE SUPPOSEDLY TWELVE OF THESE BUT I'VE ONLY EVER FOUND THREE.

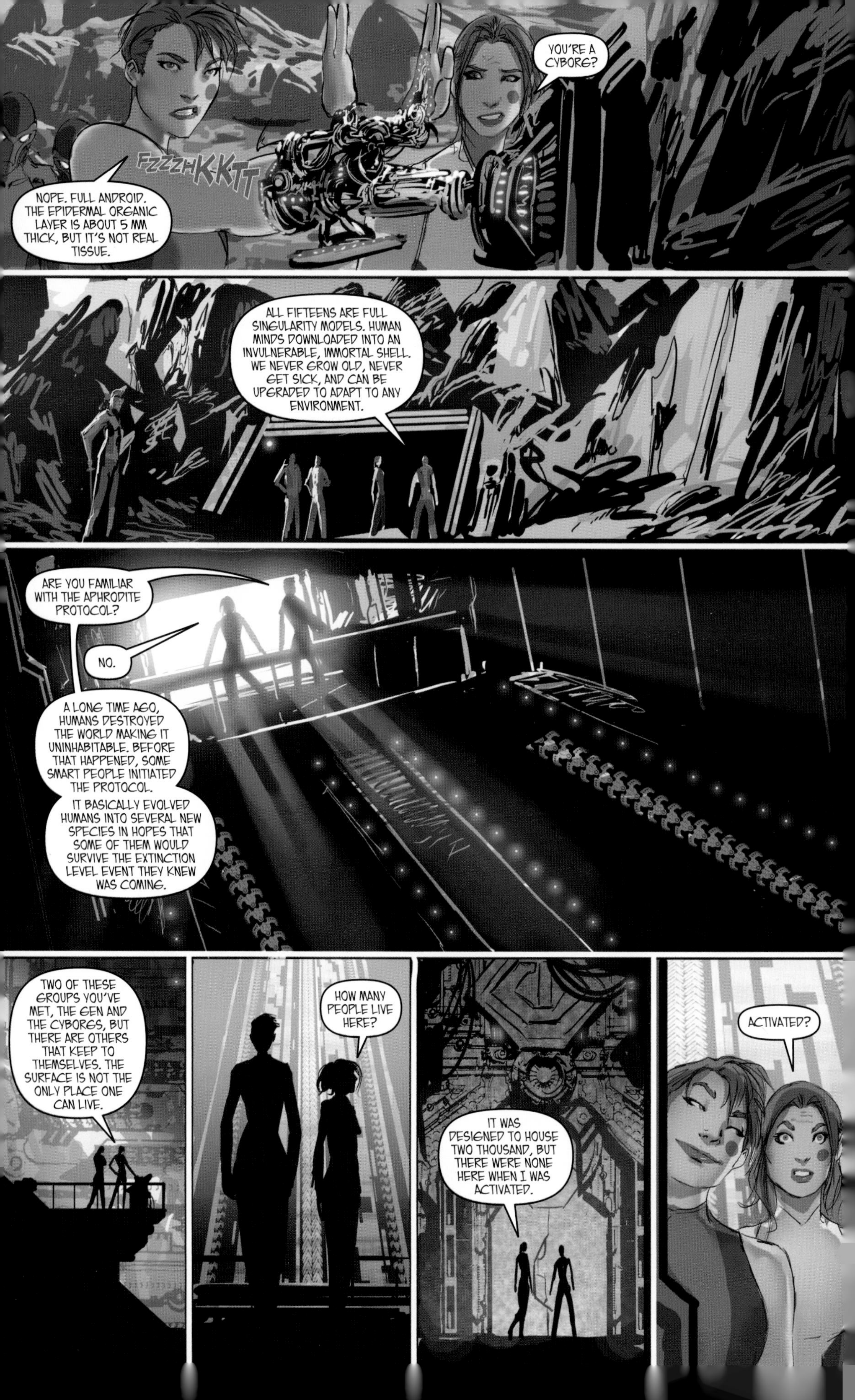
YOU'RE A CYBORG?
FZZZHKKTT
NOPE. FULL ANDROID. THE EPIDERMAL ORGANIC LAYER IS ABOUT 5 MM THICK, BUT IT'S NOT REAL TISSUE.
ALL FIFTEENS ARE FULL SINGULARITY MODELS. HUMAN MINDS DOWNLOADED INTO AN INVULNERABLE, IMMORTAL SHELL. WE NEVER GROW OLD, NEVER GET SICK, AND CAN BE UPGRADED TO ADAPT TO ANY ENVIRONMENT.
ARE YOU FAMILIAR WITH THE APHRODITE PROTOCOL?
NO.
A LONG TIME AGO, HUMANS DESTROYED THE WORLD MAKING IT UNINHABITABLE. BEFORE THAT HAPPENED, SOME SMART PEOPLE INITIATED THE PROTOCOL.
IT BASICALLY EVOLVED HUMANS INTO SEVERAL NEW SPECIES IN HOPES THAT SOME OF THEM WOULD SURVIVE THE EXTINCTION LEVEL EVENT THEY KNEW WAS COMING.
TWO OF THESE GROUPS YOU'VE MET, THE GEN AND THE CYBORGS, BUT THERE ARE OTHERS THAT KEEP TO THEMSELVES. THE SURFACE IS NOT THE ONLY PLACE ONE CAN LIVE.
HOW MANY PEOPLE LIVE HERE?
IT WAS DESIGNED TO HOUSE TWO THOUSAND, BUT THERE WERE NONE HERE WHEN I WAS ACTIVATED.
ACTIVATED?

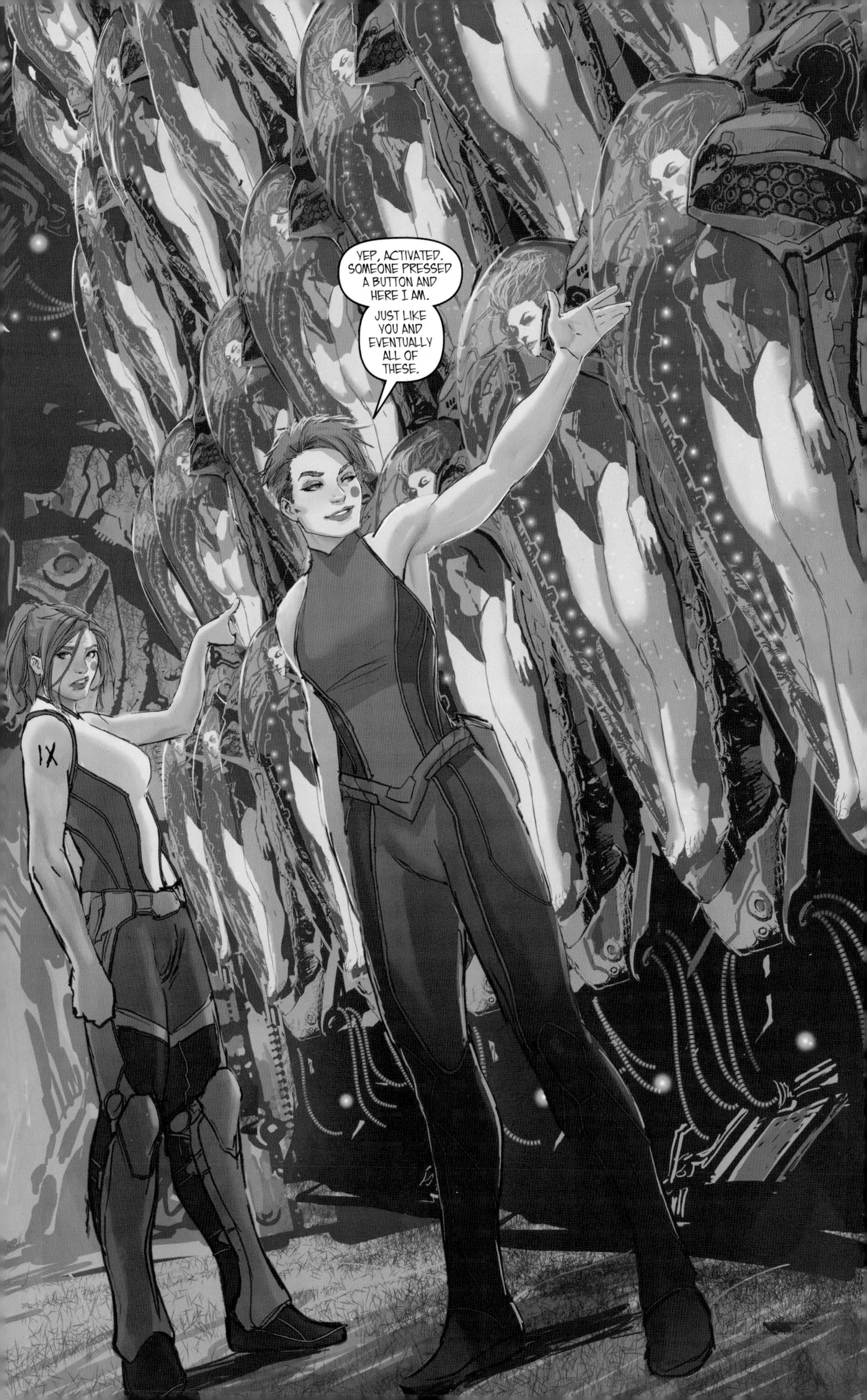
YEP, ACTIVATED. SOMEONE PRESSED A BUTTON AND HERE I AM.
JUST LIKE YOU AND EVENTUALLY ALL OF THESE.
IX

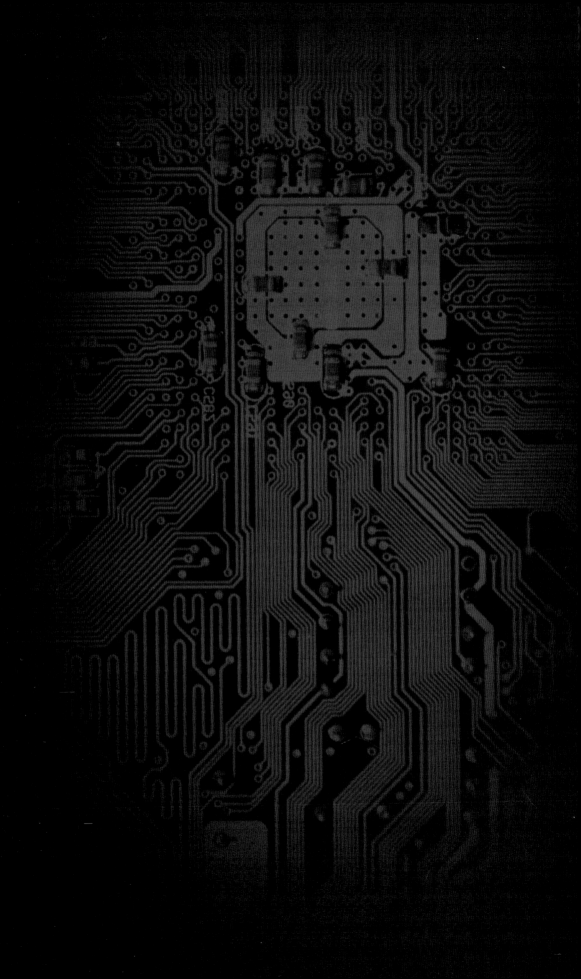

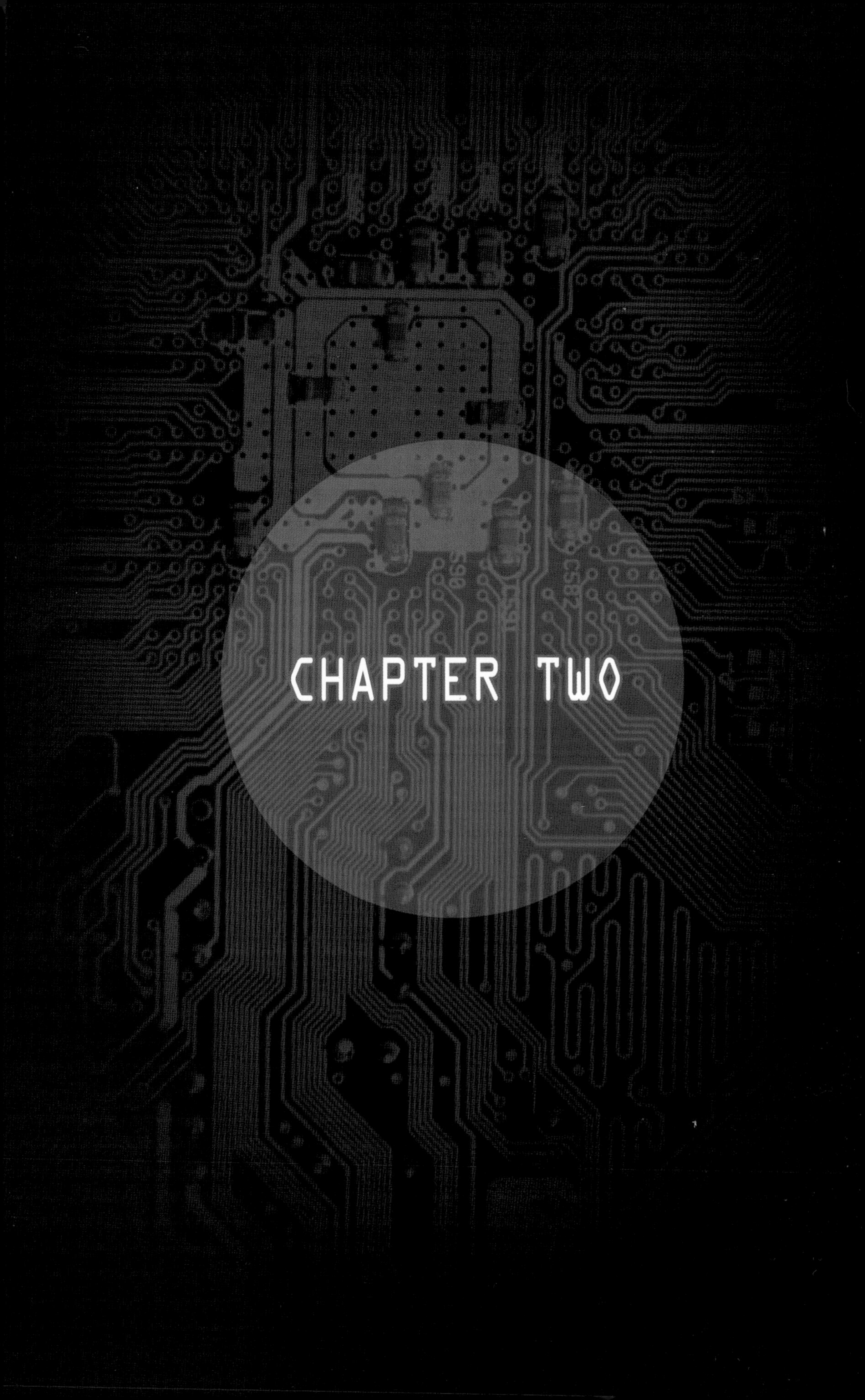

CHAPTER TWO

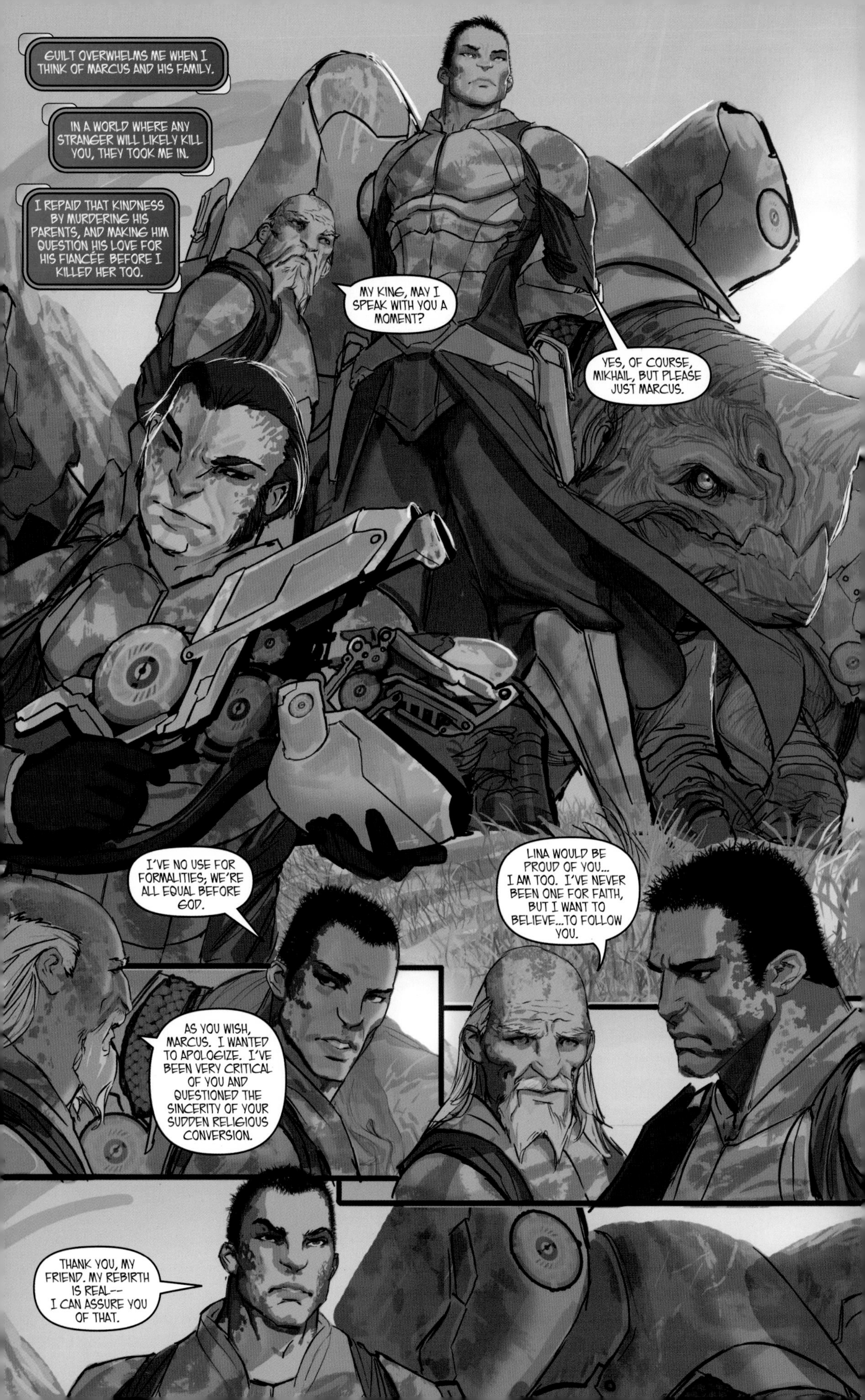
GUILT OVERWHELMS ME WHEN I THINK OF MARCUS AND HIS FAMILY.
IN A WORLD WHERE ANY STRANGER WILL LIKELY KILL YOU, THEY TOOK ME IN.
I REPAID THAT KINDNESS BY MURDERING HIS PARENTS, AND MAKING HIM QUESTION HIS LOVE FOR HIS FIANCÉE BEFORE I KILLED HER TOO.
MY KING, MAY I SPEAK WITH YOU A MOMENT?
YES, OF COURSE, MIKHAIL, BUT PLEASE JUST MARCUS.
I'VE NO USE FOR FORMALITIES; WE'RE ALL EQUAL BEFORE GOD.
AS YOU WISH, MARCUS. I WANTED TO APOLOGIZE. I'VE BEEN VERY CRITICAL OF YOU AND QUESTIONED THE SINCERITY OF YOUR SUDDEN RELIGIOUS CONVERSION.
LINA WOULD BE PROUD OF YOU... I AM TOO. I'VE NEVER BEEN ONE FOR FAITH, BUT I WANT TO BELIEVE...TO FOLLOW YOU.
THANK YOU, MY FRIEND. MY REBIRTH IS REAL-- I CAN ASSURE YOU OF THAT.

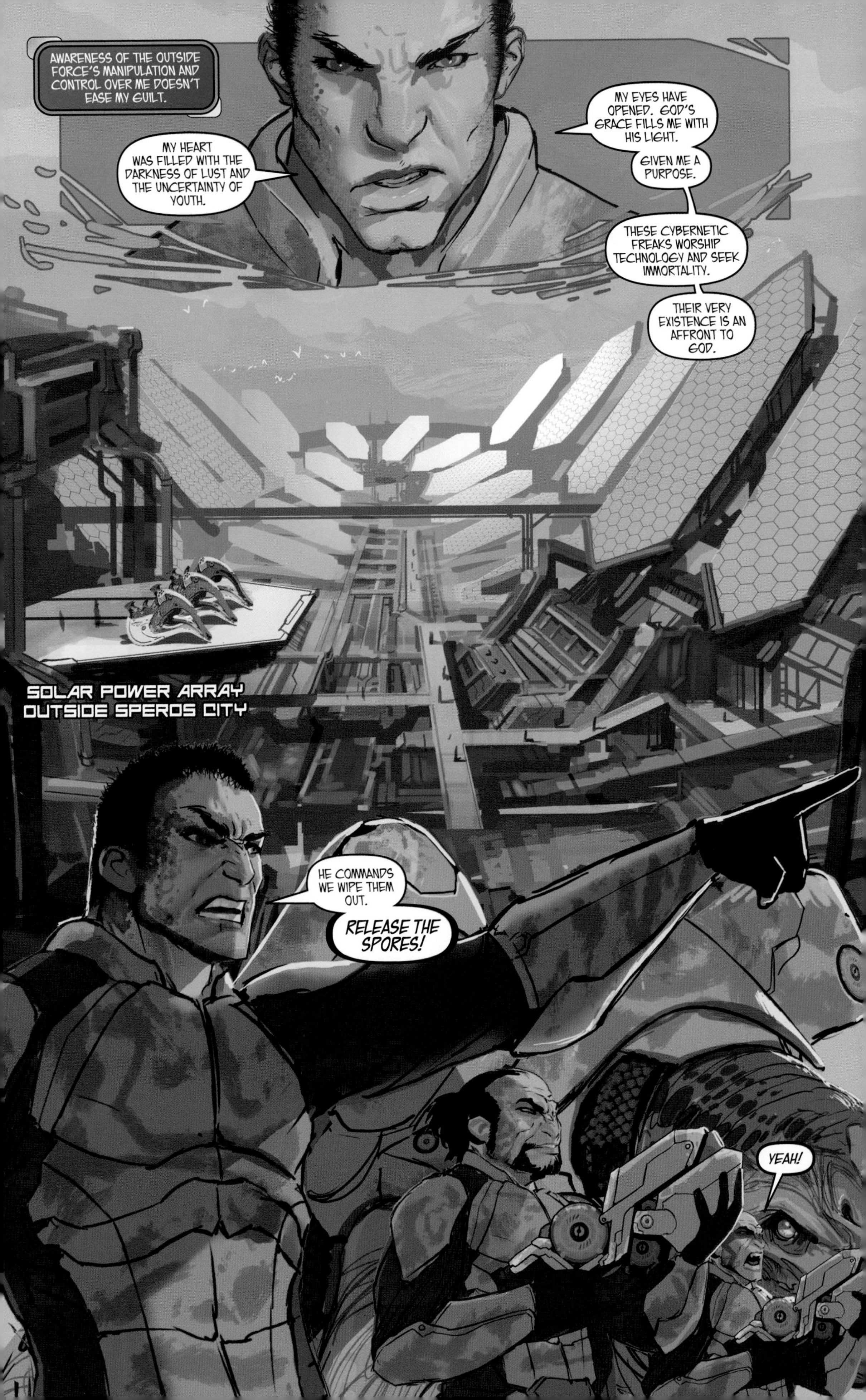
AWARENESS OF THE OUTSIDE FORCE'S MANIPULATION AND CONTROL OVER ME DOESN'T EASE MY GUILT.
MY HEART WAS FILLED WITH THE DARKNESS OF LUST AND THE UNCERTAINTY OF YOUTH.
MY EYES HAVE OPENED. GOD'S GRACE FILLS ME WITH HIS LIGHT.
GIVEN ME A PURPOSE.
THESE CYBERNETIC FREAKS WORSHIP TECHNOLOGY AND SEEK IMMORTALITY.
THEIR VERY EXISTENCE IS AN AFFRONT TO GOD.
SOLAR POWER ARRAY OUTSIDE SPEROS CITY
HE COMMANDS WE WIPE THEM OUT.
RELEASE THE SPORES!
YEAH!

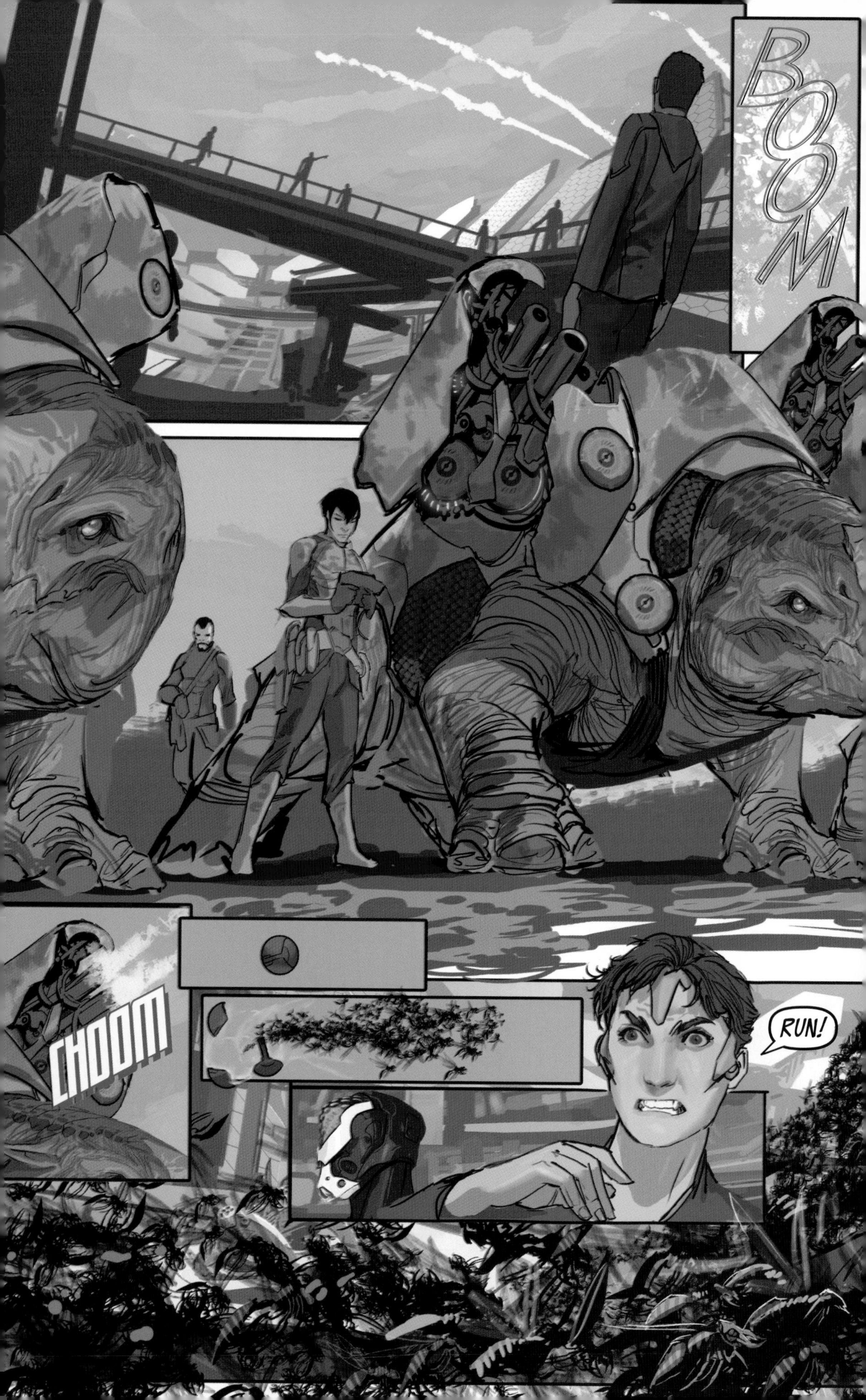
BOOOM
CHOOM
RUN!

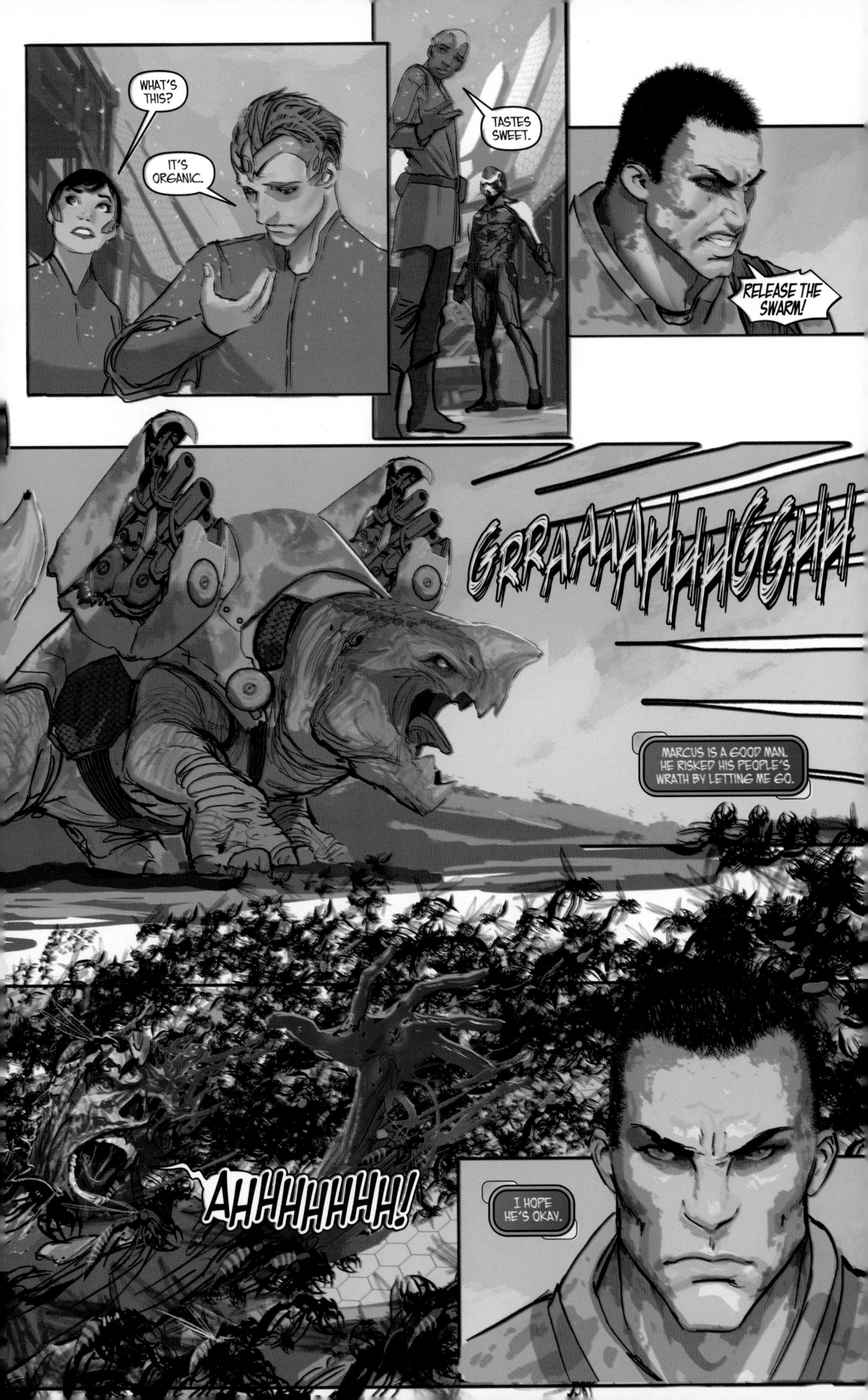
WHAT'S THIS?
IT'S ORGANIC.
TASTES SWEET.
RELEASE THE SWARM!
GRRAAAAHHHGGHH
MARCUS IS A GOOD MAN. HE RISKED HIS PEOPLE'S WRATH BY LETTING ME GO.
AHHHHHHH!
I HOPE HE'S OKAY.

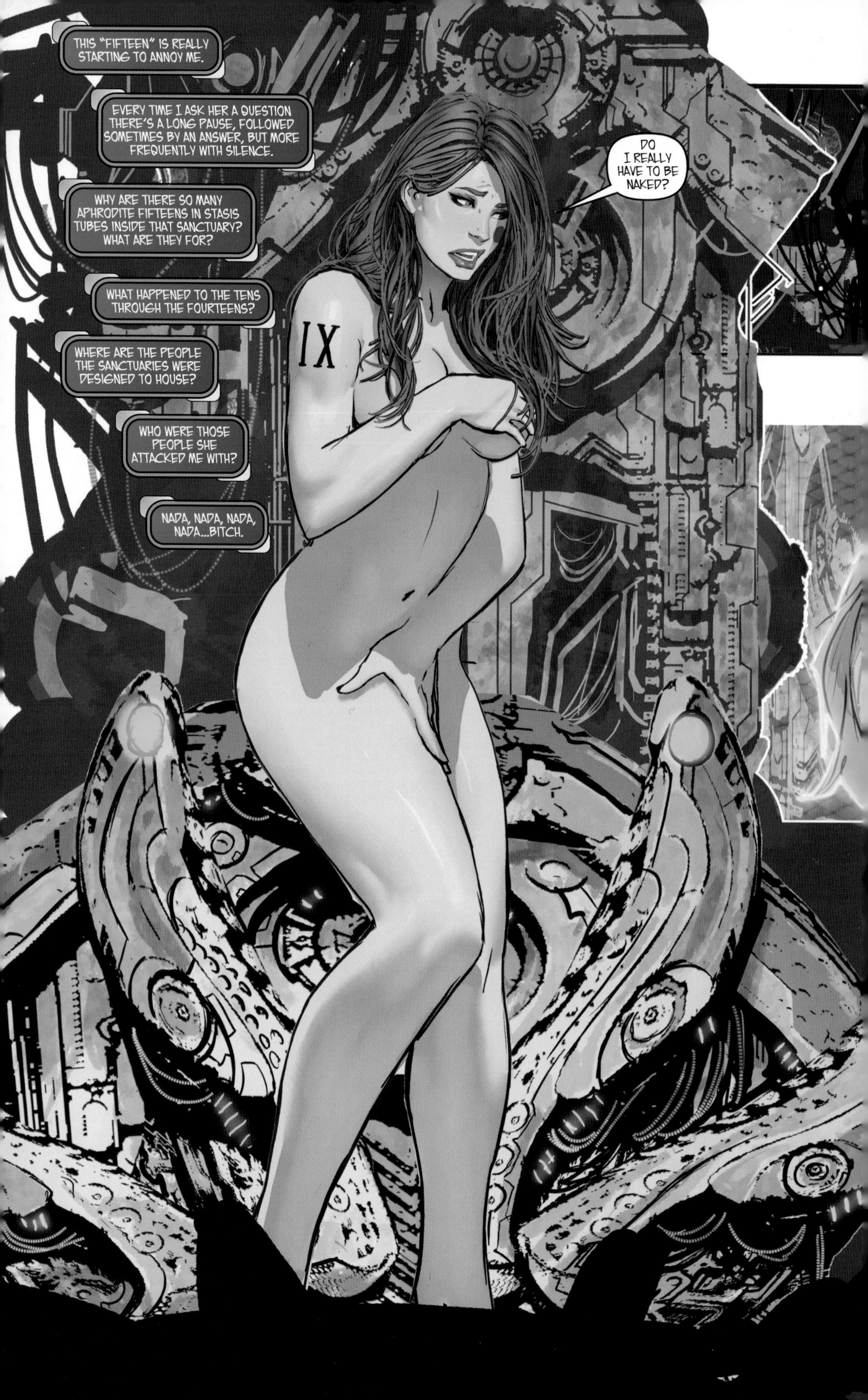
THIS "FIFTEEN" IS REALLY STARTING TO ANNOY ME.
EVERY TIME I ASK HER A QUESTION THERE'S A LONG PAUSE, FOLLOWED SOMETIMES BY AN ANSWER, BUT MORE FREQUENTLY WITH SILENCE.
DO I REALLY HAVE TO BE NAKED?
WHY ARE THERE SO MANY APHRODITE FIFTEENS IN STASIS TUBES INSIDE THAT SANCTUARY? WHAT ARE THEY FOR?
WHAT HAPPENED TO THE TENS THROUGH THE FOURTEENS?
WHERE ARE THE PEOPLE THE SANCTUARIES WERE DESIGNED TO HOUSE?
WHO WERE THOSE PEOPLE SHE ATTACKED ME WITH?
NADA, NADA, NADA, NADA...BITCH.
IX

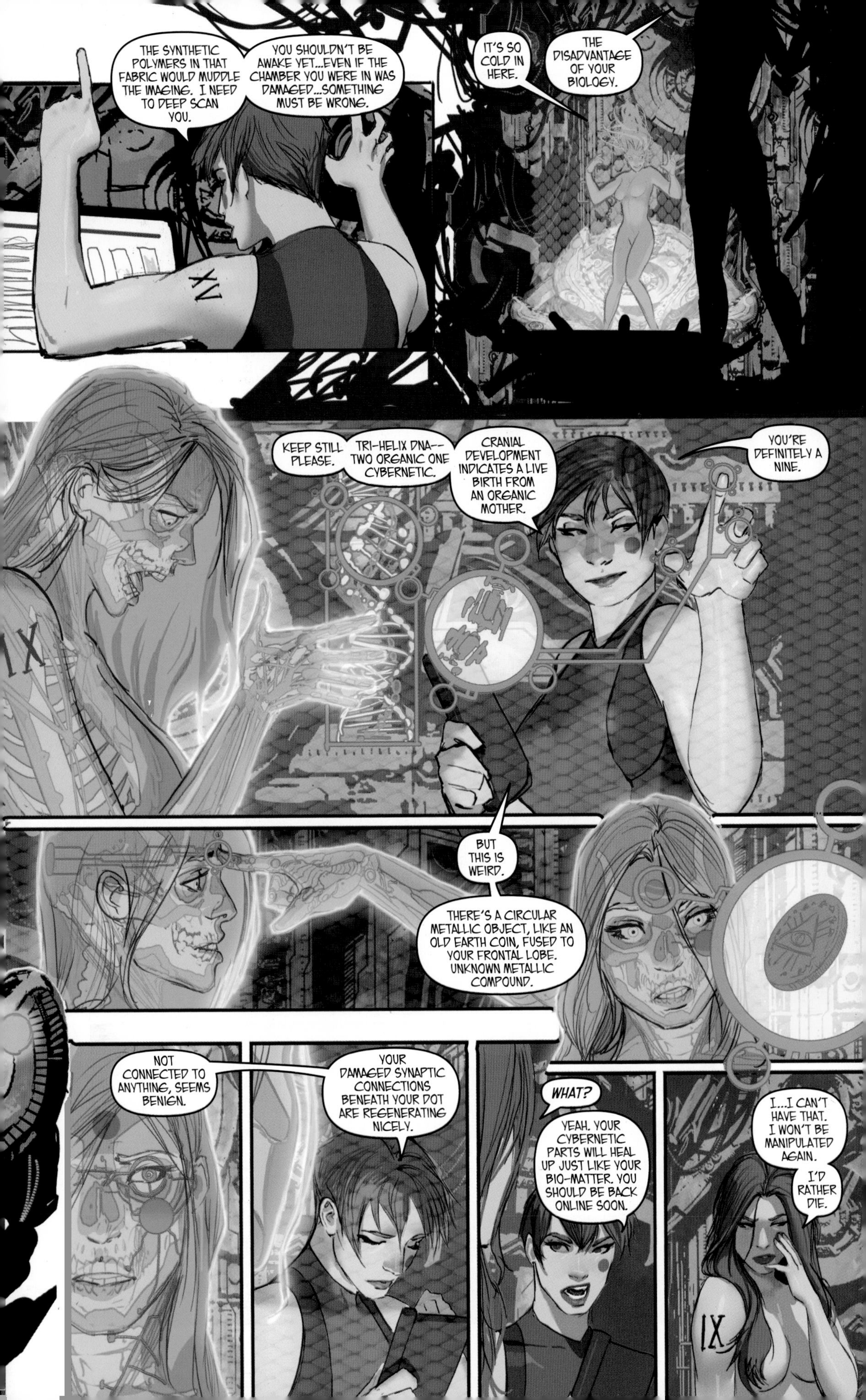

THE SYNTHETIC POLYMERS IN THAT FABRIC WOULD MUDDLE THE IMAGING. I NEED TO DEEP SCAN YOU.
YOU SHOULDN'T BE AWAKE YET...EVEN IF THE CHAMBER YOU WERE IN WAS DAMAGED...SOMETHING MUST BE WRONG.
IT'S SO COLD IN HERE.
THE DISADVANTAGE OF YOUR BIOLOGY.
XV
KEEP STILL PLEASE.
TRI-HELIX DNA--TWO ORGANIC ONE CYBERNETIC.
CRANIAL DEVELOPMENT INDICATES A LIVE BIRTH FROM AN ORGANIC MOTHER.
YOU'RE DEFINITELY A NINE.
IX
BUT THIS IS WEIRD.
THERE'S A CIRCULAR METALLIC OBJECT, LIKE AN OLD EARTH COIN, FUSED TO YOUR FRONTAL LOBE. UNKNOWN METALLIC COMPOUND.
NOT CONNECTED TO ANYTHING, SEEMS BENIGN.
YOUR DAMAGED SYNAPTIC CONNECTIONS BENEATH YOUR DOT ARE REGENERATING NICELY.
WHAT?
YEAH. YOUR CYBERNETIC PARTS WILL HEAL UP JUST LIKE YOUR BIO-MATTER. YOU SHOULD BE BACK ONLINE SOON.
I...I CAN'T HAVE THAT. I WON'T BE MANIPULATED AGAIN.
I'D RATHER DIE.
IX

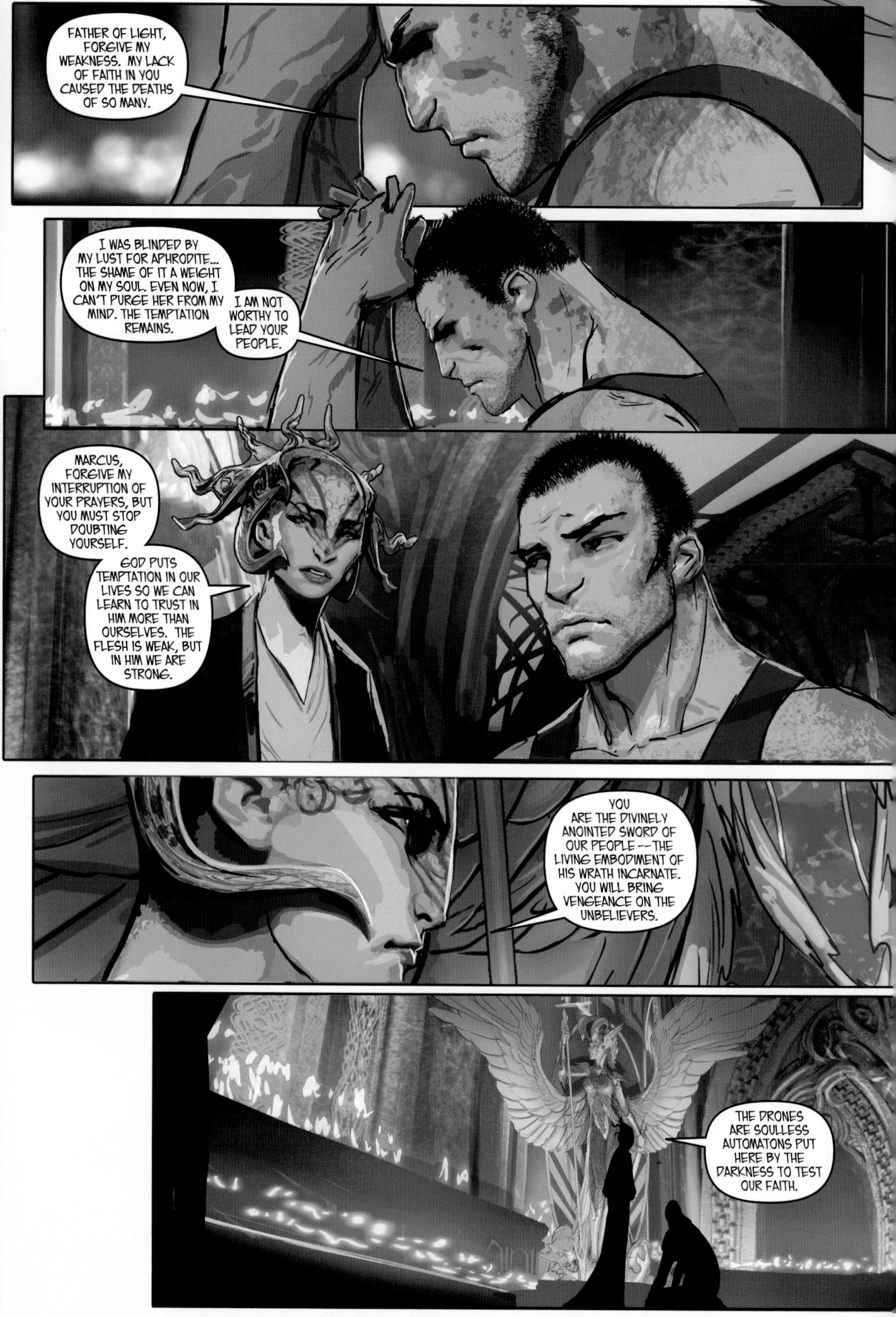
FATHER OF LIGHT, FORGIVE MY WEAKNESS. MY LACK OF FAITH IN YOU CAUSED THE DEATHS OF SO MANY.
I WAS BLINDED BY MY LUST FOR APHRODITE... THE SHAME OF IT A WEIGHT ON MY SOUL. EVEN NOW, I CAN'T PURGE HER FROM MY MIND. THE TEMPTATION REMAINS.
I AM NOT WORTHY TO LEAD YOUR PEOPLE.
MARCUS, FORGIVE MY INTERRUPTION OF YOUR PRAYERS, BUT YOU MUST STOP DOUBTING YOURSELF.
GOD PUTS TEMPTATION IN OUR LIVES SO WE CAN LEARN TO TRUST IN HIM MORE THAN OURSELVES. THE FLESH IS WEAK, BUT IN HIM WE ARE STRONG.
YOU ARE THE DIVINELY ANOINTED SWORD OF OUR PEOPLE--THE LIVING EMBODIMENT OF HIS WRATH INCARNATE. YOU WILL BRING VENGEANCE ON THE UNBELIEVERS.
THE DRONES ARE SOULLESS AUTOMATONS PUT HERE BY THE DARKNESS TO TEST OUR FAITH.

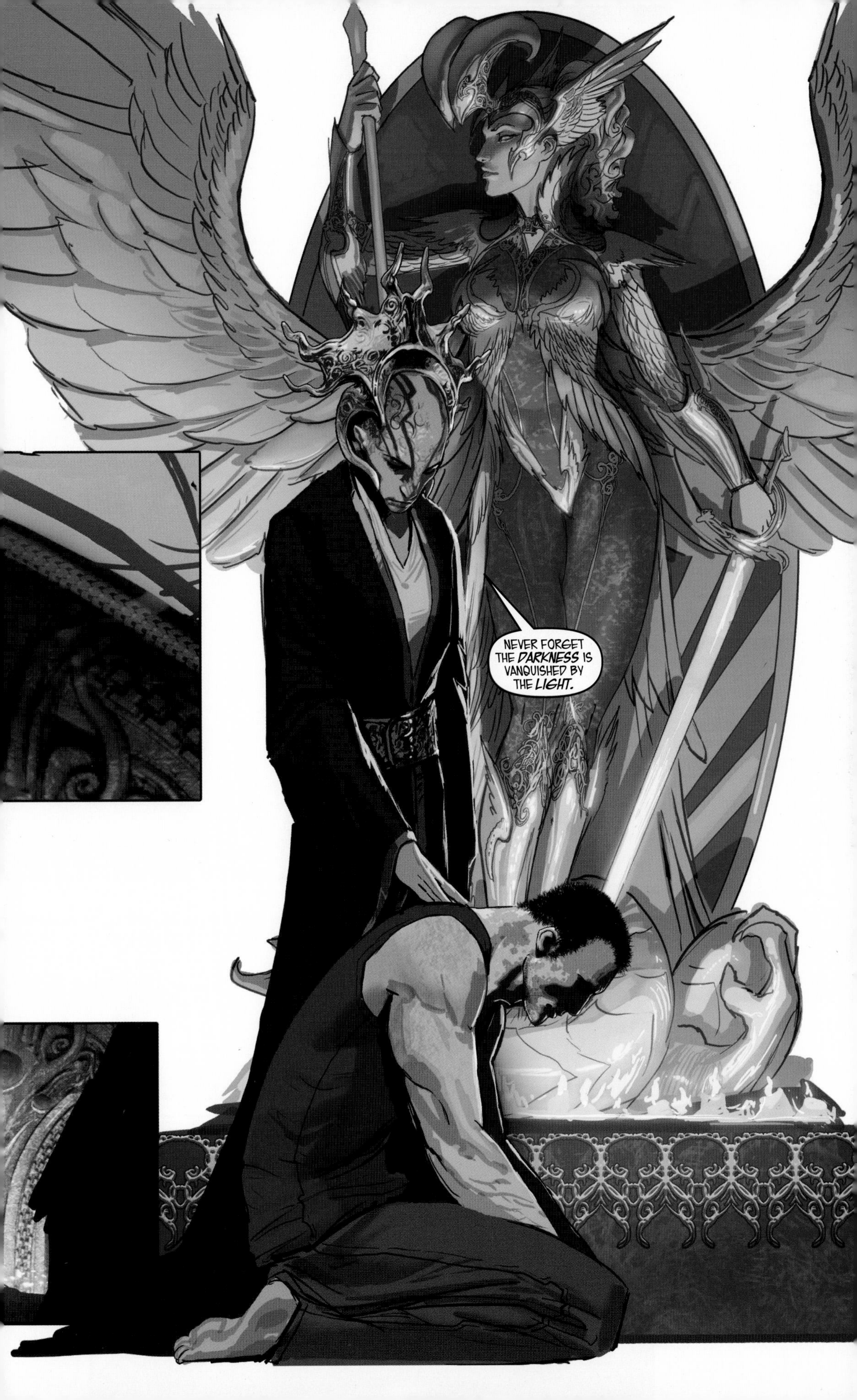
NEVER FORGET THE DARKNESS IS VANQUISHED BY THE LIGHT.

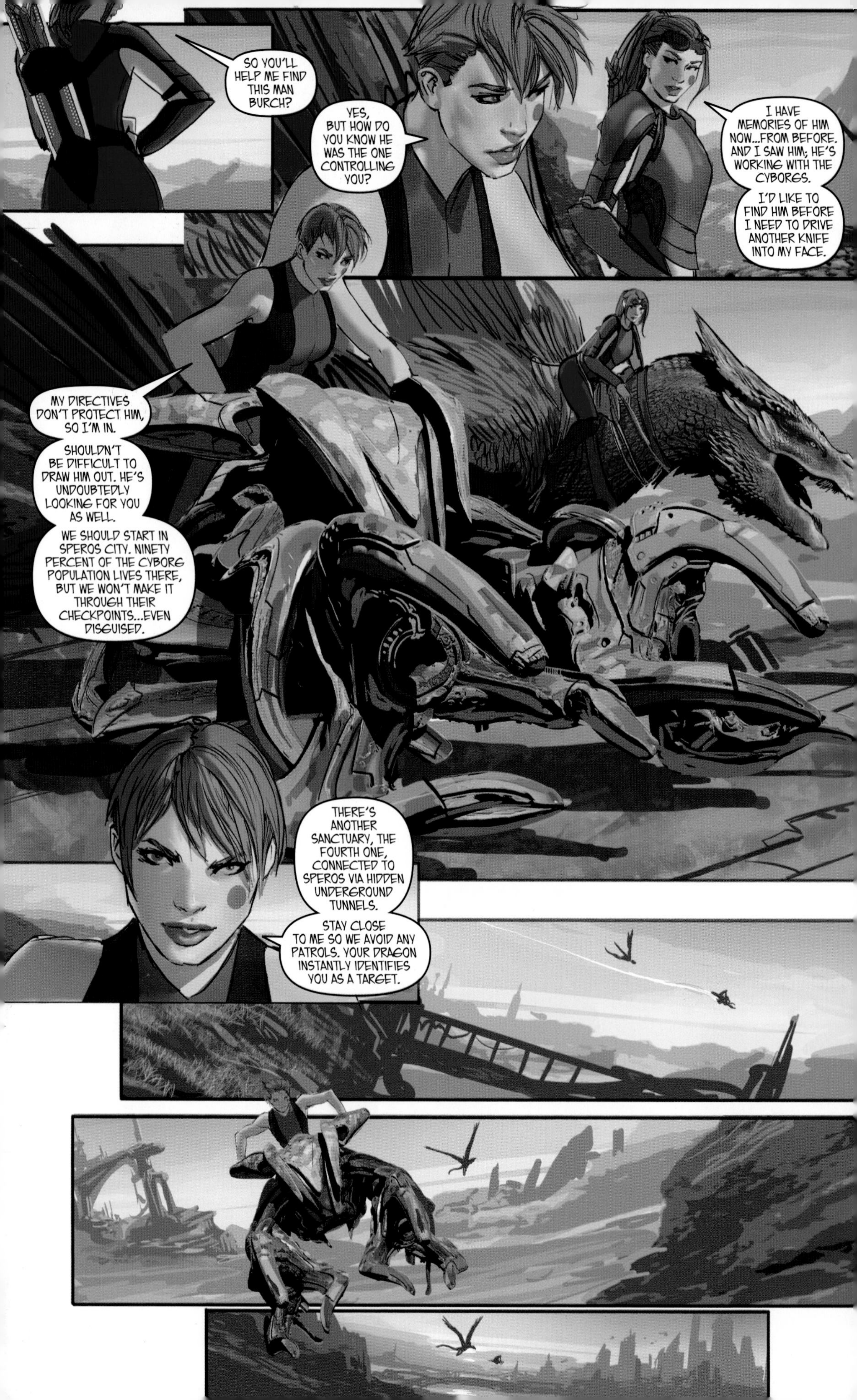
SO YOU'LL HELP ME FIND THIS MAN BURCH?
YES, BUT HOW DO YOU KNOW HE WAS THE ONE CONTROLLING YOU?
I HAVE MEMORIES OF HIM NOW...FROM BEFORE. AND I SAW HIM; HE'S WORKING WITH THE CYBORGS.
I'D LIKE TO FIND HIM BEFORE I NEED TO DRIVE ANOTHER KNIFE INTO MY FACE.
MY DIRECTIVES DON'T PROTECT HIM, SO I'M IN.
SHOULDN'T BE DIFFICULT TO DRAW HIM OUT. HE'S UNDOUBTEDLY LOOKING FOR YOU AS WELL.
WE SHOULD START IN SPEROS CITY. NINETY PERCENT OF THE CYBORG POPULATION LIVES THERE, BUT WE WON'T MAKE IT THROUGH THEIR CHECKPOINTS...EVEN DISGUISED.
THERE'S ANOTHER SANCTUARY, THE FOURTH ONE, CONNECTED TO SPEROS VIA HIDDEN UNDERGROUND TUNNELS.
STAY CLOSE TO ME SO WE AVOID ANY PATROLS. YOUR DRAGON INSTANTLY IDENTIFIES YOU AS A TARGET.

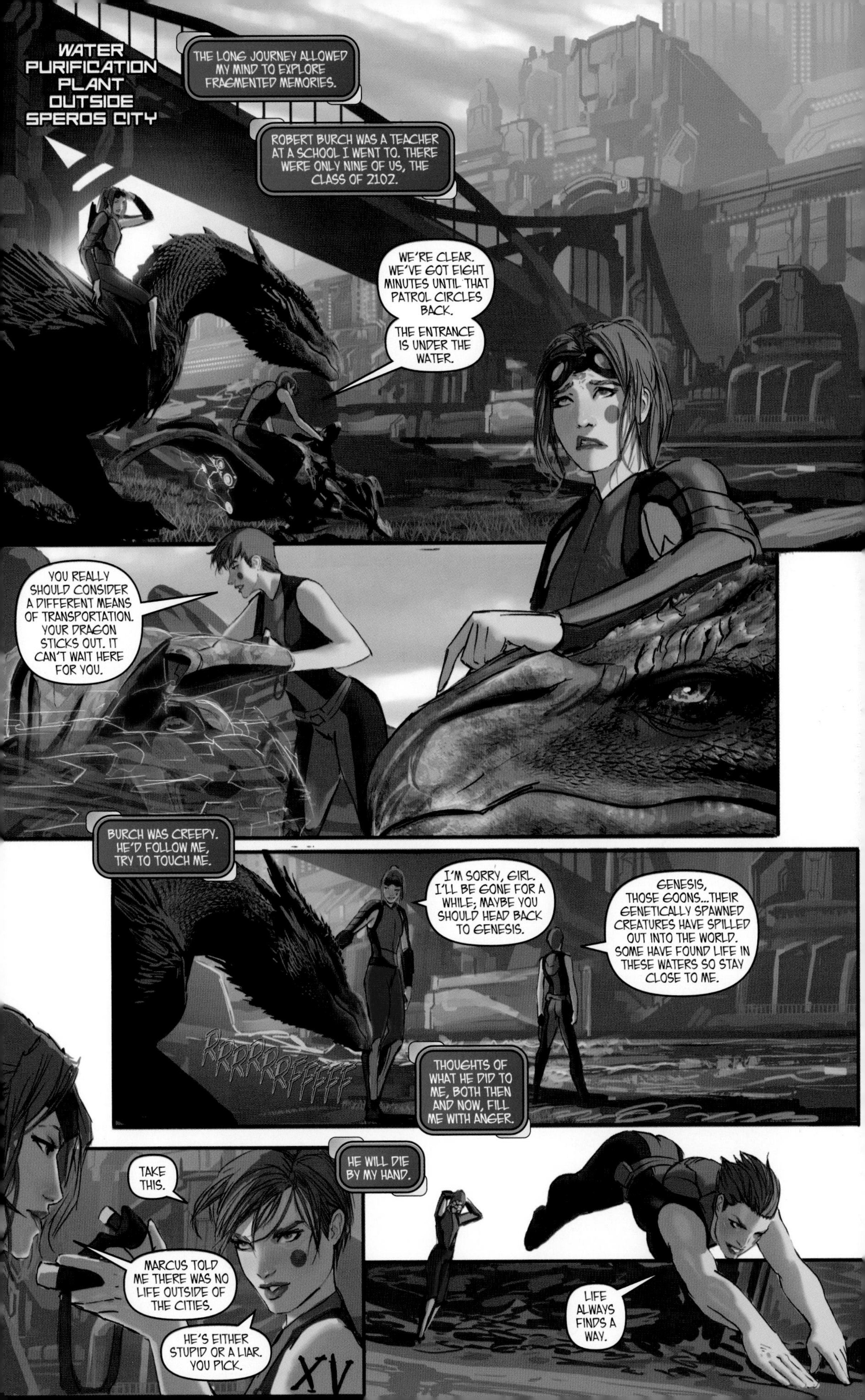
WATER PURIFICATION PLANT OUTSIDE SPEROS CITY
THE LONG JOURNEY ALLOWED MY MIND TO EXPLORE FRAGMENTED MEMORIES.
ROBERT BURCH WAS A TEACHER AT A SCHOOL I WENT TO. THERE WERE ONLY NINE OF US, THE CLASS OF 2102.
WE'RE CLEAR. WE'VE GOT EIGHT MINUTES UNTIL THAT PATROL CIRCLES BACK.
THE ENTRANCE IS UNDER THE WATER.
YOU REALLY SHOULD CONSIDER A DIFFERENT MEANS OF TRANSPORTATION. YOUR DRAGON STICKS OUT. IT CAN'T WAIT HERE FOR YOU.
BURCH WAS CREEPY. HE'D FOLLOW ME, TRY TO TOUCH ME.
I'M SORRY, GIRL. I'LL BE GONE FOR A WHILE; MAYBE YOU SHOULD HEAD BACK TO GENESIS.
GENESIS, THOSE GOONS...THEIR GENETICALLY SPAWNED CREATURES HAVE SPILLED OUT INTO THE WORLD. SOME HAVE FOUND LIFE IN THESE WATERS SO STAY CLOSE TO ME.
RRRRRRFFFFFF
THOUGHTS OF WHAT HE DID TO ME, BOTH THEN AND NOW, FILL ME WITH ANGER.
HE WILL DIE BY MY HAND.
TAKE THIS.
MARCUS TOLD ME THERE WAS NO LIFE OUTSIDE OF THE CITIES.
HE'S EITHER STUPID OR A LIAR. YOU PICK.
XV
LIFE ALWAYS FINDS A WAY.

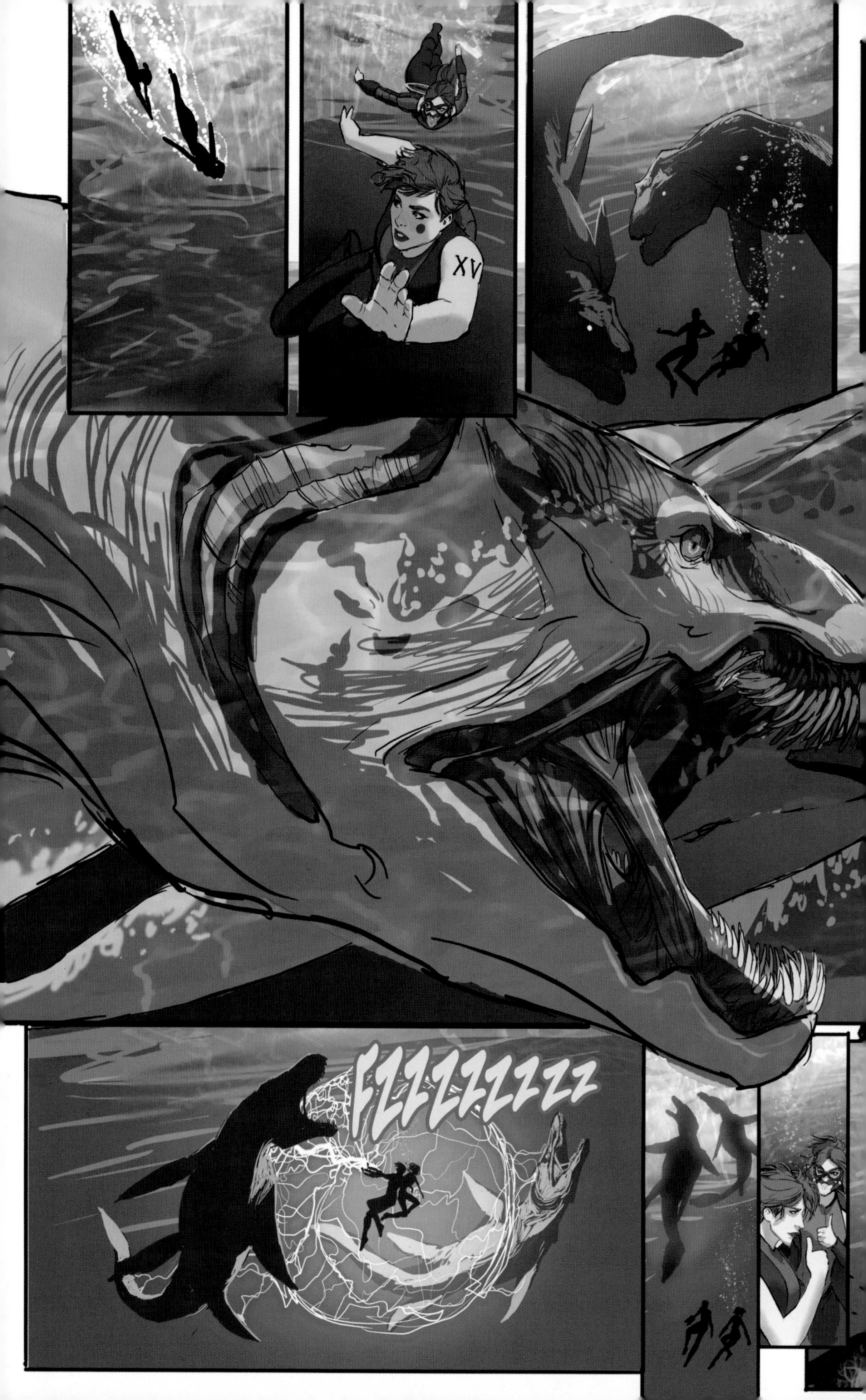

XV
FZZZZZZZZZ

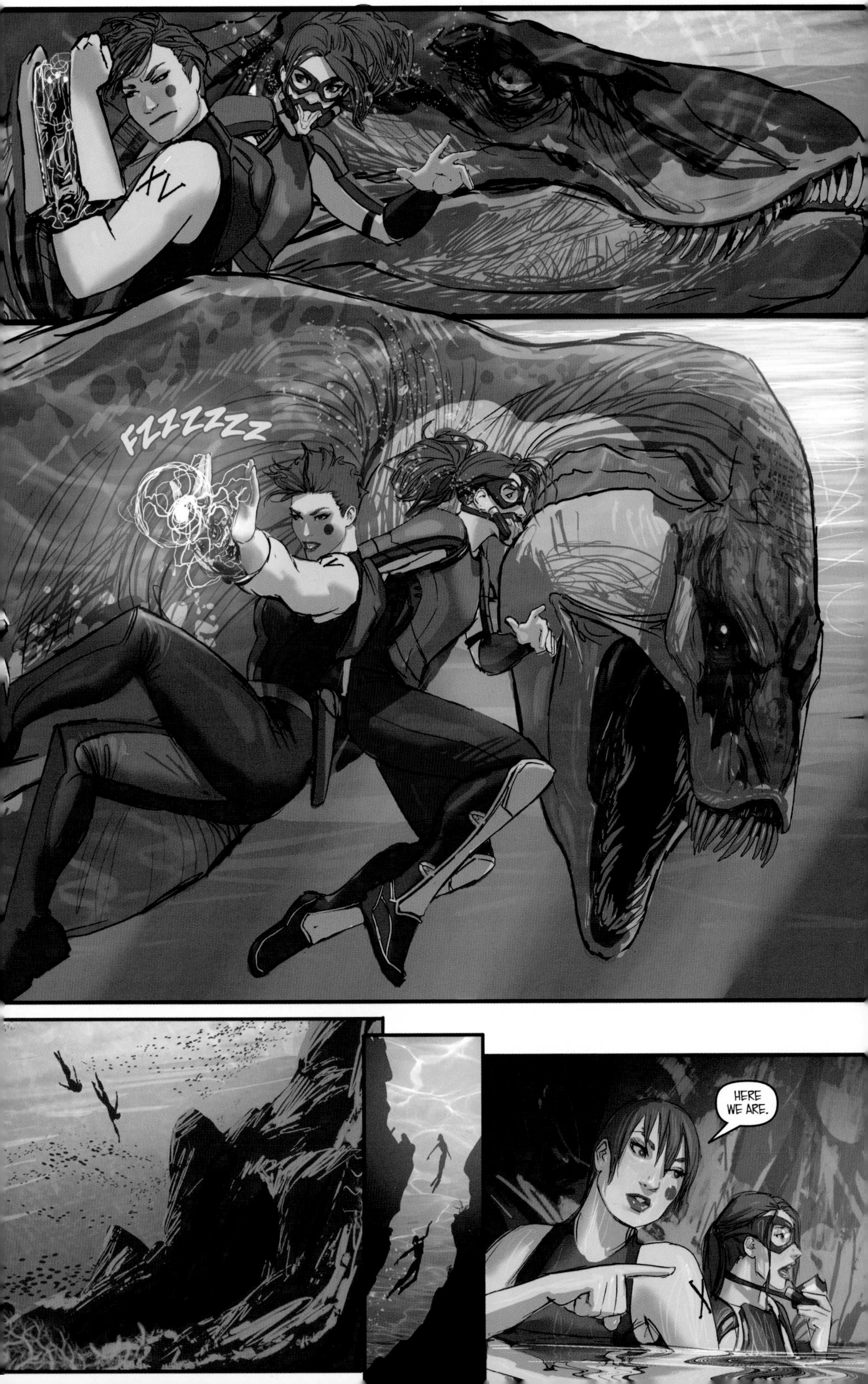
FZZZZZZZ
HERE WE ARE.

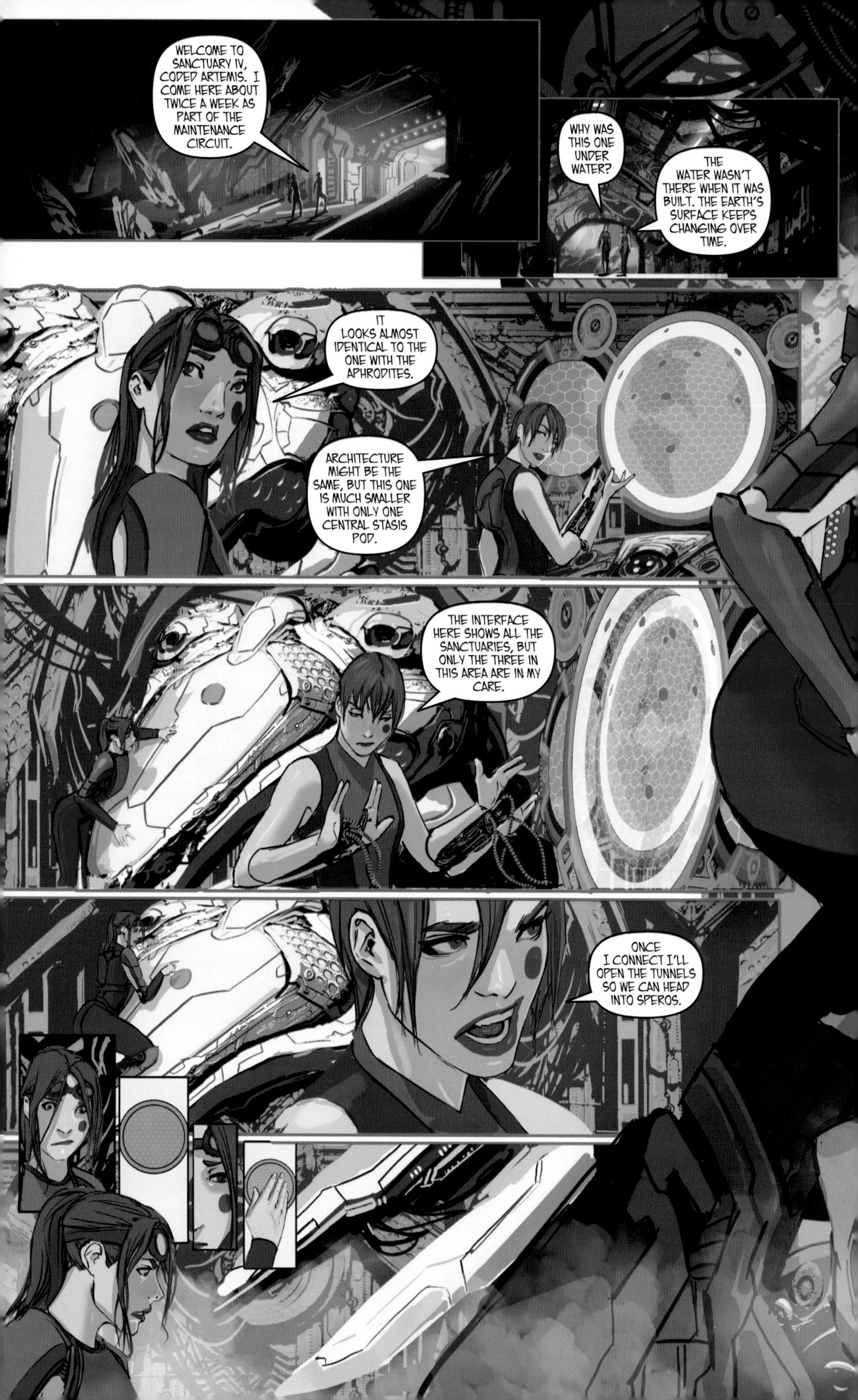
WELCOME TO SANCTUARY IV, CODED ARTEMIS. I COME HERE ABOUT TWICE A WEEK AS PART OF THE MAINTENANCE CIRCUIT.
WHY WAS THIS ONE UNDER WATER?
THE WATER WASN'T THERE WHEN IT WAS BUILT. THE EARTH'S SURFACE KEEPS CHANGING OVER TIME.
IT LOOKS ALMOST IDENTICAL TO THE ONE WITH THE APHRODITES.
ARCHITECTURE MIGHT BE THE SAME, BUT THIS ONE IS MUCH SMALLER WITH ONLY ONE CENTRAL STASIS POD.
THE INTERFACE HERE SHOWS ALL THE SANCTUARIES, BUT ONLY THE THREE IN THIS AREA ARE IN MY CARE.
ONCE I CONNECT I'LL OPEN THE TUNNELS SO WE CAN HEAD INTO SPEROS.

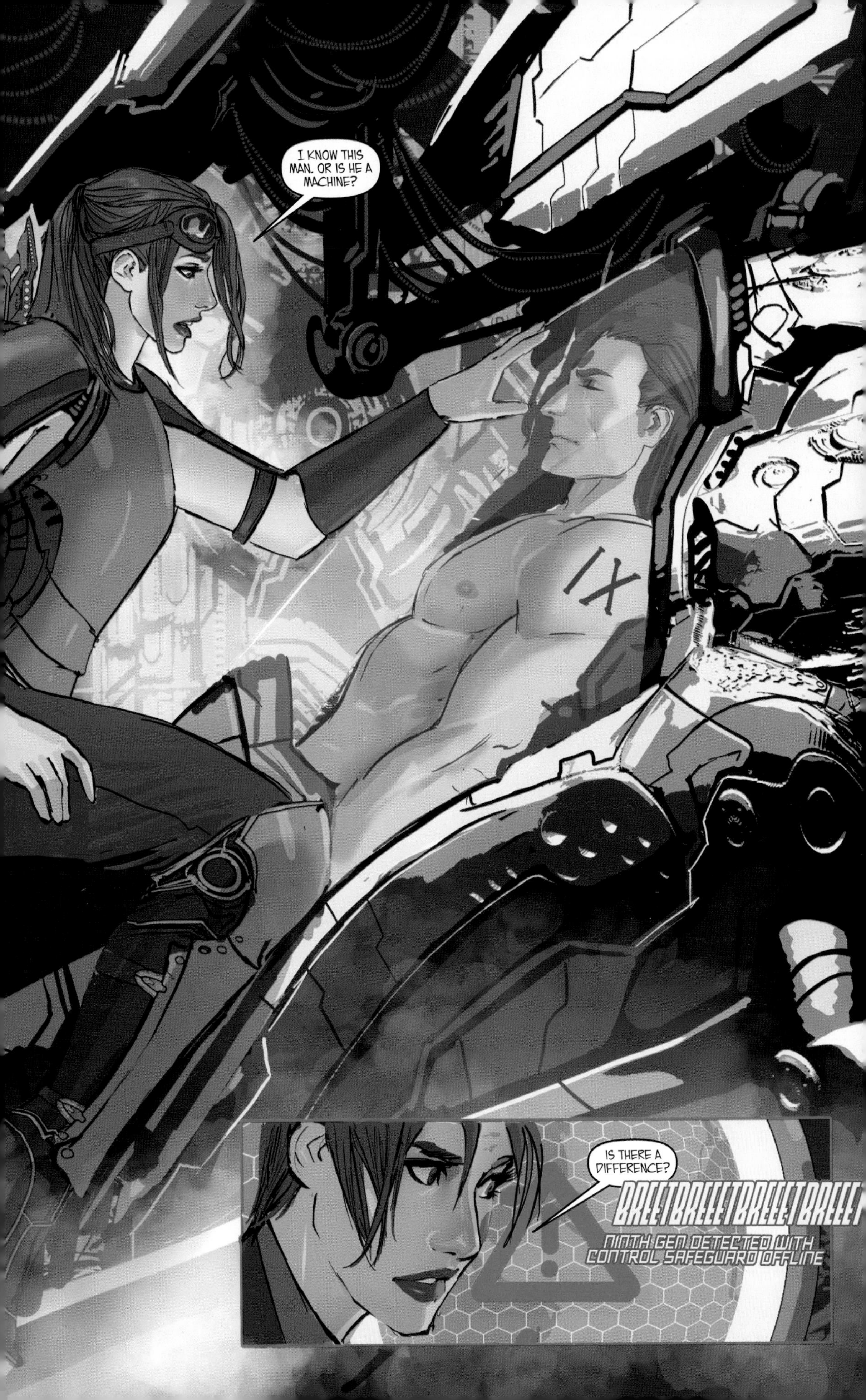
I KNOW THIS MAN. OR IS HE A MACHINE?
IS THERE A DIFFERENCE?
BREETBREEETBREEETBREEET
NINTH GEN DETECTED WITH CONTROL SAFEGUARD OFFLINE

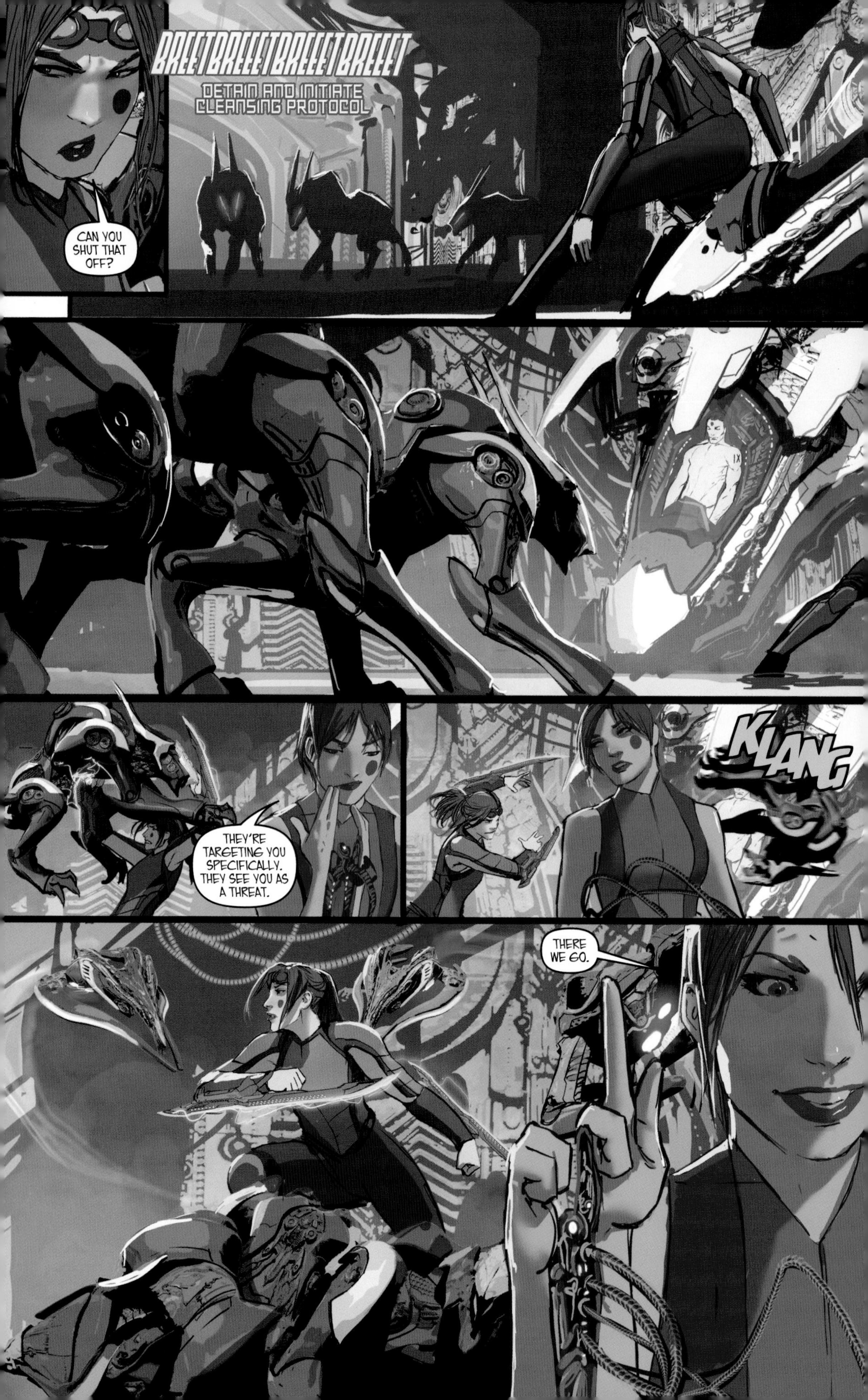
BREETBREEETBREEETBREEET
DETAIN AND INITIATE CLEANSING PROTOCOL
CAN YOU SHUT THAT OFF?
THEY'RE TARGETING YOU SPECIFICALLY. THEY SEE YOU AS A THREAT.
KLANG
THERE WE GO.

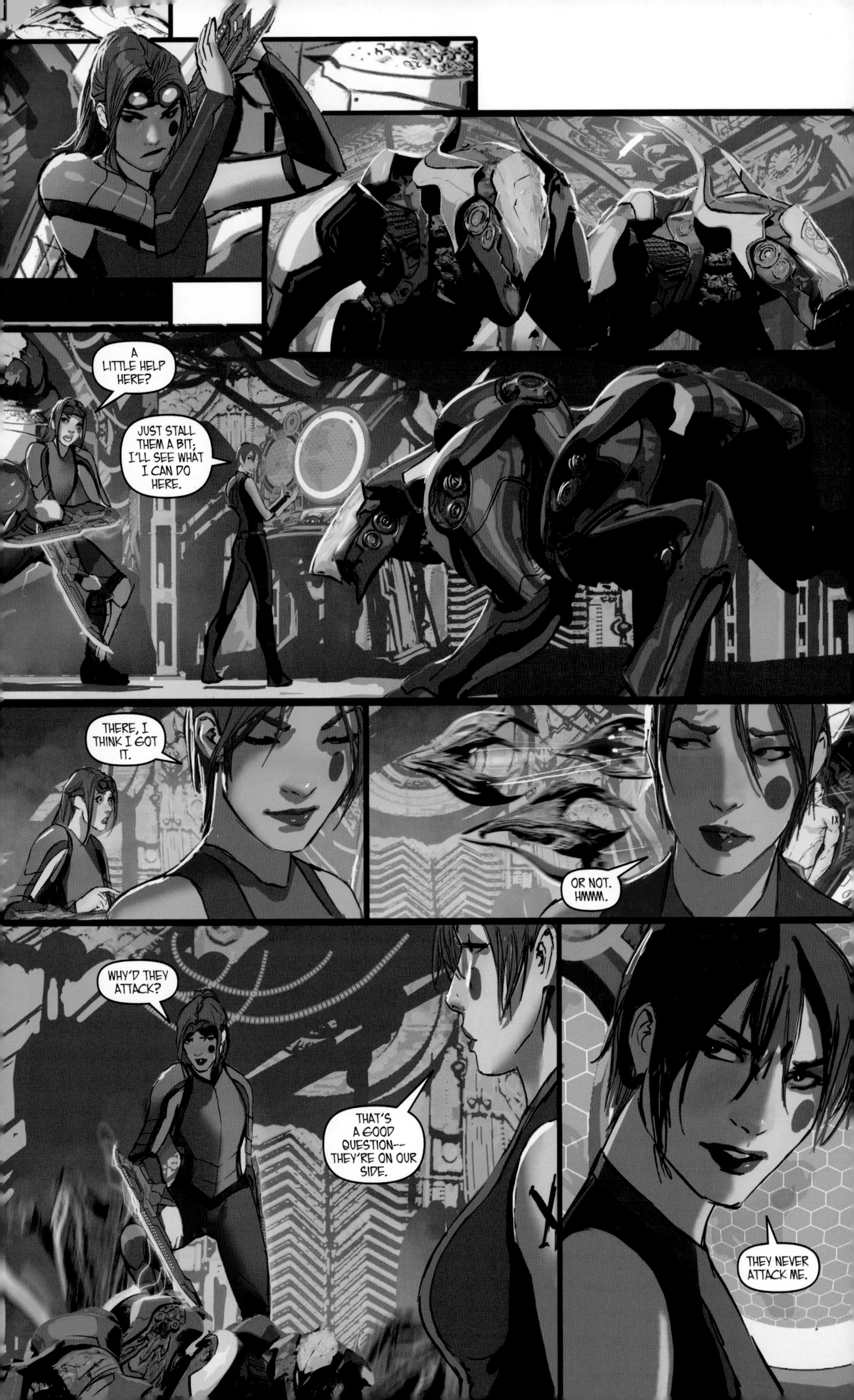
A LITTLE HELP HERE?
JUST STALL THEM A BIT; I'LL SEE WHAT I CAN DO HERE.
THERE, I THINK I GOT IT.
OR NOT. HMMM.
WHY'D THEY ATTACK?
THAT'S A GOOD QUESTION-- THEY'RE ON OUR SIDE.
THEY NEVER ATTACK ME.

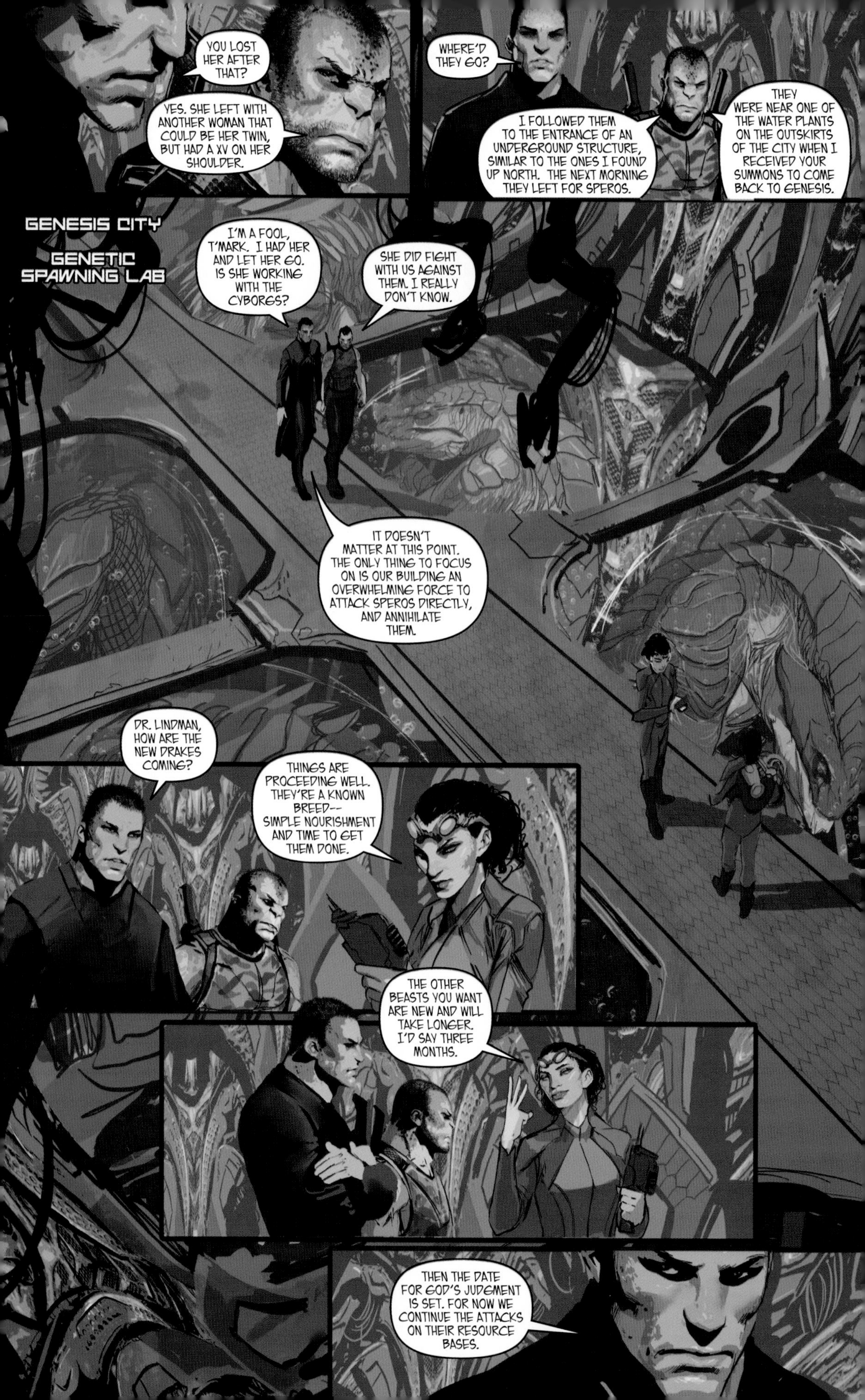
YOU LOST HER AFTER THAT?
YES. SHE LEFT WITH ANOTHER WOMAN THAT COULD BE HER TWIN, BUT HAD A XV ON HER SHOULDER.
WHERE'D THEY GO?
I FOLLOWED THEM TO THE ENTRANCE OF AN UNDERGROUND STRUCTURE, SIMILAR TO THE ONES I FOUND UP NORTH. THE NEXT MORNING THEY LEFT FOR SPEROS.
THEY WERE NEAR ONE OF THE WATER PLANTS ON THE OUTSKIRTS OF THE CITY WHEN I RECEIVED YOUR SUMMONS TO COME BACK TO GENESIS.
GENESIS CITY
GENETIC SPAWNING LAB
I'M A FOOL, T'MARK. I HAD HER AND LET HER GO. IS SHE WORKING WITH THE CYBORGS?
SHE DID FIGHT WITH US AGAINST THEM. I REALLY DON'T KNOW.
IT DOESN'T MATTER AT THIS POINT. THE ONLY THING TO FOCUS ON IS OUR BUILDING AN OVERWHELMING FORCE TO ATTACK SPEROS DIRECTLY, AND ANNIHILATE THEM.
DR. LINDMAN, HOW ARE THE NEW DRAKES COMING?
THINGS ARE PROCEEDING WELL. THEY'RE A KNOWN BREED-- SIMPLE NOURISHMENT AND TIME TO GET THEM DONE.
THE OTHER BEASTS YOU WANT ARE NEW AND WILL TAKE LONGER. I'D SAY THREE MONTHS.
THEN THE DATE FOR GOD'S JUDGMENT IS SET. FOR NOW WE CONTINUE THE ATTACKS ON THEIR RESOURCE BASES.

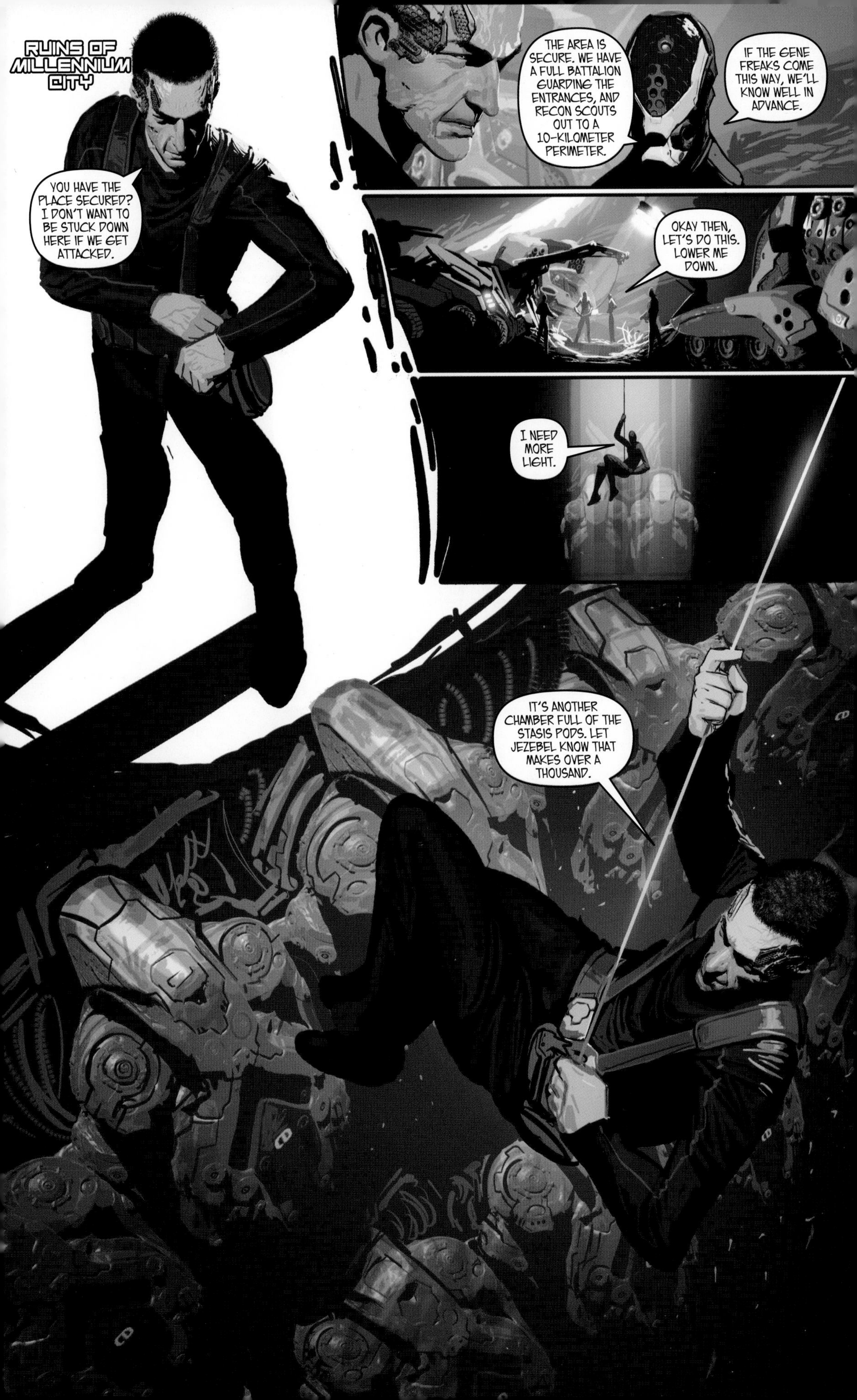
RUINS OF MILLENNIUM CITY
YOU HAVE THE PLACE SECURED? I DON'T WANT TO BE STUCK DOWN HERE IF WE GET ATTACKED.
THE AREA IS SECURE. WE HAVE A FULL BATTALION GUARDING THE ENTRANCES, AND RECON SCOUTS OUT TO A 10-KILOMETER PERIMETER.
IF THE GENE FREAKS COME THIS WAY, WE'LL KNOW WELL IN ADVANCE.
OKAY THEN, LET'S DO THIS. LOWER ME DOWN.
I NEED MORE LIGHT.
IT'S ANOTHER CHAMBER FULL OF THE STASIS PODS. LET JEZEBEL KNOW THAT MAKES OVER A THOUSAND.

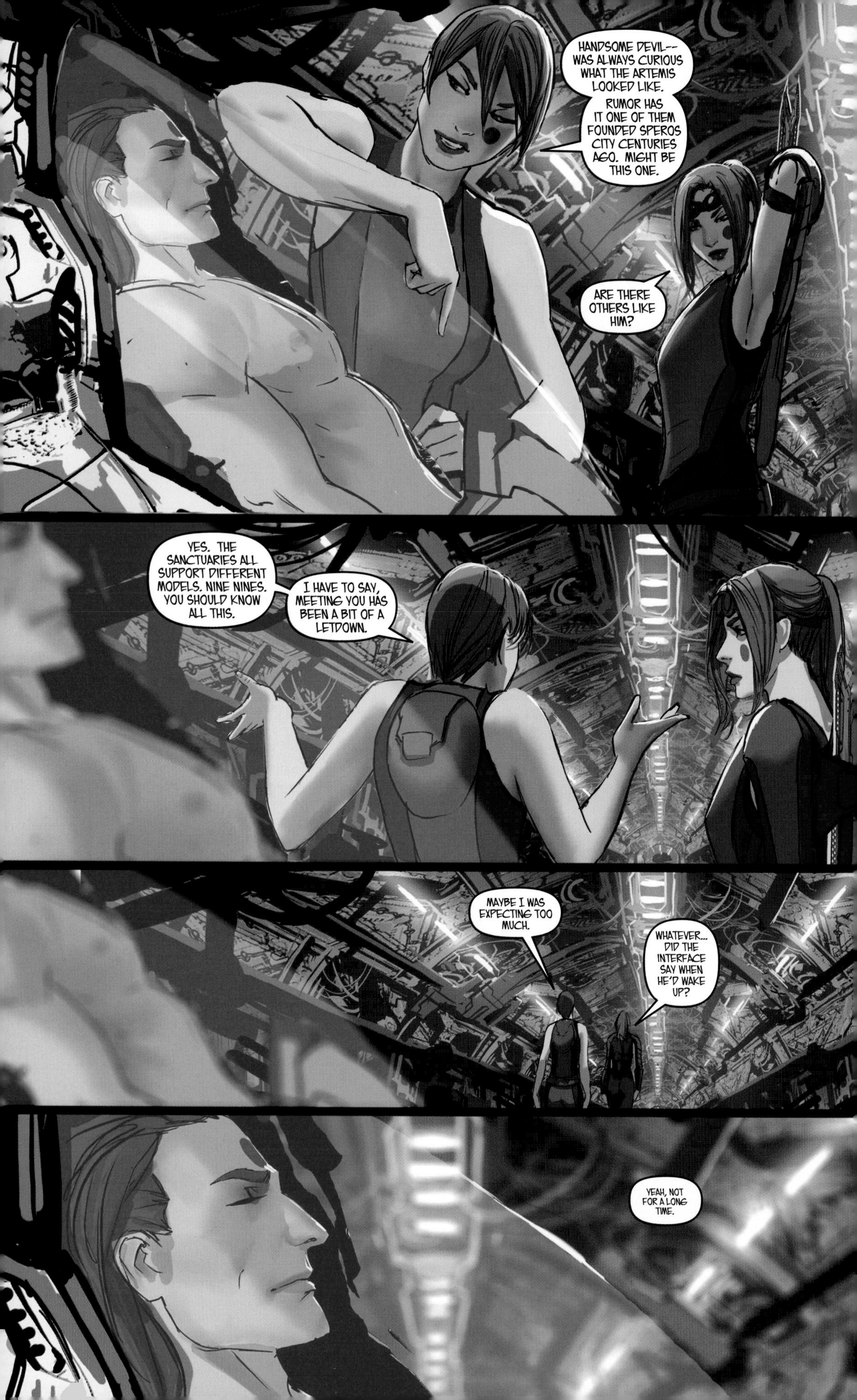
HANDSOME DEVIL-- WAS ALWAYS CURIOUS WHAT THE ARTEMIS LOOKED LIKE.
RUMOR HAS IT ONE OF THEM FOUNDED SPEROS CITY CENTURIES AGO. MIGHT BE THIS ONE.
ARE THERE OTHERS LIKE HIM?
YES. THE SANCTUARIES ALL SUPPORT DIFFERENT MODELS. NINE NINES. YOU SHOULD KNOW ALL THIS.
I HAVE TO SAY, MEETING YOU HAS BEEN A BIT OF A LETDOWN.
MAYBE I WAS EXPECTING TOO MUCH.
WHATEVER... DID THE INTERFACE SAY WHEN HE'D WAKE UP?
YEAH, NOT FOR A LONG TIME.

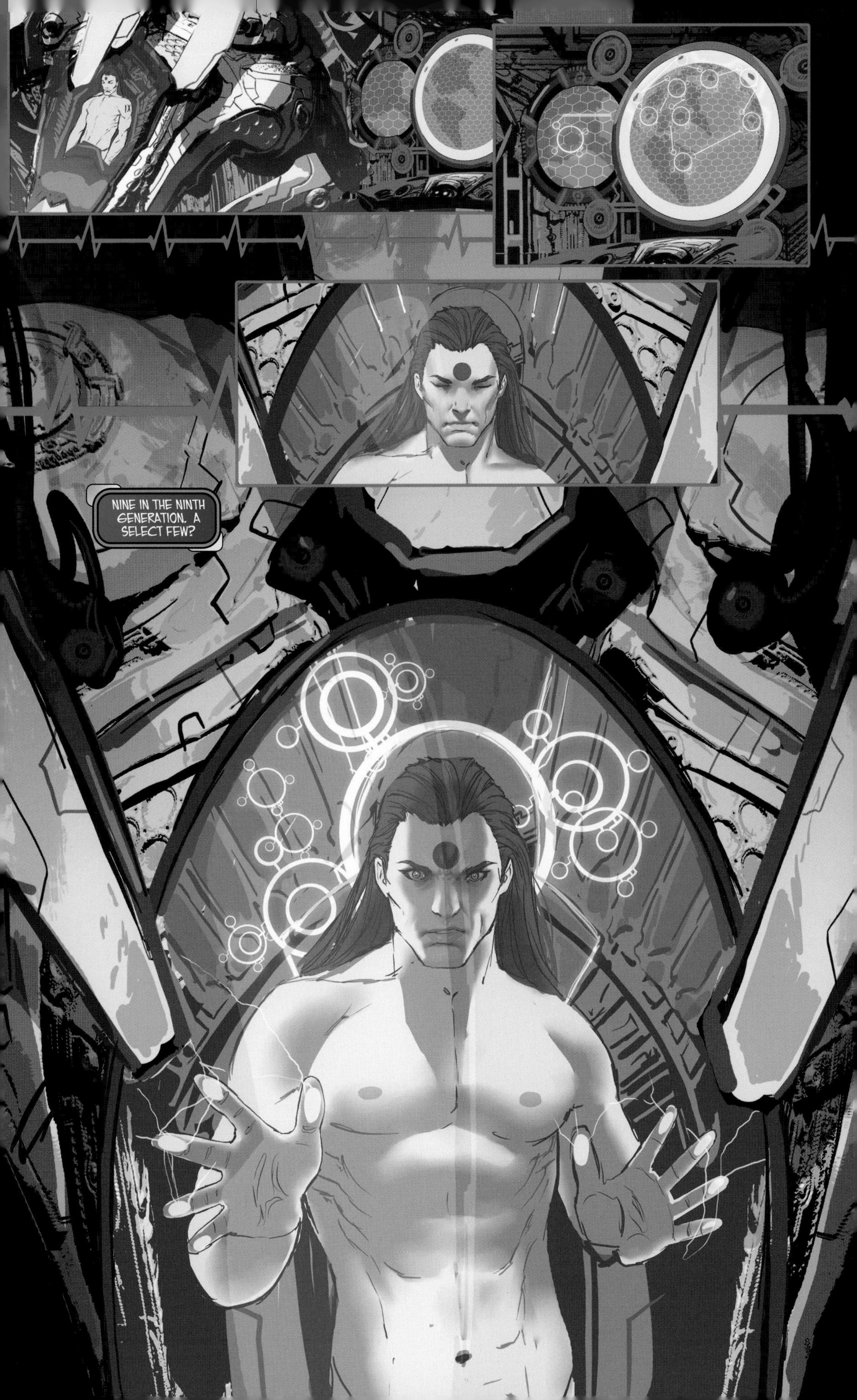
NINE IN THE NINTH GENERATION. A SELECT FEW?

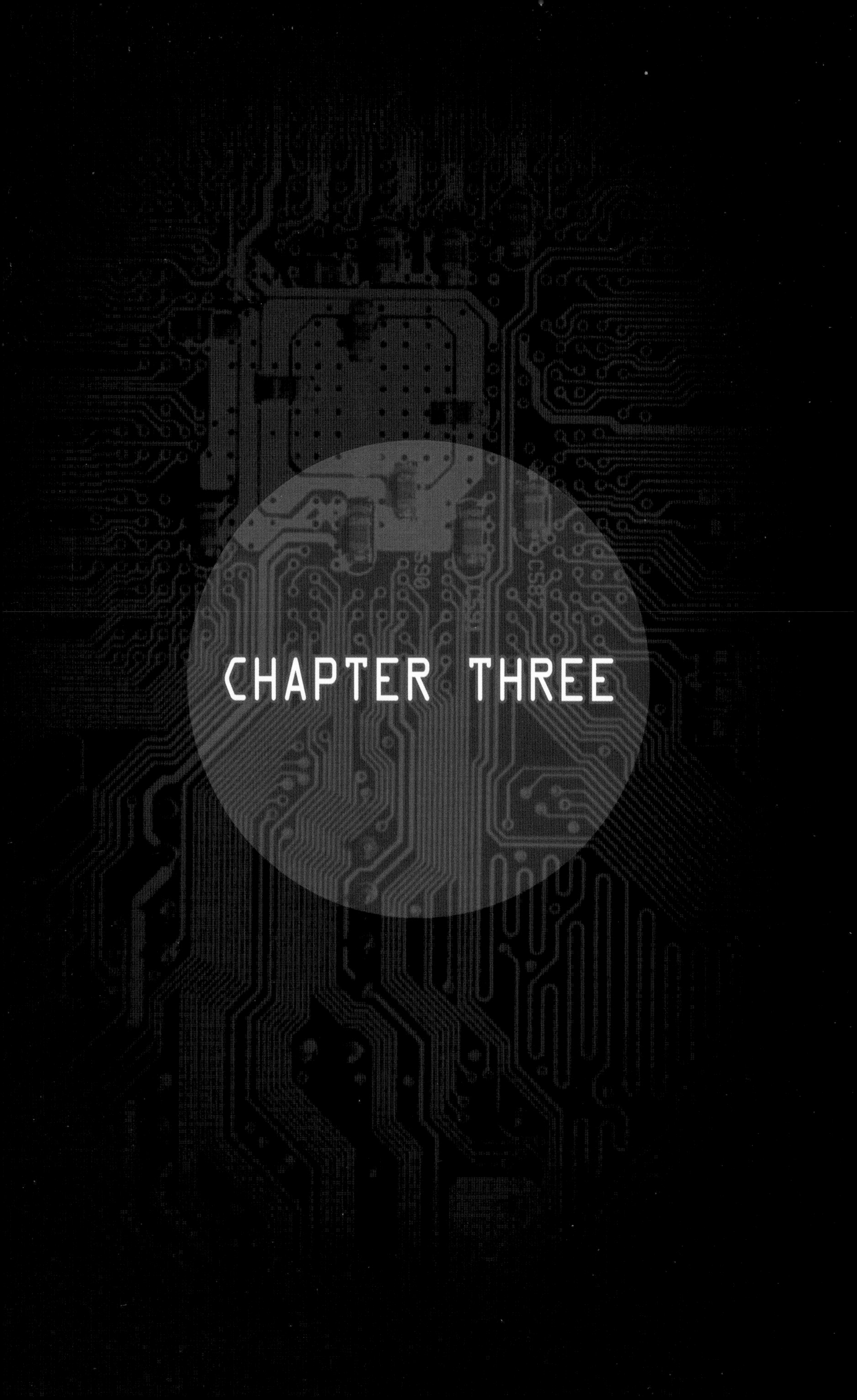

CHAPTER THREE

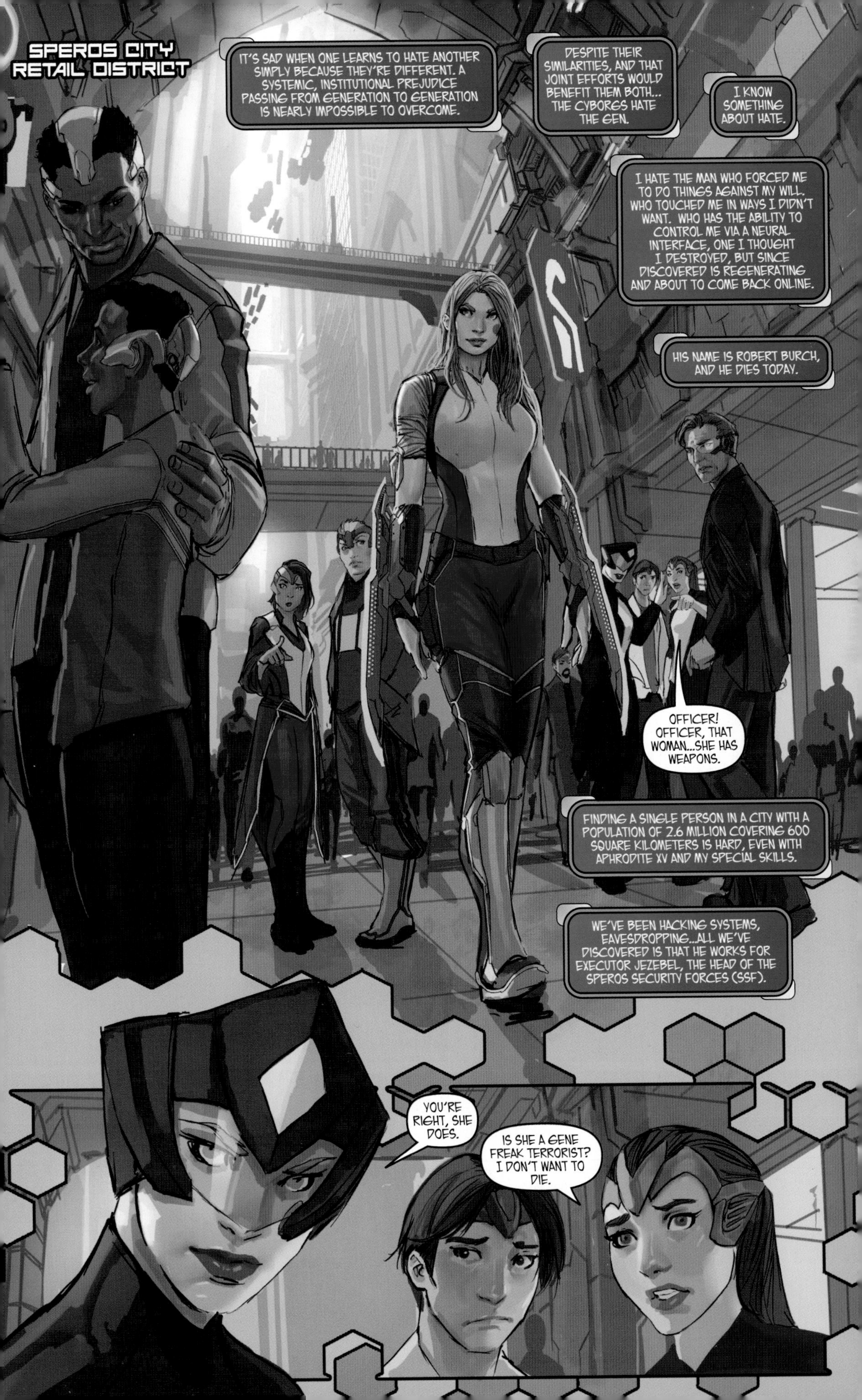
SPEROS CITY RETAIL DISTRICT
IT'S SAD WHEN ONE LEARNS TO HATE ANOTHER SIMPLY BECAUSE THEY'RE DIFFERENT. A SYSTEMIC, INSTITUTIONAL PREJUDICE PASSING FROM GENERATION TO GENERATION IS NEARLY IMPOSSIBLE TO OVERCOME.
DESPITE THEIR SIMILARITIES, AND THAT JOINT EFFORTS WOULD BENEFIT THEM BOTH... THE CYBORGS HATE THE GEN.
I KNOW SOMETHING ABOUT HATE.
I HATE THE MAN WHO FORCED ME TO DO THINGS AGAINST MY WILL. WHO TOUCHED ME IN WAYS I DIDN'T WANT. WHO HAS THE ABILITY TO CONTROL ME VIA A NEURAL INTERFACE, ONE I THOUGHT I DESTROYED, BUT SINCE DISCOVERED IS REGENERATING AND ABOUT TO COME BACK ONLINE.
HIS NAME IS ROBERT BURCH, AND HE DIES TODAY.
OFFICER! OFFICER, THAT WOMAN...SHE HAS WEAPONS.
FINDING A SINGLE PERSON IN A CITY WITH A POPULATION OF 2.6 MILLION COVERING 600 SQUARE KILOMETERS IS HARD, EVEN WITH APHRODITE XV AND MY SPECIAL SKILLS.
WE'VE BEEN HACKING SYSTEMS, EAVESDROPPING...ALL WE'VE DISCOVERED IS THAT HE WORKS FOR EXECUTOR JEZEBEL, THE HEAD OF THE SPEROS SECURITY FORCES (SSF).
YOU'RE RIGHT, SHE DOES.
IS SHE A GENE FREAK TERRORIST? I DON'T WANT TO DIE.

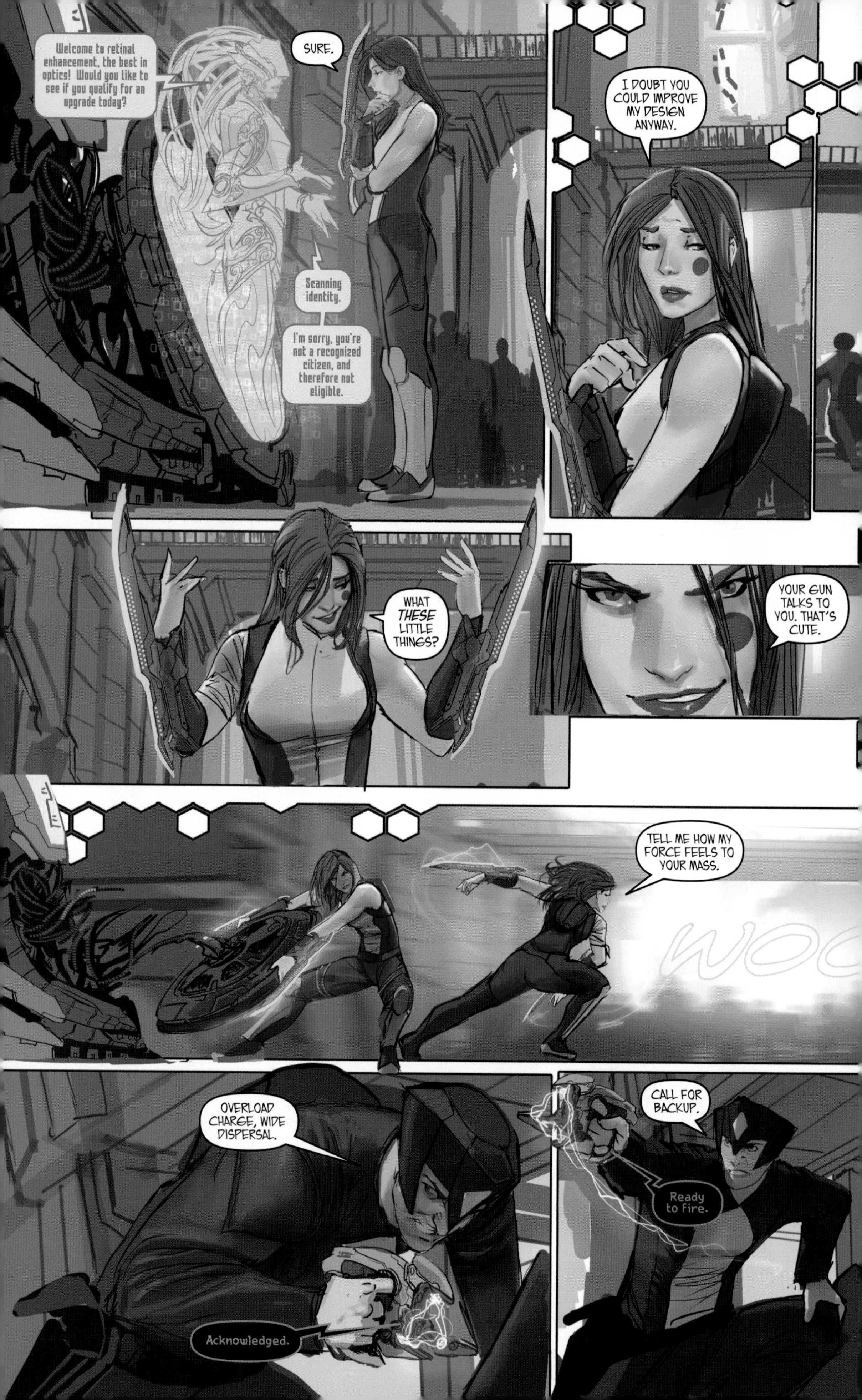
Welcome to retinal enhancement, the best in optics! Would you like to see if you qualify for an upgrade today?
SURE.
Scanning identity.
I'm sorry, you're not a recognized citizen, and therefore not eligible.
I DOUBT YOU COULD IMPROVE MY DESIGN ANYWAY.
WHAT THESE LITTLE THINGS?
YOUR GUN TALKS TO YOU. THAT'S CUTE.
TELL ME HOW MY FORCE FEELS TO YOUR MASS.
WOO
OVERLOAD CHARGE, WIDE DISPERSAL.
Acknowledged.
CALL FOR BACKUP.
Ready to fire.

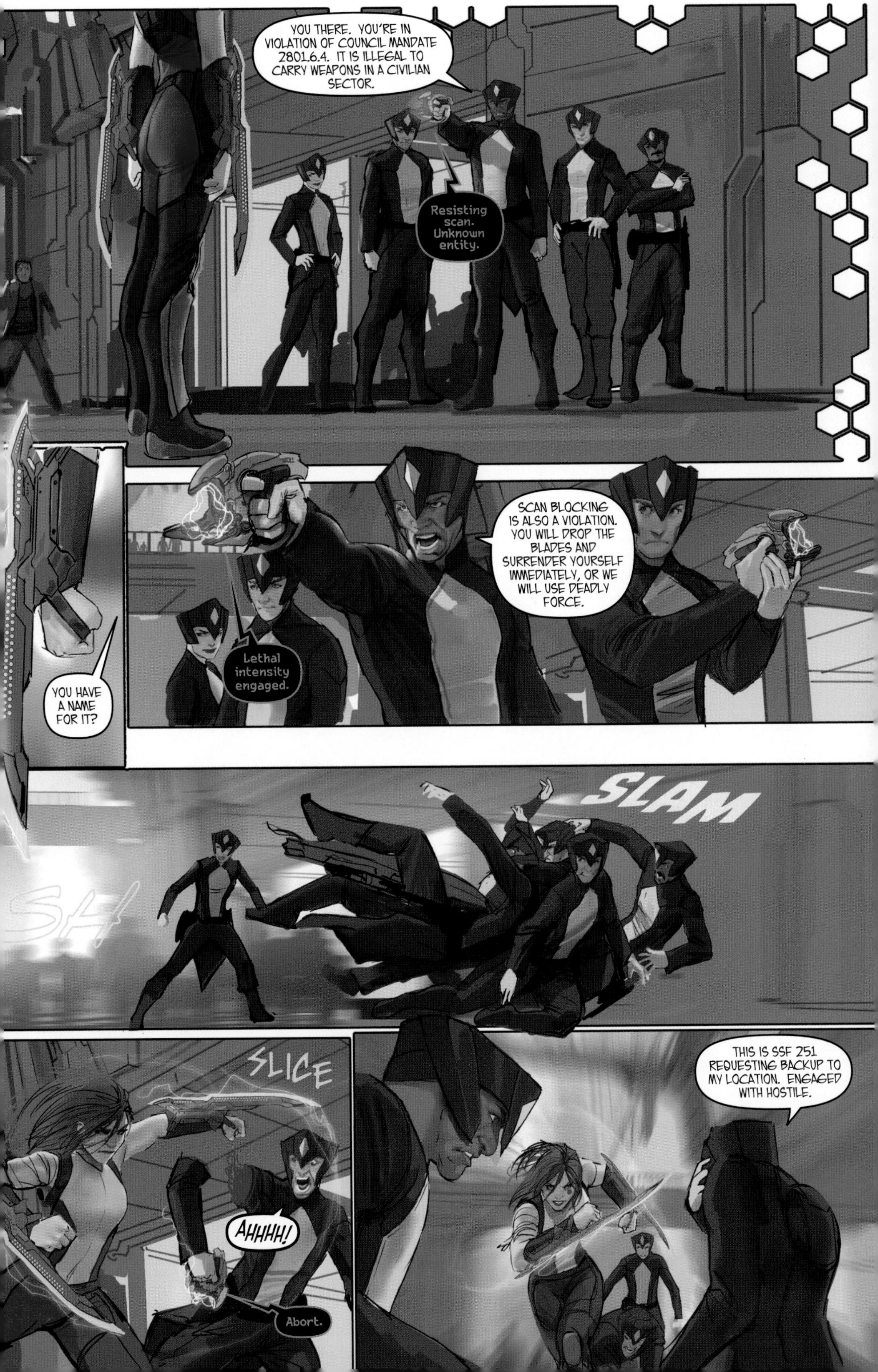
YOU THERE. YOU'RE IN VIOLATION OF COUNCIL MANDATE 2801.6.4. IT IS ILLEGAL TO CARRY WEAPONS IN A CIVILIAN SECTOR.
Resisting scan. Unknown entity.
YOU HAVE A NAME FOR IT?
SCAN BLOCKING IS ALSO A VIOLATION. YOU WILL DROP THE BLADES AND SURRENDER YOURSELF IMMEDIATELY, OR WE WILL USE DEADLY FORCE.
Lethal intensity engaged.
SLAM
SH
SLICE
AHHHH!
Abort.
THIS IS SSF 251 REQUESTING BACKUP TO MY LOCATION. ENGAGED WITH HOSTILE.

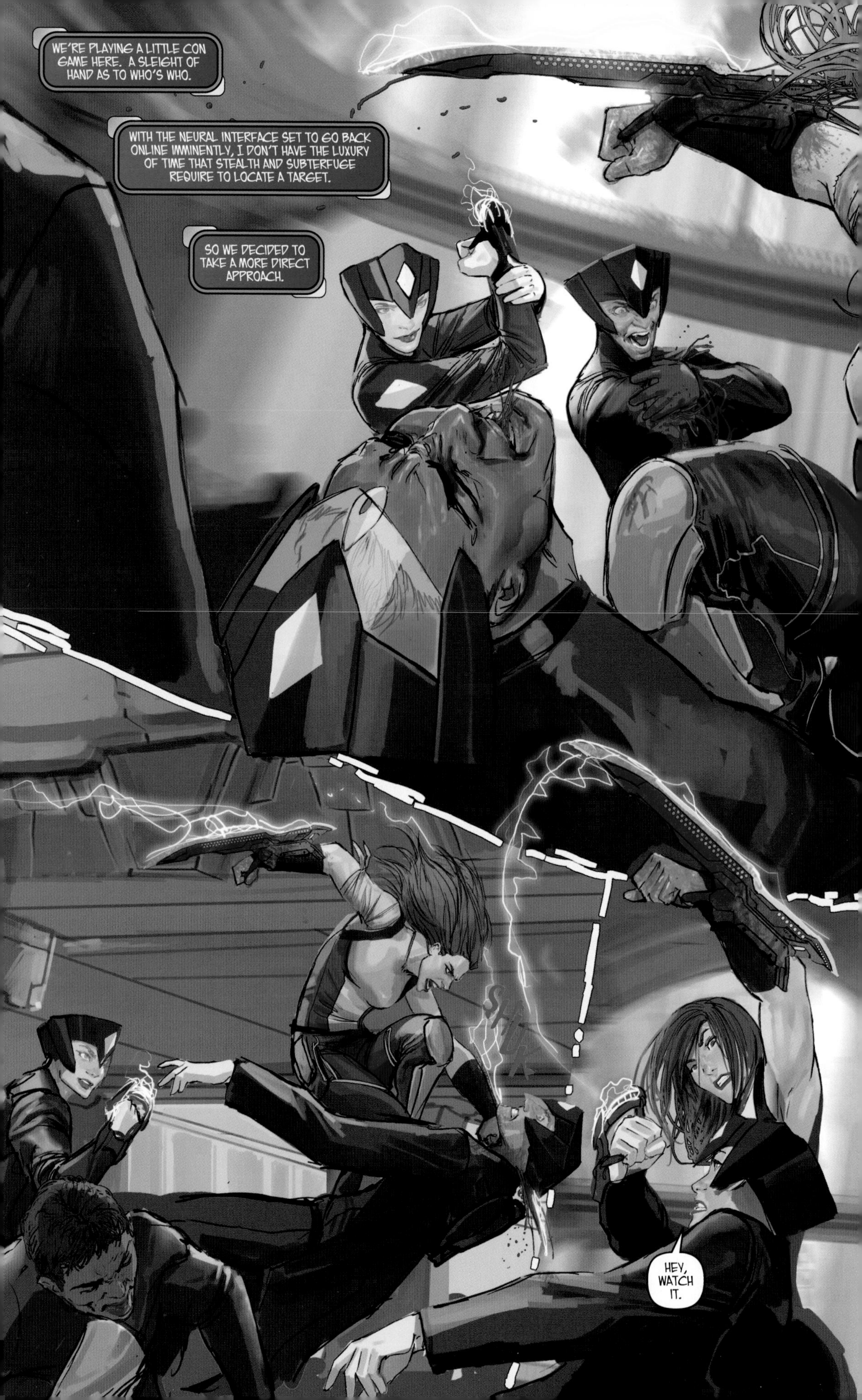
WE'RE PLAYING A LITTLE CON GAME HERE. A SLEIGHT OF HAND AS TO WHO'S WHO.
WITH THE NEURAL INTERFACE SET TO GO BACK ONLINE IMMINENTLY, I DON'T HAVE THE LUXURY OF TIME THAT STEALTH AND SUBTERFUGE REQUIRE TO LOCATE A TARGET.
SO WE DECIDED TO TAKE A MORE DIRECT APPROACH.
HEY, WATCH IT.

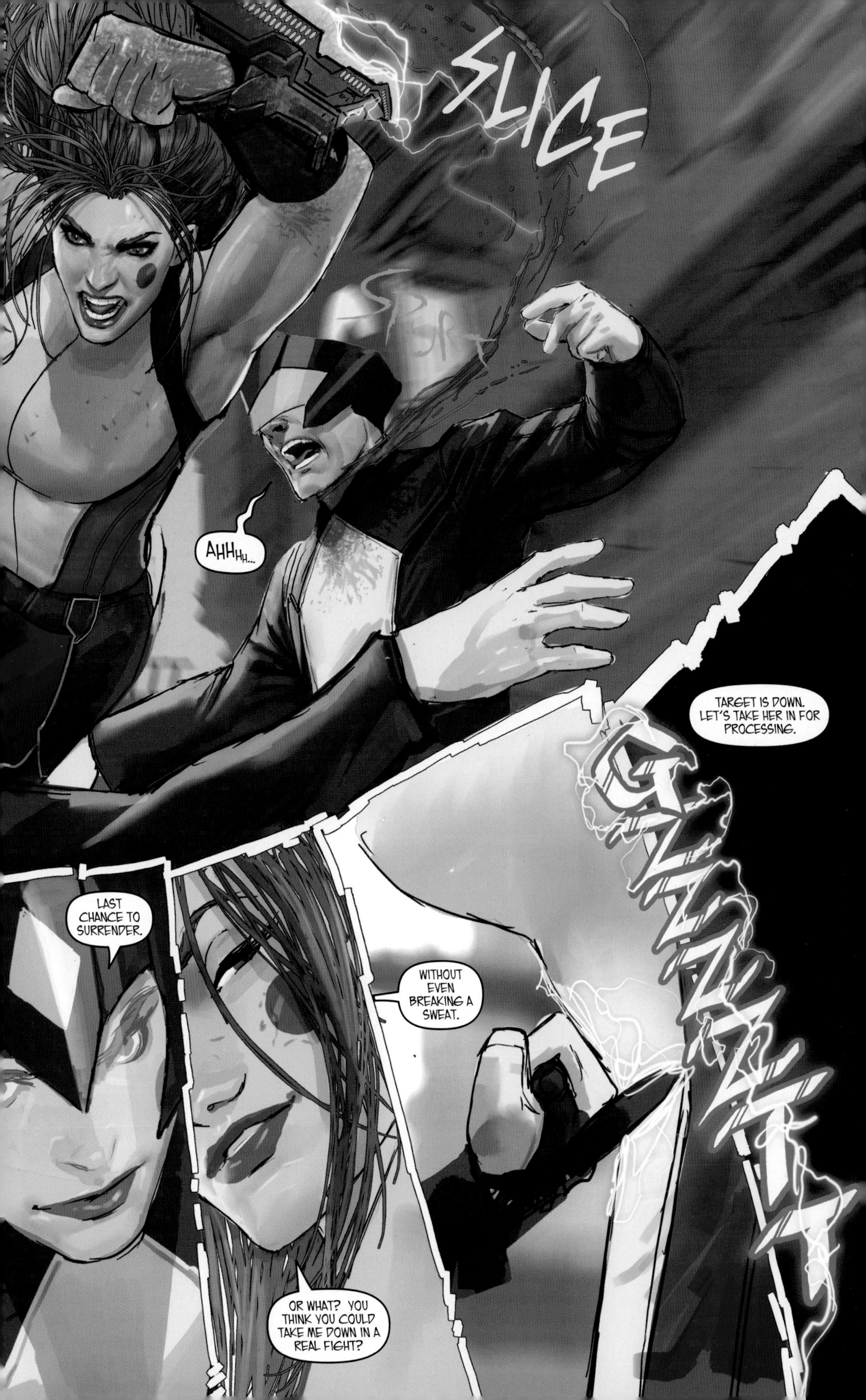
SLICE
SPURT
AHHHH...
TARGET IS DOWN. LET'S TAKE HER IN FOR PROCESSING.
LAST CHANCE TO SURRENDER.
WITHOUT EVEN BREAKING A SWEAT.
OR WHAT? YOU THINK YOU COULD TAKE ME DOWN IN A REAL FIGHT?

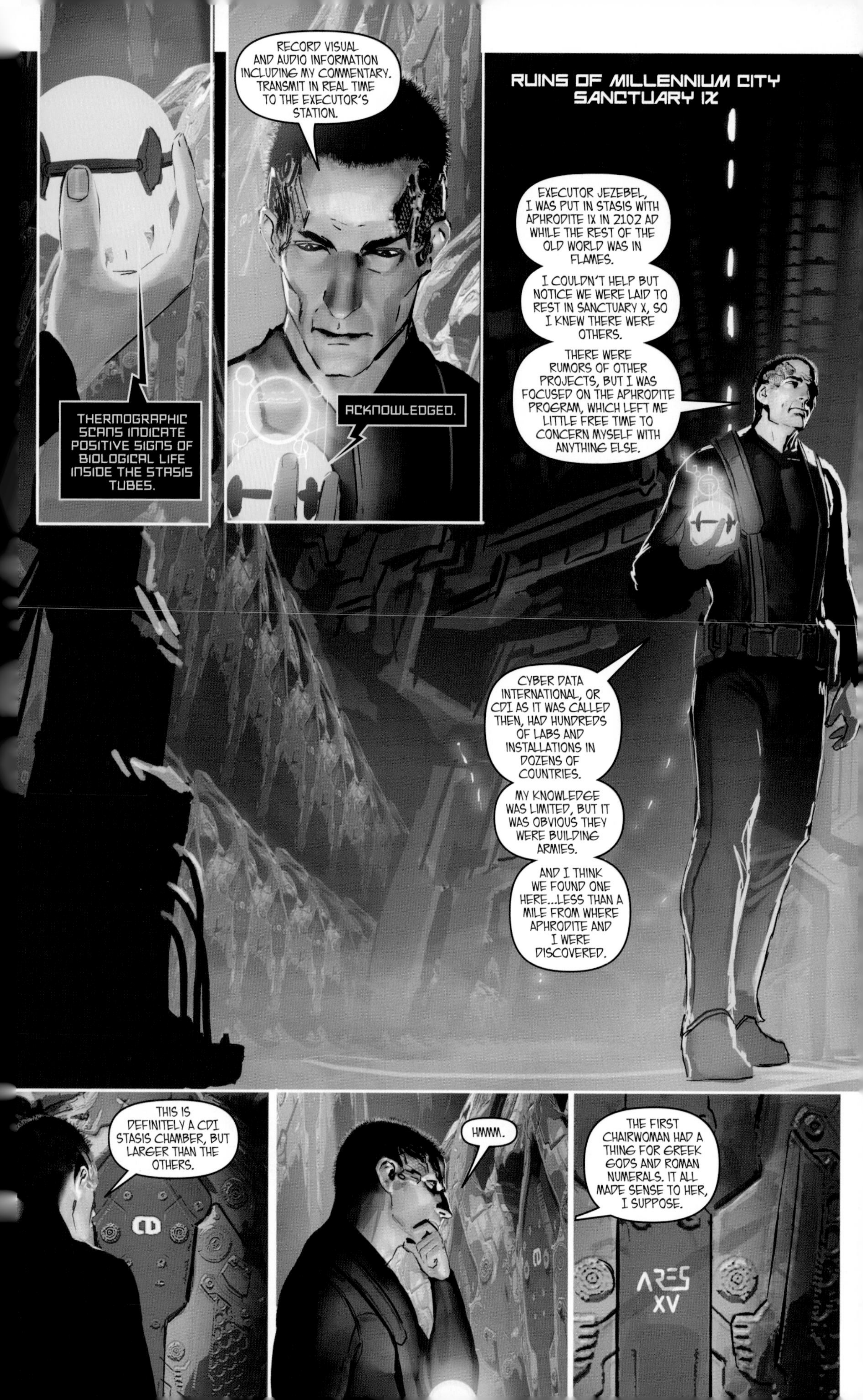
THERMOGRAPHIC SCANS INDICATE POSITIVE SIGNS OF BIOLOGICAL LIFE INSIDE THE STASIS TUBES.
RECORD VISUAL AND AUDIO INFORMATION INCLUDING MY COMMENTARY. TRANSMIT IN REAL TIME TO THE EXECUTOR'S STATION.
ACKNOWLEDGED.
RUINS OF MILLENNIUM CITY SANCTUARY IX
EXECUTOR JEZEBEL, I WAS PUT IN STASIS WITH APHRODITE IX IN 2102 AD WHILE THE REST OF THE OLD WORLD WAS IN FLAMES.
I COULDN'T HELP BUT NOTICE WE WERE LAID TO REST IN SANCTUARY X, SO I KNEW THERE WERE OTHERS.
THERE WERE RUMORS OF OTHER PROJECTS, BUT I WAS FOCUSED ON THE APHRODITE PROGRAM, WHICH LEFT ME LITTLE FREE TIME TO CONCERN MYSELF WITH ANYTHING ELSE.
CYBER DATA INTERNATIONAL, OR CDI AS IT WAS CALLED THEN, HAD HUNDREDS OF LABS AND INSTALLATIONS IN DOZENS OF COUNTRIES.
MY KNOWLEDGE WAS LIMITED, BUT IT WAS OBVIOUS THEY WERE BUILDING ARMIES.
AND I THINK WE FOUND ONE HERE...LESS THAN A MILE FROM WHERE APHRODITE AND I WERE DISCOVERED.
THIS IS DEFINITELY A CDI STASIS CHAMBER, BUT LARGER THAN THE OTHERS.
HMMM.
THE FIRST CHAIRWOMAN HAD A THING FOR GREEK GODS AND ROMAN NUMERALS. IT ALL MADE SENSE TO HER, I SUPPOSE.
ARES
XV

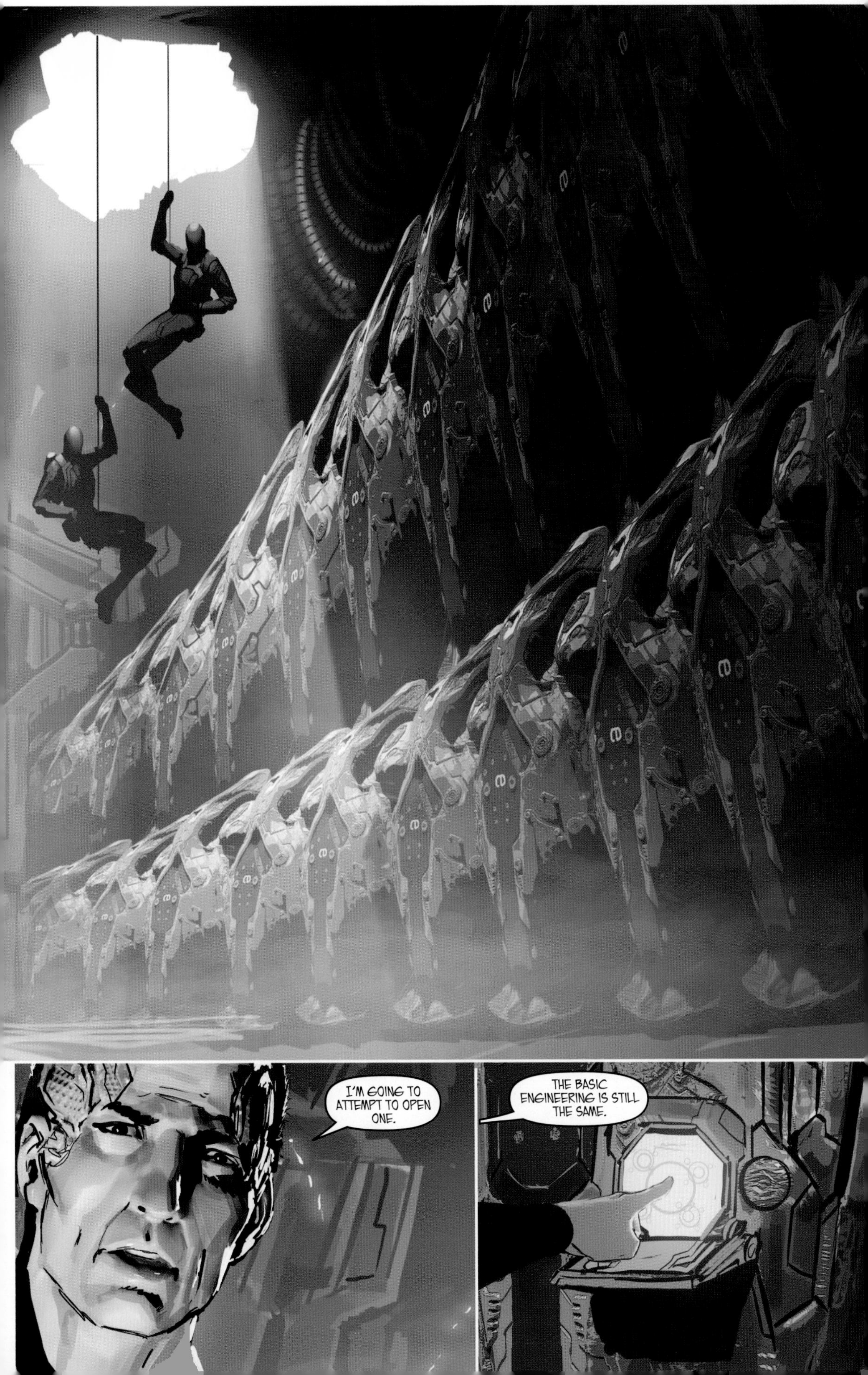
I'M GOING TO ATTEMPT TO OPEN ONE.
THE BASIC ENGINEERING IS STILL THE SAME.

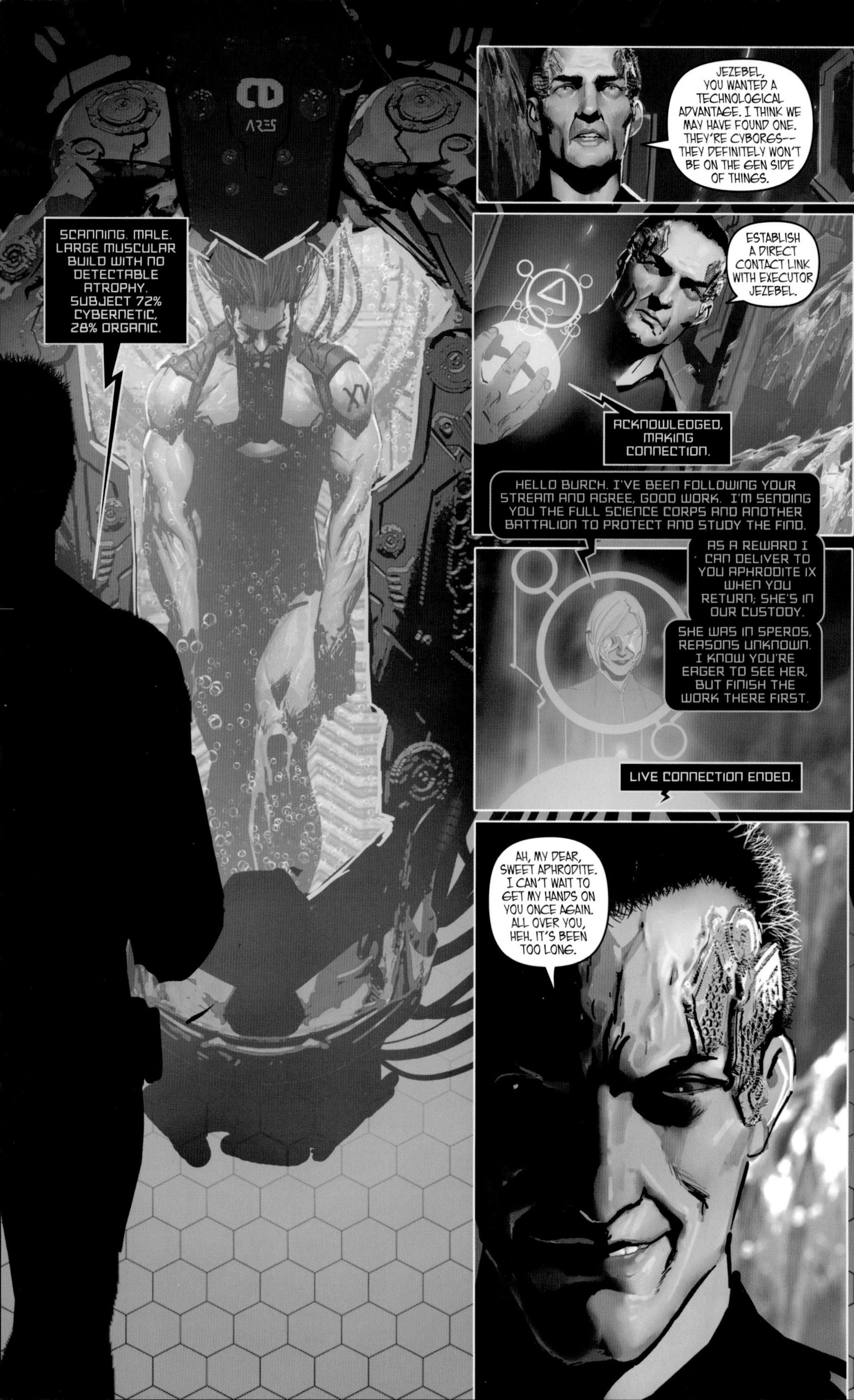
SCANNING. MALE. LARGE MUSCULAR BUILD WITH NO DETECTABLE ATROPHY. SUBJECT 72% CYBERNETIC, 28% ORGANIC.
JEZEBEL, YOU WANTED A TECHNOLOGICAL ADVANTAGE. I THINK WE MAY HAVE FOUND ONE. THEY'RE CYBORGS-- THEY DEFINITELY WON'T BE ON THE GEN SIDE OF THINGS.
ESTABLISH A DIRECT CONTACT LINK WITH EXECUTOR JEZEBEL.
ACKNOWLEDGED, MAKING CONNECTION.
HELLO BURCH. I'VE BEEN FOLLOWING YOUR STREAM AND AGREE, GOOD WORK. I'M SENDING YOU THE FULL SCIENCE CORPS AND ANOTHER BATTALION TO PROTECT AND STUDY THE FIND.
AS A REWARD I CAN DELIVER TO YOU APHRODITE IX WHEN YOU RETURN; SHE'S IN OUR CUSTODY.
SHE WAS IN SPEROS, REASONS UNKNOWN. I KNOW YOU'RE EAGER TO SEE HER, BUT FINISH THE WORK THERE FIRST.
LIVE CONNECTION ENDED.
AH, MY DEAR, SWEET APHRODITE. I CAN'T WAIT TO GET MY HANDS ON YOU ONCE AGAIN. ALL OVER YOU, HEH. IT'S BEEN TOO LONG.

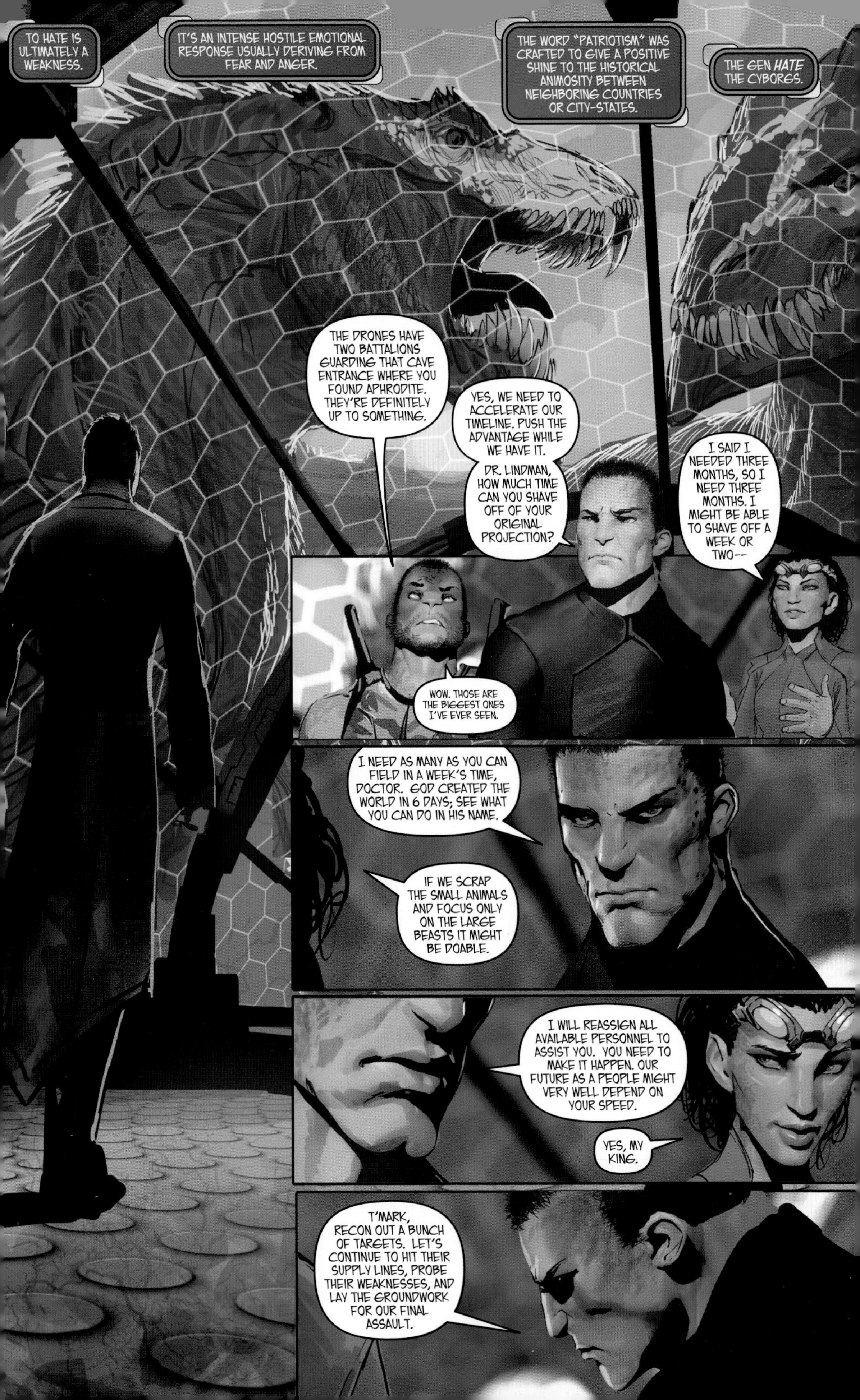

TO HATE IS ULTIMATELY A WEAKNESS.
IT'S AN INTENSE HOSTILE EMOTIONAL RESPONSE USUALLY DERIVING FROM FEAR AND ANGER.
THE WORD "PATRIOTISM" WAS CRAFTED TO GIVE A POSITIVE SHINE TO THE HISTORICAL ANIMOSITY BETWEEN NEIGHBORING COUNTRIES OR CITY-STATES.
THE GEN *HATE* THE CYBORGS.
THE DRONES HAVE TWO BATTALIONS GUARDING THAT CAVE ENTRANCE WHERE YOU FOUND APHRODITE. THEY'RE DEFINITELY UP TO SOMETHING.
YES, WE NEED TO ACCELERATE OUR TIMELINE. PUSH THE ADVANTAGE WHILE WE HAVE IT.
DR. LINDMAN, HOW MUCH TIME CAN YOU SHAVE OFF OF YOUR ORIGINAL PROJECTION?
I SAID I NEEDED THREE MONTHS, SO I NEED THREE MONTHS. I MIGHT BE ABLE TO SHAVE OFF A WEEK OR TWO--
WOW. THOSE ARE THE BIGGEST ONES I'VE EVER SEEN.
I NEED AS MANY AS YOU CAN FIELD IN A WEEK'S TIME, DOCTOR. GOD CREATED THE WORLD IN 6 DAYS; SEE WHAT YOU CAN DO IN HIS NAME.
IF WE SCRAP THE SMALL ANIMALS AND FOCUS ONLY ON THE LARGE BEASTS IT MIGHT BE DOABLE.
I WILL REASSIGN ALL AVAILABLE PERSONNEL TO ASSIST YOU. YOU NEED TO MAKE IT HAPPEN. OUR FUTURE AS A PEOPLE MIGHT VERY WELL DEPEND ON YOUR SPEED.
YES, MY KING.
T'MARK, RECON OUT A BUNCH OF TARGETS. LET'S CONTINUE TO HIT THEIR SUPPLY LINES, PROBE THEIR WEAKNESSES, AND LAY THE GROUNDWORK FOR OUR FINAL ASSAULT.

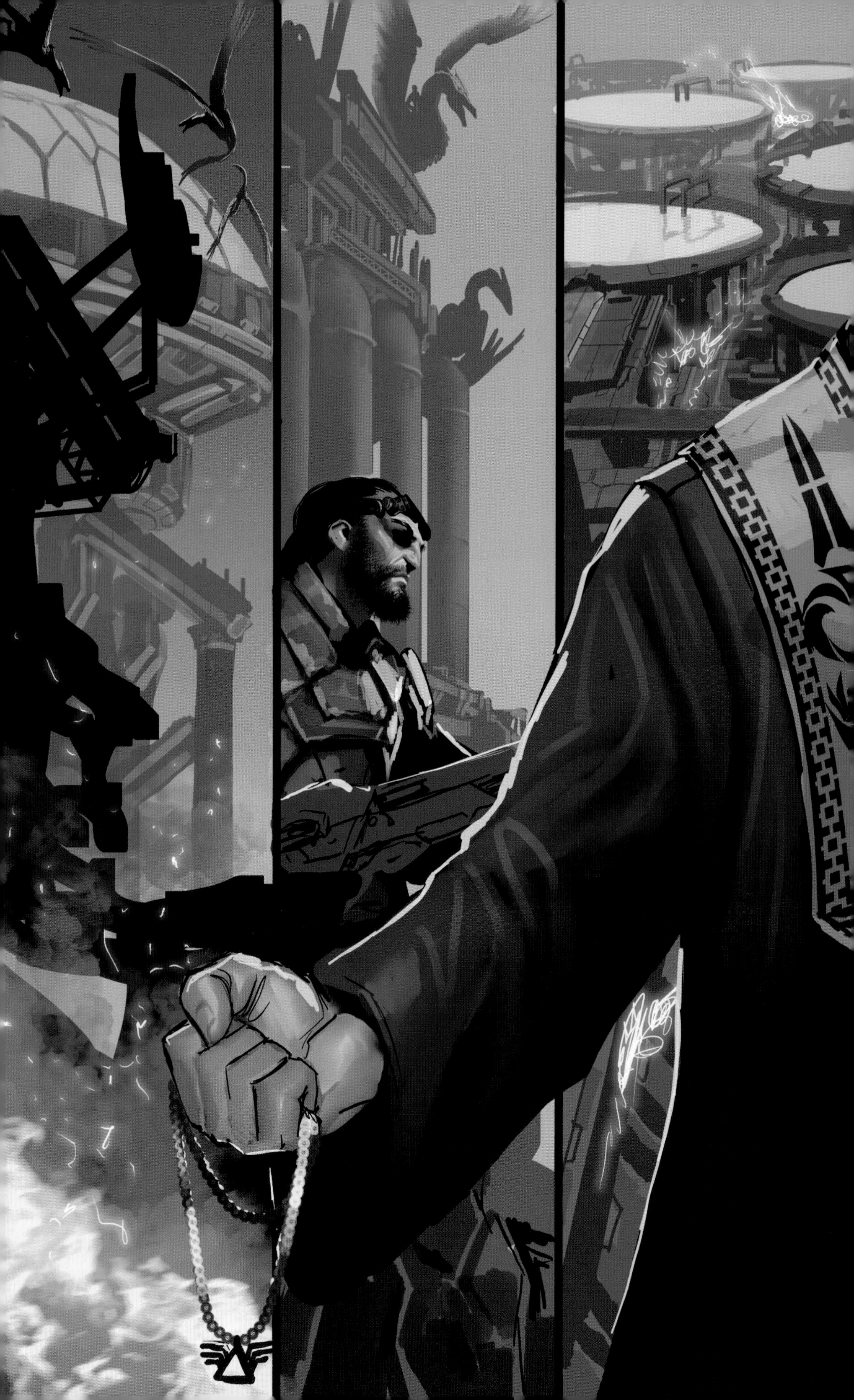

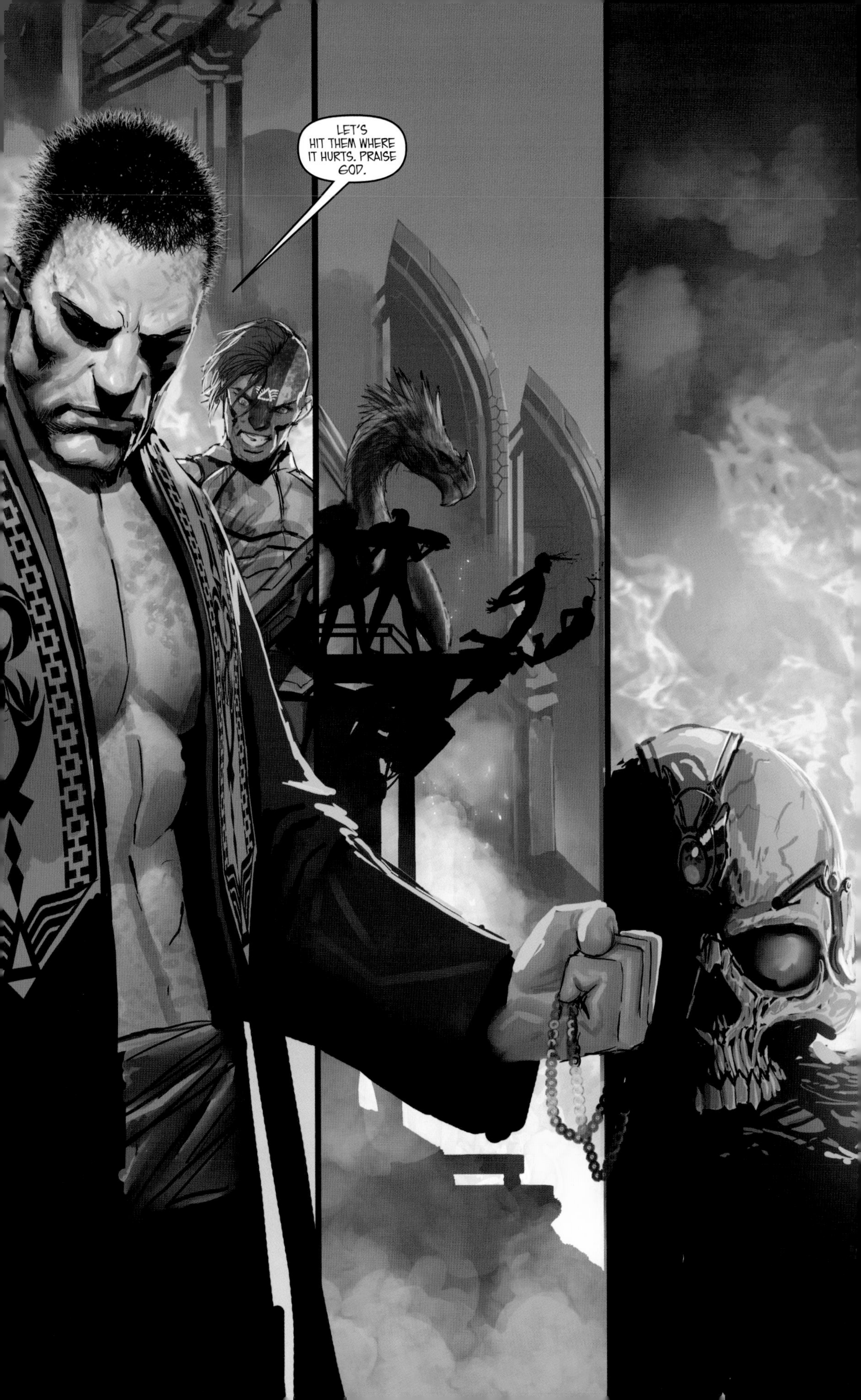
LET'S HIT THEM WHERE IT HURTS. PRAISE GOD.

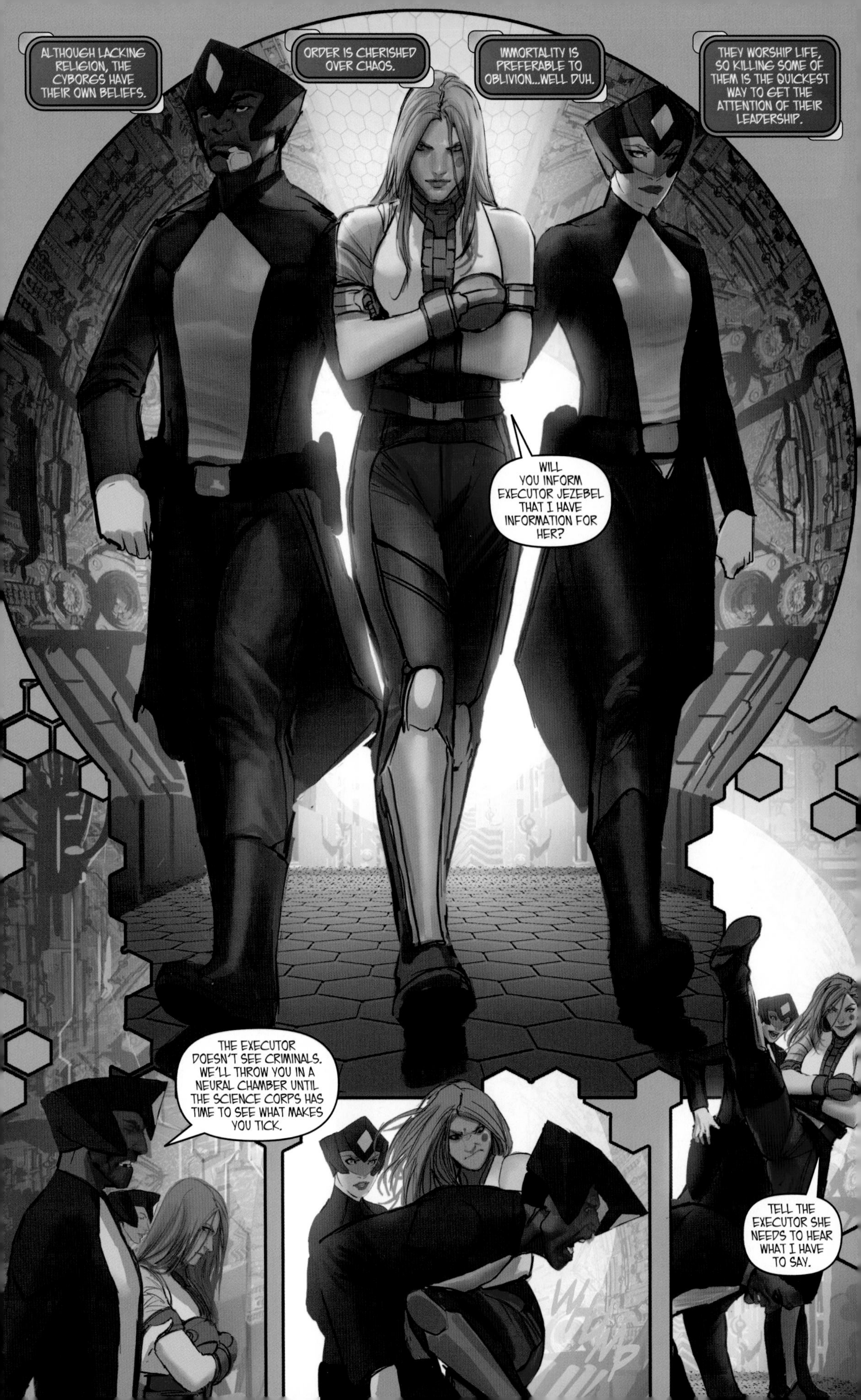
ALTHOUGH LACKING RELIGION, THE CYBORGS HAVE THEIR OWN BELIEFS.
ORDER IS CHERISHED OVER CHAOS.
IMMORTALITY IS PREFERABLE TO OBLIVION...WELL DUH.
THEY WORSHIP LIFE, SO KILLING SOME OF THEM IS THE QUICKEST WAY TO GET THE ATTENTION OF THEIR LEADERSHIP.
WILL YOU INFORM EXECUTOR JEZEBEL THAT I HAVE INFORMATION FOR HER?
THE EXECUTOR DOESN'T SEE CRIMINALS. WE'LL THROW YOU IN A NEURAL CHAMBER UNTIL THE SCIENCE CORPS HAS TIME TO SEE WHAT MAKES YOU TICK.
TELL THE EXECUTOR SHE NEEDS TO HEAR WHAT I HAVE TO SAY.

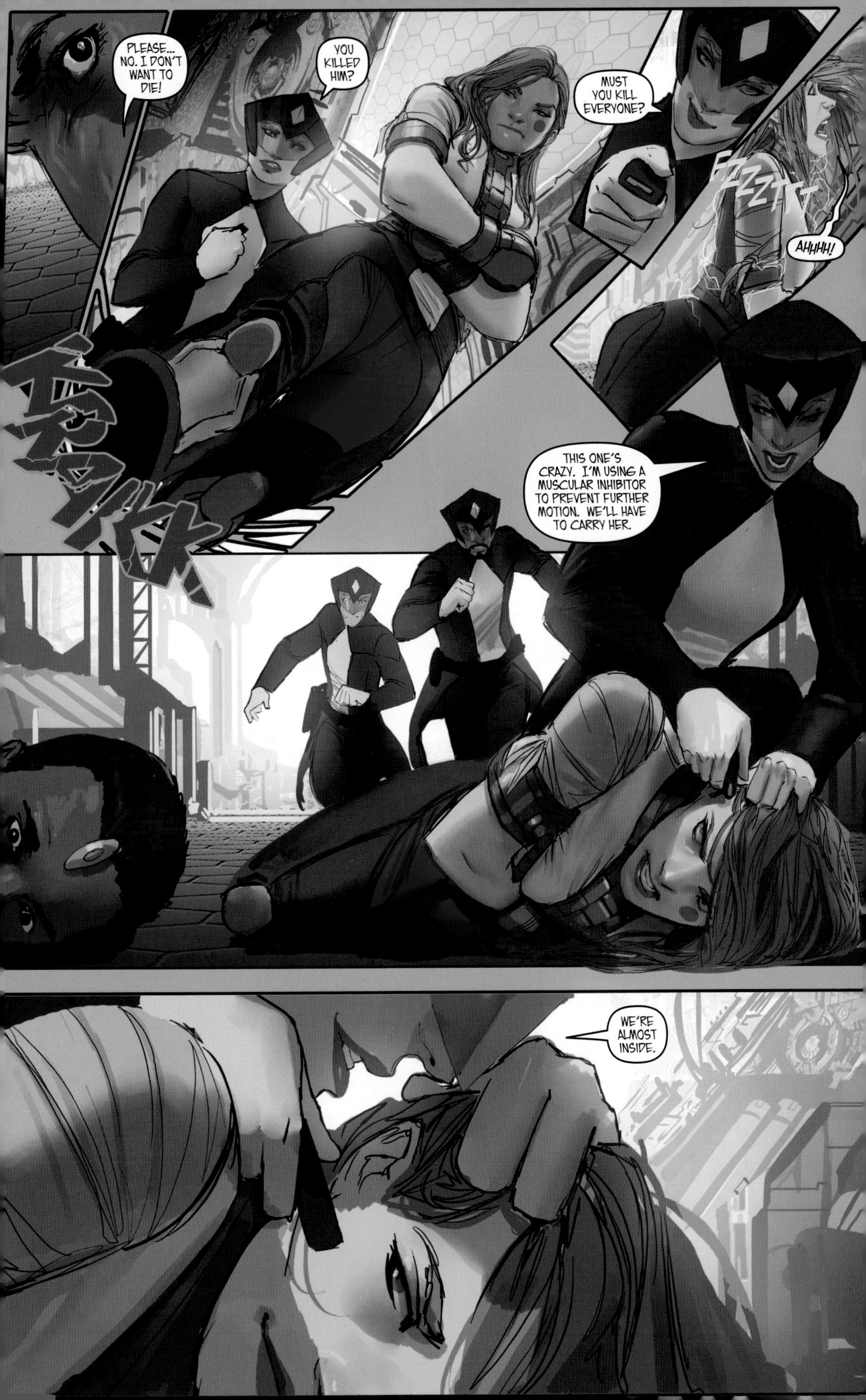
PLEASE... NO. I DON'T WANT TO DIE!
YOU KILLED HIM?
MUST YOU KILL EVERYONE?
FZZZTTT
AHHHH!
THIS ONE'S CRAZY. I'M USING A MUSCULAR INHIBITOR TO PREVENT FURTHER MOTION. WE'LL HAVE TO CARRY HER.
WE'RE ALMOST INSIDE.

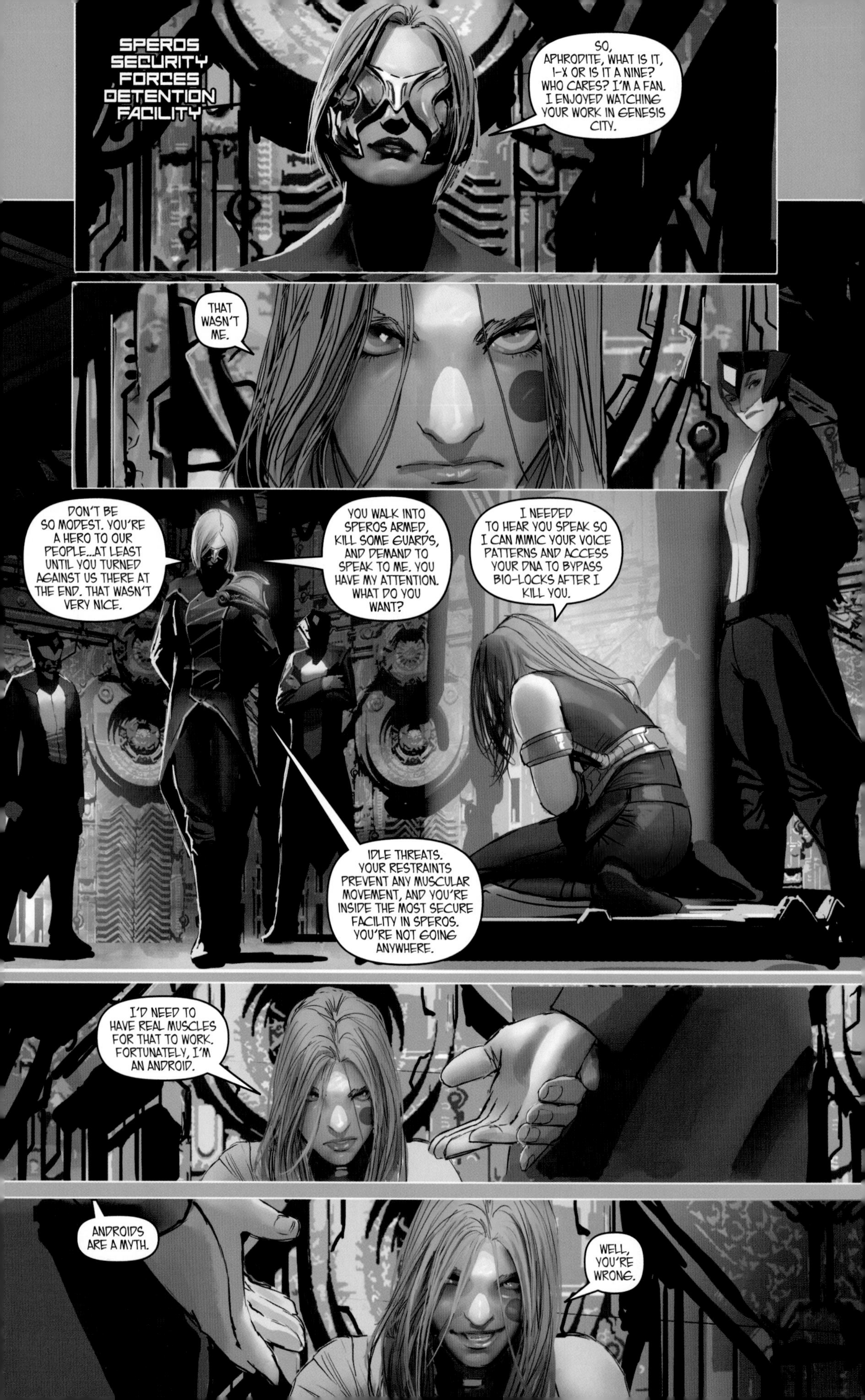
SPEROS SECURITY FORCES DETENTION FACILITY
SO, APHRODITE, WHAT IS IT, I-X OR IS IT A NINE? WHO CARES? I'M A FAN. I ENJOYED WATCHING YOUR WORK IN GENESIS CITY.
THAT WASN'T ME.
DON'T BE SO MODEST. YOU'RE A HERO TO OUR PEOPLE...AT LEAST UNTIL YOU TURNED AGAINST US THERE AT THE END. THAT WASN'T VERY NICE.
YOU WALK INTO SPEROS ARMED, KILL SOME GUARDS, AND DEMAND TO SPEAK TO ME. YOU HAVE MY ATTENTION. WHAT DO YOU WANT?
I NEEDED TO HEAR YOU SPEAK SO I CAN MIMIC YOUR VOICE PATTERNS AND ACCESS YOUR DNA TO BYPASS BIO-LOCKS AFTER I KILL YOU.
IDLE THREATS. YOUR RESTRAINTS PREVENT ANY MUSCULAR MOVEMENT, AND YOU'RE INSIDE THE MOST SECURE FACILITY IN SPEROS. YOU'RE NOT GOING ANYWHERE.
I'D NEED TO HAVE REAL MUSCLES FOR THAT TO WORK. FORTUNATELY, I'M AN ANDROID.
ANDROIDS ARE A MYTH.
WELL, YOU'RE WRONG.

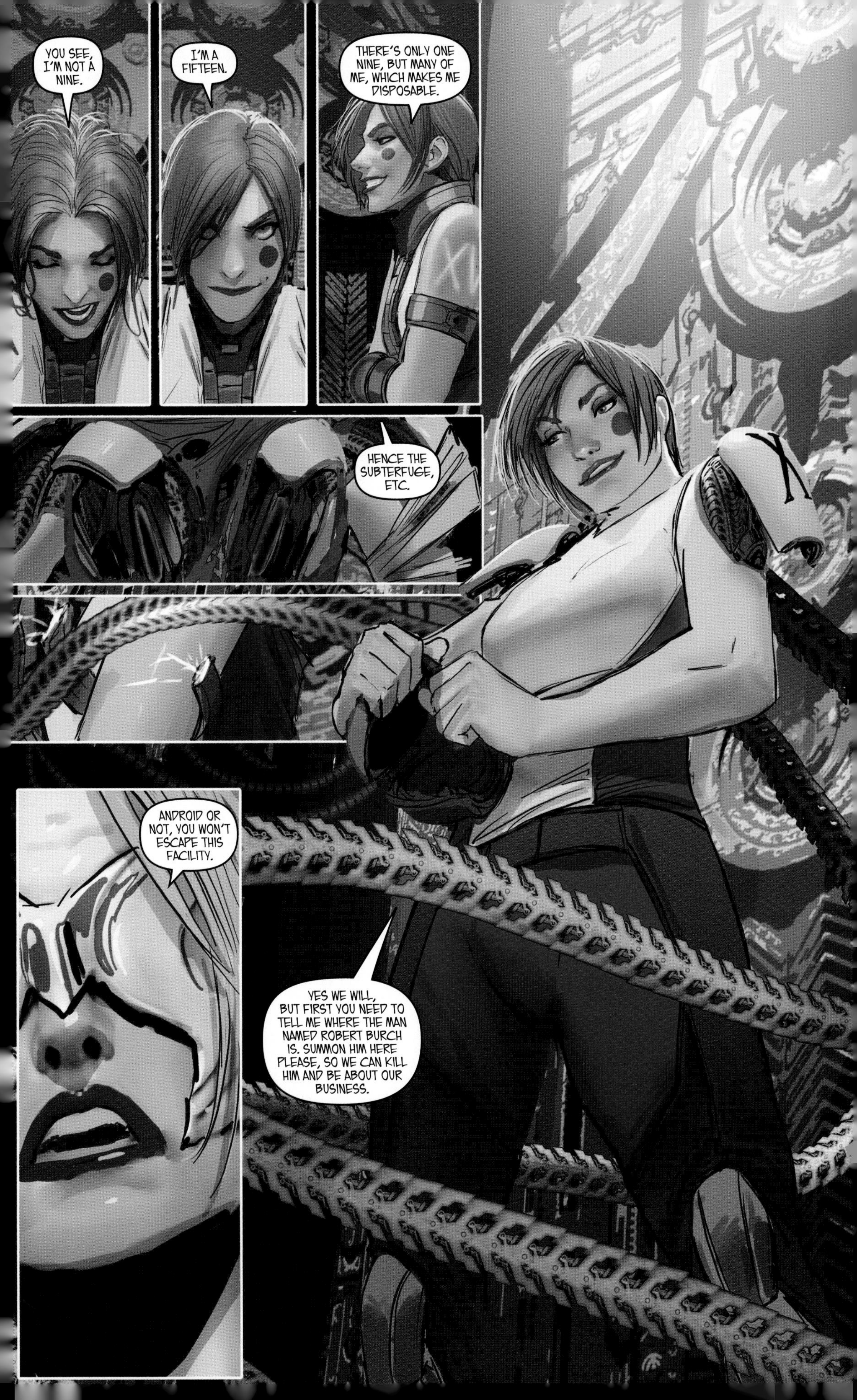
YOU SEE, I'M NOT A NINE.
I'M A FIFTEEN.
THERE'S ONLY ONE NINE, BUT MANY OF ME, WHICH MAKES ME DISPOSABLE.
HENCE THE SUBTERFUGE, ETC.
ANDROID OR NOT, YOU WON'T ESCAPE THIS FACILITY.
YES WE WILL, BUT FIRST YOU NEED TO TELL ME WHERE THE MAN NAMED ROBERT BURCH IS. SUMMON HIM HERE PLEASE, SO WE CAN KILL HIM AND BE ABOUT OUR BUSINESS.

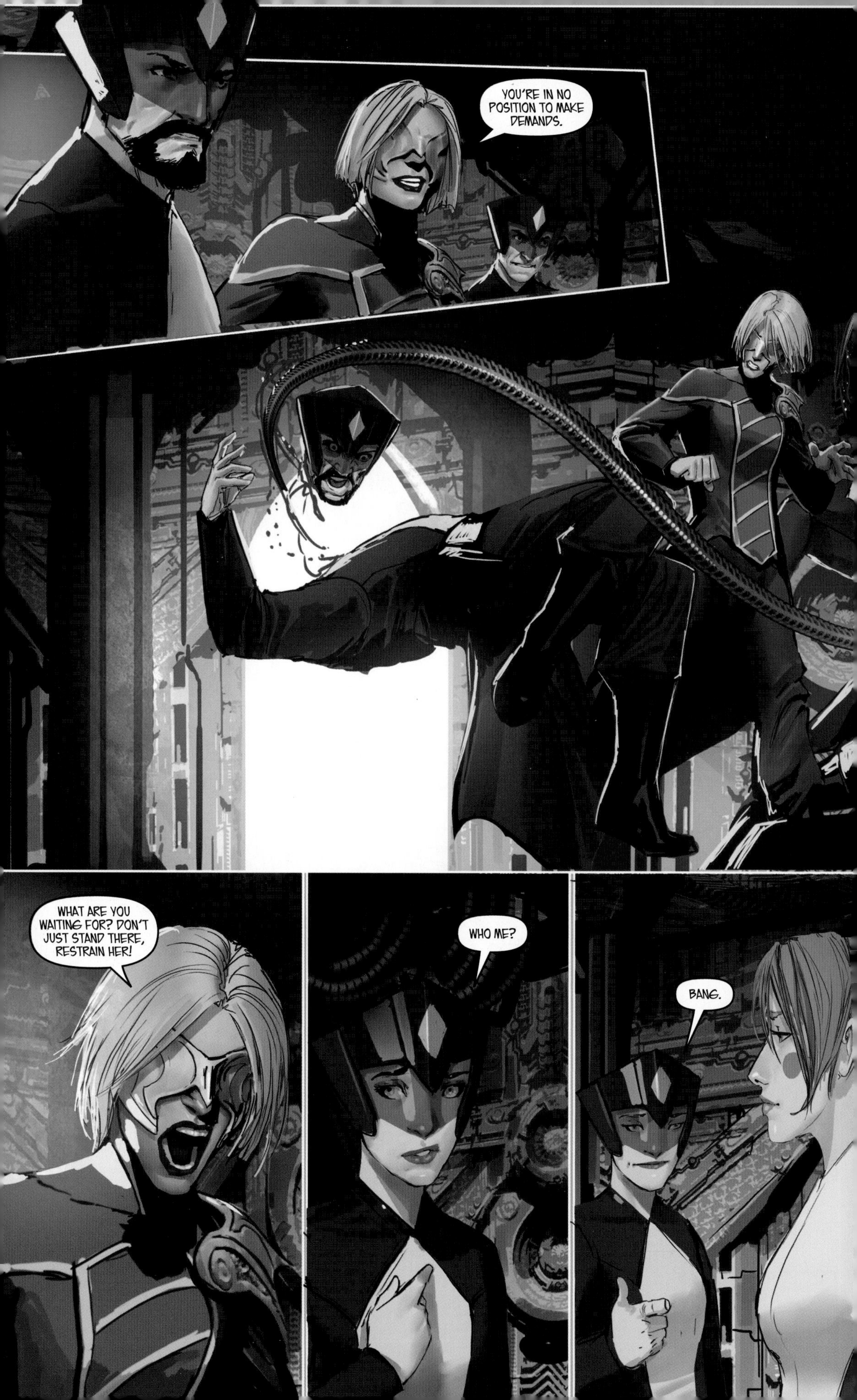
YOU'RE IN NO POSITION TO MAKE DEMANDS.
WHAT ARE YOU WAITING FOR? DON'T JUST STAND THERE, RESTRAIN HER!
WHO ME?
BANG.

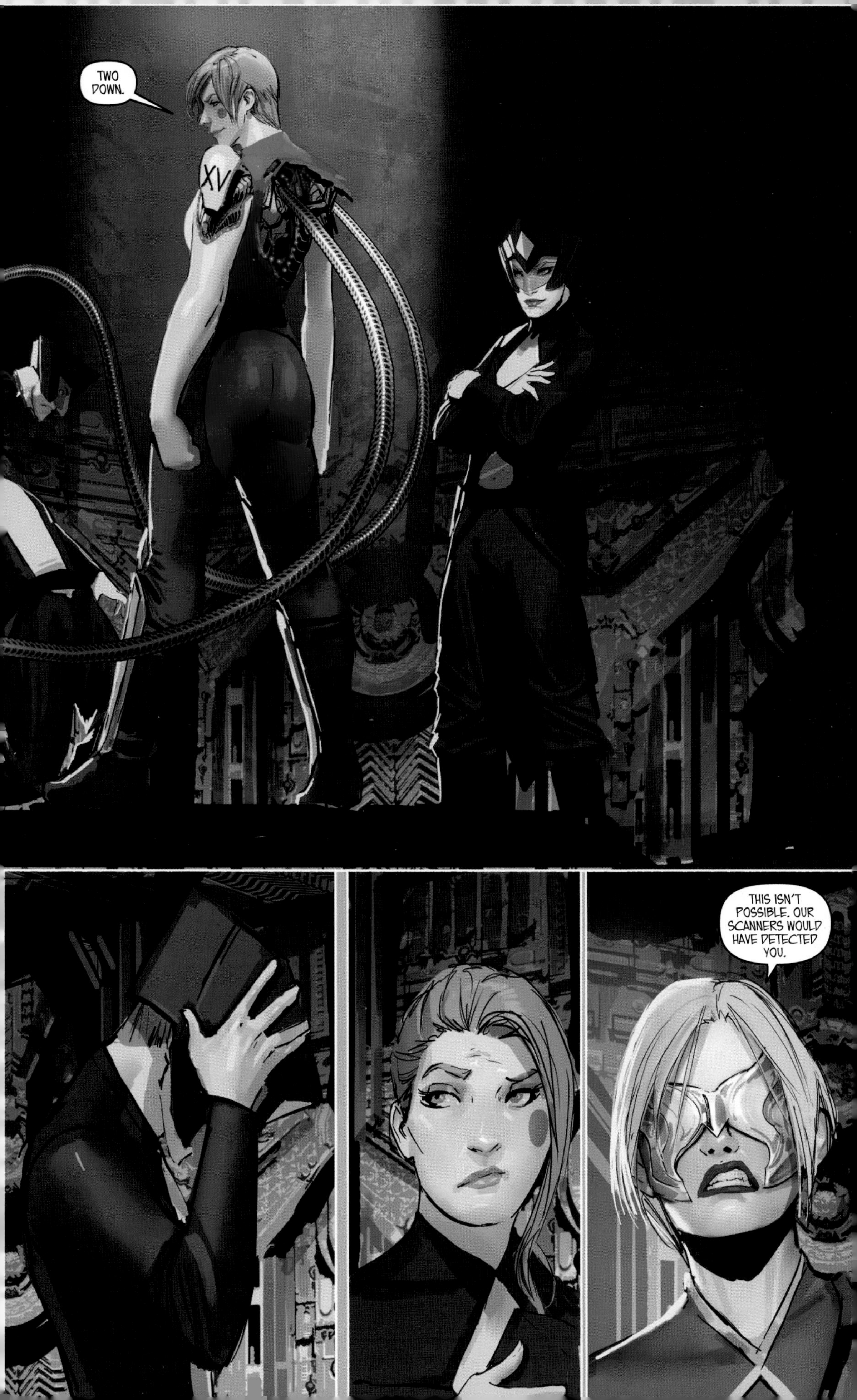
TWO DOWN.
XV
THIS ISN'T POSSIBLE. OUR SCANNERS WOULD HAVE DETECTED YOU.

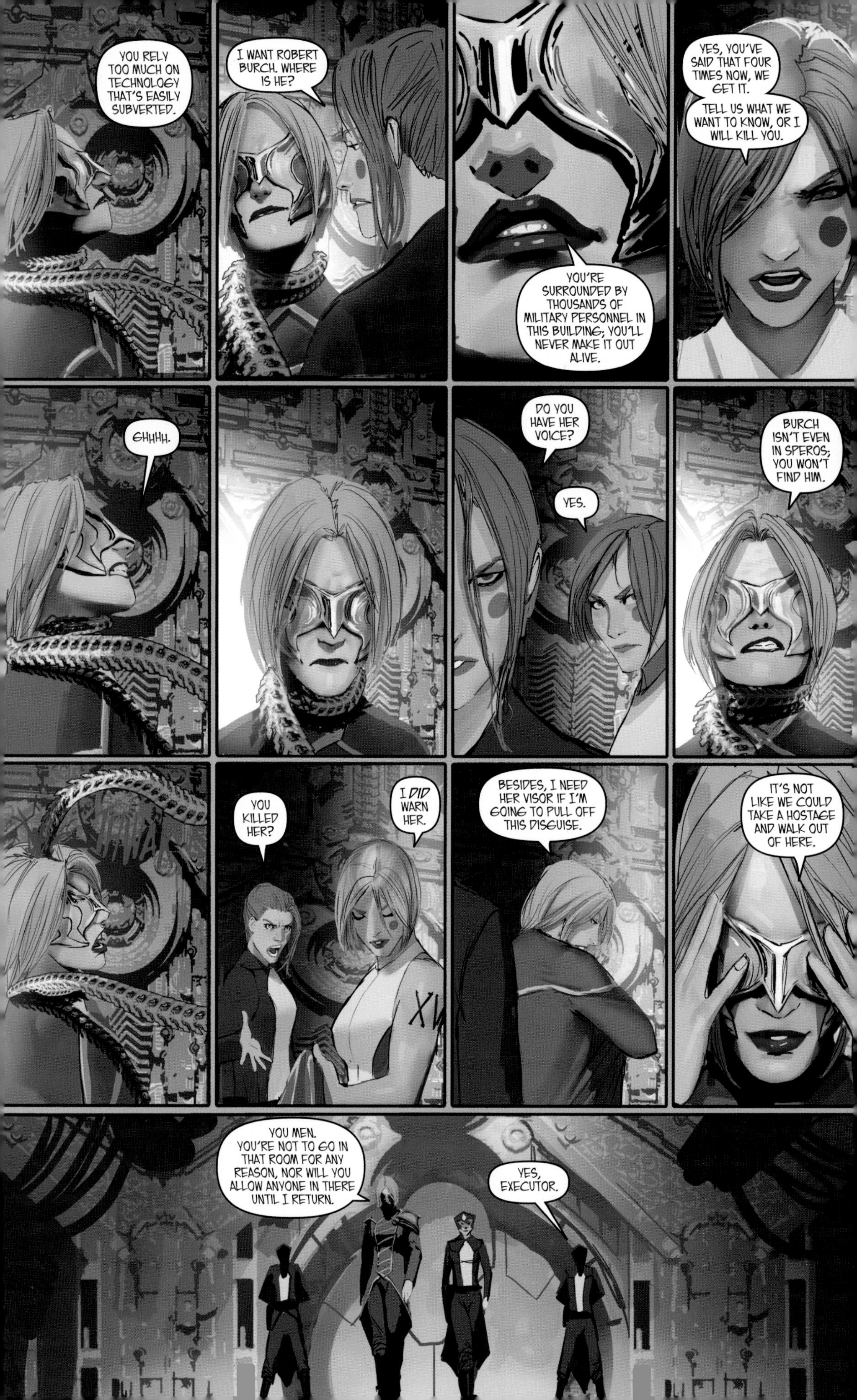
YOU RELY TOO MUCH ON TECHNOLOGY THAT'S EASILY SUBVERTED.
I WANT ROBERT BURCH. WHERE IS HE?
YOU'RE SURROUNDED BY THOUSANDS OF MILITARY PERSONNEL IN THIS BUILDING; YOU'LL NEVER MAKE IT OUT ALIVE.
YES, YOU'VE SAID THAT FOUR TIMES NOW, WE GET IT.
TELL US WHAT WE WANT TO KNOW, OR I WILL KILL YOU.
GHHHH.
DO YOU HAVE HER VOICE?
YES.
BURCH ISN'T EVEN IN SPEROS; YOU WON'T FIND HIM.
YOU KILLED HER?
I DID WARN HER.
BESIDES, I NEED HER VISOR IF I'M GOING TO PULL OFF THIS DISGUISE.
IT'S NOT LIKE WE COULD TAKE A HOSTAGE AND WALK OUT OF HERE.
YOU MEN. YOU'RE NOT TO GO IN THAT ROOM FOR ANY REASON, NOR WILL YOU ALLOW ANYONE IN THERE UNTIL I RETURN.
YES, EXECUTOR.

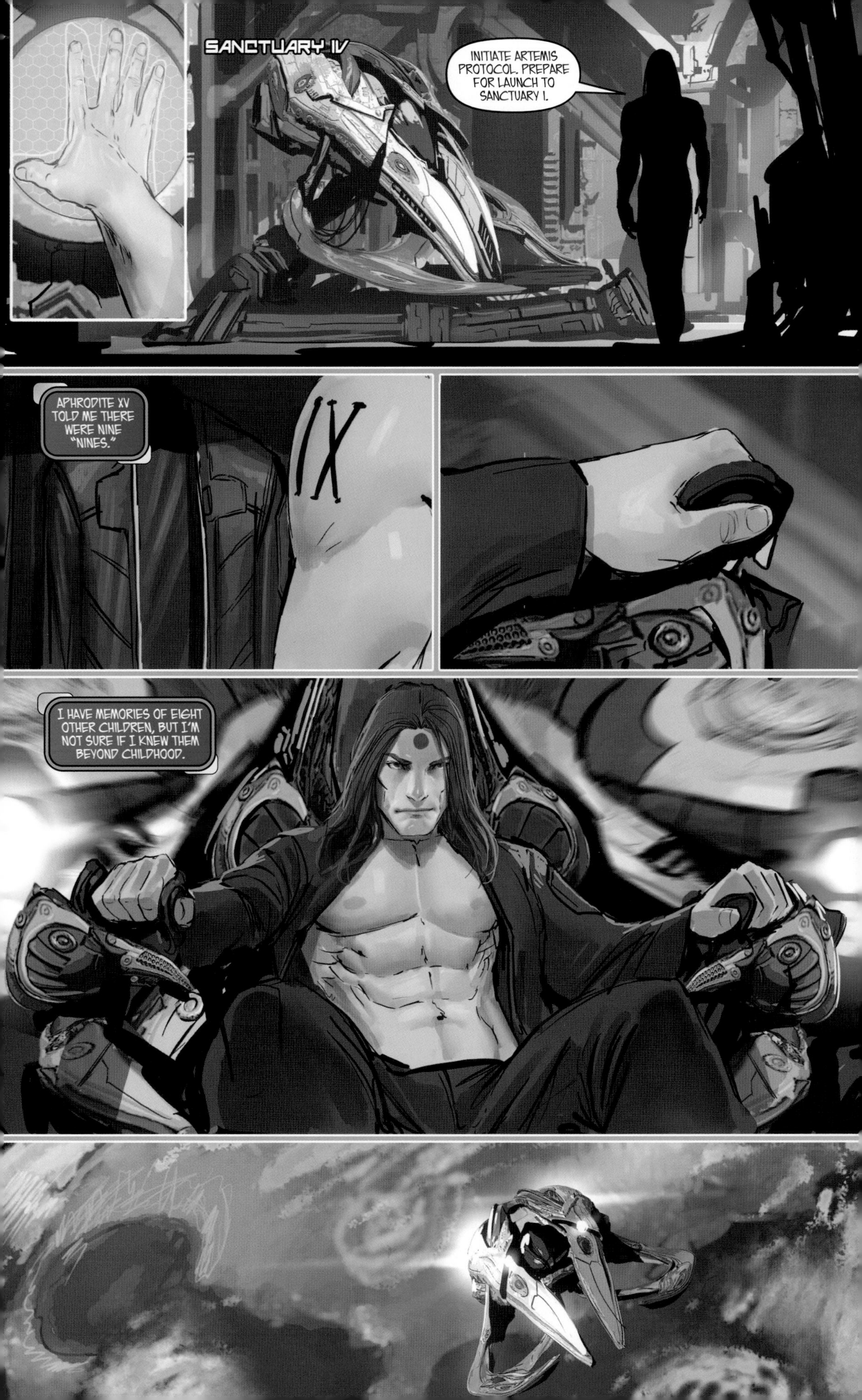
SANCTUARY IV
INITIATE ARTEMIS PROTOCOL. PREPARE FOR LAUNCH TO SANCTUARY I.
APHRODITE XV TOLD ME THERE WERE NINE "NINES."
IX
I HAVE MEMORIES OF EIGHT OTHER CHILDREN, BUT I'M NOT SURE IF I KNEW THEM BEYOND CHILDHOOD.

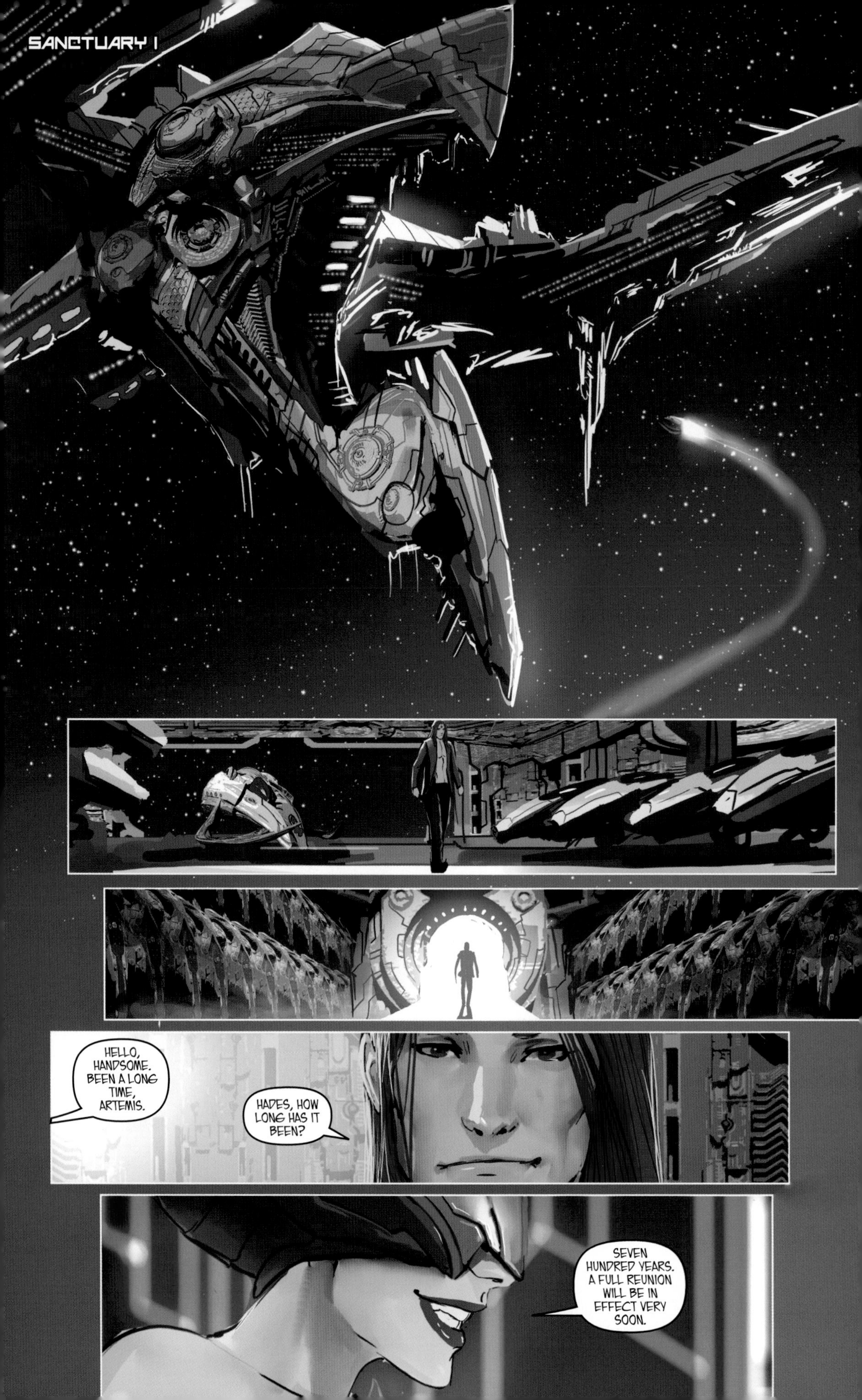
SANCTUARY I
HELLO, HANDSOME. BEEN A LONG TIME, ARTEMIS.
HADES, HOW LONG HAS IT BEEN?
SEVEN HUNDRED YEARS. A FULL REUNION WILL BE IN EFFECT VERY SOON.

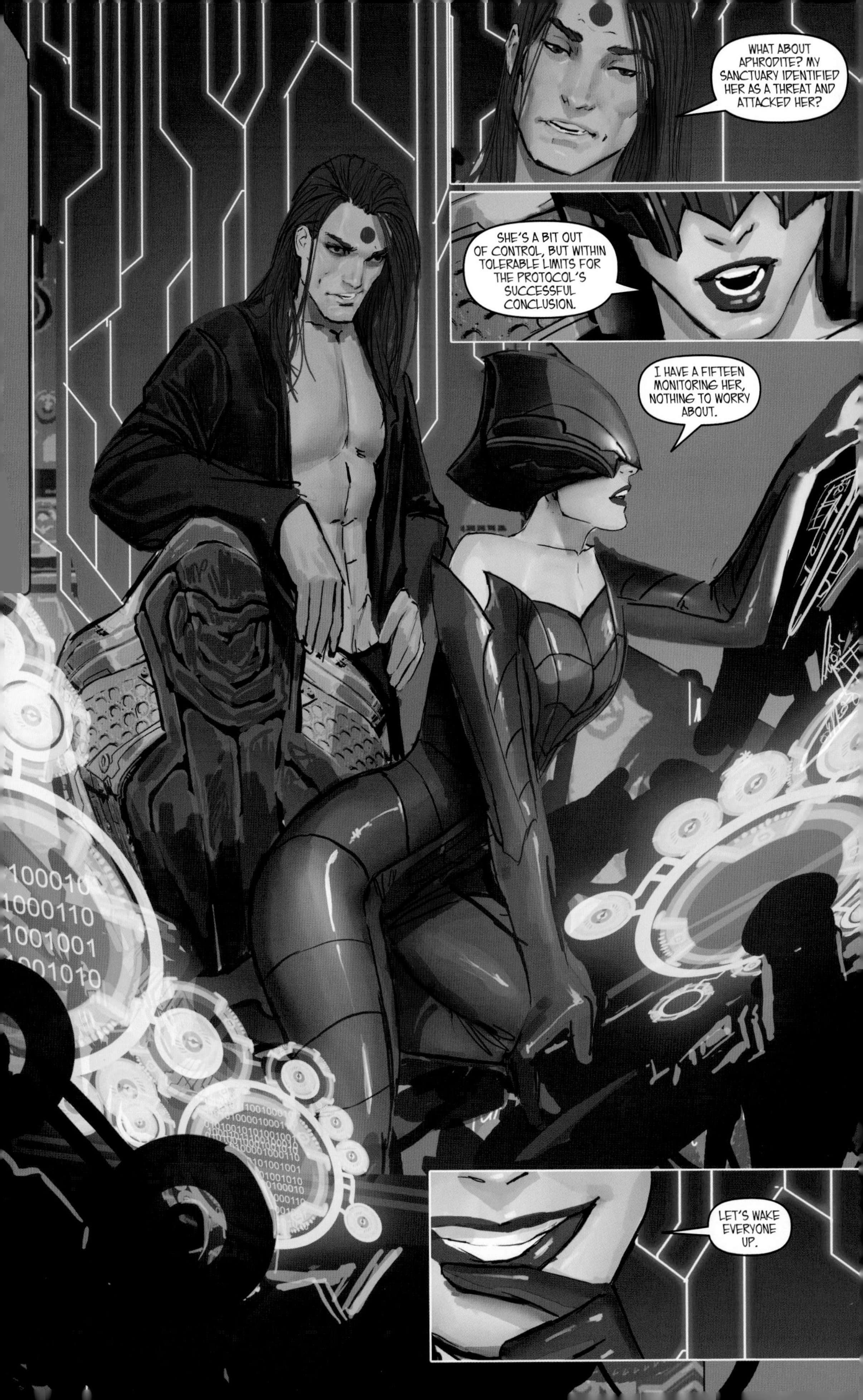
WHAT ABOUT APHRODITE? MY SANCTUARY IDENTIFIED HER AS A THREAT AND ATTACKED HER?
SHE'S A BIT OUT OF CONTROL, BUT WITHIN TOLERABLE LIMITS FOR THE PROTOCOL'S SUCCESSFUL CONCLUSION.
I HAVE A FIFTEEN MONITORING HER, NOTHING TO WORRY ABOUT.
LET'S WAKE EVERYONE UP.

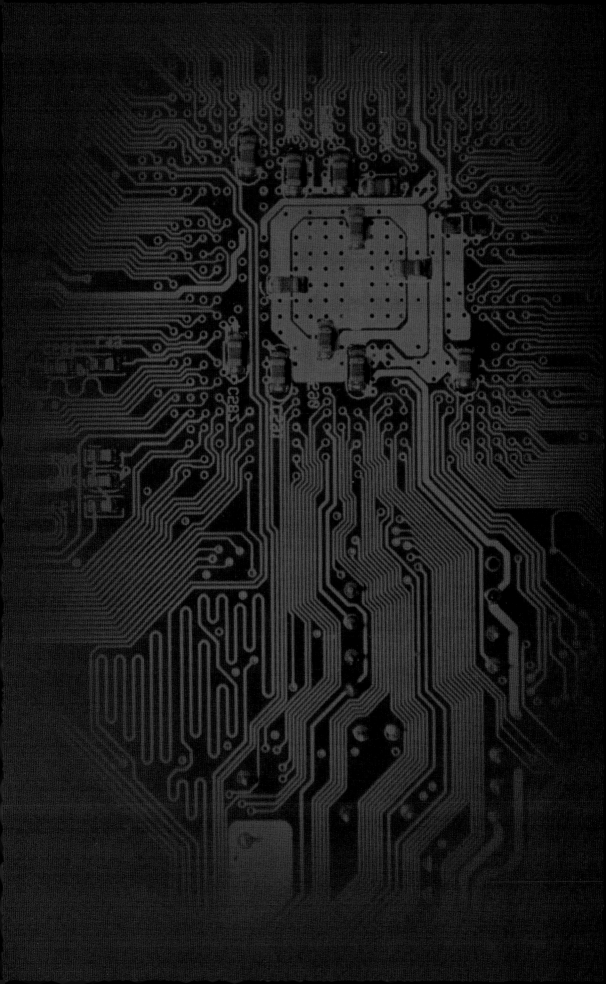

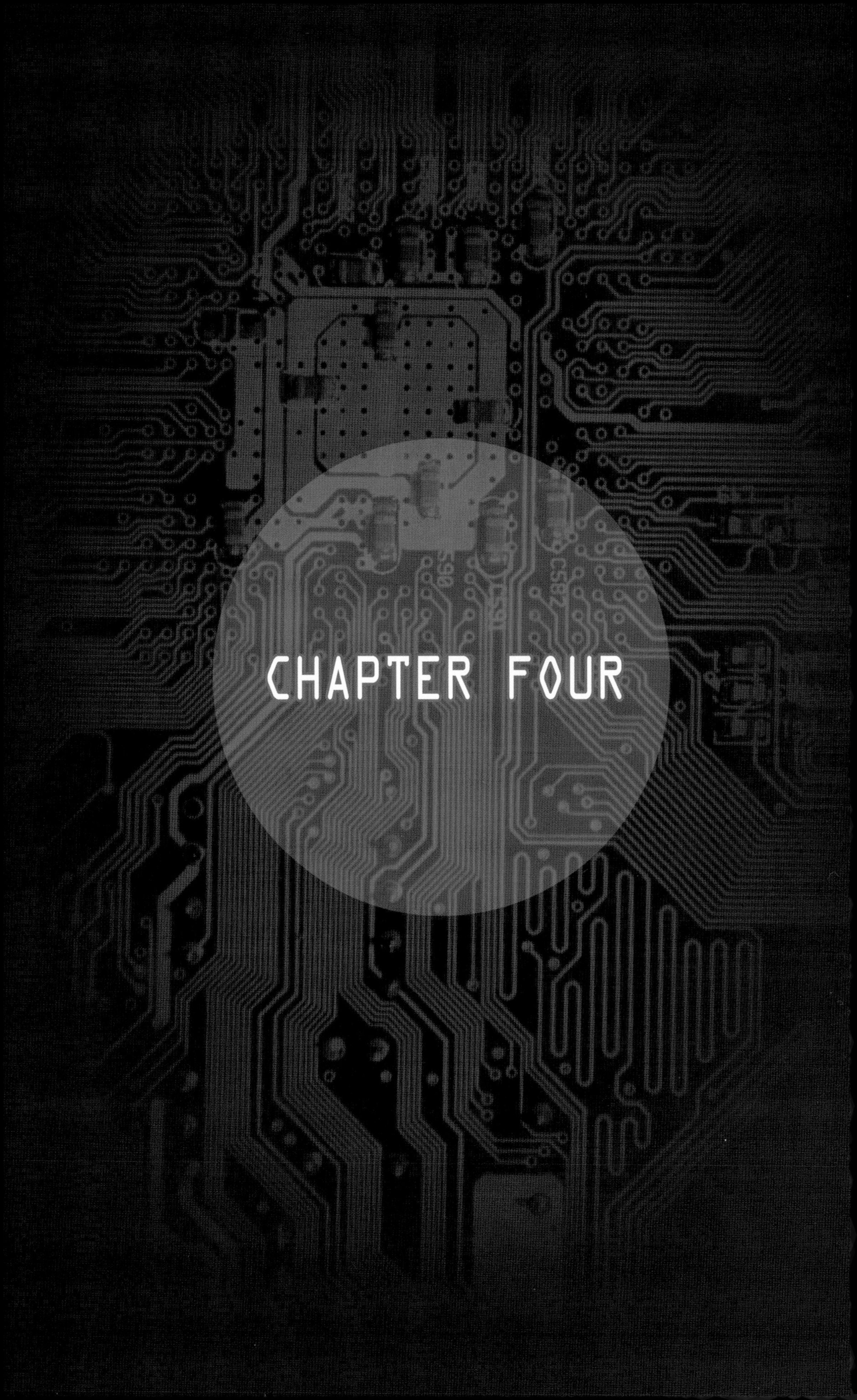

CHAPTER FOUR

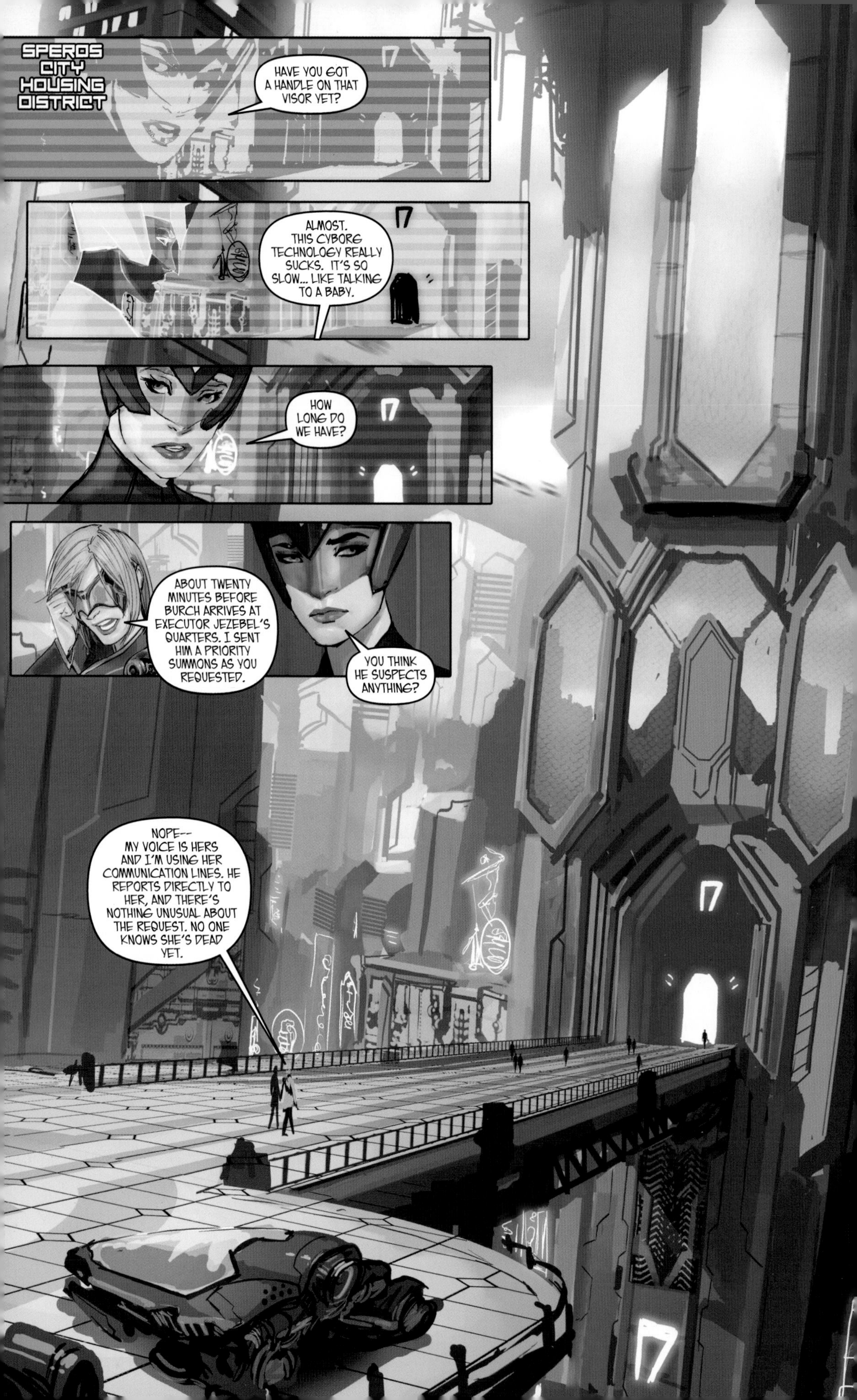
SPEROS CITY HOUSING DISTRICT
HAVE YOU GOT A HANDLE ON THAT VISOR YET?
ALMOST. THIS CYBORG TECHNOLOGY REALLY SUCKS. IT'S SO SLOW... LIKE TALKING TO A BABY.
HOW LONG DO WE HAVE?
ABOUT TWENTY MINUTES BEFORE BURCH ARRIVES AT EXECUTOR JEZEBEL'S QUARTERS. I SENT HIM A PRIORITY SUMMONS AS YOU REQUESTED.
YOU THINK HE SUSPECTS ANYTHING?
NOPE-- MY VOICE IS HERS AND I'M USING HER COMMUNICATION LINES. HE REPORTS DIRECTLY TO HER, AND THERE'S NOTHING UNUSUAL ABOUT THE REQUEST. NO ONE KNOWS SHE'S DEAD YET.

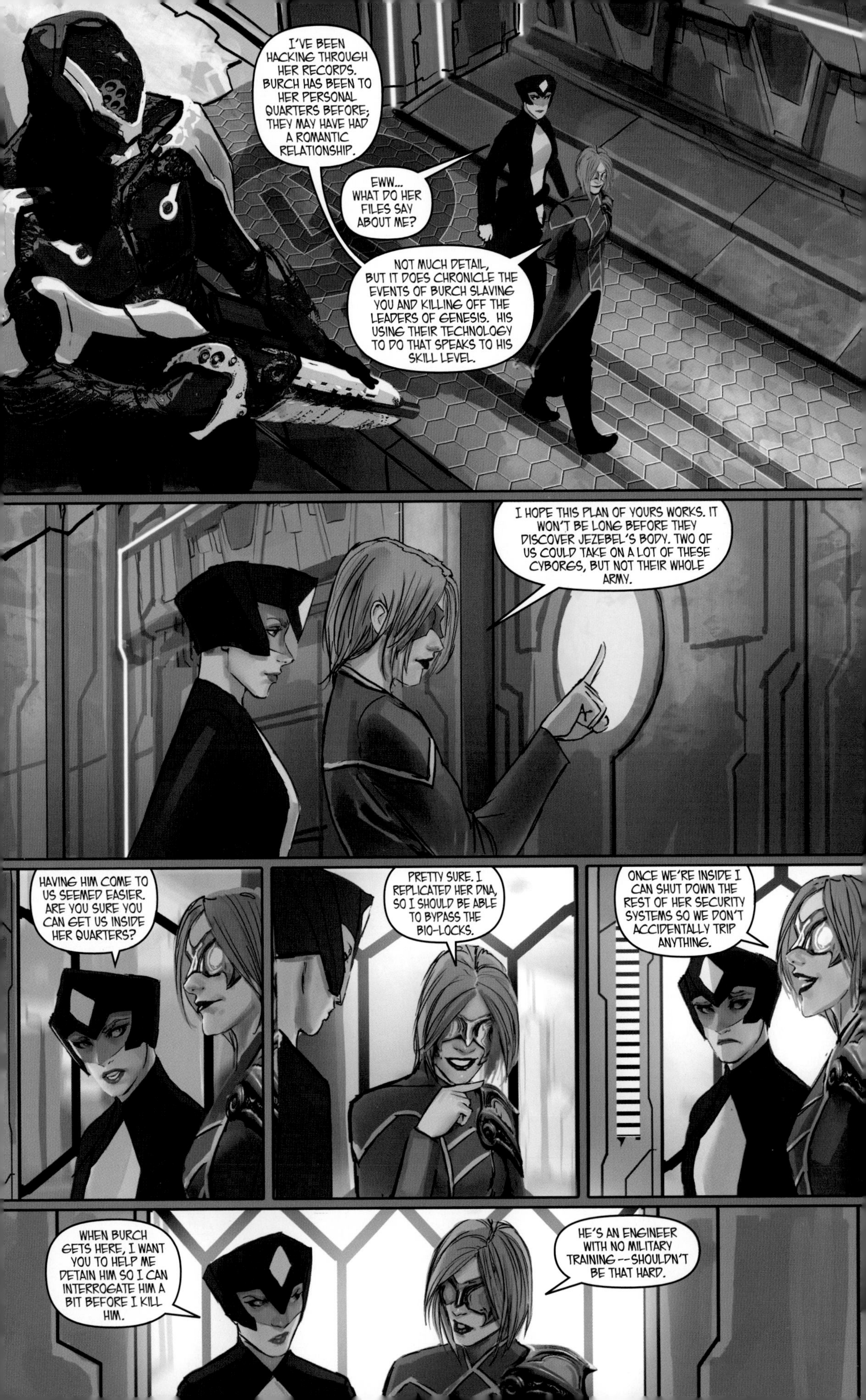
I'VE BEEN HACKING THROUGH HER RECORDS. BURCH HAS BEEN TO HER PERSONAL QUARTERS BEFORE; THEY MAY HAVE HAD A ROMANTIC RELATIONSHIP.
EWW... WHAT DO HER FILES SAY ABOUT ME?
NOT MUCH DETAIL, BUT IT DOES CHRONICLE THE EVENTS OF BURCH SLAVING YOU AND KILLING OFF THE LEADERS OF GENESIS. HIS USING THEIR TECHNOLOGY TO DO THAT SPEAKS TO HIS SKILL LEVEL.
I HOPE THIS PLAN OF YOURS WORKS. IT WON'T BE LONG BEFORE THEY DISCOVER JEZEBEL'S BODY. TWO OF US COULD TAKE ON A LOT OF THESE CYBORGS, BUT NOT THEIR WHOLE ARMY.
HAVING HIM COME TO US SEEMED EASIER. ARE YOU SURE YOU CAN GET US INSIDE HER QUARTERS?
PRETTY SURE. I REPLICATED HER DNA, SO I SHOULD BE ABLE TO BYPASS THE BIO-LOCKS.
ONCE WE'RE INSIDE I CAN SHUT DOWN THE REST OF HER SECURITY SYSTEMS SO WE DON'T ACCIDENTALLY TRIP ANYTHING.
WHEN BURCH GETS HERE, I WANT YOU TO HELP ME DETAIN HIM SO I CAN INTERROGATE HIM A BIT BEFORE I KILL HIM.
HE'S AN ENGINEER WITH NO MILITARY TRAINING--SHOULDN'T BE THAT HARD.

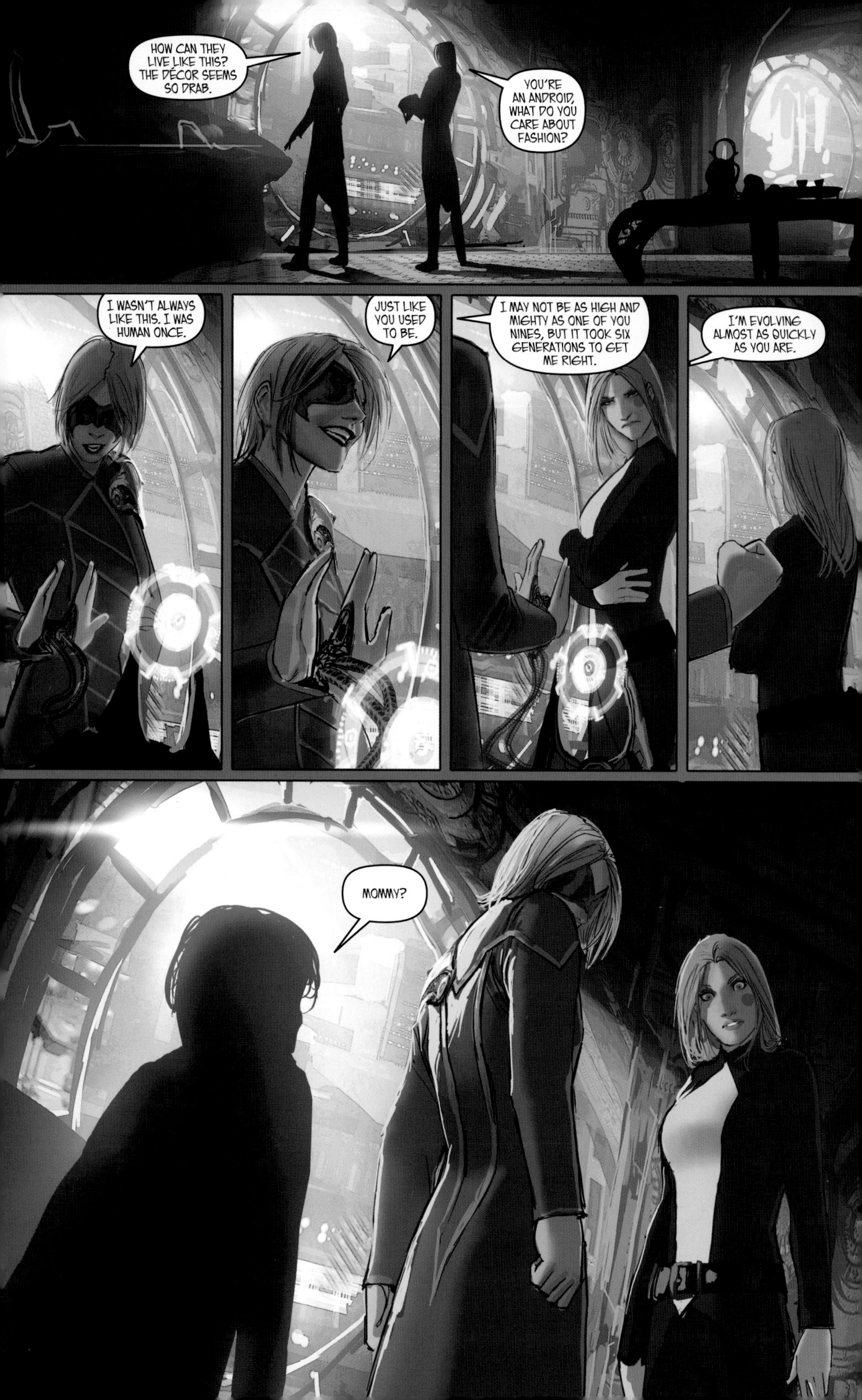
HOW CAN THEY LIVE LIKE THIS? THE DÉCOR SEEMS SO DRAB.
YOU'RE AN ANDROID, WHAT DO YOU CARE ABOUT FASHION?
I WASN'T ALWAYS LIKE THIS. I WAS HUMAN ONCE.
JUST LIKE YOU USED TO BE.
I MAY NOT BE AS HIGH AND MIGHTY AS ONE OF YOU NINES, BUT IT TOOK SIX GENERATIONS TO GET ME RIGHT.
I'M EVOLVING ALMOST AS QUICKLY AS YOU ARE.
MOMMY?

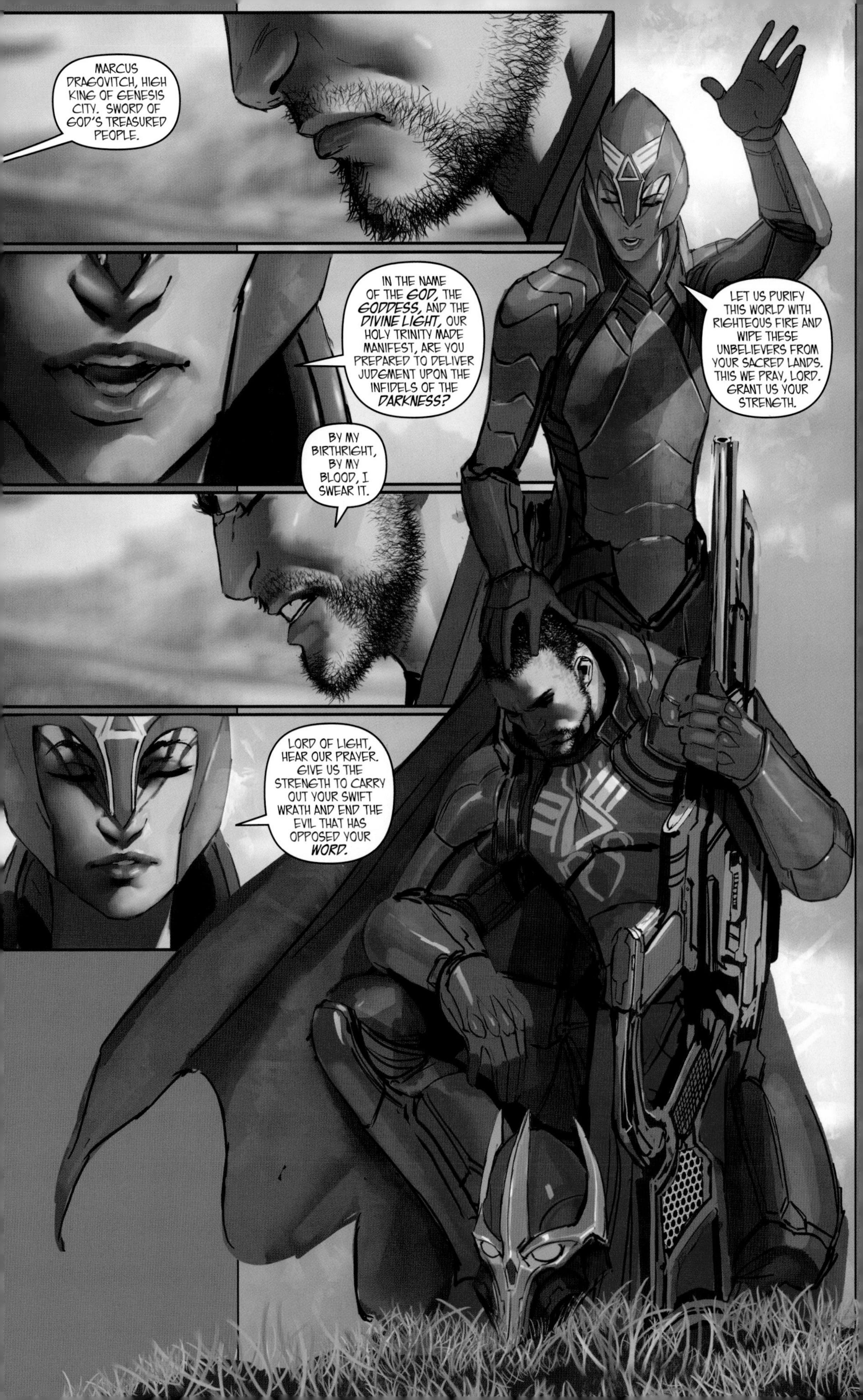
MARCUS DRAGOVITCH, HIGH KING OF GENESIS CITY. SWORD OF GOD'S TREASURED PEOPLE.
IN THE NAME OF THE GOD, THE GODDESS, AND THE DIVINE LIGHT, OUR HOLY TRINITY MADE MANIFEST, ARE YOU PREPARED TO DELIVER JUDGMENT UPON THE INFIDELS OF THE DARKNESS?
BY MY BIRTHRIGHT, BY MY BLOOD, I SWEAR IT.
LORD OF LIGHT, HEAR OUR PRAYER. GIVE US THE STRENGTH TO CARRY OUT YOUR SWIFT WRATH AND END THE EVIL THAT HAS OPPOSED YOUR WORD.
LET US PURIFY THIS WORLD WITH RIGHTEOUS FIRE AND WIPE THESE UNBELIEVERS FROM YOUR SACRED LANDS. THIS WE PRAY, LORD. GRANT US YOUR STRENGTH.

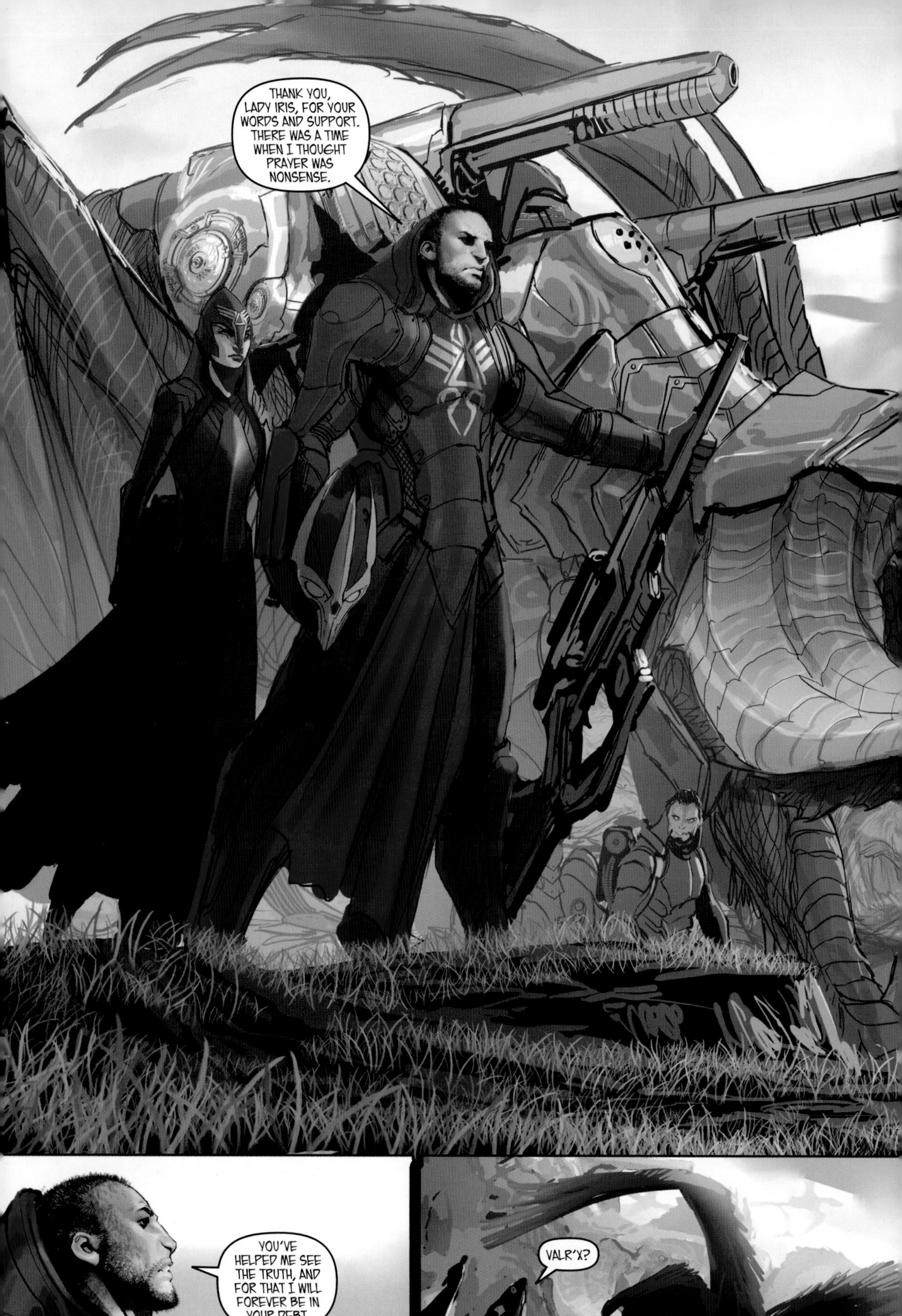
THANK YOU, LADY IRIS, FOR YOUR WORDS AND SUPPORT. THERE WAS A TIME WHEN I THOUGHT PRAYER WAS NONSENSE.

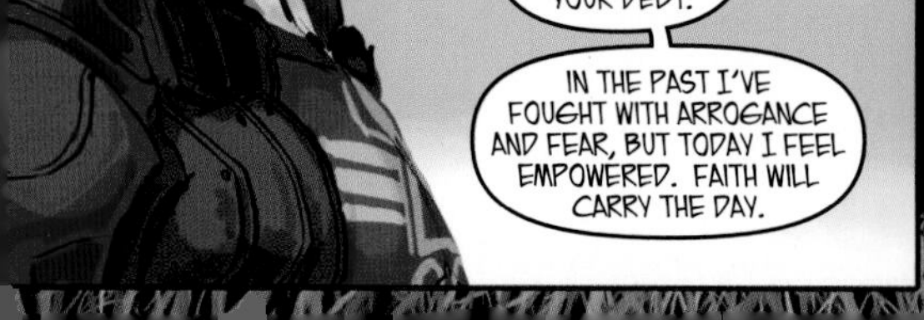
YOU'VE HELPED ME SEE THE TRUTH, AND FOR THAT I WILL FOREVER BE IN YOUR DEBT.
IN THE PAST I'VE FOUGHT WITH ARROGANCE AND FEAR, BUT TODAY I FEEL EMPOWERED. FAITH WILL CARRY THE DAY.

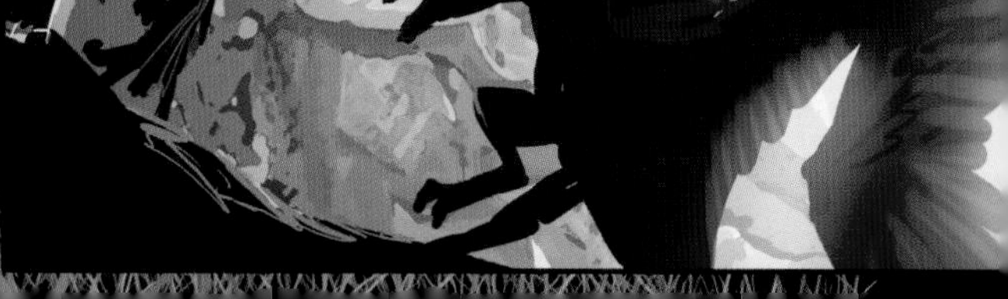
VALR'X?

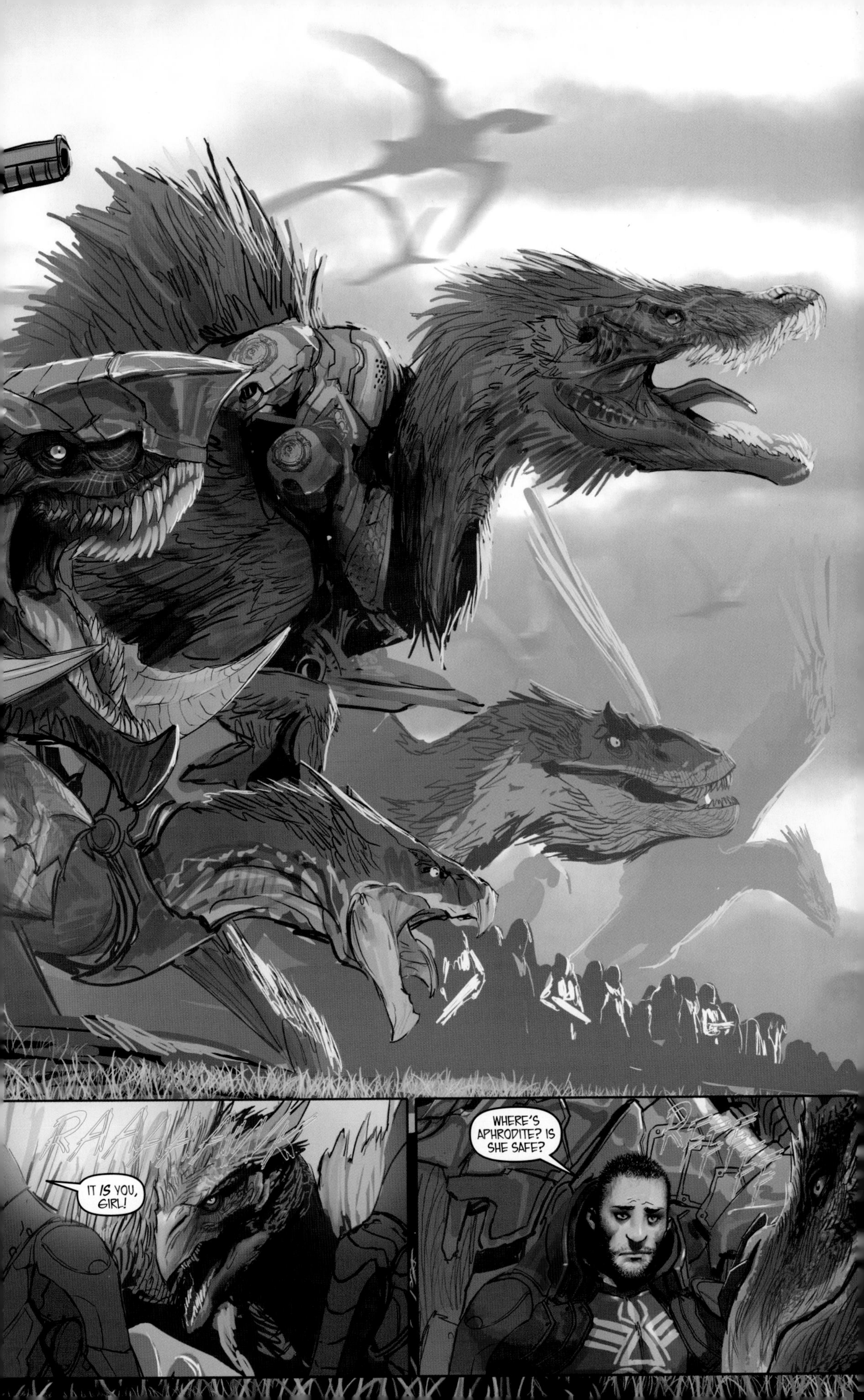
IT IS YOU, GIRL!
WHERE'S APHRODITE? IS SHE SAFE?

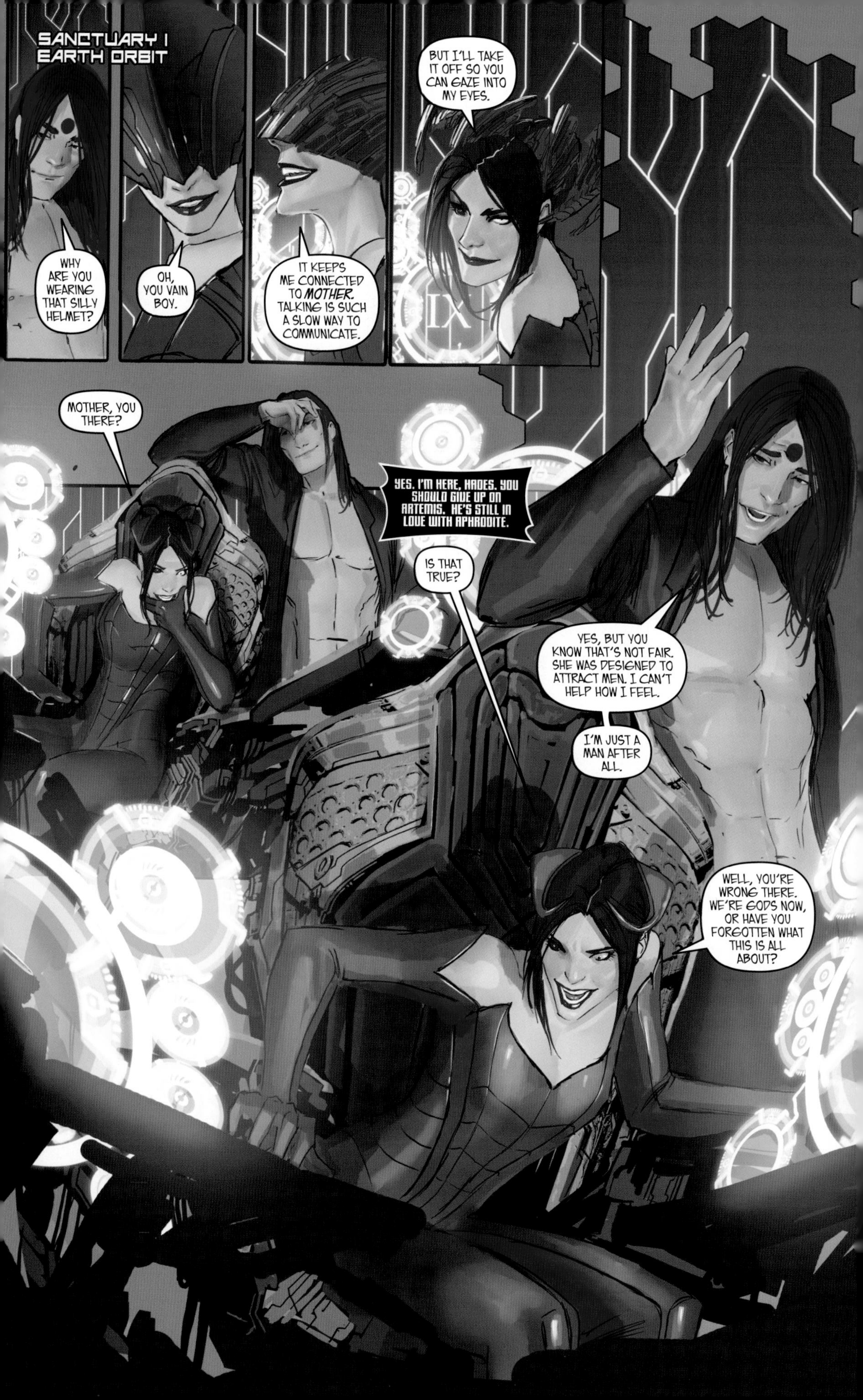
SANCTUARY I
EARTH ORBIT
WHY ARE YOU WEARING THAT SILLY HELMET?
OH, YOU VAIN BOY.
IT KEEPS ME CONNECTED TO MOTHER. TALKING IS SUCH A SLOW WAY TO COMMUNICATE.
BUT I'LL TAKE IT OFF SO YOU CAN GAZE INTO MY EYES.
IX
MOTHER, YOU THERE?
YES. I'M HERE, HADES. YOU SHOULD GIVE UP ON ARTEMIS. HE'S STILL IN LOVE WITH APHRODITE.
IS THAT TRUE?
YES, BUT YOU KNOW THAT'S NOT FAIR. SHE WAS DESIGNED TO ATTRACT MEN. I CAN'T HELP HOW I FEEL.
I'M JUST A MAN AFTER ALL.
WELL, YOU'RE WRONG THERE. WE'RE GODS NOW, OR HAVE YOU FORGOTTEN WHAT THIS IS ALL ABOUT?

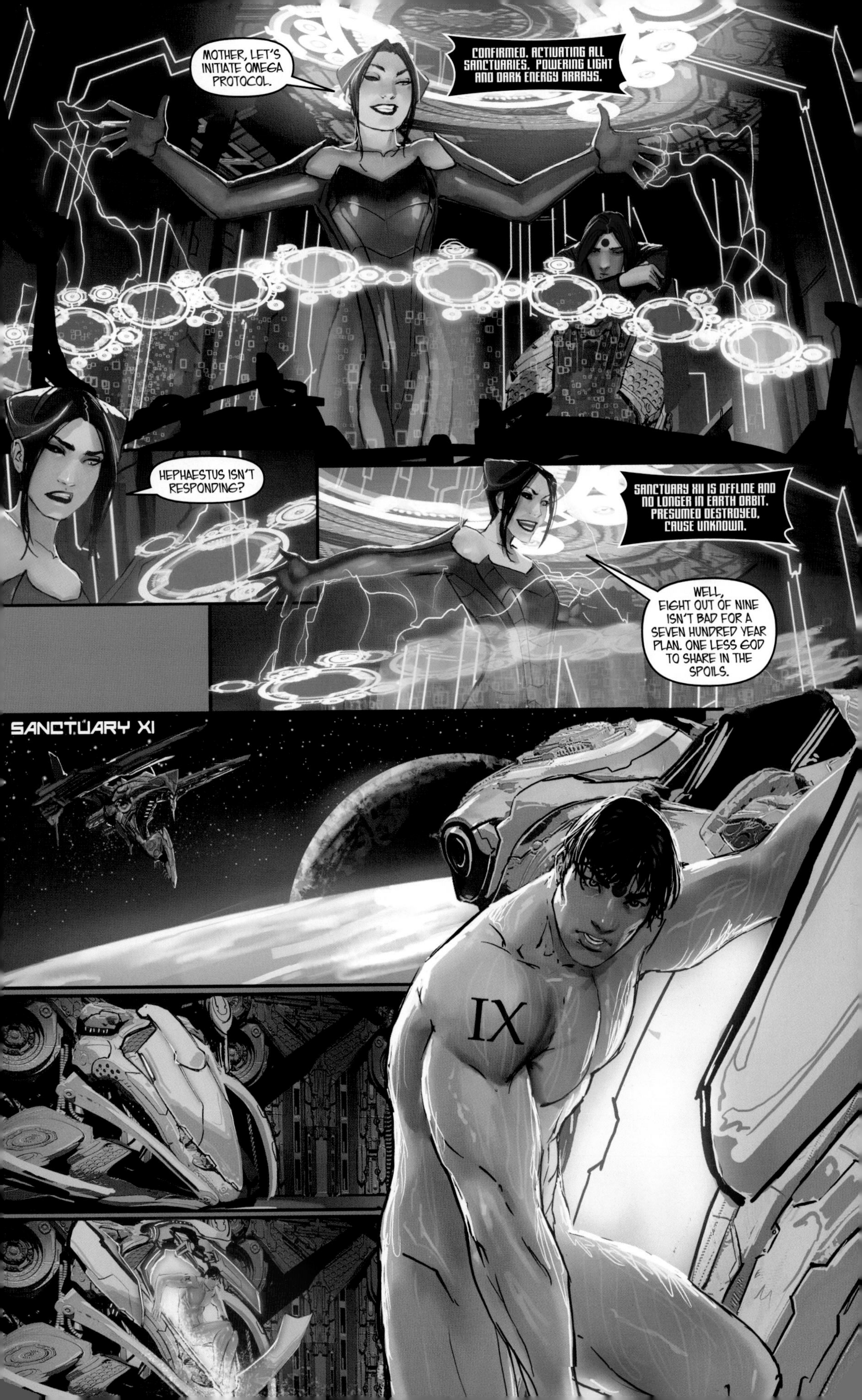
MOTHER, LET'S INITIATE OMEGA PROTOCOL.
CONFIRMED. ACTIVATING ALL SANCTUARIES. POWERING LIGHT AND DARK ENERGY ARRAYS.
HEPHAESTUS ISN'T RESPONDING?
SANCTUARY XII IS OFFLINE AND NO LONGER IN EARTH ORBIT. PRESUMED DESTROYED, CAUSE UNKNOWN.
WELL, EIGHT OUT OF NINE ISN'T BAD FOR A SEVEN HUNDRED YEAR PLAN. ONE LESS GOD TO SHARE IN THE SPOILS.
SANCTUARY XI
IX

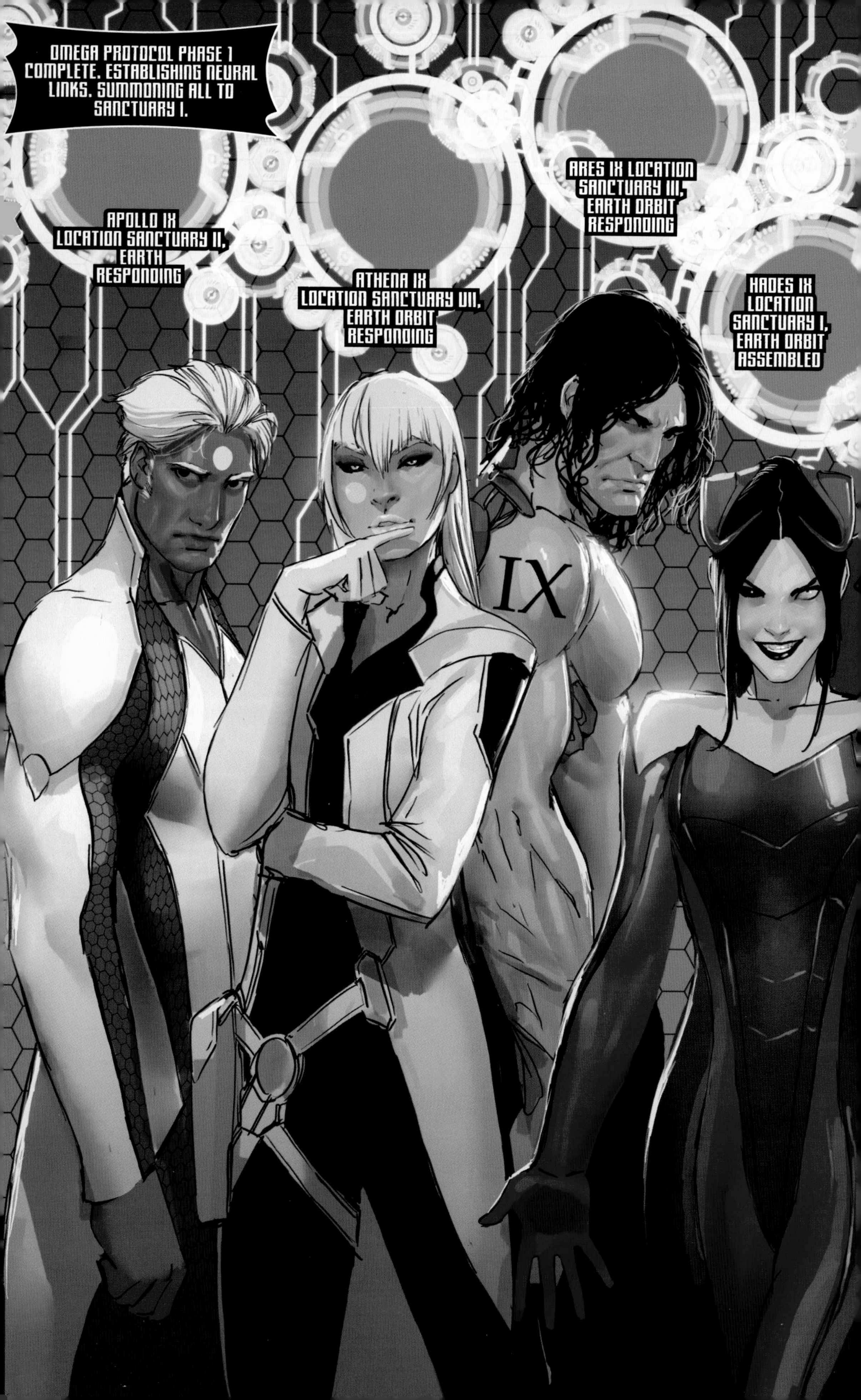

OMEGA PROTOCOL PHASE 1 COMPLETE. ESTABLISHING NEURAL LINKS. SUMMONING ALL TO SANCTUARY I.
APOLLO IX LOCATION SANCTUARY II, EARTH RESPONDING
ATHENA IX LOCATION SANCTUARY VII, EARTH ORBIT RESPONDING
ARES IX LOCATION SANCTUARY III, EARTH ORBIT RESPONDING
HADES IX LOCATION SANCTUARY I, EARTH ORBIT ASSEMBLED
IX

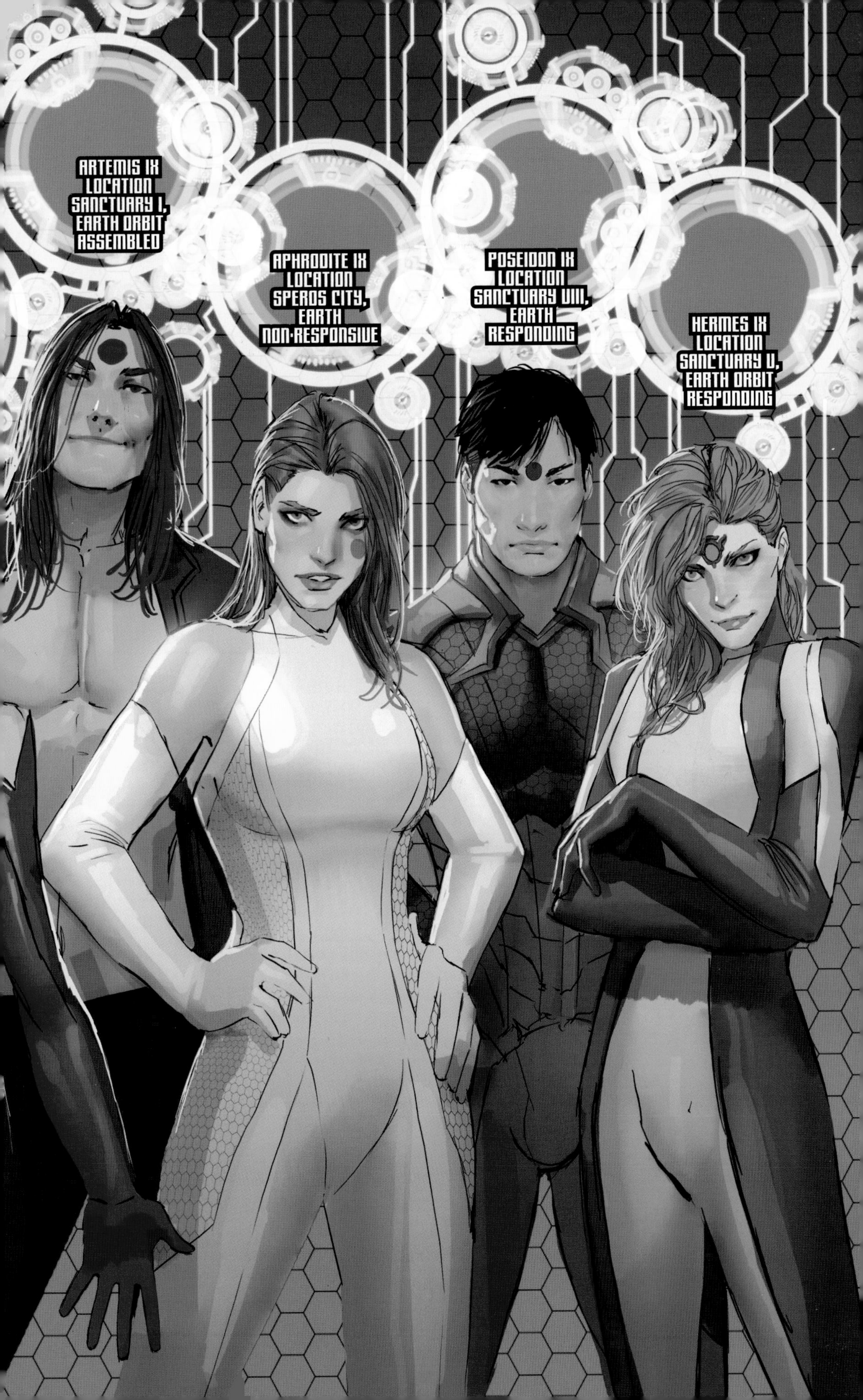
ARTEMIS IX
LOCATION
SANCTUARY I,
EARTH ORBIT
ASSEMBLED
APHRODITE IX
LOCATION
SPEROS CITY,
EARTH
NON-RESPONSIVE
POSEIDON IX
LOCATION
SANCTUARY VIII,
EARTH
RESPONDING
HERMES IX
LOCATION
SANCTUARY V,
EARTH ORBIT
RESPONDING

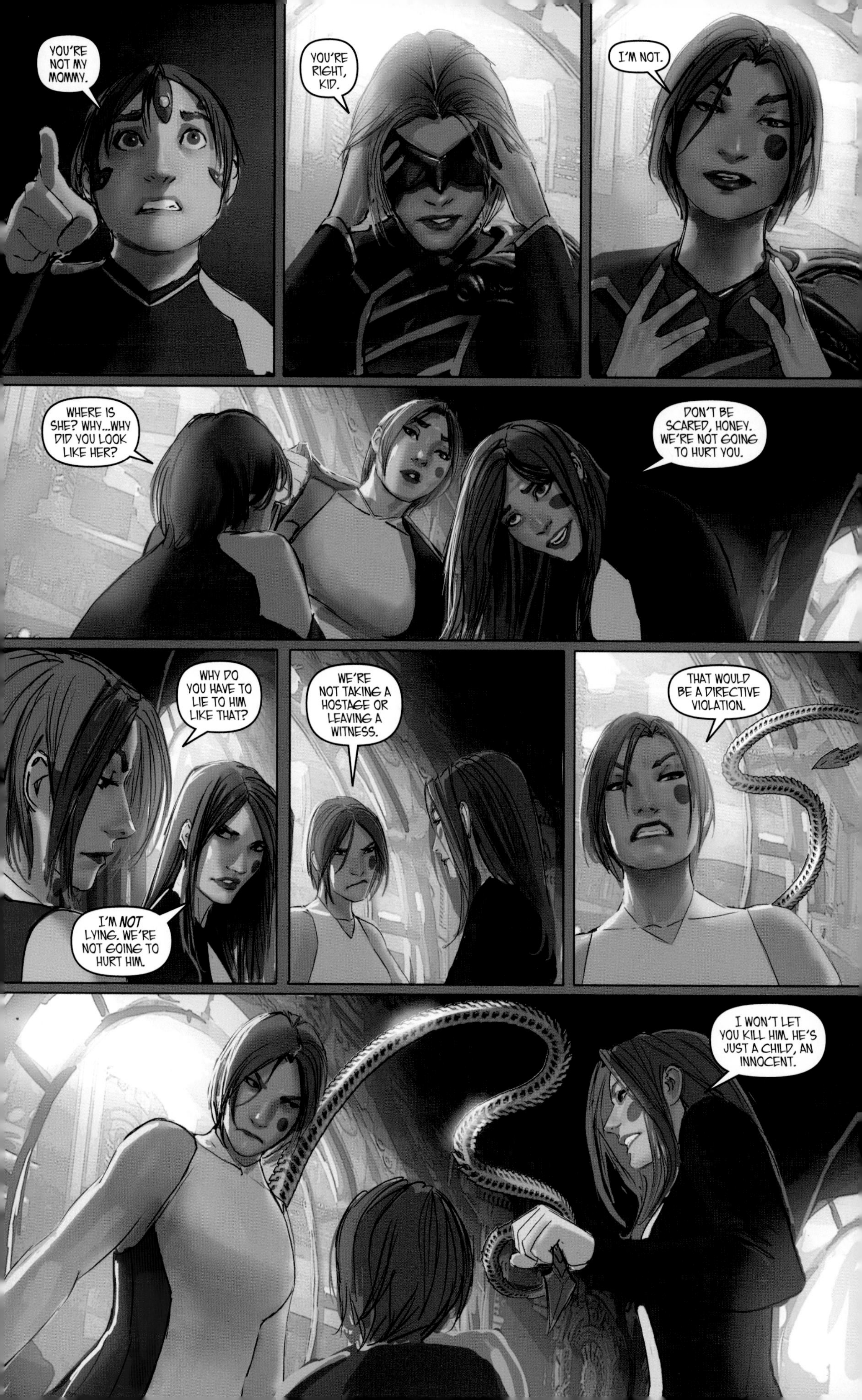
YOU'RE NOT MY MOMMY.
YOU'RE RIGHT, KID.
I'M NOT.
WHERE IS SHE? WHY...WHY DID YOU LOOK LIKE HER?
DON'T BE SCARED, HONEY. WE'RE NOT GOING TO HURT YOU.
WHY DO YOU HAVE TO LIE TO HIM LIKE THAT?
I'M *NOT* LYING. WE'RE NOT GOING TO HURT HIM.
WE'RE NOT TAKING A HOSTAGE OR LEAVING A WITNESS.
THAT WOULD BE A DIRECTIVE VIOLATION.
I WON'T LET YOU KILL HIM. HE'S JUST A CHILD, AN INNOCENT.

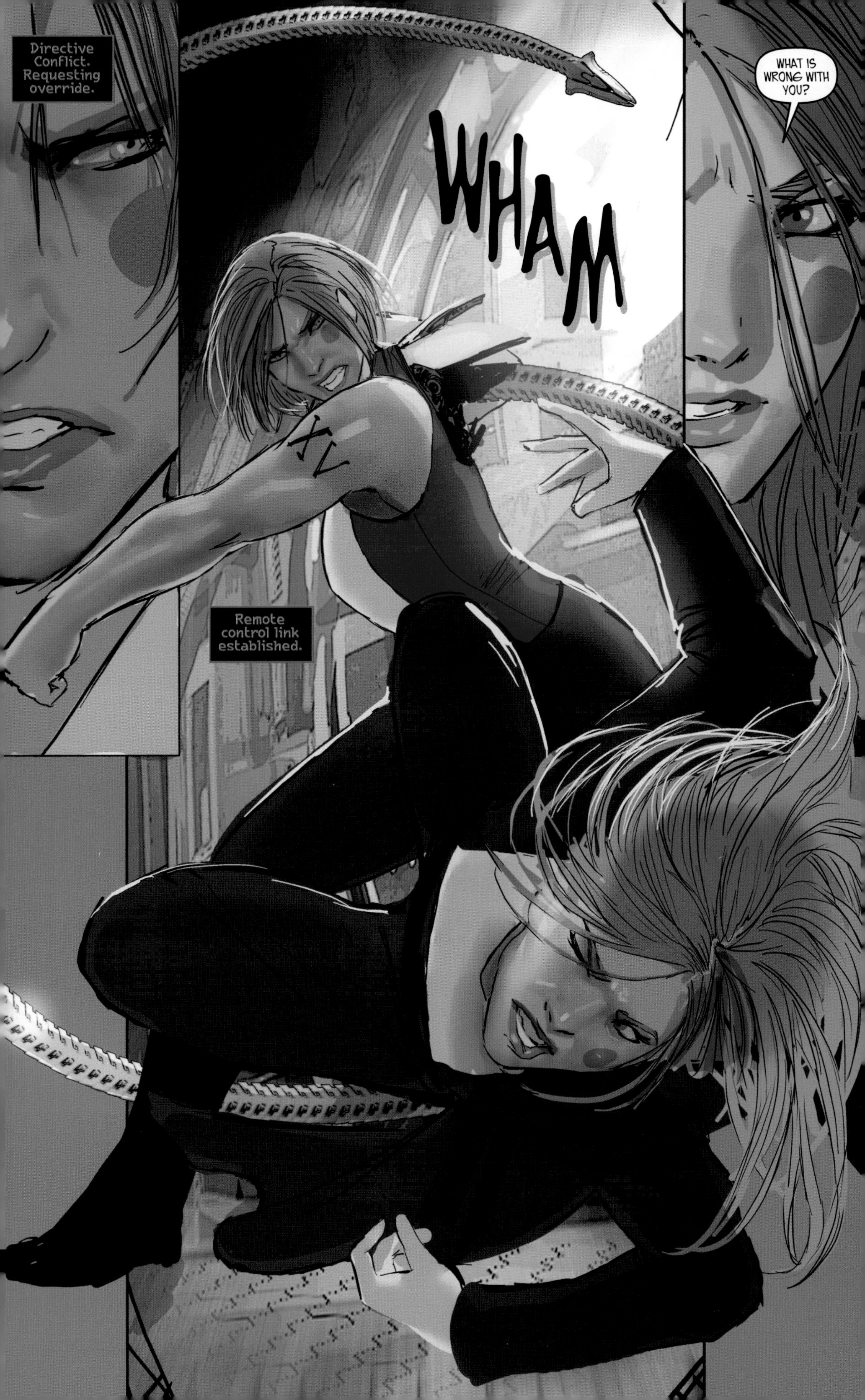
Directive Conflict. Requesting override.
WHAM
WHAT IS WRONG WITH YOU?
Remote control link established.

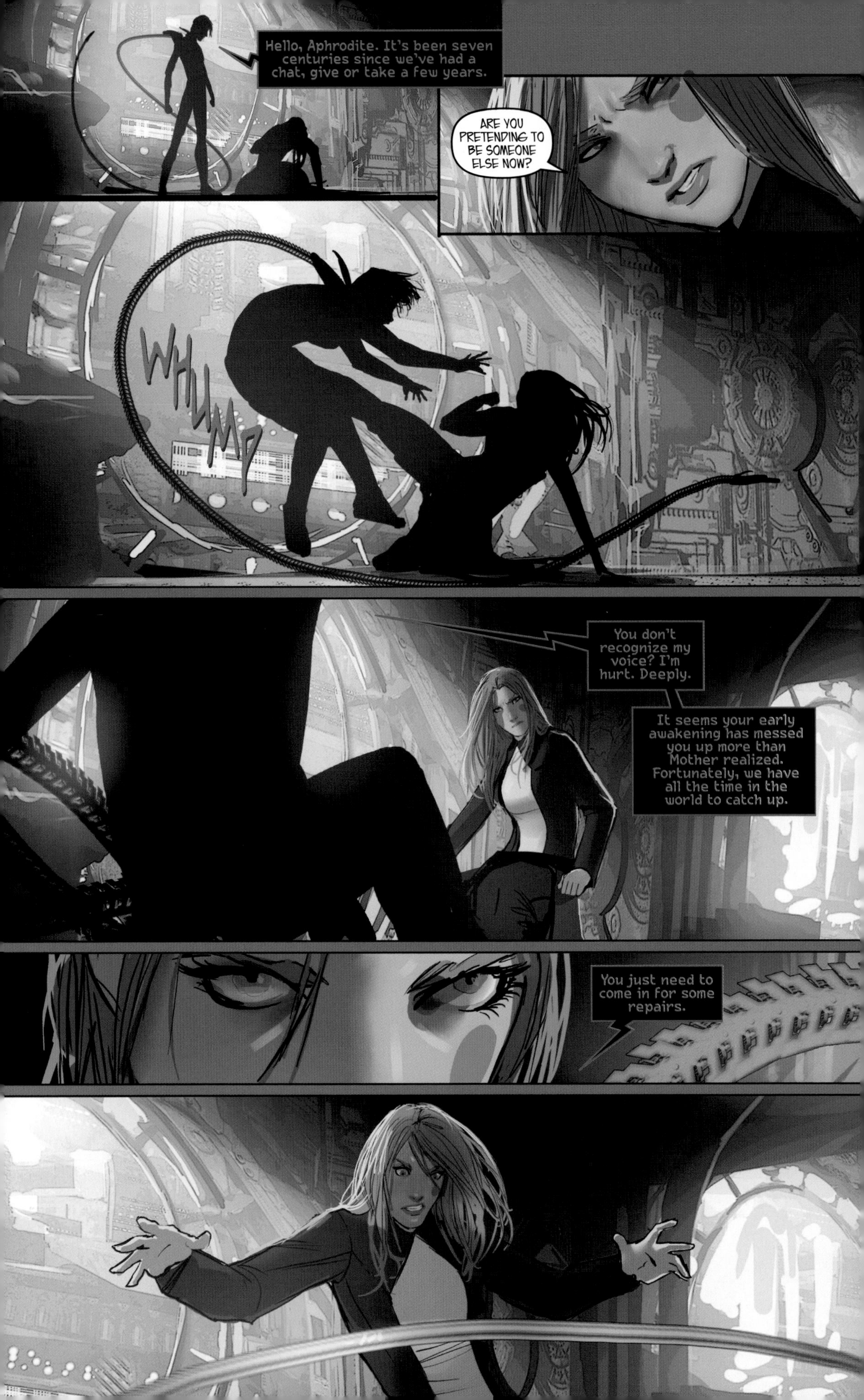
Hello, Aphrodite. It's been seven centuries since we've had a chat, give or take a few years.
ARE YOU PRETENDING TO BE SOMEONE ELSE NOW?
WHUMP
You don't recognize my voice? I'm hurt. Deeply.
It seems your early awakening has messed you up more than Mother realized. Fortunately, we have all the time in the world to catch up.
You just need to come in for some repairs.

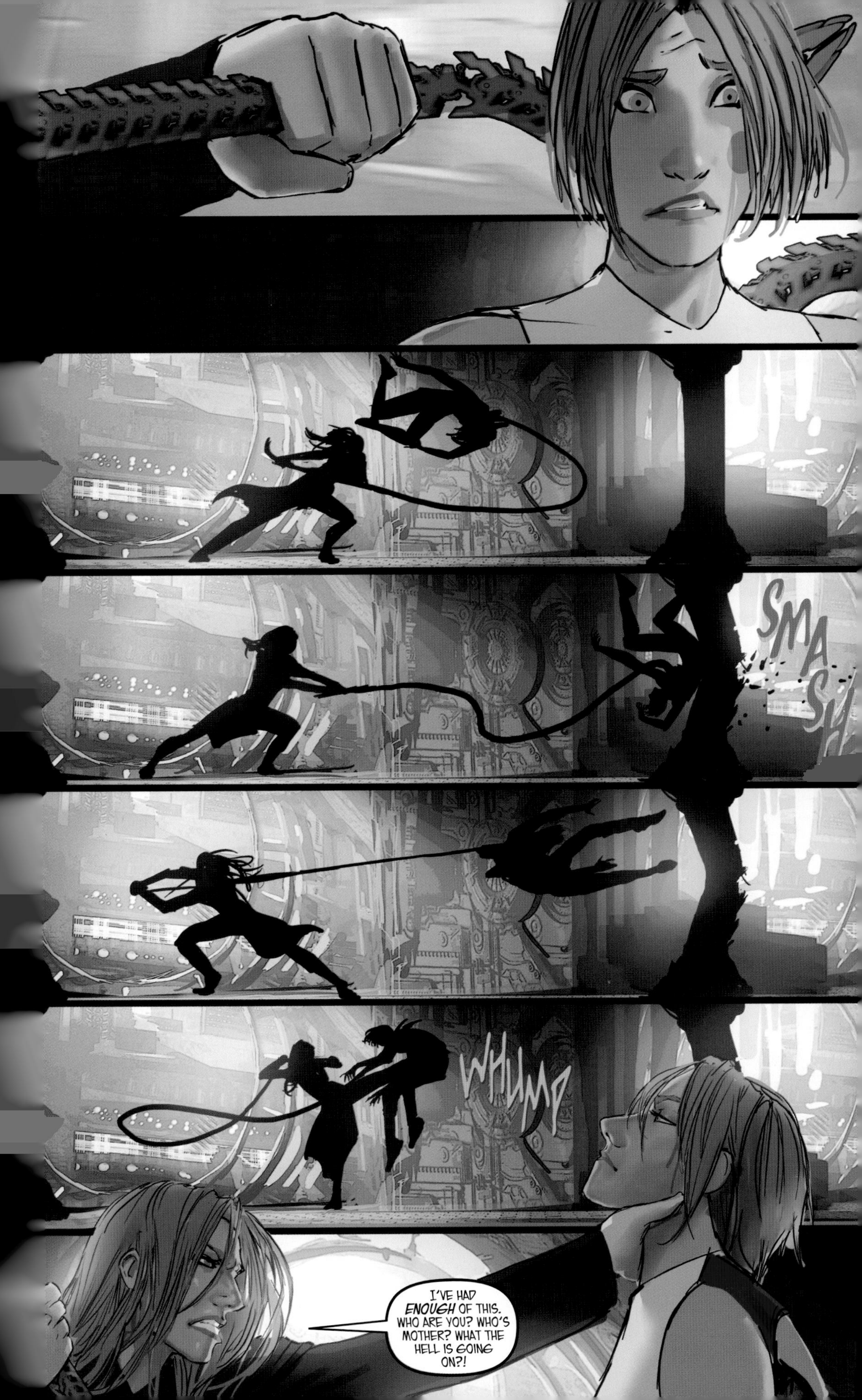
SMASH
WHUMP
I'VE HAD ENOUGH OF THIS. WHO ARE YOU? WHO'S MOTHER? WHAT THE HELL IS GOING ON?!

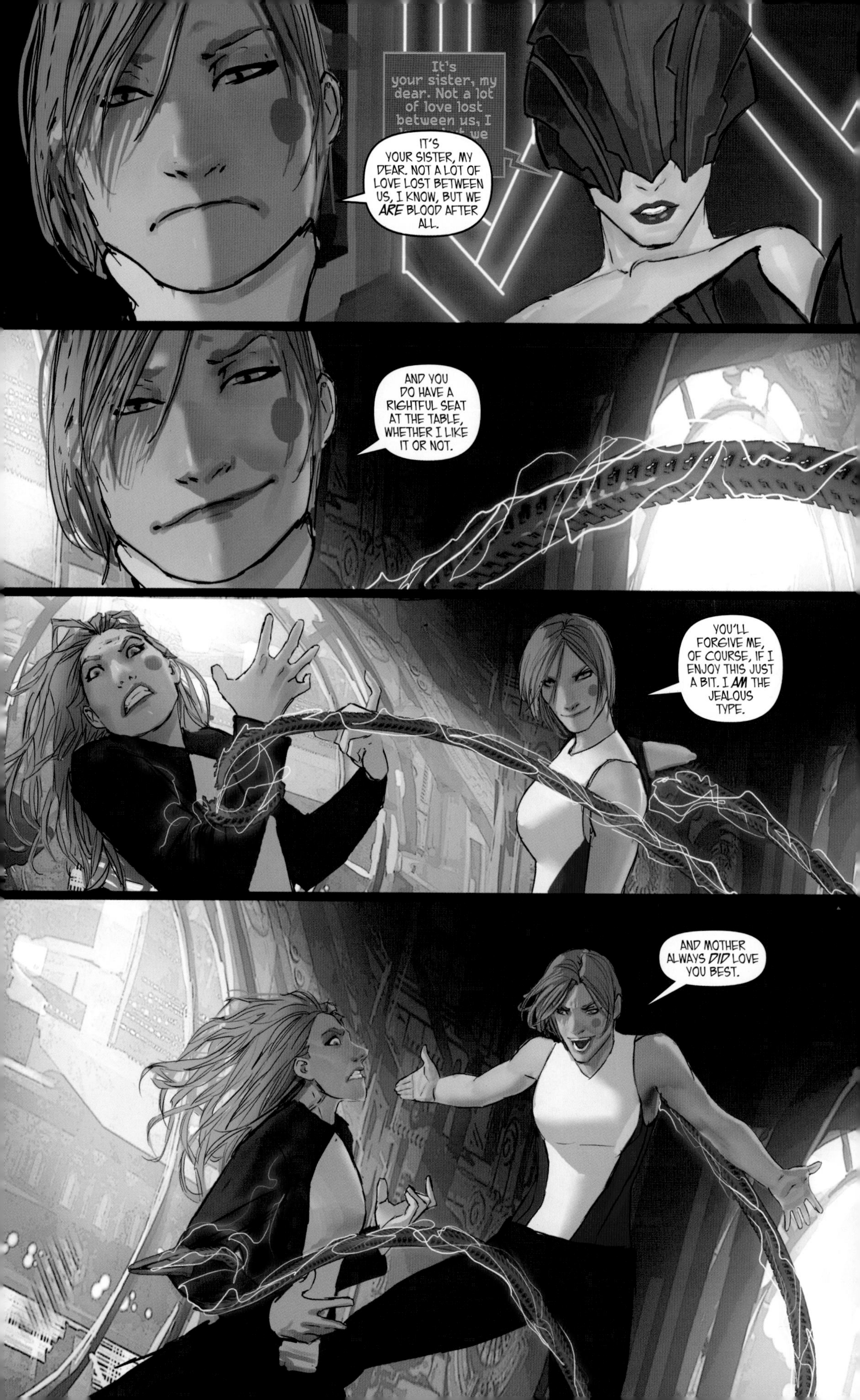
It's your sister, my dear. Not a lot of love lost between us, I
IT'S YOUR SISTER, MY DEAR. NOT A LOT OF LOVE LOST BETWEEN US, I KNOW, BUT WE *ARE* BLOOD AFTER ALL.
AND YOU DO HAVE A RIGHTFUL SEAT AT THE TABLE, WHETHER I LIKE IT OR NOT.
YOU'LL FORGIVE ME, OF COURSE, IF I ENJOY THIS JUST A BIT. I *AM* THE JEALOUS TYPE.
AND MOTHER ALWAYS *DID* LOVE YOU BEST.

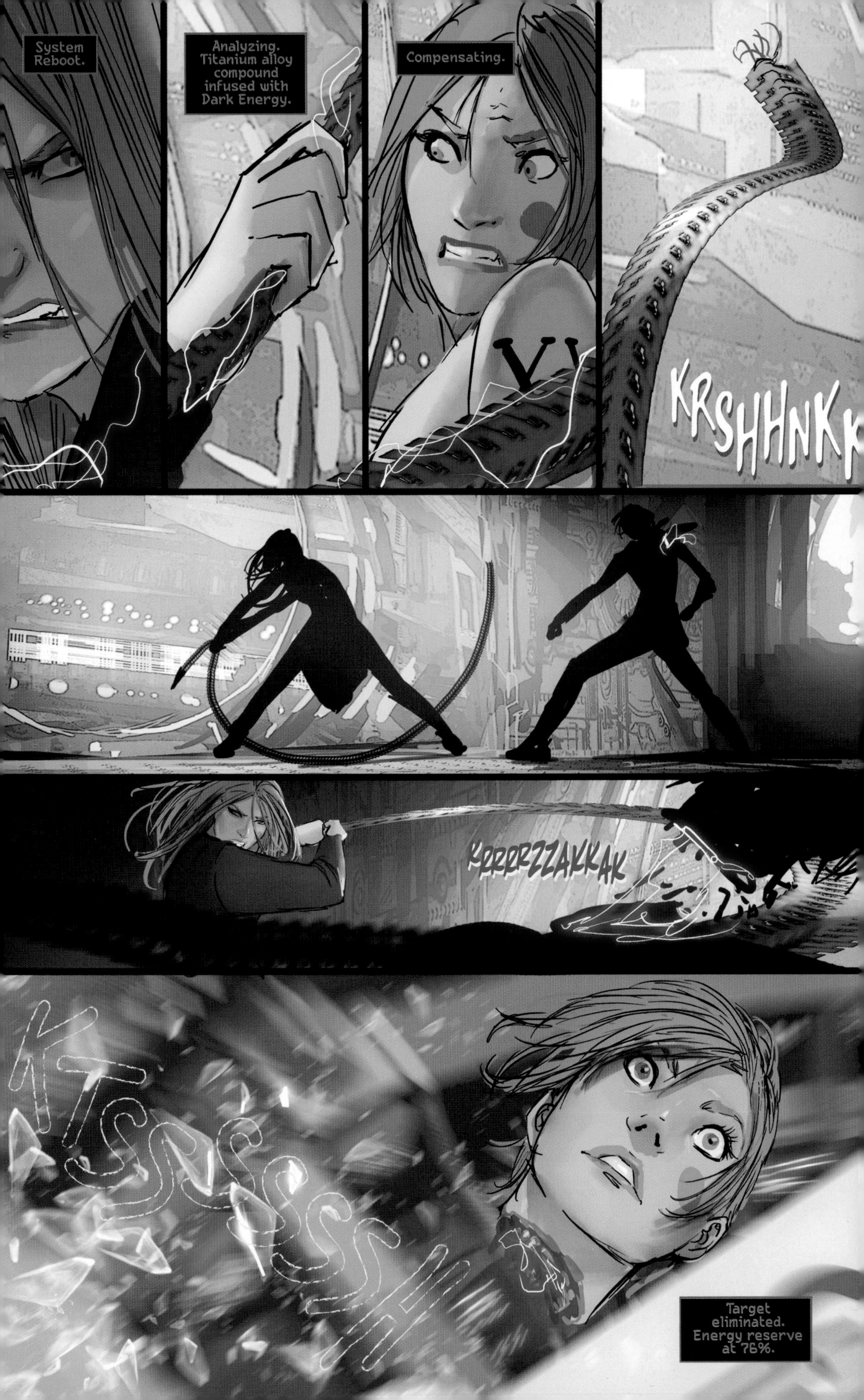
System Reboot.
Analyzing. Titanium alloy compound infused with Dark Energy.
Compensating.
KRSHHNKK
KRRRRZZAKKAK
KTSSSSSH
Target eliminated. Energy reserve at 76%.

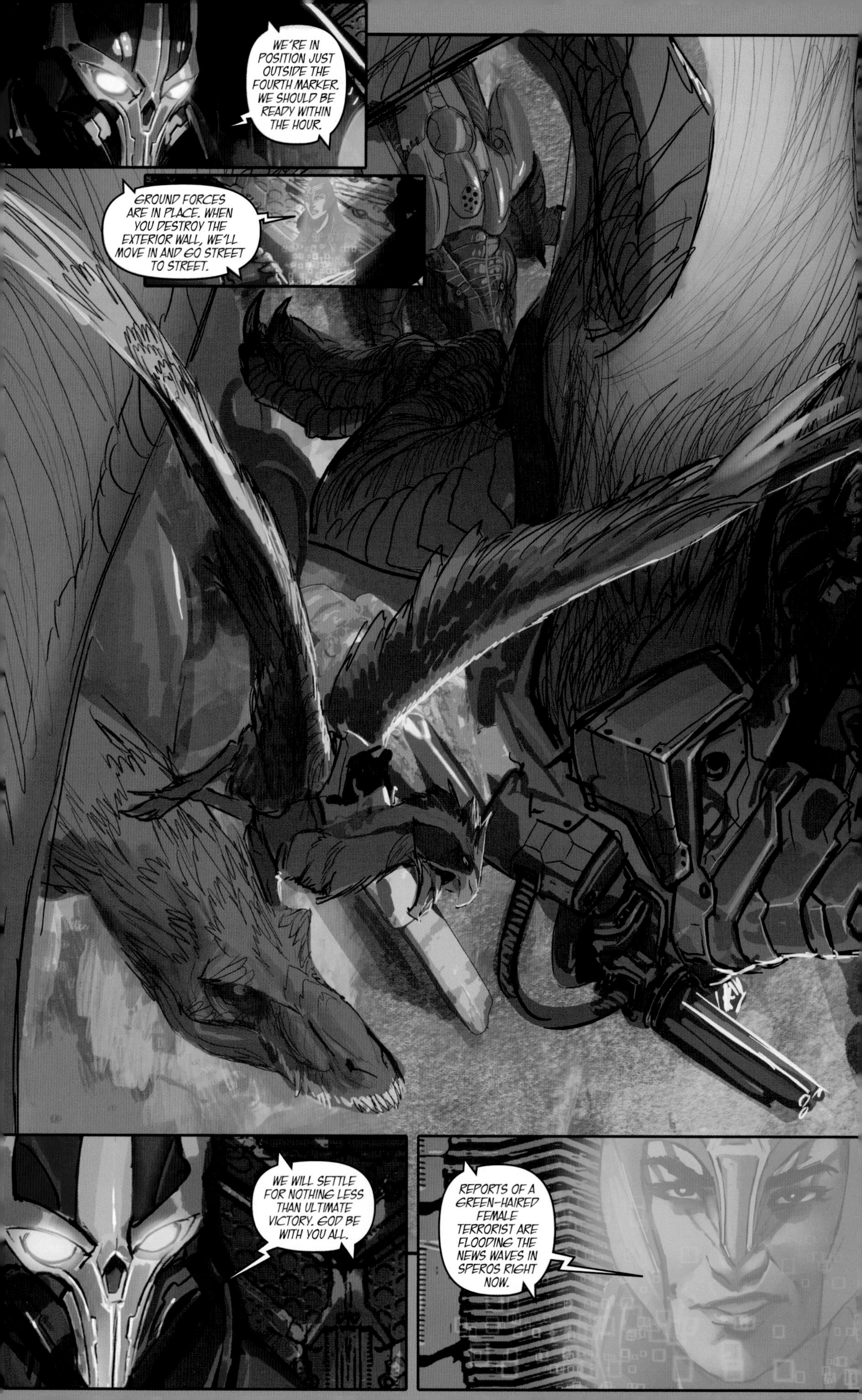
WE'RE IN POSITION JUST OUTSIDE THE FOURTH MARKER. WE SHOULD BE READY WITHIN THE HOUR.
GROUND FORCES ARE IN PLACE. WHEN YOU DESTROY THE EXTERIOR WALL, WE'LL MOVE IN AND GO STREET TO STREET.
WE WILL SETTLE FOR NOTHING LESS THAN ULTIMATE VICTORY. GOD BE WITH YOU ALL.
REPORTS OF A GREEN-HAIRED FEMALE TERRORIST ARE FLOODING THE NEWS WAVES IN SPEROS RIGHT NOW.

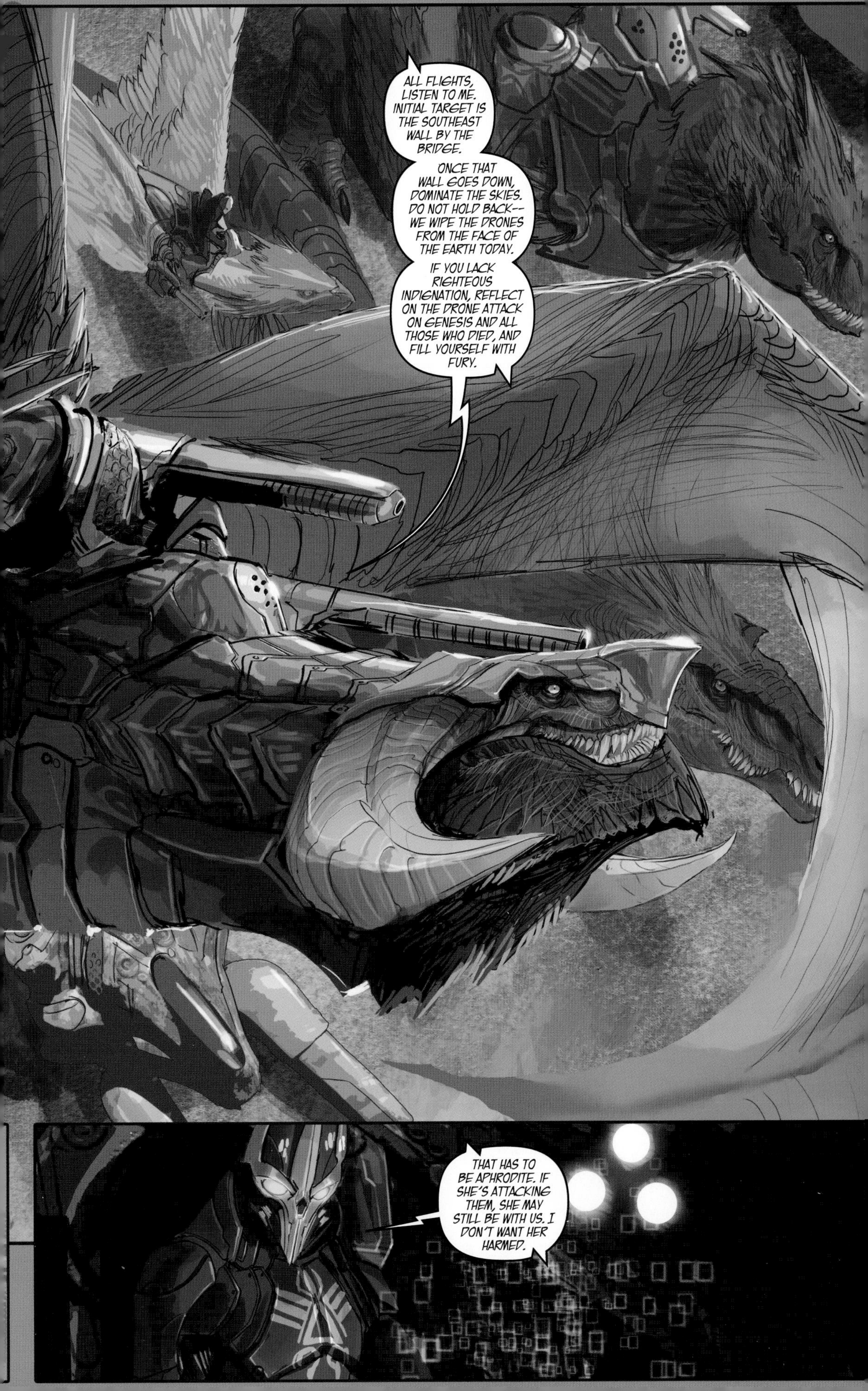
ALL FLIGHTS, LISTEN TO ME. INITIAL TARGET IS THE SOUTHEAST WALL BY THE BRIDGE.
ONCE THAT WALL GOES DOWN, DOMINATE THE SKIES. DO NOT HOLD BACK-- WE WIPE THE DRONES FROM THE FACE OF THE EARTH TODAY.
IF YOU LACK RIGHTEOUS INDIGNATION, REFLECT ON THE DRONE ATTACK ON GENESIS AND ALL THOSE WHO DIED, AND FILL YOURSELF WITH FURY.
THAT HAS TO BE APHRODITE. IF SHE'S ATTACKING THEM, SHE MAY STILL BE WITH US. I DON'T WANT HER HARMED.

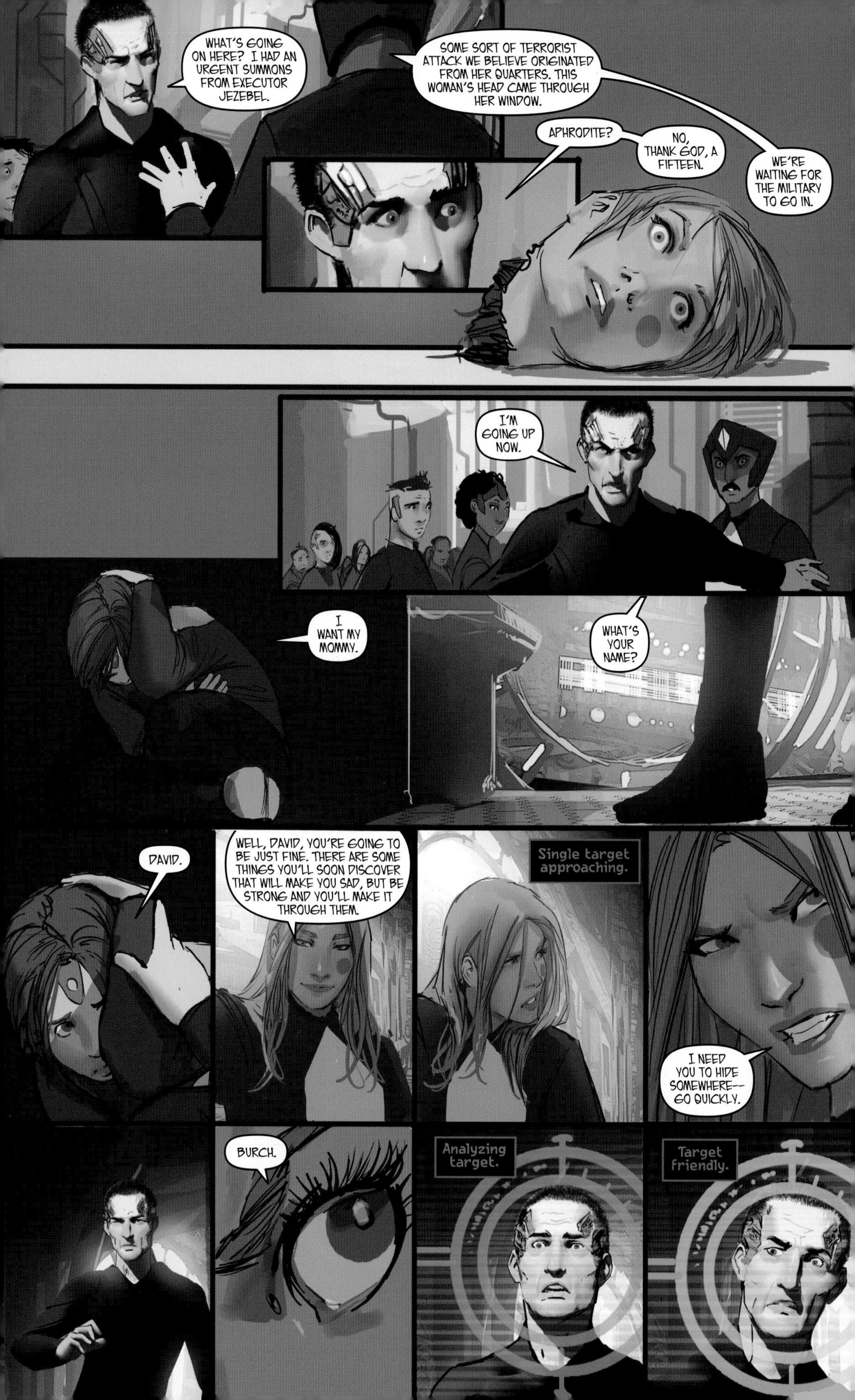
WHAT'S GOING ON HERE? I HAD AN URGENT SUMMONS FROM EXECUTOR JEZEBEL.
SOME SORT OF TERRORIST ATTACK WE BELIEVE ORIGINATED FROM HER QUARTERS. THIS WOMAN'S HEAD CAME THROUGH HER WINDOW.
APHRODITE?
NO, THANK GOD, A FIFTEEN.
WE'RE WAITING FOR THE MILITARY TO GO IN.
I'M GOING UP NOW.
I WANT MY MOMMY.
WHAT'S YOUR NAME?
DAVID.
WELL, DAVID, YOU'RE GOING TO BE JUST FINE. THERE ARE SOME THINGS YOU'LL SOON DISCOVER THAT WILL MAKE YOU SAD, BUT BE STRONG AND YOU'LL MAKE IT THROUGH THEM.
Single target approaching.
I NEED YOU TO HIDE SOMEWHERE-- GO QUICKLY.
BURCH.
Analyzing target.
Target friendly.

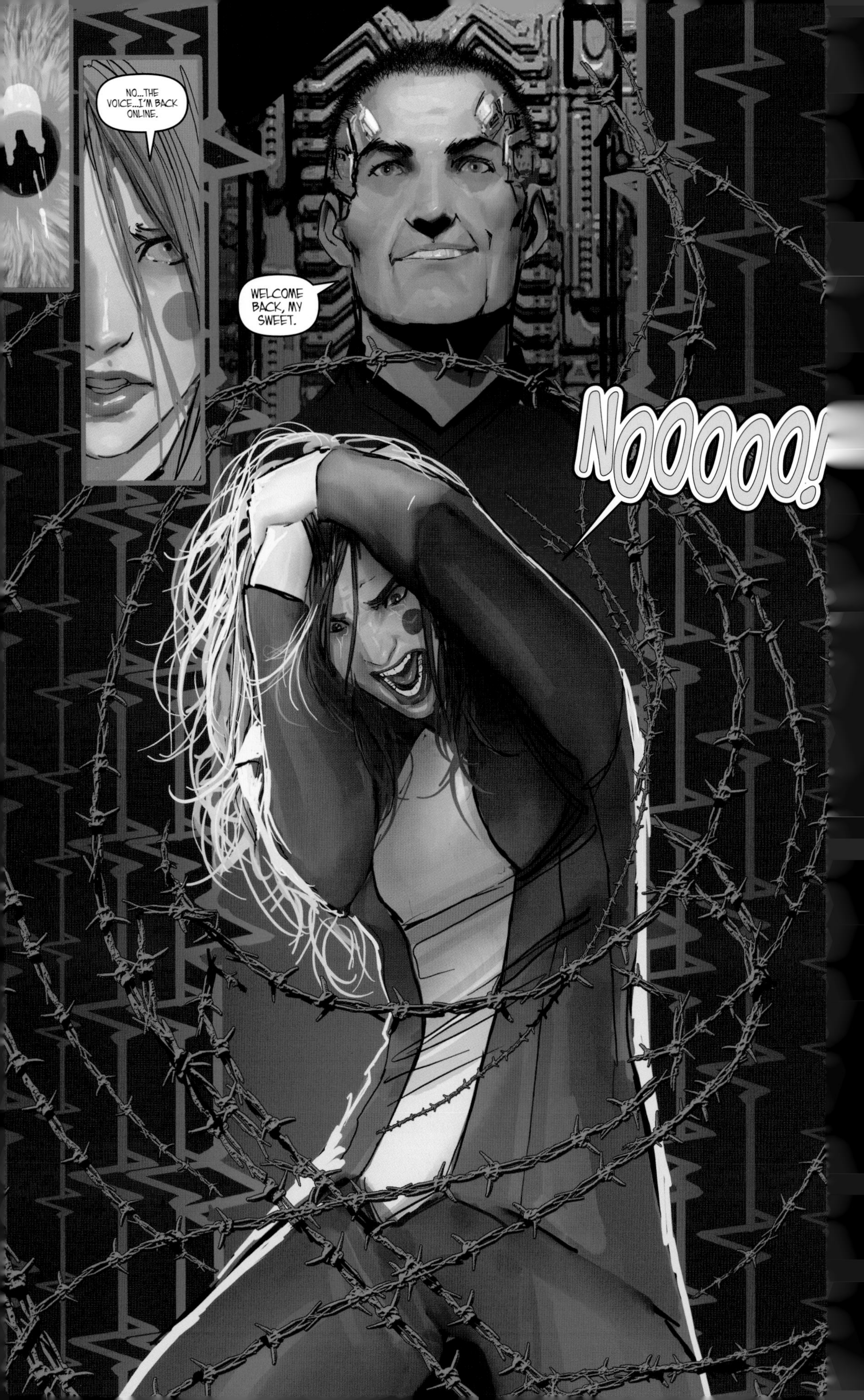
NO...THE VOICE...I'M BACK ONLINE.
WELCOME BACK, MY SWEET.
NOOOOO!

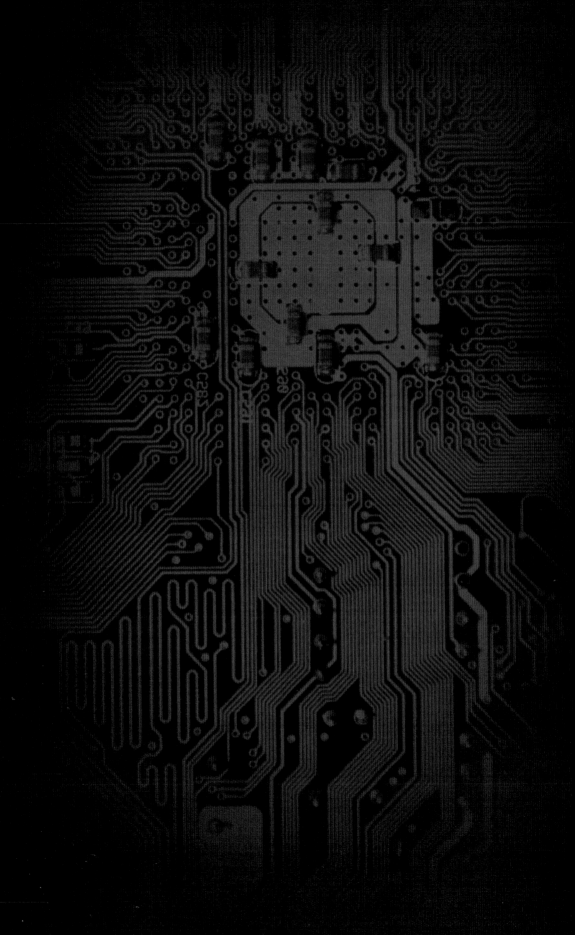

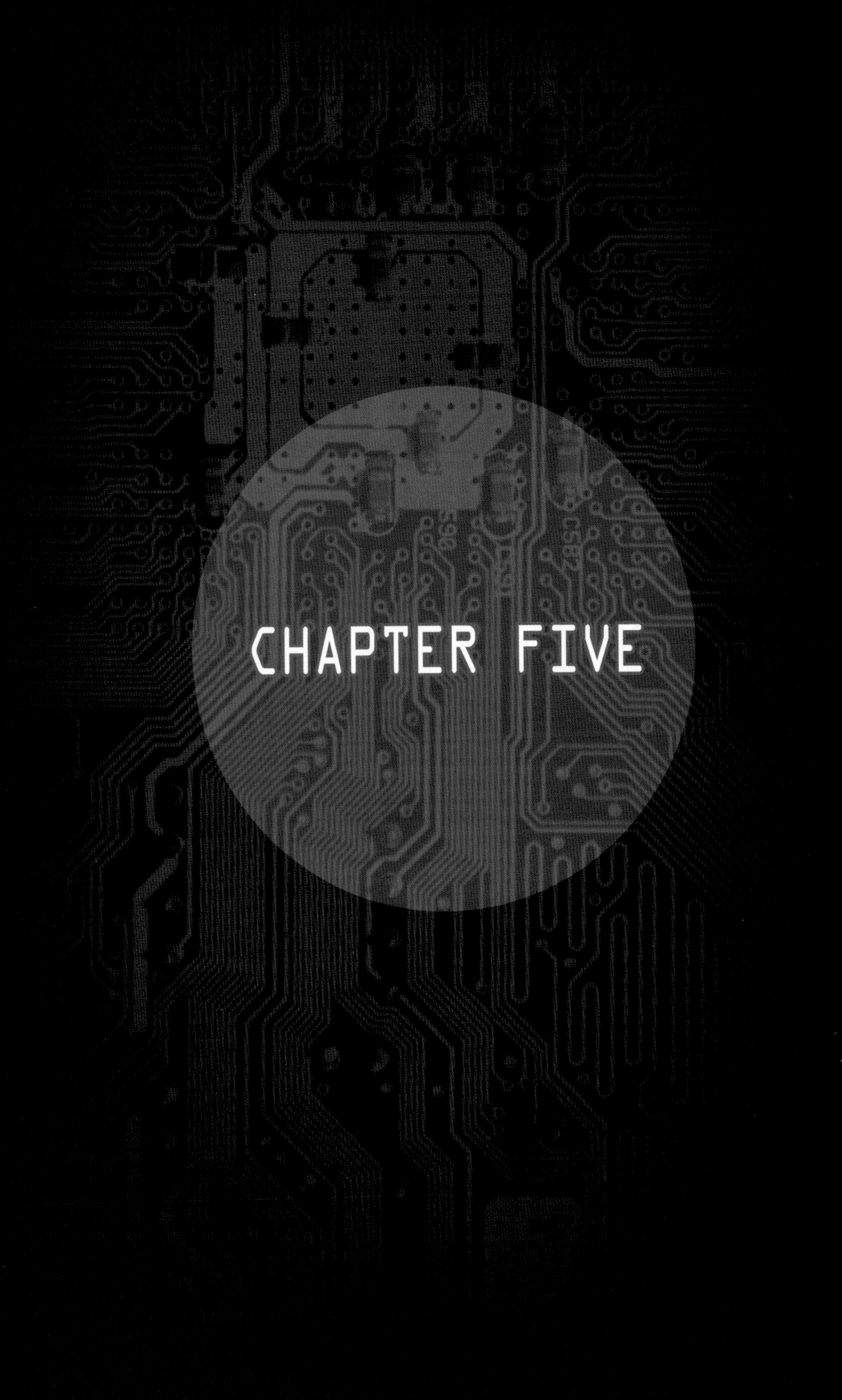

CHAPTER FIVE

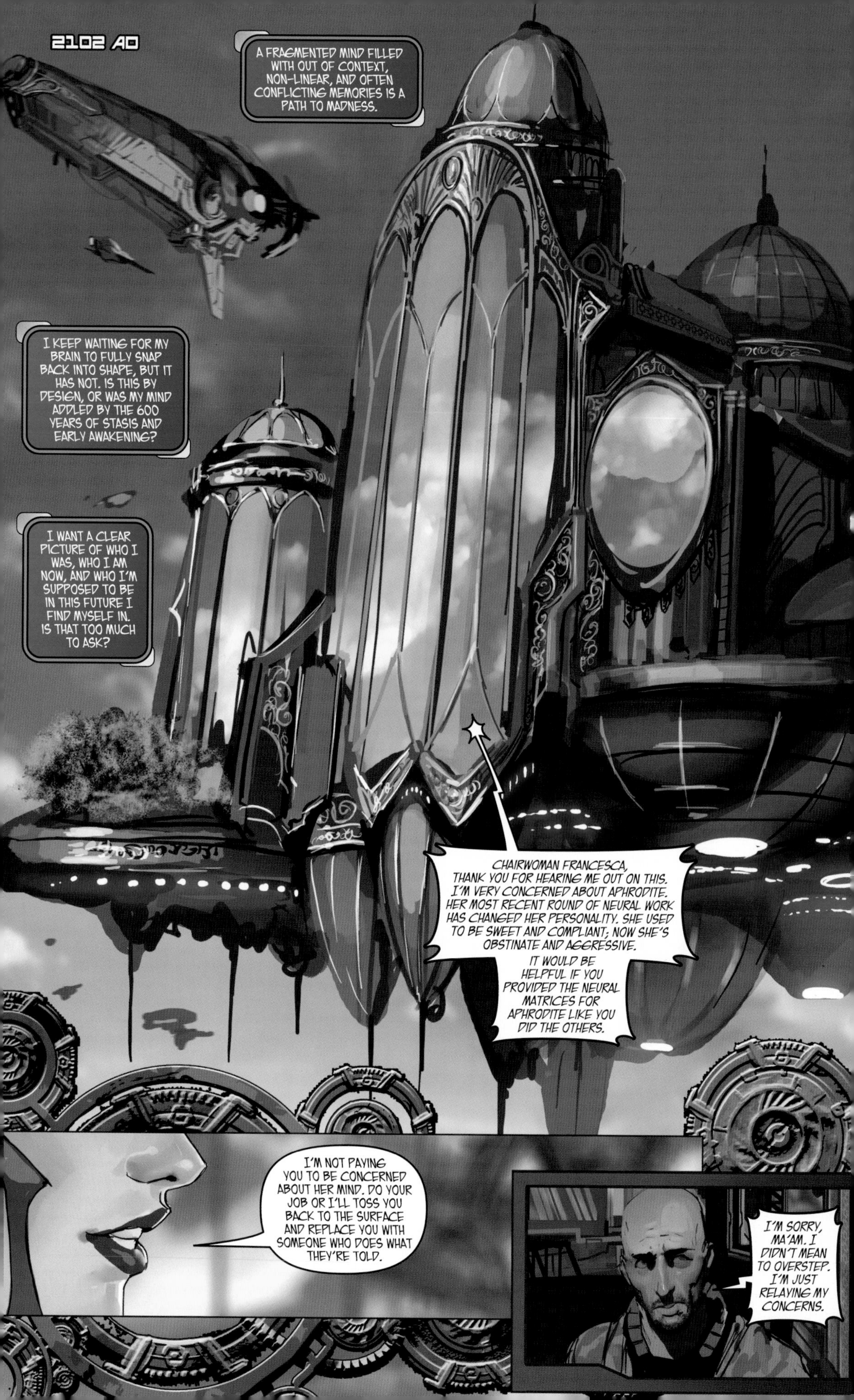

2102 AD
A FRAGMENTED MIND FILLED WITH OUT OF CONTEXT, NON-LINEAR, AND OFTEN CONFLICTING MEMORIES IS A PATH TO MADNESS.
I KEEP WAITING FOR MY BRAIN TO FULLY SNAP BACK INTO SHAPE, BUT IT HAS NOT. IS THIS BY DESIGN, OR WAS MY MIND ADDLED BY THE 600 YEARS OF STASIS AND EARLY AWAKENING?
I WANT A CLEAR PICTURE OF WHO I WAS, WHO I AM NOW, AND WHO I'M SUPPOSED TO BE IN THIS FUTURE I FIND MYSELF IN. IS THAT TOO MUCH TO ASK?
CHAIRWOMAN FRANCESCA, THANK YOU FOR HEARING ME OUT ON THIS. I'M VERY CONCERNED ABOUT APHRODITE. HER MOST RECENT ROUND OF NEURAL WORK HAS CHANGED HER PERSONALITY. SHE USED TO BE SWEET AND COMPLIANT; NOW SHE'S OBSTINATE AND AGGRESSIVE.
IT WOULD BE HELPFUL IF YOU PROVIDED THE NEURAL MATRICES FOR APHRODITE LIKE YOU DID THE OTHERS.
I'M NOT PAYING YOU TO BE CONCERNED ABOUT HER MIND. DO YOUR JOB OR I'LL TOSS YOU BACK TO THE SURFACE AND REPLACE YOU WITH SOMEONE WHO DOES WHAT THEY'RE TOLD.
I'M SORRY, MA'AM. I DIDN'T MEAN TO OVERSTEP. I'M JUST RELAYING MY CONCERNS.

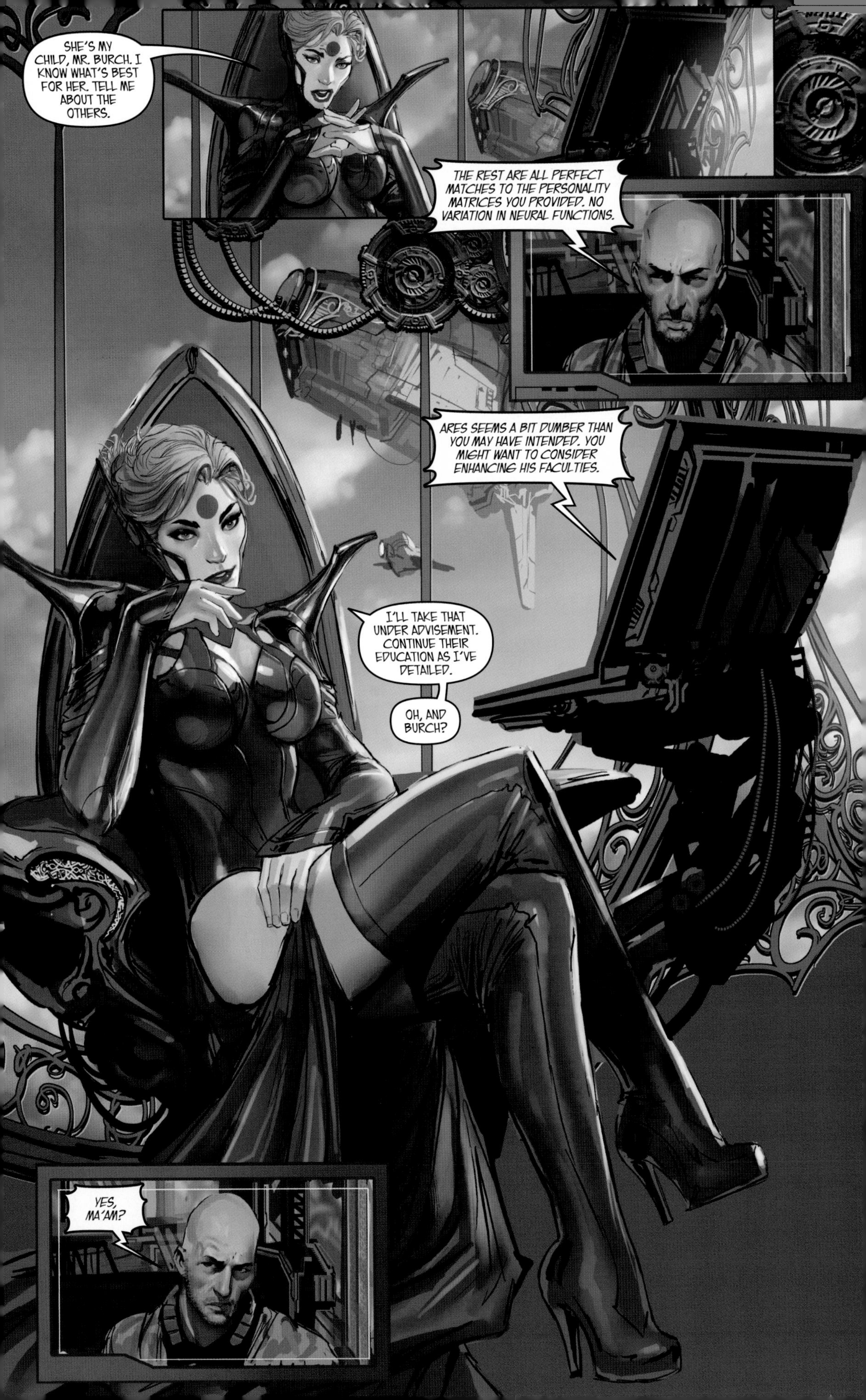
SHE'S MY CHILD, MR. BURCH. I KNOW WHAT'S BEST FOR HER. TELL ME ABOUT THE OTHERS.
THE REST ARE ALL PERFECT MATCHES TO THE PERSONALITY MATRICES YOU PROVIDED. NO VARIATION IN NEURAL FUNCTIONS.
ARES SEEMS A BIT DUMBER THAN YOU MAY HAVE INTENDED. YOU MIGHT WANT TO CONSIDER ENHANCING HIS FACULTIES.
I'LL TAKE THAT UNDER ADVISEMENT. CONTINUE THEIR EDUCATION AS I'VE DETAILED.
OH, AND BURCH?
YES, MA'AM?

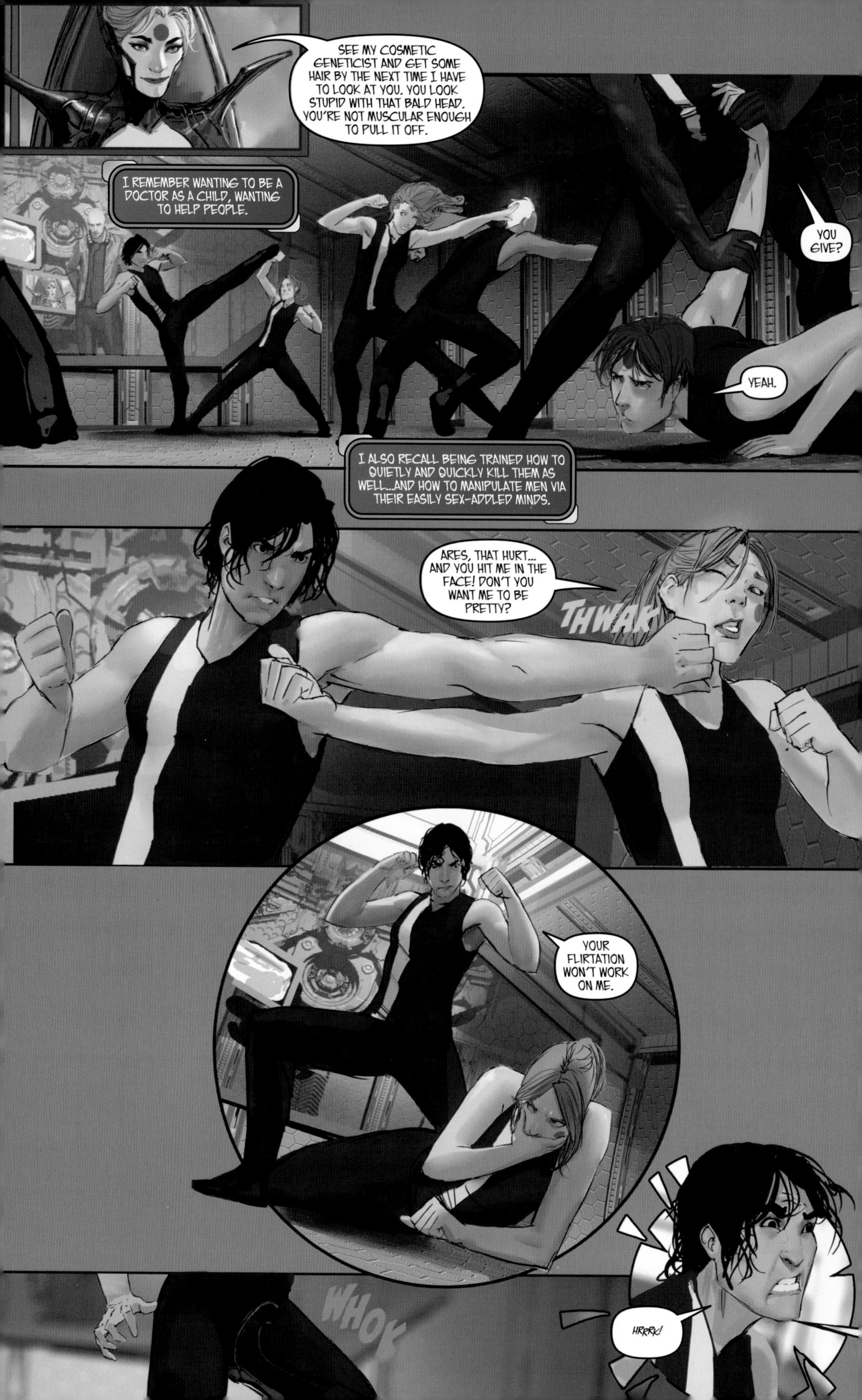
SEE MY COSMETIC GENETICIST AND GET SOME HAIR BY THE NEXT TIME I HAVE TO LOOK AT YOU. YOU LOOK STUPID WITH THAT BALD HEAD. YOU'RE NOT MUSCULAR ENOUGH TO PULL IT OFF.
I REMEMBER WANTING TO BE A DOCTOR AS A CHILD, WANTING TO HELP PEOPLE.
YOU GIVE?
YEAH.
I ALSO RECALL BEING TRAINED HOW TO QUIETLY AND QUICKLY KILL THEM AS WELL...AND HOW TO MANIPULATE MEN VIA THEIR EASILY SEX-ADDLED MINDS.
ARES, THAT HURT... AND YOU HIT ME IN THE FACE! DON'T YOU WANT ME TO BE PRETTY?
THWAK
YOUR FLIRTATION WON'T WORK ON ME.
WHOK
HRRRK!

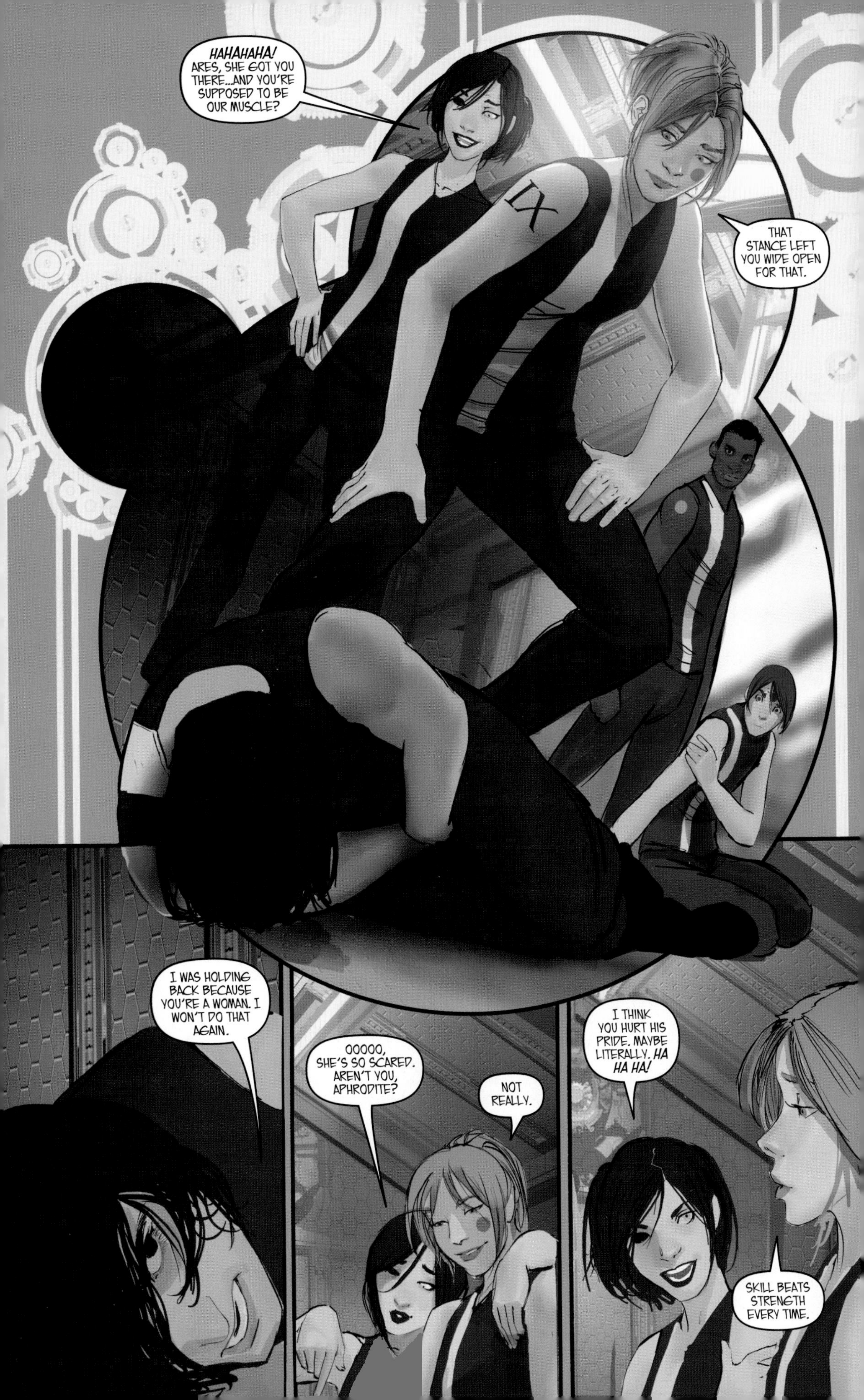
HAHAHAHA! ARES, SHE GOT YOU THERE...AND YOU'RE SUPPOSED TO BE OUR MUSCLE?
THAT STANCE LEFT YOU WIDE OPEN FOR THAT.
I WAS HOLDING BACK BECAUSE YOU'RE A WOMAN. I WON'T DO THAT AGAIN.
OOOOO, SHE'S SO SCARED. AREN'T YOU, APHRODITE?
NOT REALLY.
I THINK YOU HURT HIS PRIDE. MAYBE LITERALLY. HA HA HA!
SKILL BEATS STRENGTH EVERY TIME.

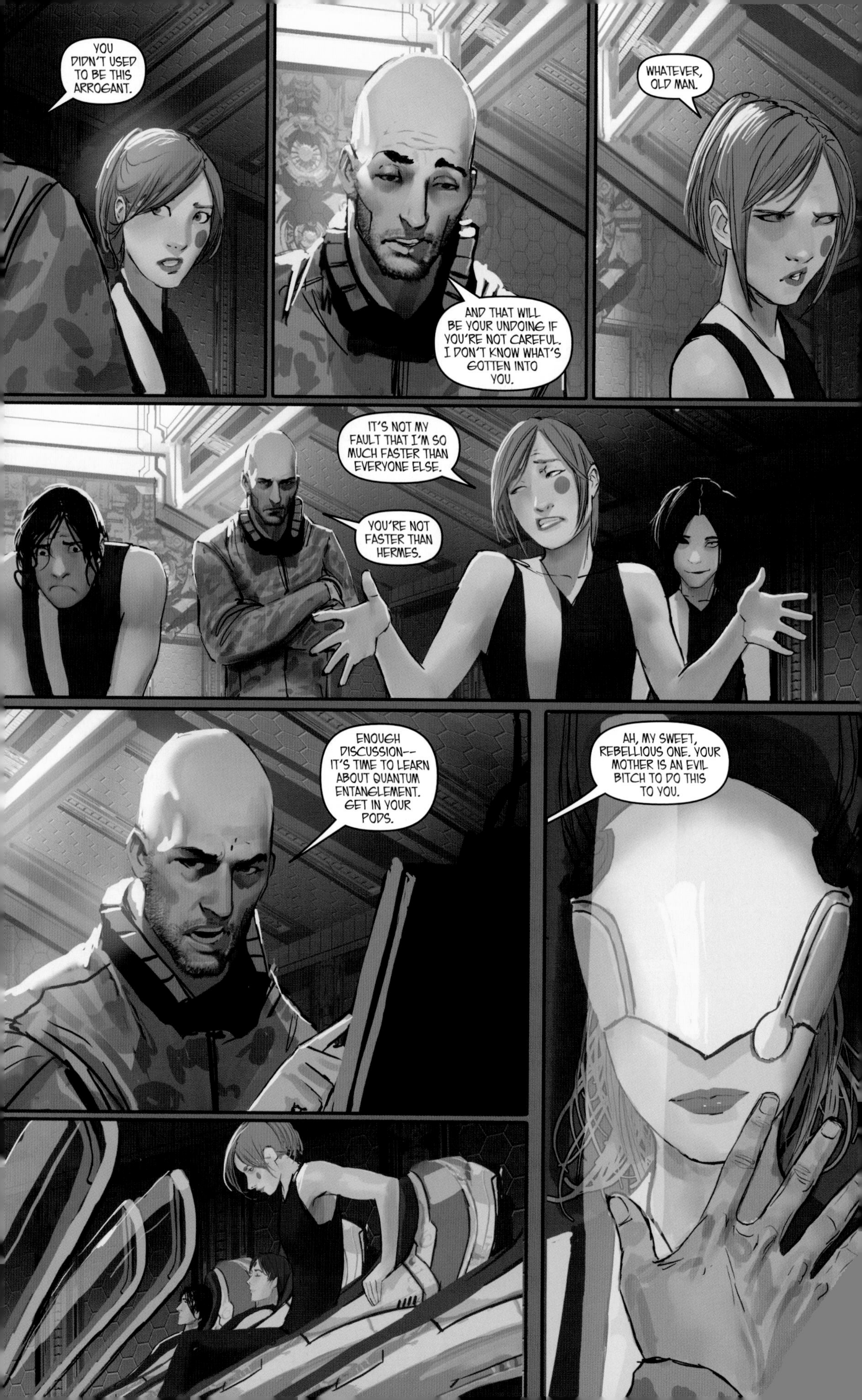
YOU DIDN'T USED TO BE THIS ARROGANT.
AND THAT WILL BE YOUR UNDOING IF YOU'RE NOT CAREFUL. I DON'T KNOW WHAT'S GOTTEN INTO YOU.
WHATEVER, OLD MAN.
IT'S NOT MY FAULT THAT I'M SO MUCH FASTER THAN EVERYONE ELSE.
YOU'RE NOT FASTER THAN HERMES.
ENOUGH DISCUSSION-- IT'S TIME TO LEARN ABOUT QUANTUM ENTANGLEMENT. GET IN YOUR PODS.
AH, MY SWEET, REBELLIOUS ONE. YOUR MOTHER IS AN EVIL BITCH TO DO THIS TO YOU.

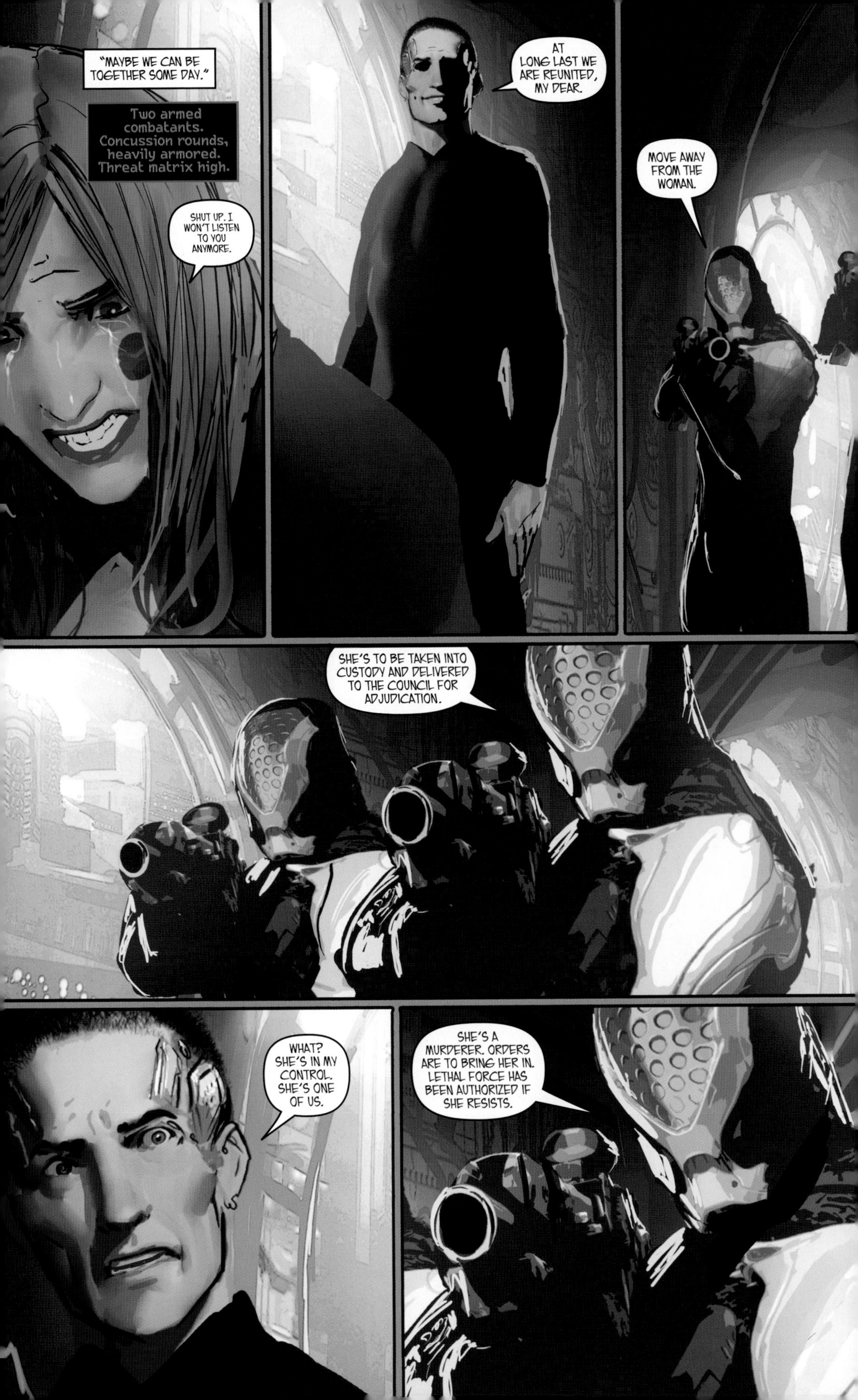
"MAYBE WE CAN BE TOGETHER SOME DAY."
Two armed combatants. Concussion rounds, heavily armored. Threat matrix high.
SHUT UP. I WON'T LISTEN TO YOU ANYMORE.
AT LONG LAST WE ARE REUNITED, MY DEAR.
MOVE AWAY FROM THE WOMAN.
SHE'S TO BE TAKEN INTO CUSTODY AND DELIVERED TO THE COUNCIL FOR ADJUDICATION.
WHAT? SHE'S IN MY CONTROL. SHE'S ONE OF US.
SHE'S A MURDERER. ORDERS ARE TO BRING HER IN. LETHAL FORCE HAS BEEN AUTHORIZED IF SHE RESISTS.

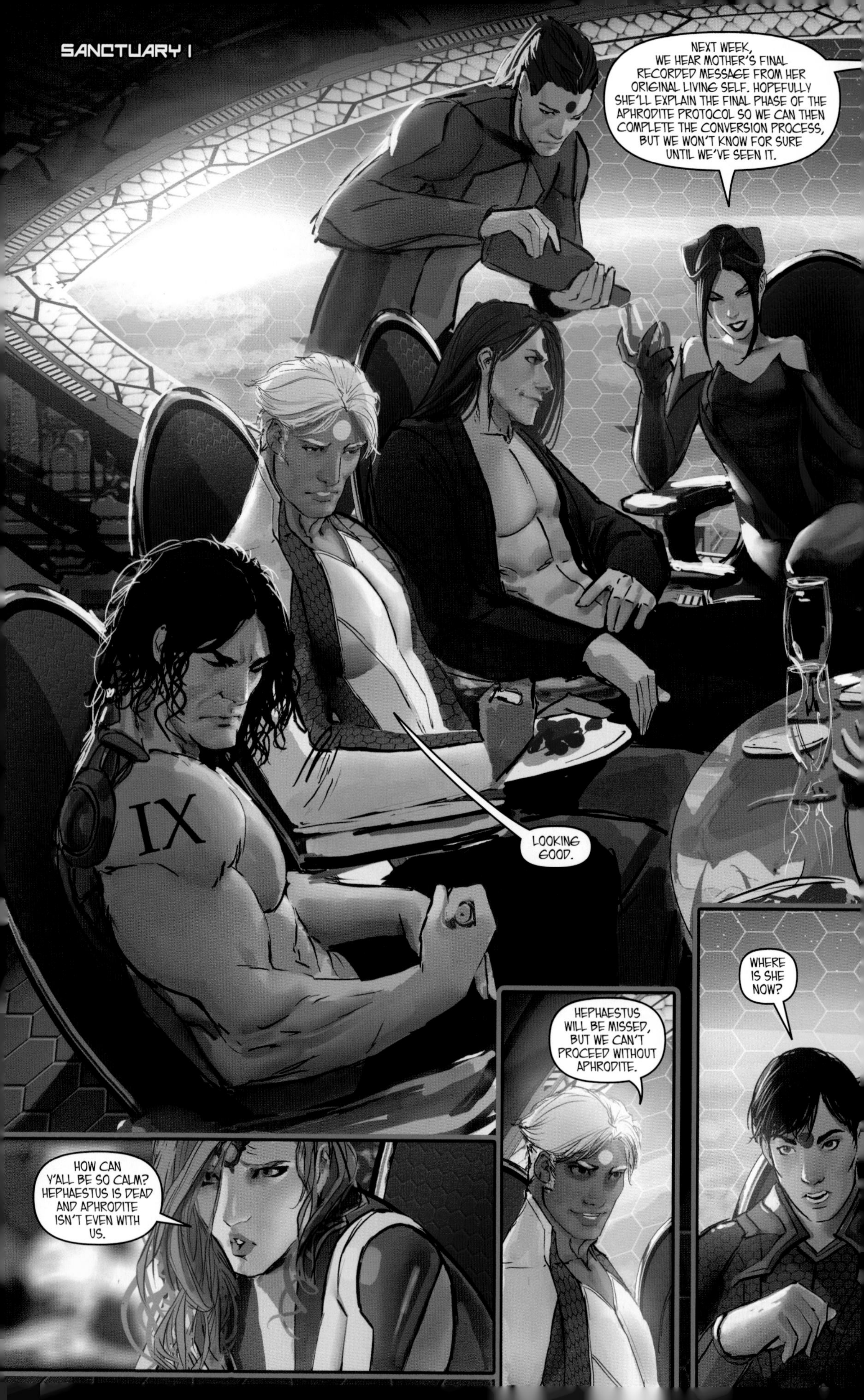
NEXT WEEK, WE HEAR MOTHER'S FINAL RECORDED MESSAGE FROM HER ORIGINAL LIVING SELF. HOPEFULLY SHE'LL EXPLAIN THE FINAL PHASE OF THE APHRODITE PROTOCOL SO WE CAN THEN COMPLETE THE CONVERSION PROCESS, BUT WE WON'T KNOW FOR SURE UNTIL WE'VE SEEN IT.
IX
LOOKING GOOD.
WHERE IS SHE NOW?
HEPHAESTUS WILL BE MISSED, BUT WE CAN'T PROCEED WITHOUT APHRODITE.
HOW CAN Y'ALL BE SO CALM? HEPHAESTUS IS DEAD AND APHRODITE ISN'T EVEN WITH US.

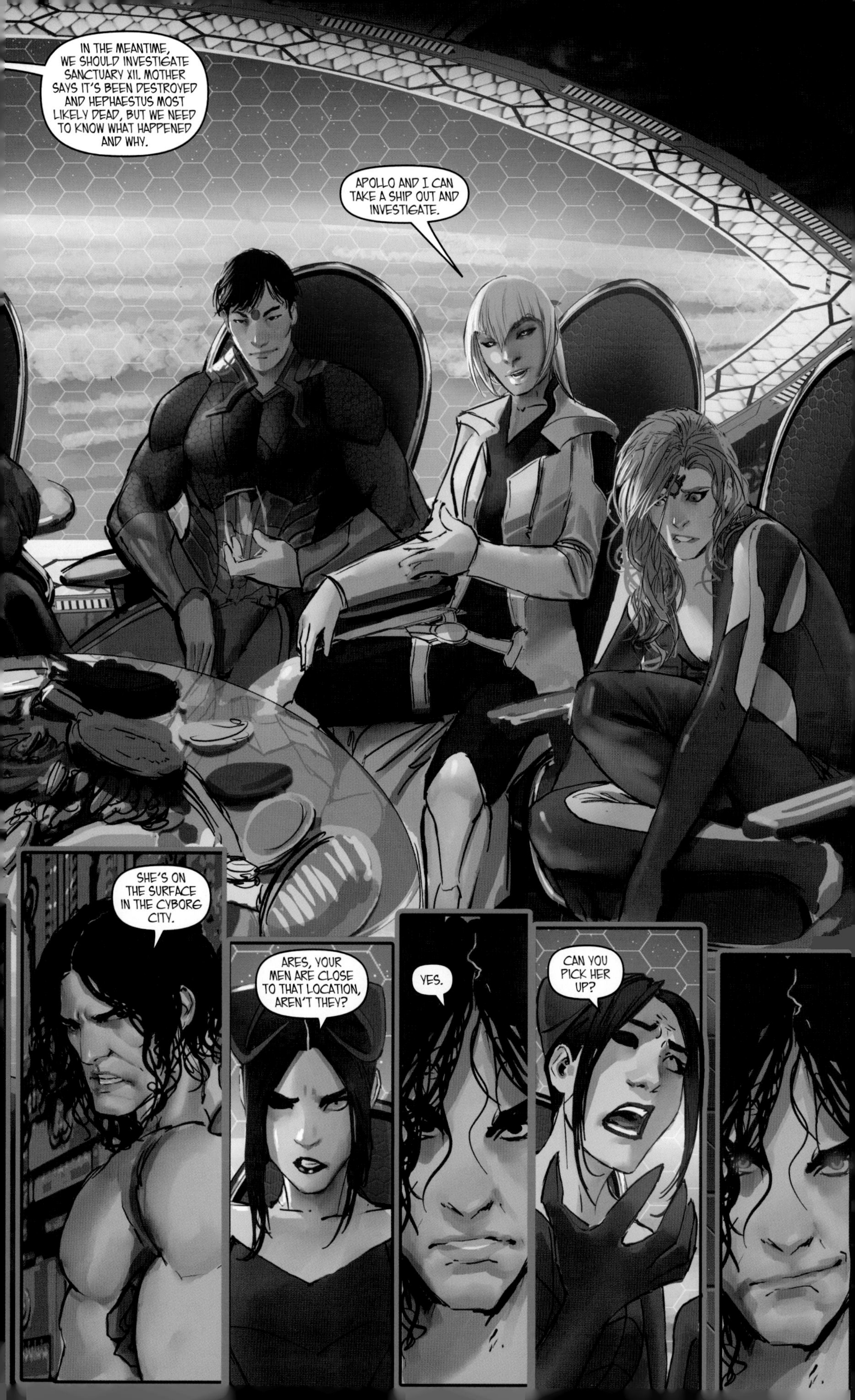
IN THE MEANTIME, WE SHOULD INVESTIGATE SANCTUARY XII. MOTHER SAYS IT'S BEEN DESTROYED AND HEPHAESTUS MOST LIKELY DEAD, BUT WE NEED TO KNOW WHAT HAPPENED AND WHY.
APOLLO AND I CAN TAKE A SHIP OUT AND INVESTIGATE.
SHE'S ON THE SURFACE IN THE CYBORG CITY.
ARES, YOUR MEN ARE CLOSE TO THAT LOCATION, AREN'T THEY?
YES.
CAN YOU PICK HER UP?

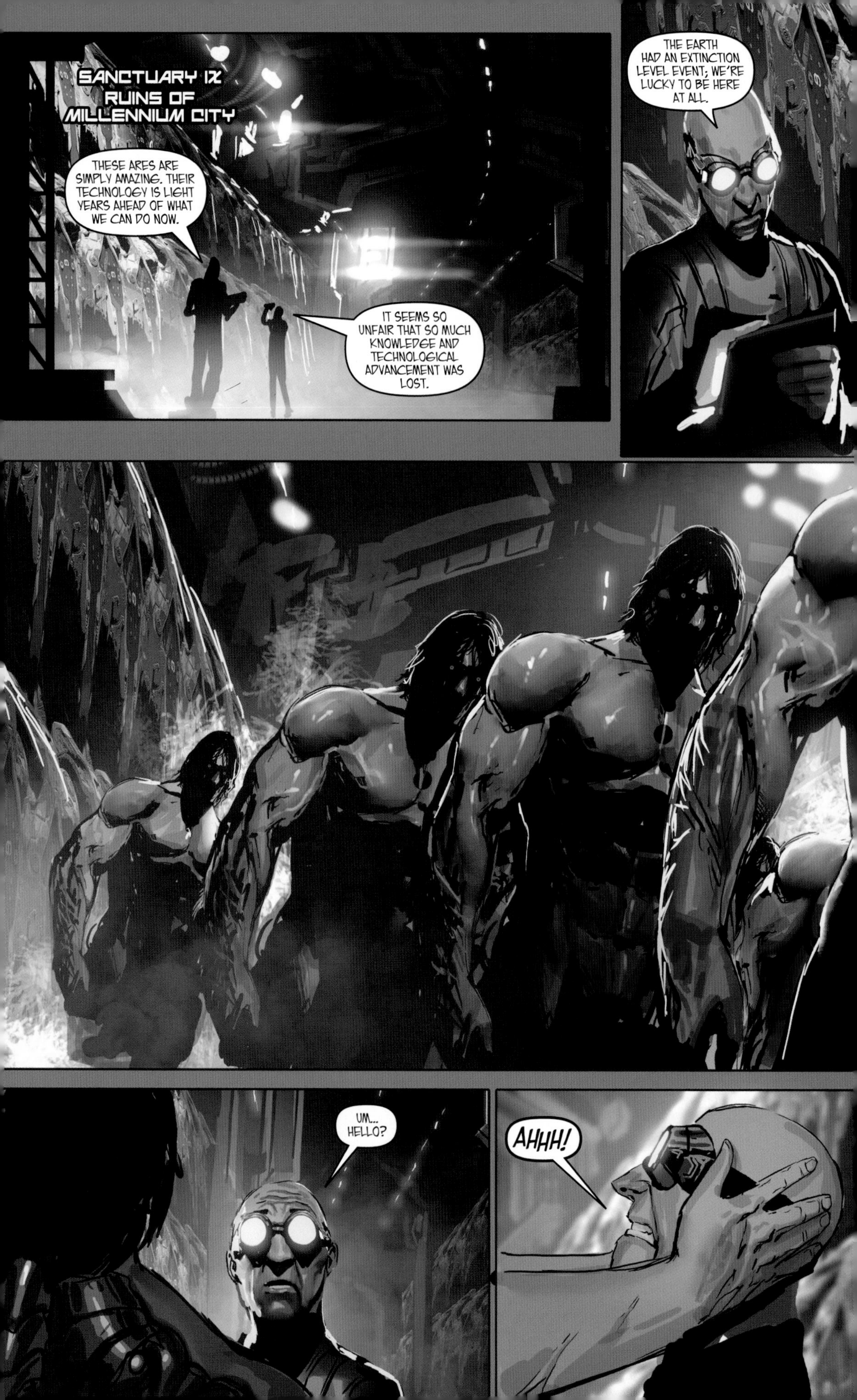
SANCTUARY IX
RUINS OF
MILLENNIUM CITY
THESE ARES ARE SIMPLY AMAZING. THEIR TECHNOLOGY IS LIGHT YEARS AHEAD OF WHAT WE CAN DO NOW.
IT SEEMS SO UNFAIR THAT SO MUCH KNOWLEDGE AND TECHNOLOGICAL ADVANCEMENT WAS LOST.
THE EARTH HAD AN EXTINCTION LEVEL EVENT; WE'RE LUCKY TO BE HERE AT ALL.
UM... HELLO?
AHHH!

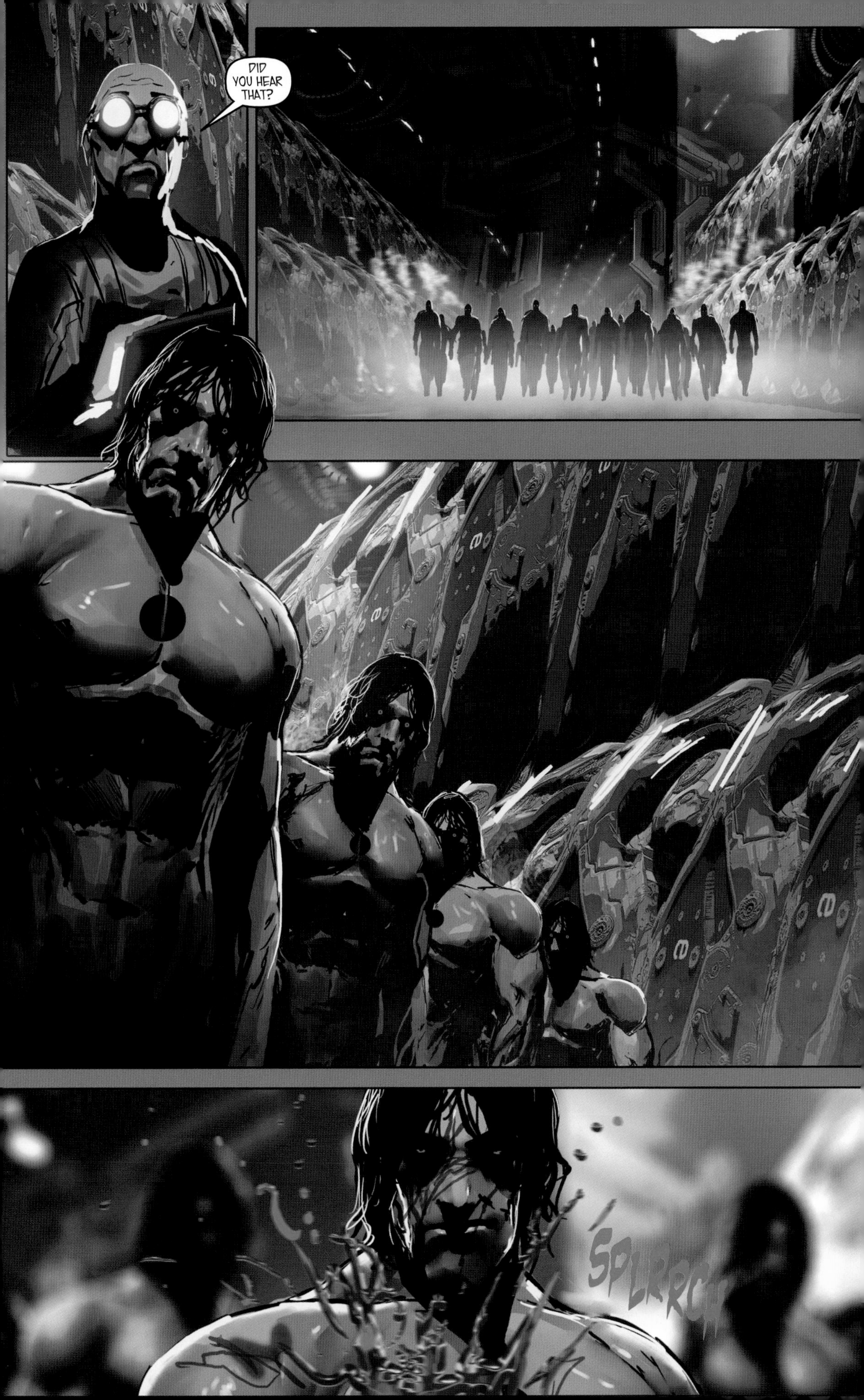
DID YOU HEAR THAT?
SPLRRCH

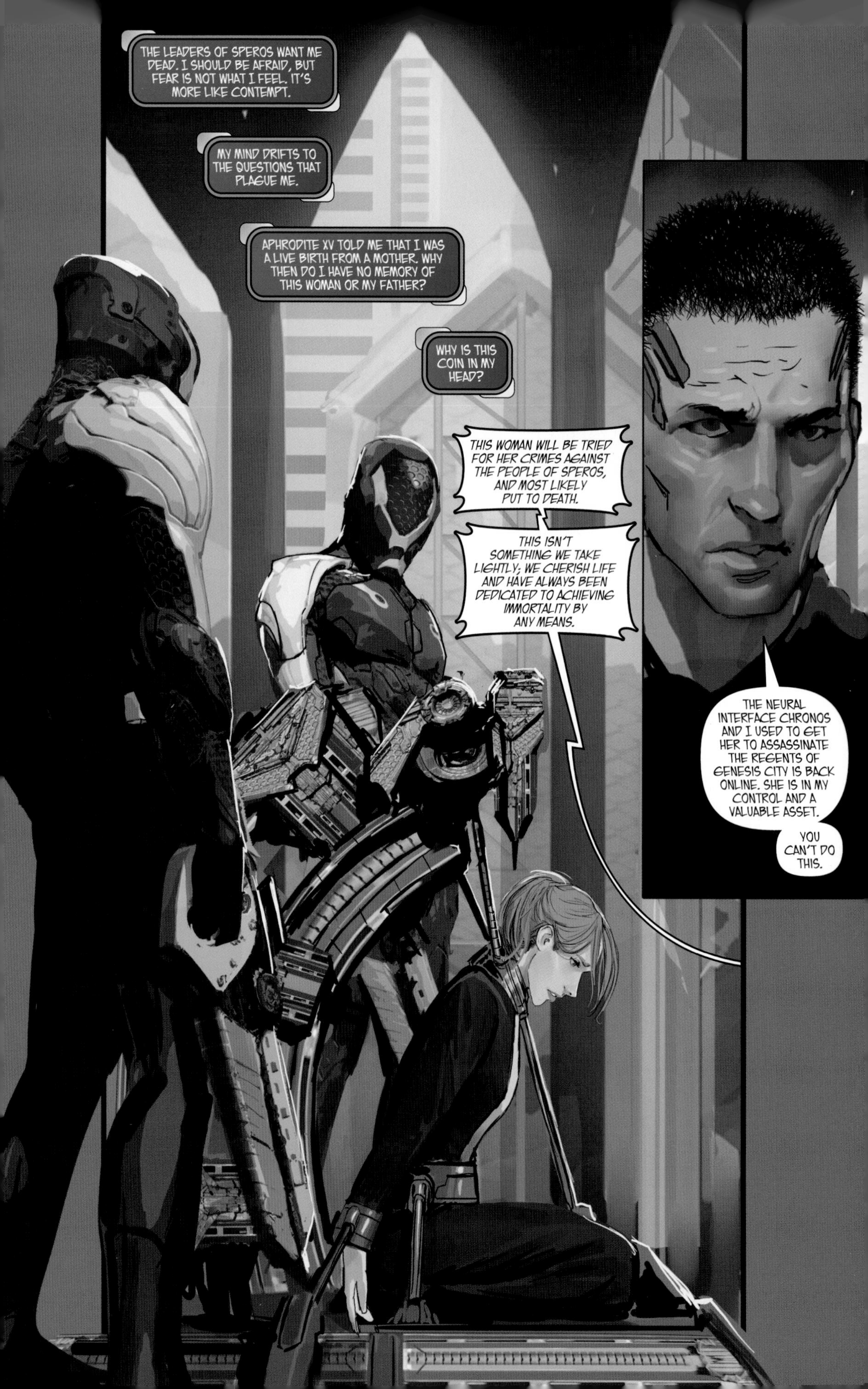
THE LEADERS OF SPEROS WANT ME DEAD. I SHOULD BE AFRAID, BUT FEAR IS NOT WHAT I FEEL. IT'S MORE LIKE CONTEMPT.
MY MIND DRIFTS TO THE QUESTIONS THAT PLAGUE ME.
APHRODITE XV TOLD ME THAT I WAS A LIVE BIRTH FROM A MOTHER. WHY THEN DO I HAVE NO MEMORY OF THIS WOMAN OR MY FATHER?
WHY IS THIS COIN IN MY HEAD?
THIS WOMAN WILL BE TRIED FOR HER CRIMES AGAINST THE PEOPLE OF SPEROS, AND MOST LIKELY PUT TO DEATH.
THIS ISN'T SOMETHING WE TAKE LIGHTLY; WE CHERISH LIFE AND HAVE ALWAYS BEEN DEDICATED TO ACHIEVING IMMORTALITY BY ANY MEANS.
THE NEURAL INTERFACE CHRONOS AND I USED TO GET HER TO ASSASSINATE THE REGENTS OF GENESIS CITY IS BACK ONLINE. SHE IS IN MY CONTROL AND A VALUABLE ASSET.
YOU CAN'T DO THIS.

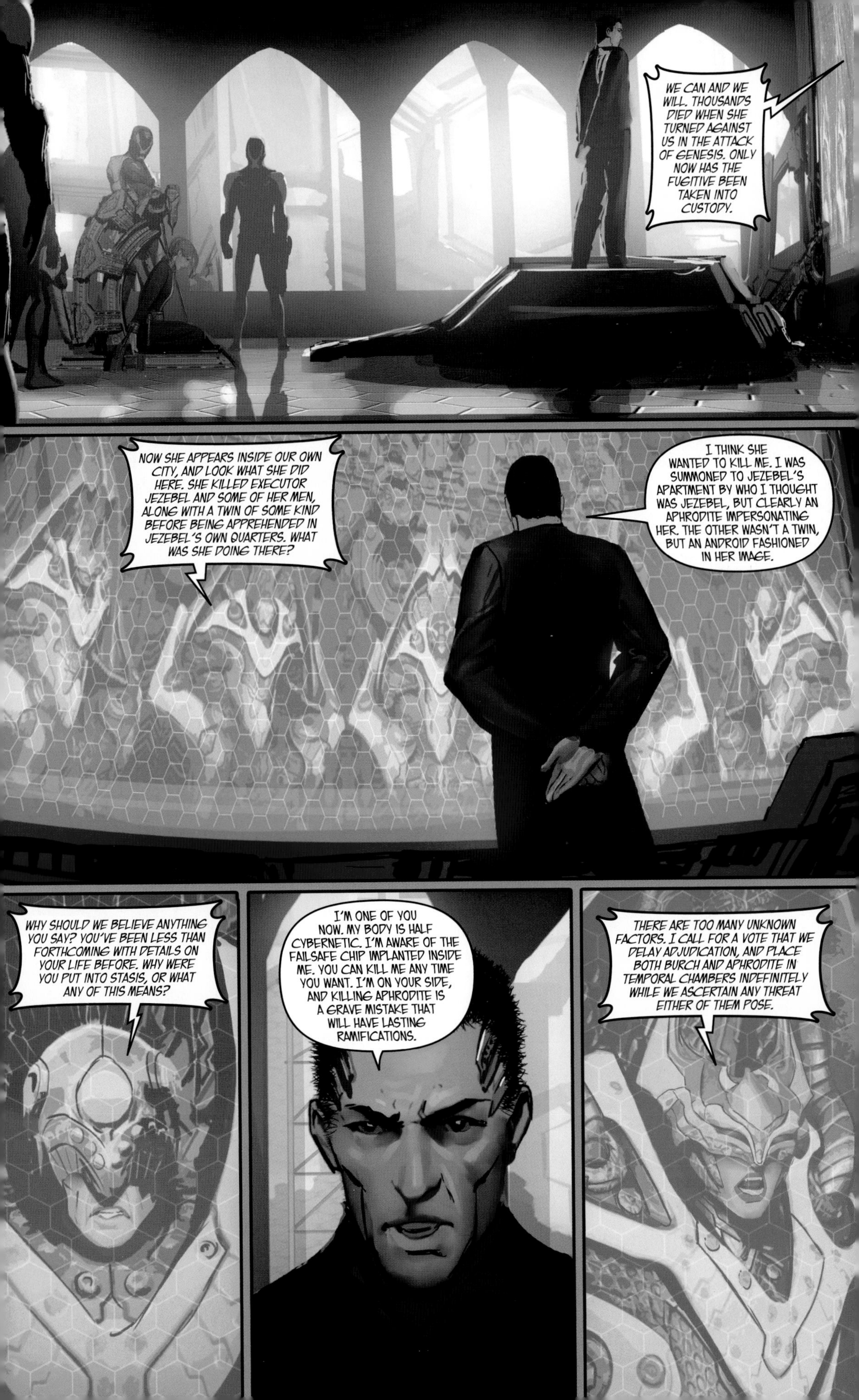
WE CAN AND WE WILL. THOUSANDS DIED WHEN SHE TURNED AGAINST US IN THE ATTACK OF GENESIS. ONLY NOW HAS THE FUGITIVE BEEN TAKEN INTO CUSTODY.
NOW SHE APPEARS INSIDE OUR OWN CITY, AND LOOK WHAT SHE DID HERE. SHE KILLED EXECUTOR JEZEBEL AND SOME OF HER MEN, ALONG WITH A TWIN OF SOME KIND BEFORE BEING APPREHENDED IN JEZEBEL'S OWN QUARTERS. WHAT WAS SHE DOING THERE?
I THINK SHE WANTED TO KILL ME. I WAS SUMMONED TO JEZEBEL'S APARTMENT BY WHO I THOUGHT WAS JEZEBEL, BUT CLEARLY AN APHRODITE IMPERSONATING HER. THE OTHER WASN'T A TWIN, BUT AN ANDROID FASHIONED IN HER IMAGE.
WHY SHOULD WE BELIEVE ANYTHING YOU SAY? YOU'VE BEEN LESS THAN FORTHCOMING WITH DETAILS ON YOUR LIFE BEFORE. WHY WERE YOU PUT INTO STASIS, OR WHAT ANY OF THIS MEANS?
I'M ONE OF YOU NOW. MY BODY IS HALF CYBERNETIC. I'M AWARE OF THE FAILSAFE CHIP IMPLANTED INSIDE ME. YOU CAN KILL ME ANY TIME YOU WANT. I'M ON YOUR SIDE, AND KILLING APHRODITE IS A GRAVE MISTAKE THAT WILL HAVE LASTING RAMIFICATIONS.
THERE ARE TOO MANY UNKNOWN FACTORS. I CALL FOR A VOTE THAT WE DELAY ADJUDICATION, AND PLACE BOTH BURCH AND APHRODITE IN TEMPORAL CHAMBERS INDEFINITELY WHILE WE ASCERTAIN ANY THREAT EITHER OF THEM POSE.

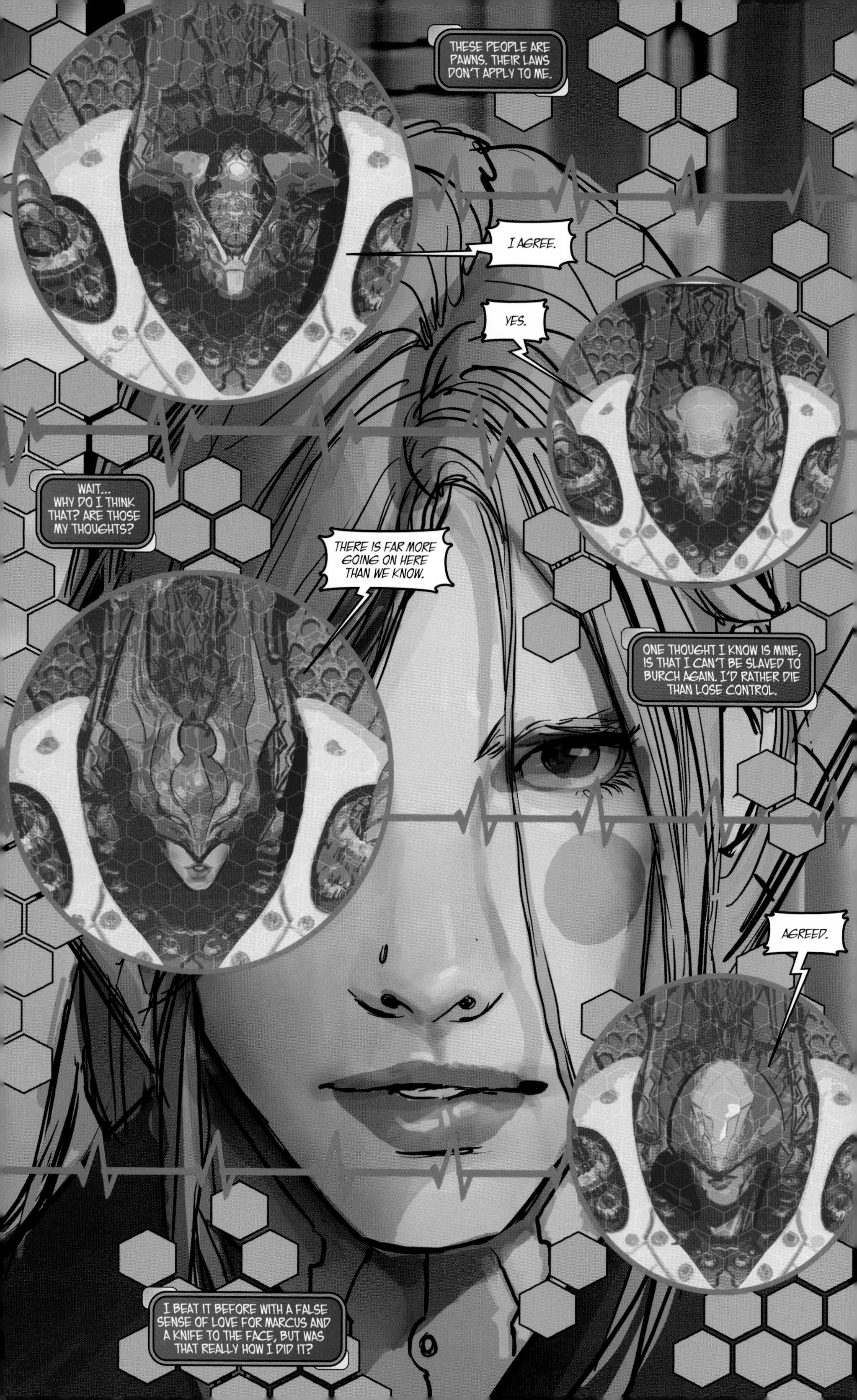
THESE PEOPLE ARE PAWNS. THEIR LAWS DON'T APPLY TO ME.
I AGREE.
YES.
WAIT... WHY DO I THINK THAT? ARE THOSE MY THOUGHTS?
THERE IS FAR MORE GOING ON HERE THAN WE KNOW.
ONE THOUGHT I KNOW IS MINE, IS THAT I CAN'T BE SLAVED TO BURCH AGAIN. I'D RATHER DIE THAN LOSE CONTROL.
AGREED.
I BEAT IT BEFORE WITH A FALSE SENSE OF LOVE FOR MARCUS AND A KNIFE TO THE FACE, BUT WAS THAT REALLY HOW I DID IT?

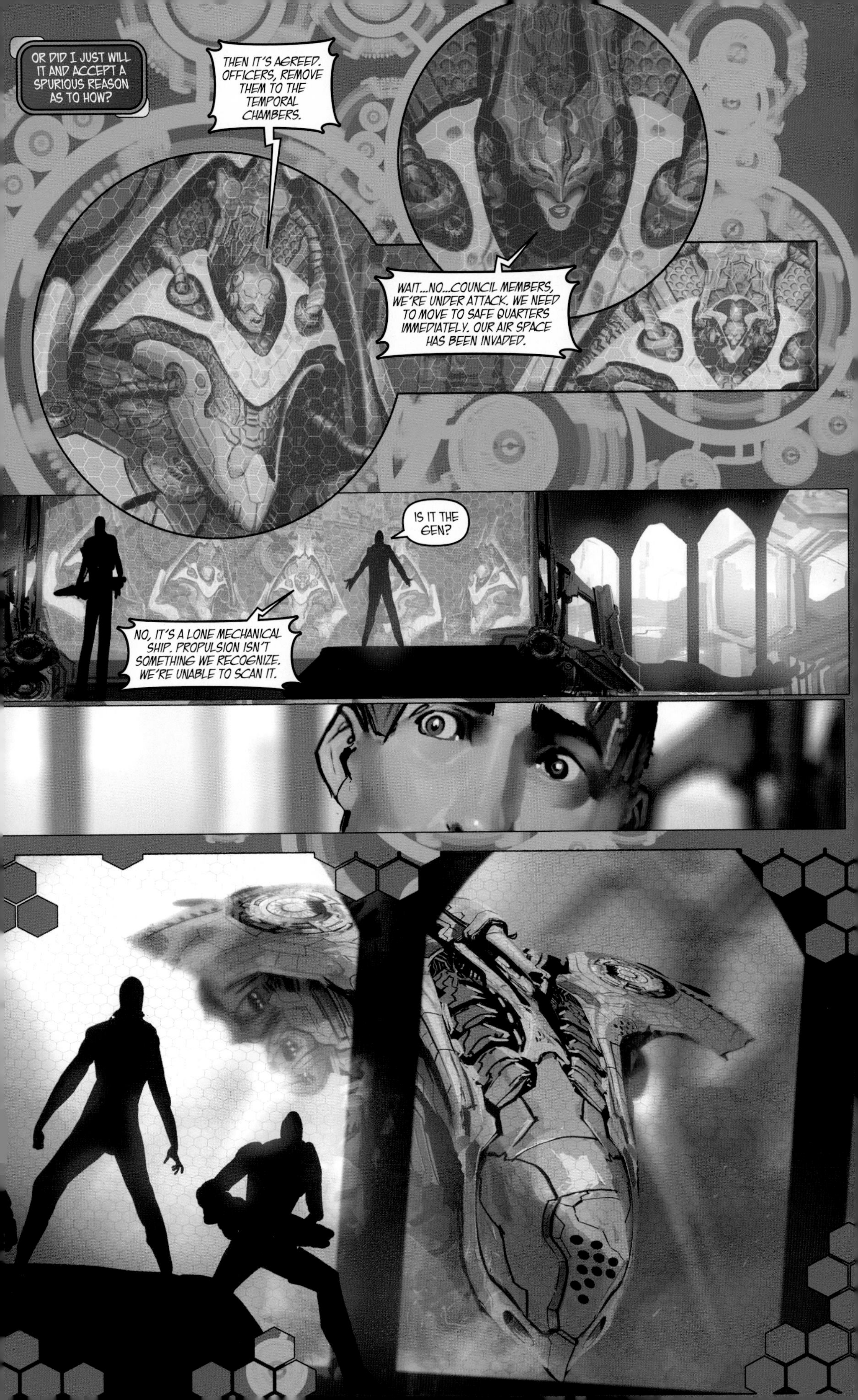
OR DID I JUST WILL IT AND ACCEPT A SPURIOUS REASON AS TO HOW?
THEN IT'S AGREED. OFFICERS, REMOVE THEM TO THE TEMPORAL CHAMBERS.
WAIT...NO...COUNCIL MEMBERS, WE'RE UNDER ATTACK. WE NEED TO MOVE TO SAFE QUARTERS IMMEDIATELY. OUR AIR SPACE HAS BEEN INVADED.
IS IT THE GEN?
NO, IT'S A LONE MECHANICAL SHIP. PROPULSION ISN'T SOMETHING WE RECOGNIZE. WE'RE UNABLE TO SCAN IT.

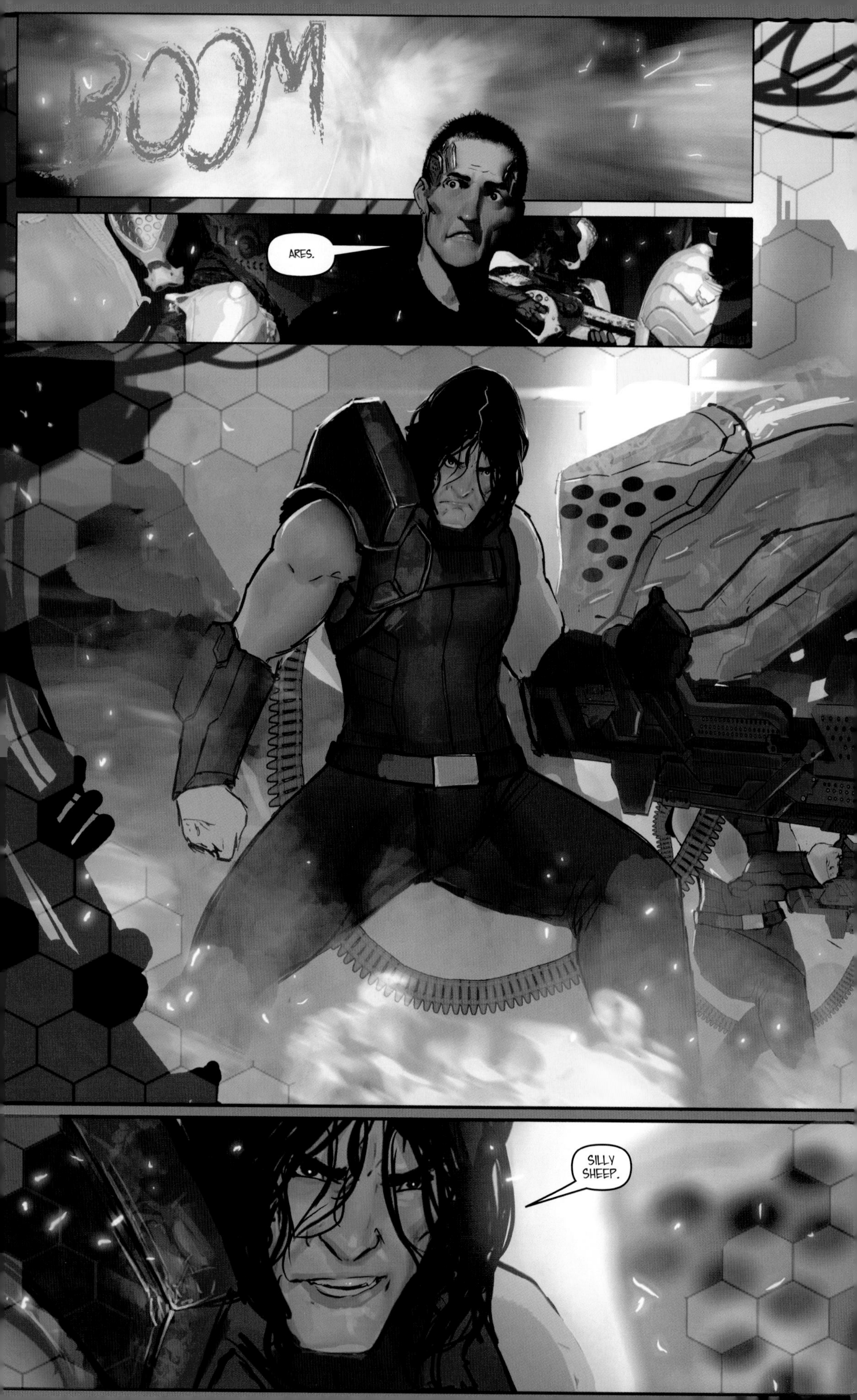
BOOM
ARES.
SILLY SHEEP.

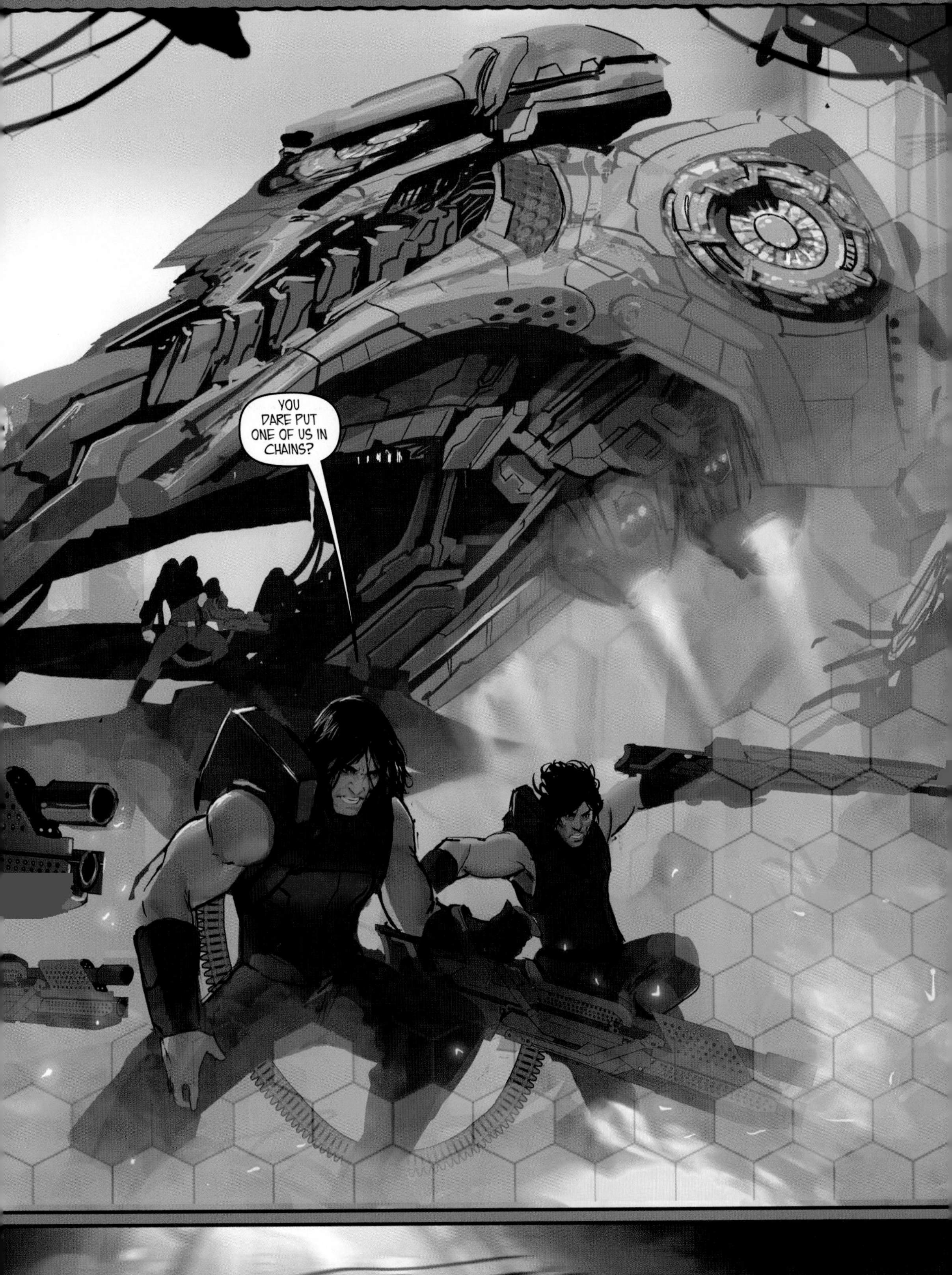
YOU DARE PUT ONE OF US IN CHAINS?
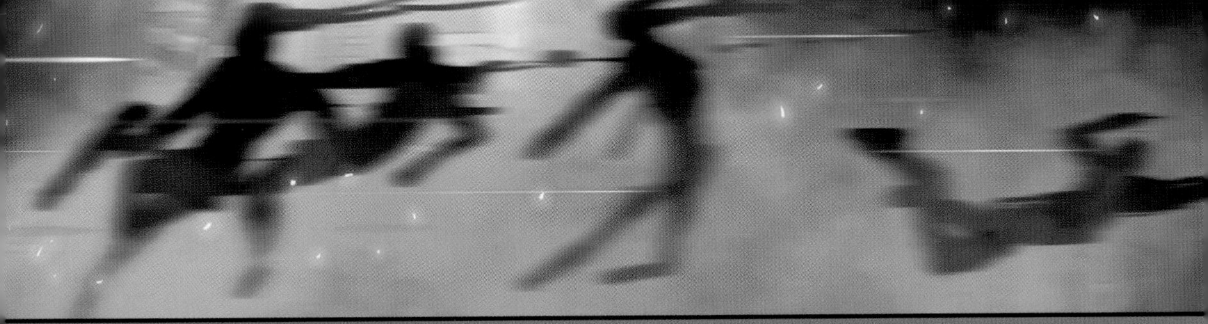

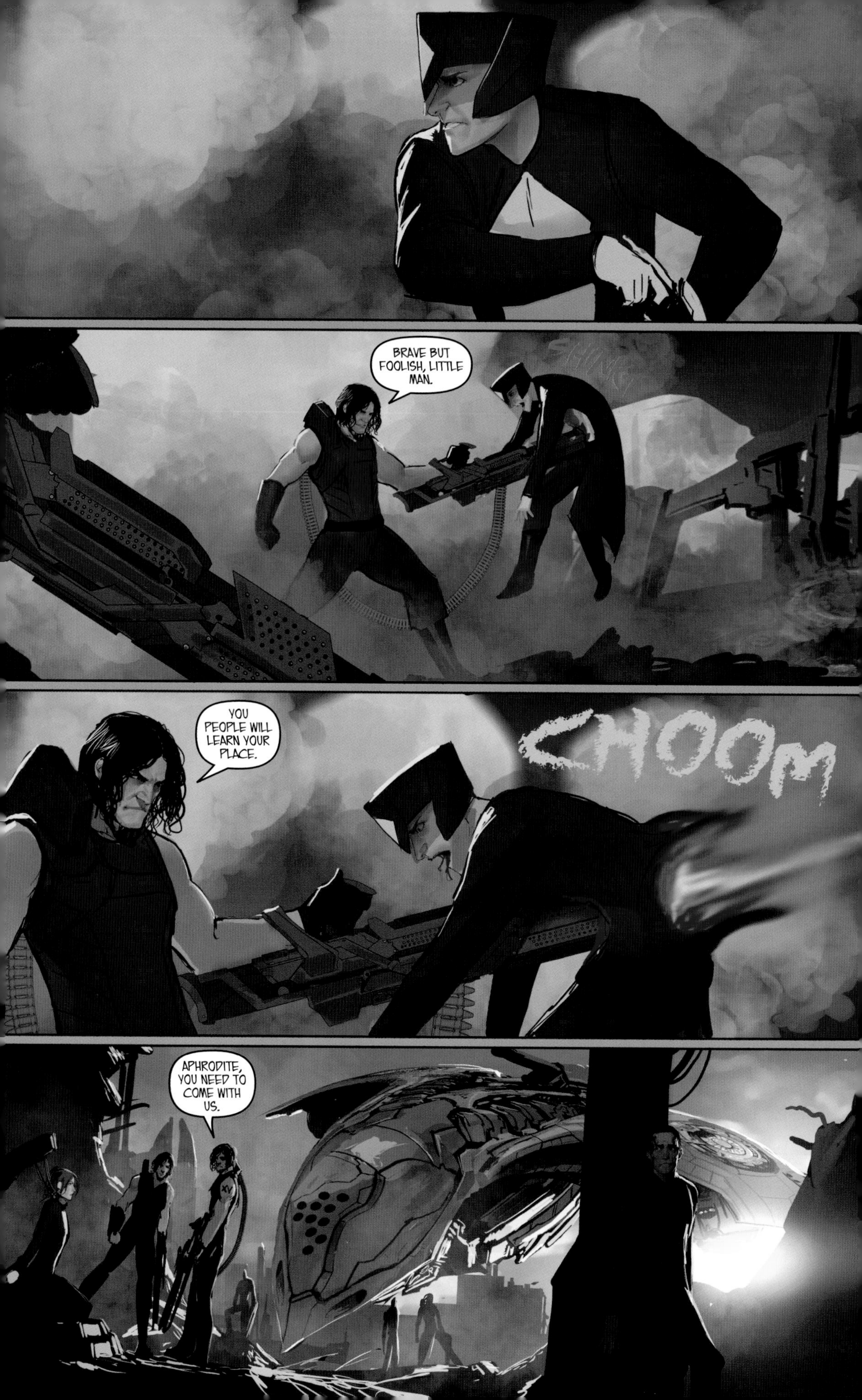
BRAVE BUT FOOLISH, LITTLE MAN.
YOU PEOPLE WILL LEARN YOUR PLACE.
CHOOM
APHRODITE, YOU NEED TO COME WITH US.

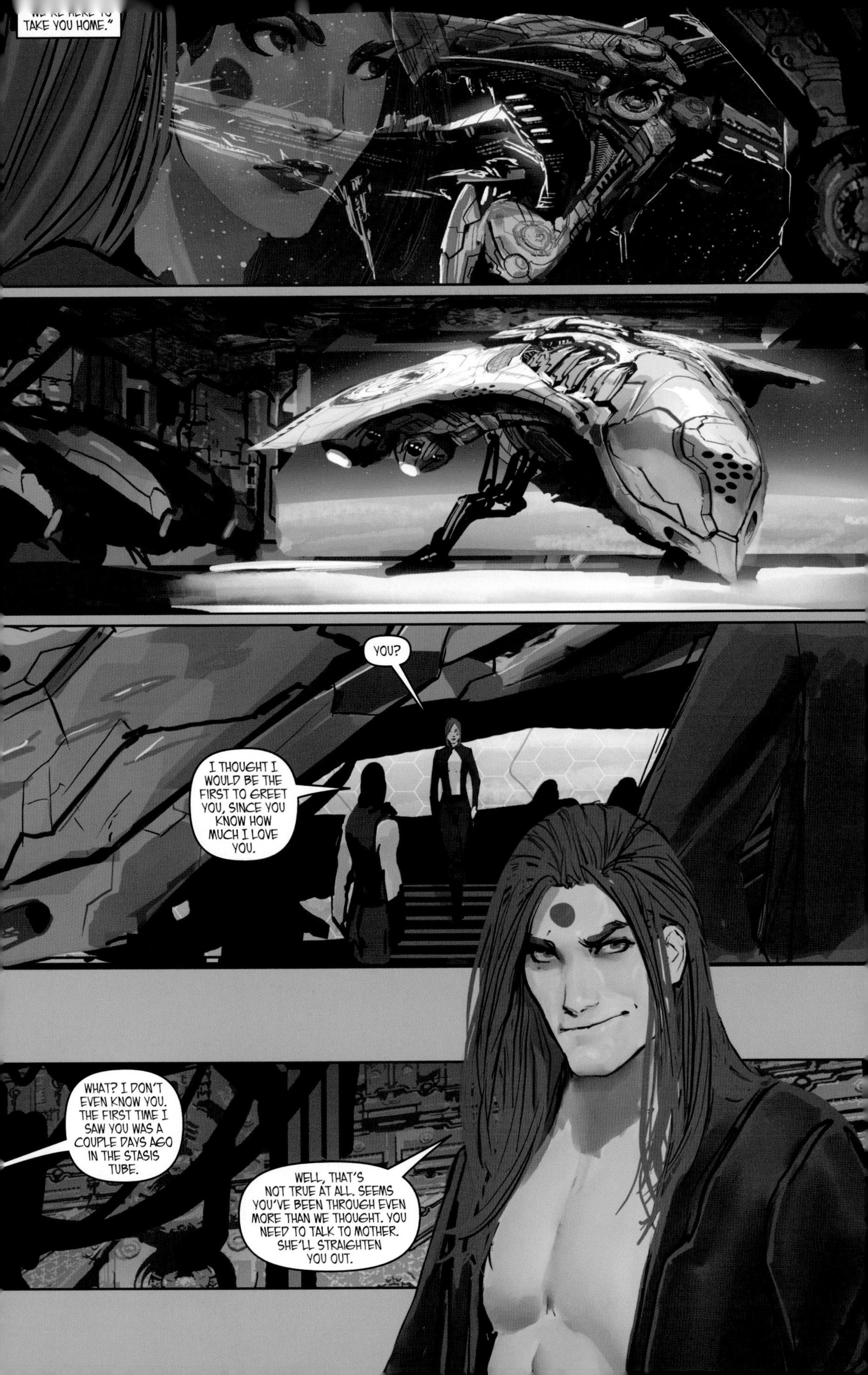
TAKE YOU HOME."
YOU?
I THOUGHT I WOULD BE THE FIRST TO GREET YOU, SINCE YOU KNOW HOW MUCH I LOVE YOU.
WHAT? I DON'T EVEN KNOW YOU. THE FIRST TIME I SAW YOU WAS A COUPLE DAYS AGO IN THE STASIS TUBE.
WELL, THAT'S NOT TRUE AT ALL. SEEMS YOU'VE BEEN THROUGH EVEN MORE THAN WE THOUGHT. YOU NEED TO TALK TO MOTHER. SHE'LL STRAIGHTEN YOU OUT.

IF THE ARES ARE AWAKE, THEY ALL MUST BE. I'M TOO LATE TO SAVE HER. TO BE WITH MY LITTLE APRIL.

THOSE WERE THE MEN FROM THE UNDERGROUND BUNKER AT THE CITY RUINS WE'VE BEEN EXCAVATING. THEY TORE THROUGH US LIKE WE WERE INSECTS TO BE SWATTED ASIDE. DO YOU KNOW WHO THEY ARE?

ARES MODELS. ARES XV TO BE PRECISE. THE BRUTE FORCE OF THE NINES. FOOTSOLDIERS.

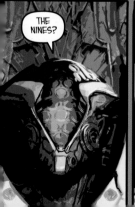

THE NINES?

YES. NINE IXs SET TO RULE THE FUTURE BY A CRAZY WOMAN.

WHAT ARE YOU BABBLING ABOUT?

A WOMAN, SEVEN HUNDRED YEARS AGO, DESIGNED A PLAN TO DESTROY THE WORLD.

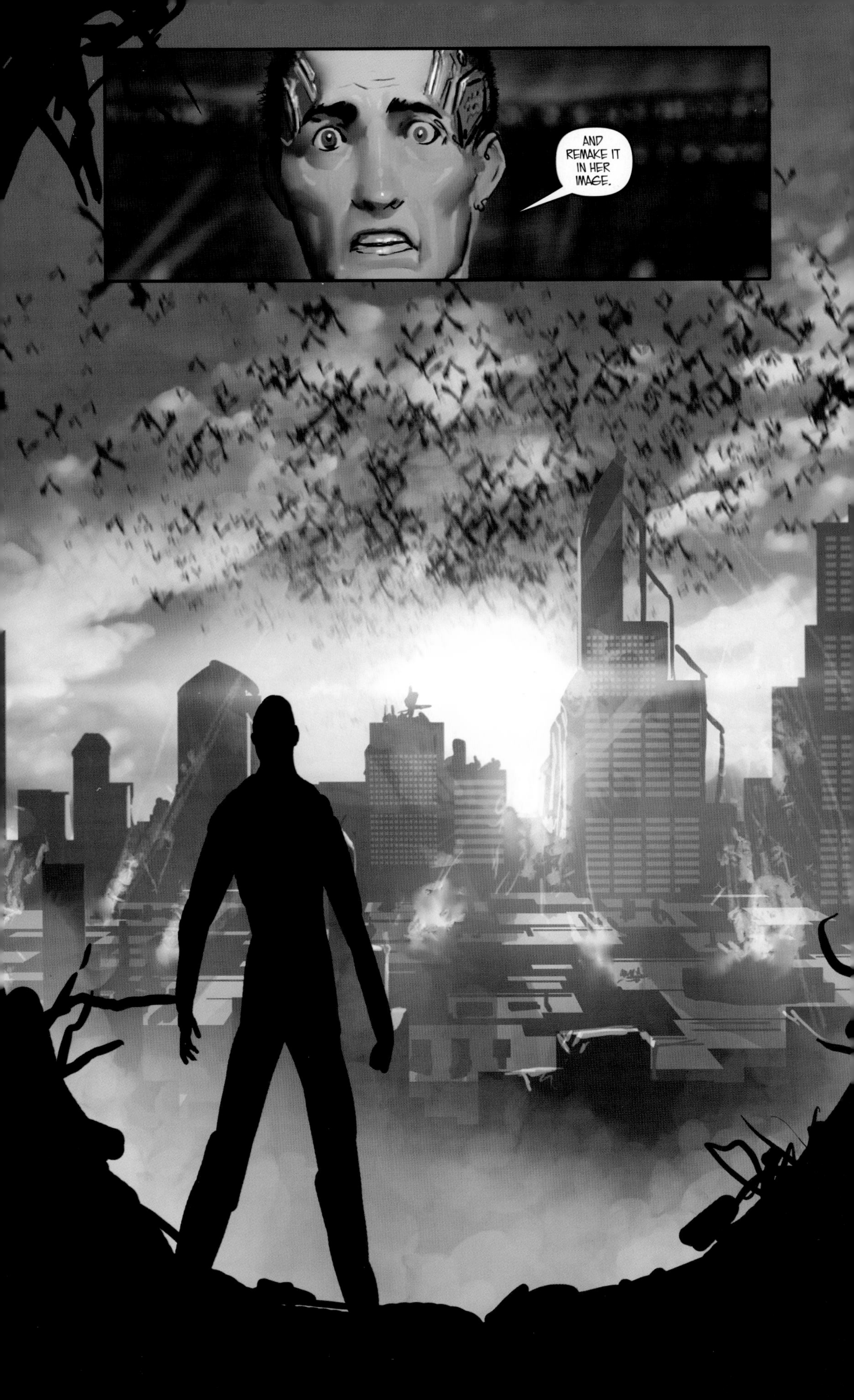
AND REMAKE IT IN HER IMAGE.

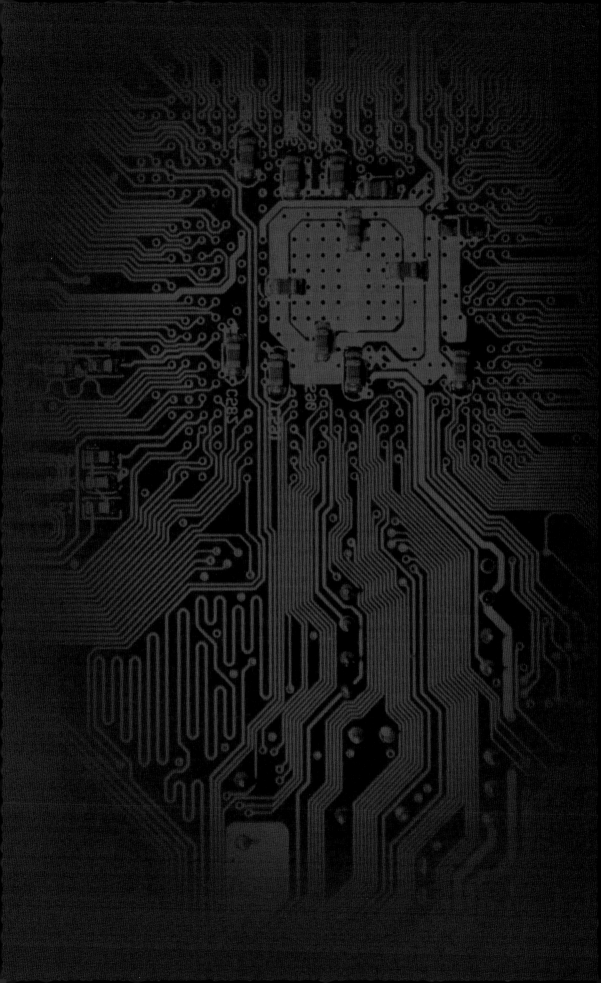

CHAPTER SIX

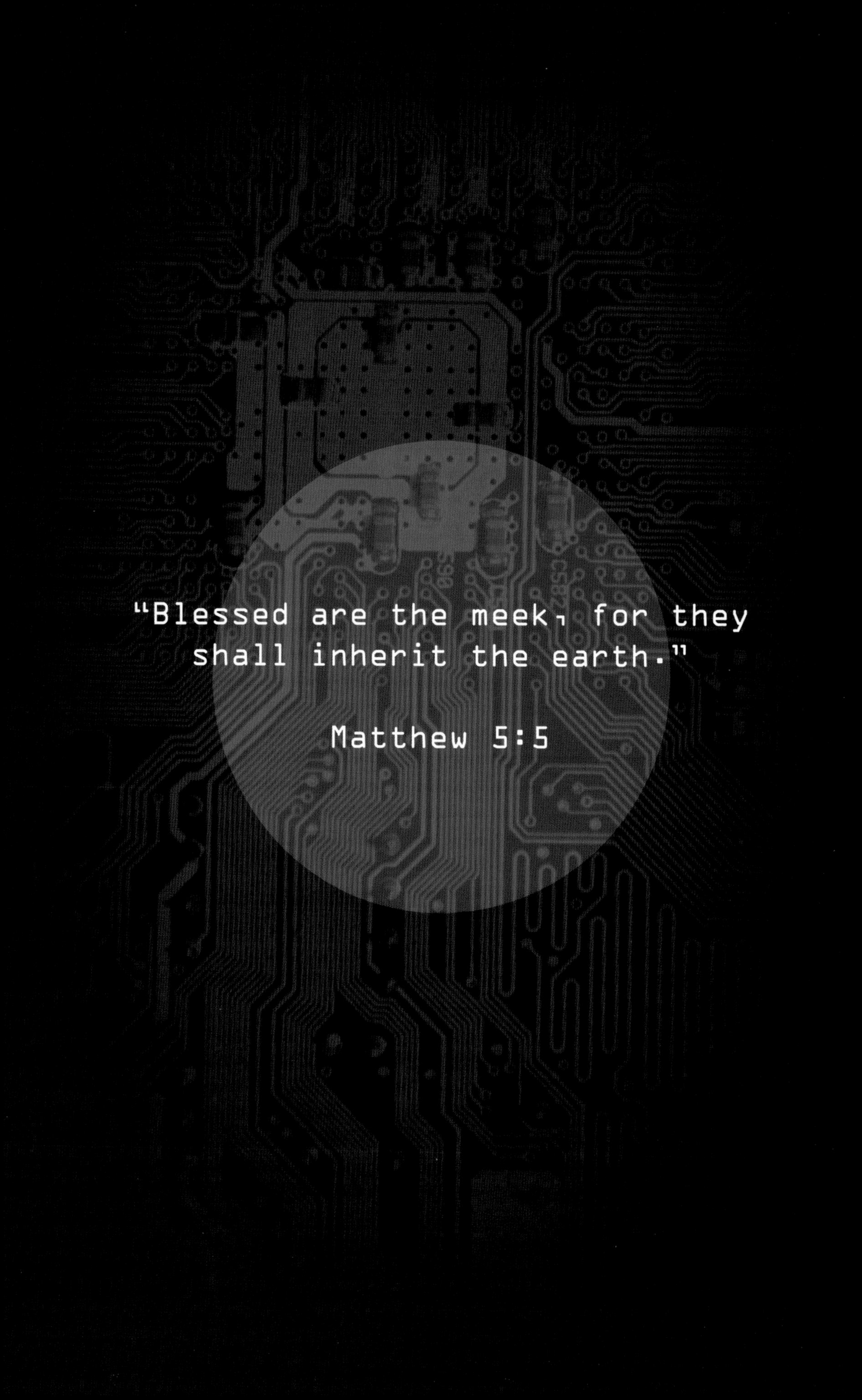

"Blessed are the meek, for they shall inherit the earth."

Matthew 5:5

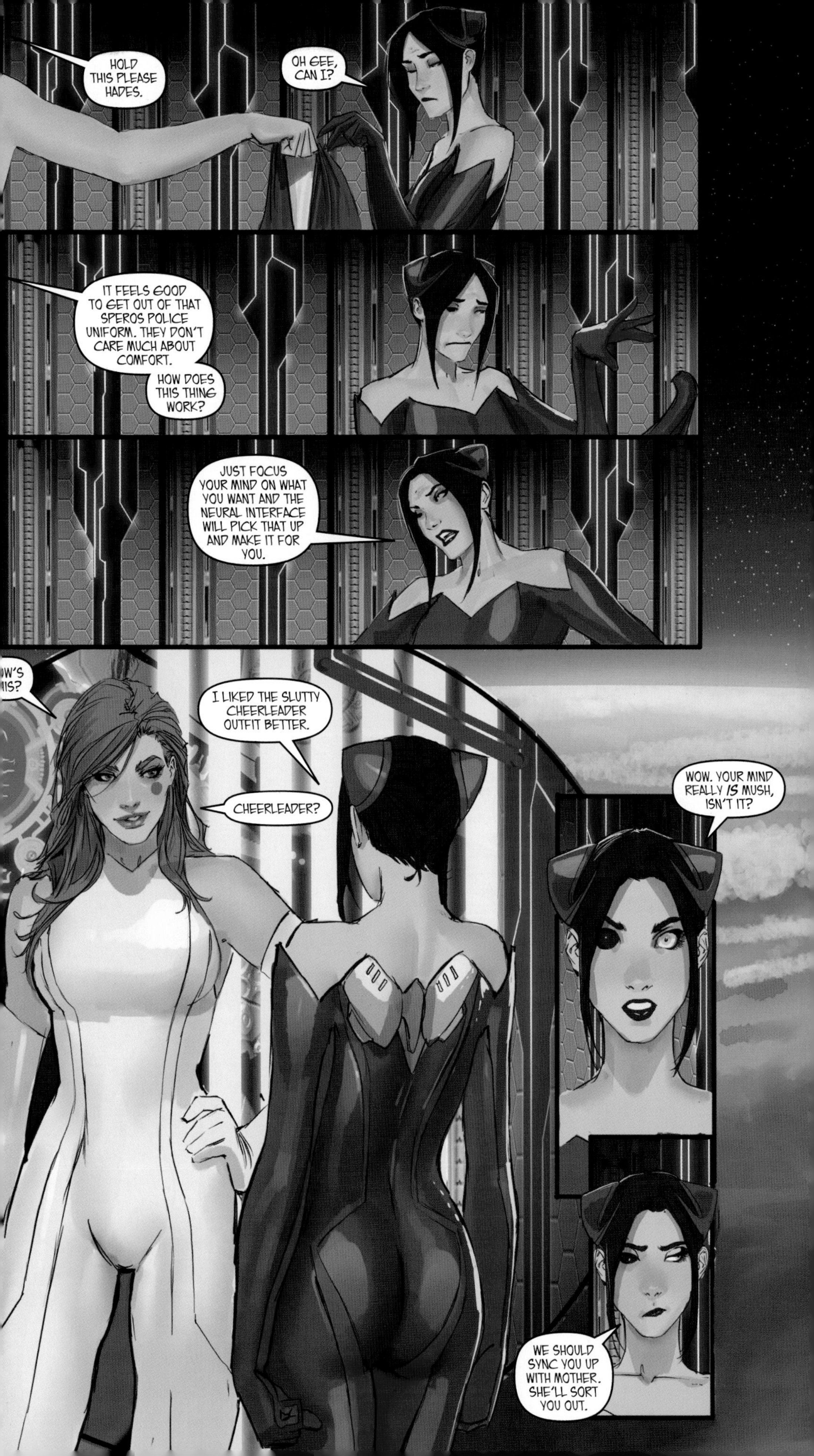
HOLD THIS PLEASE HADES.
OH GEE, CAN I?
IT FEELS GOOD TO GET OUT OF THAT SPEROS POLICE UNIFORM. THEY DON'T CARE MUCH ABOUT COMFORT.
HOW DOES THIS THING WORK?
JUST FOCUS YOUR MIND ON WHAT YOU WANT AND THE NEURAL INTERFACE WILL PICK THAT UP AND MAKE IT FOR YOU.
OW'S HIS?
I LIKED THE SLUTTY CHEERLEADER OUTFIT BETTER.
CHEERLEADER?
WOW. YOUR MIND REALLY *IS* MUSH, ISN'T IT?
WE SHOULD SYNC YOU UP WITH MOTHER. SHE'LL SORT YOU OUT.

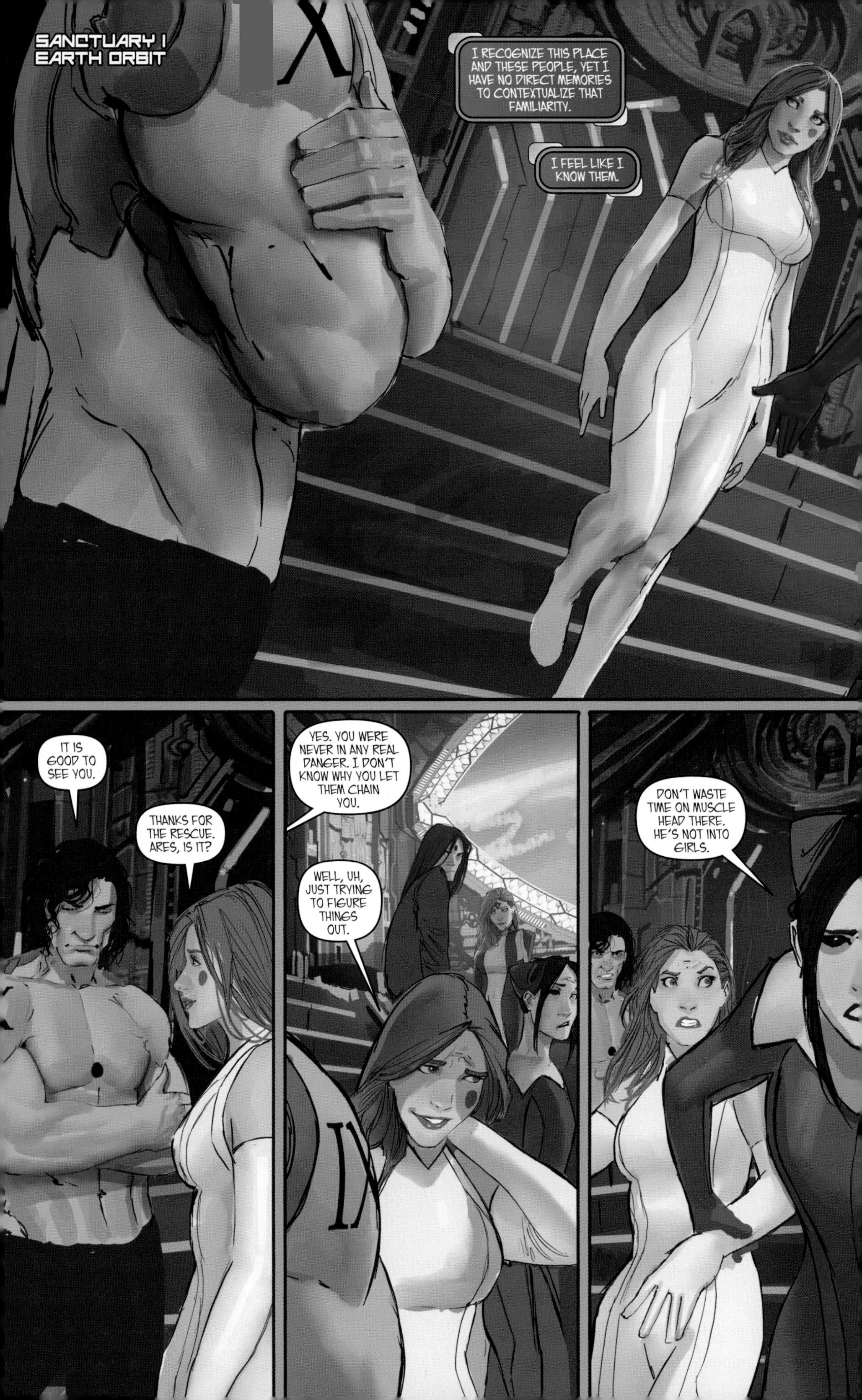
SANCTUARY I
EARTH ORBIT
I RECOGNIZE THIS PLACE AND THESE PEOPLE, YET I HAVE NO DIRECT MEMORIES TO CONTEXTUALIZE THAT FAMILIARITY.
I FEEL LIKE I KNOW THEM.
IT IS GOOD TO SEE YOU.
THANKS FOR THE RESCUE. ARES, IS IT?
YES. YOU WERE NEVER IN ANY REAL DANGER. I DON'T KNOW WHY YOU LET THEM CHAIN YOU.
WELL, UH, JUST TRYING TO FIGURE THINGS OUT.
DON'T WASTE TIME ON MUSCLE HEAD THERE. HE'S NOT INTO GIRLS.

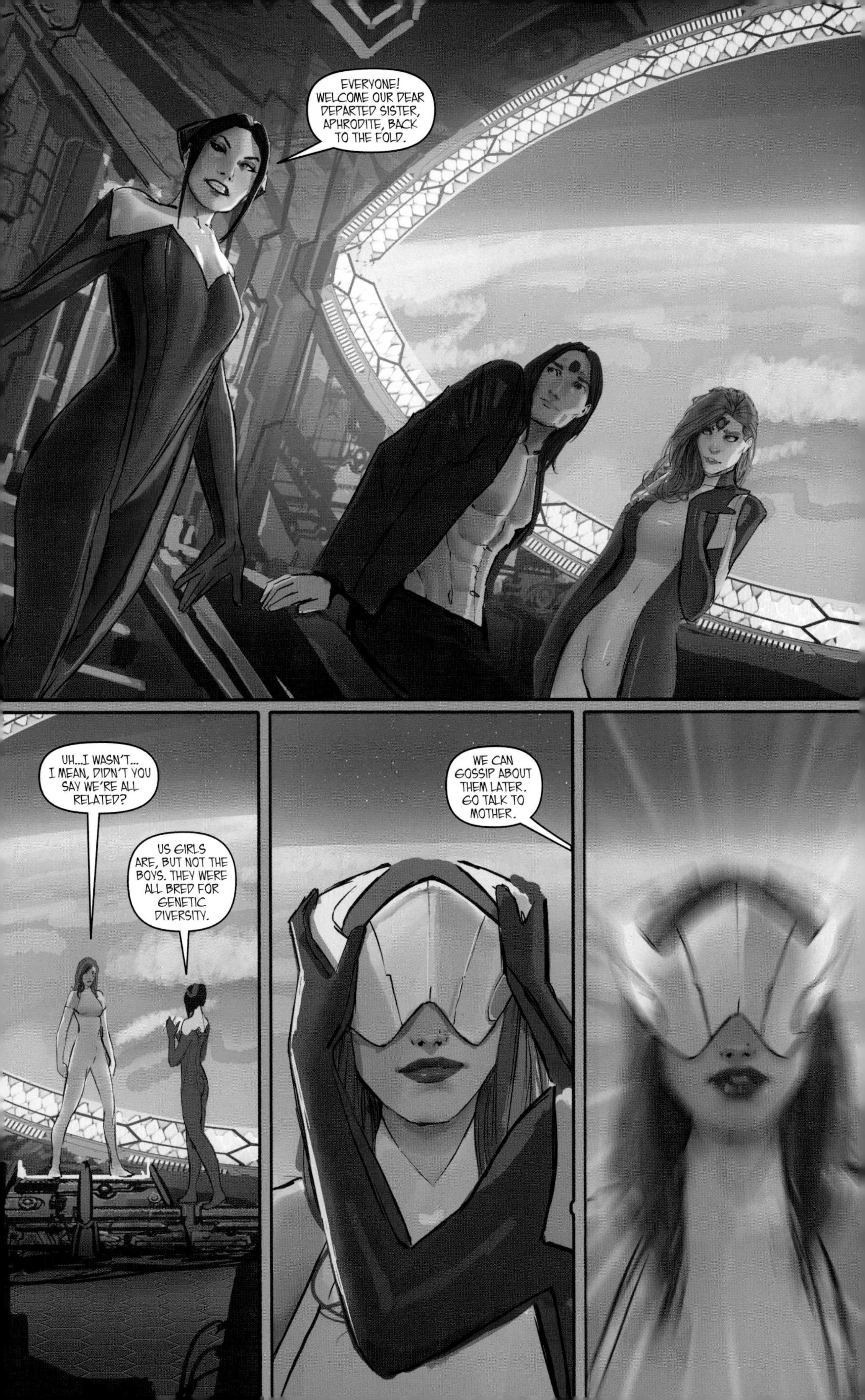
EVERYONE! WELCOME OUR DEAR DEPARTED SISTER, APHRODITE, BACK TO THE FOLD.
UH...I WASN'T... I MEAN, DIDN'T YOU SAY WE'RE ALL RELATED?
US GIRLS ARE, BUT NOT THE BOYS. THEY WERE ALL BRED FOR GENETIC DIVERSITY.
WE CAN GOSSIP ABOUT THEM LATER. GO TALK TO MOTHER.

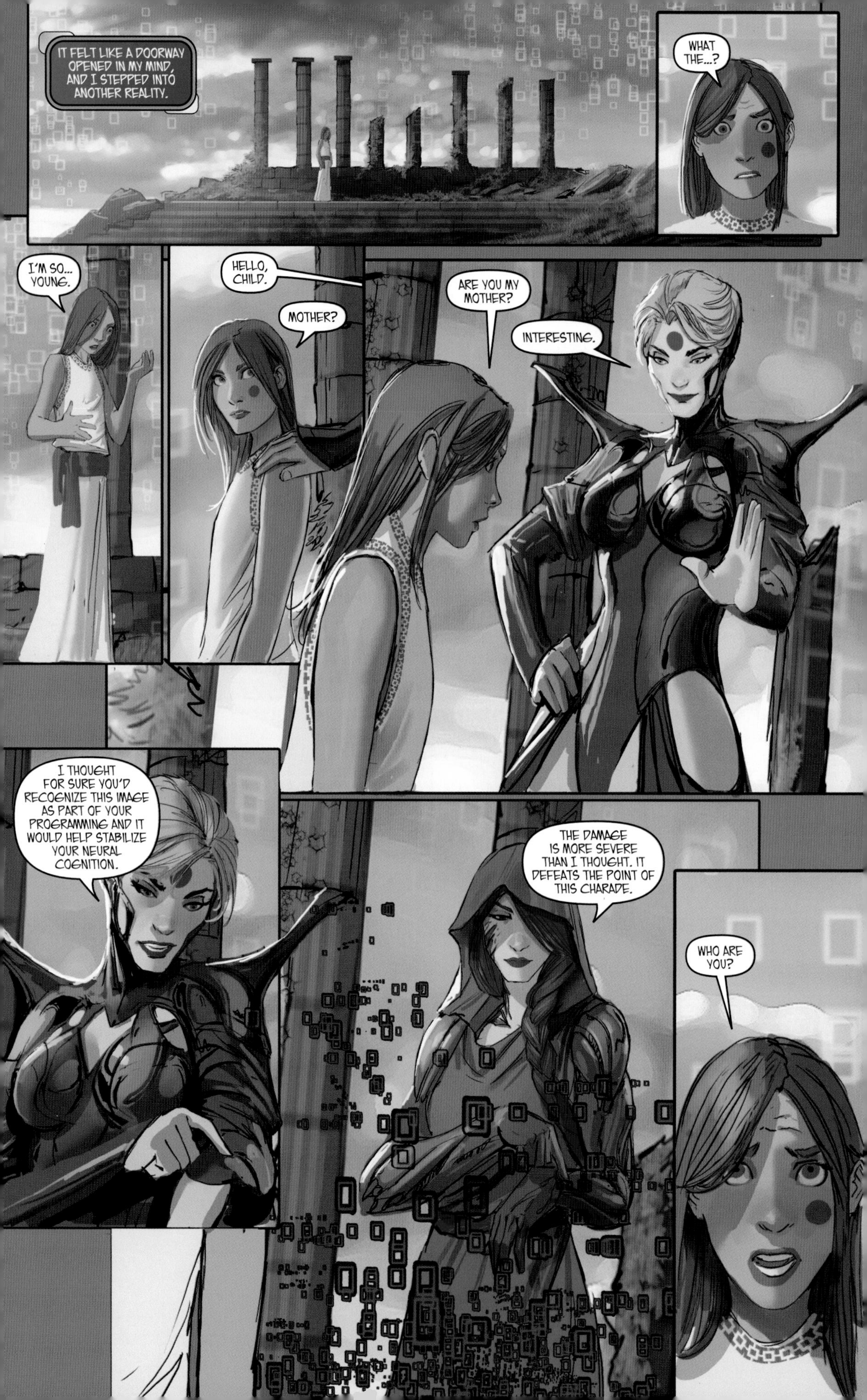
IT FELT LIKE A DOORWAY OPENED IN MY MIND, AND I STEPPED INTO ANOTHER REALITY.
WHAT THE...?
I'M SO... YOUNG.
HELLO, CHILD.
MOTHER?
ARE YOU MY MOTHER?
INTERESTING.
I THOUGHT FOR SURE YOU'D RECOGNIZE THIS IMAGE AS PART OF YOUR PROGRAMMING AND IT WOULD HELP STABILIZE YOUR NEURAL COGNITION.
THE DAMAGE IS MORE SEVERE THAN I THOUGHT. IT DEFEATS THE POINT OF THIS CHARADE.
WHO ARE YOU?

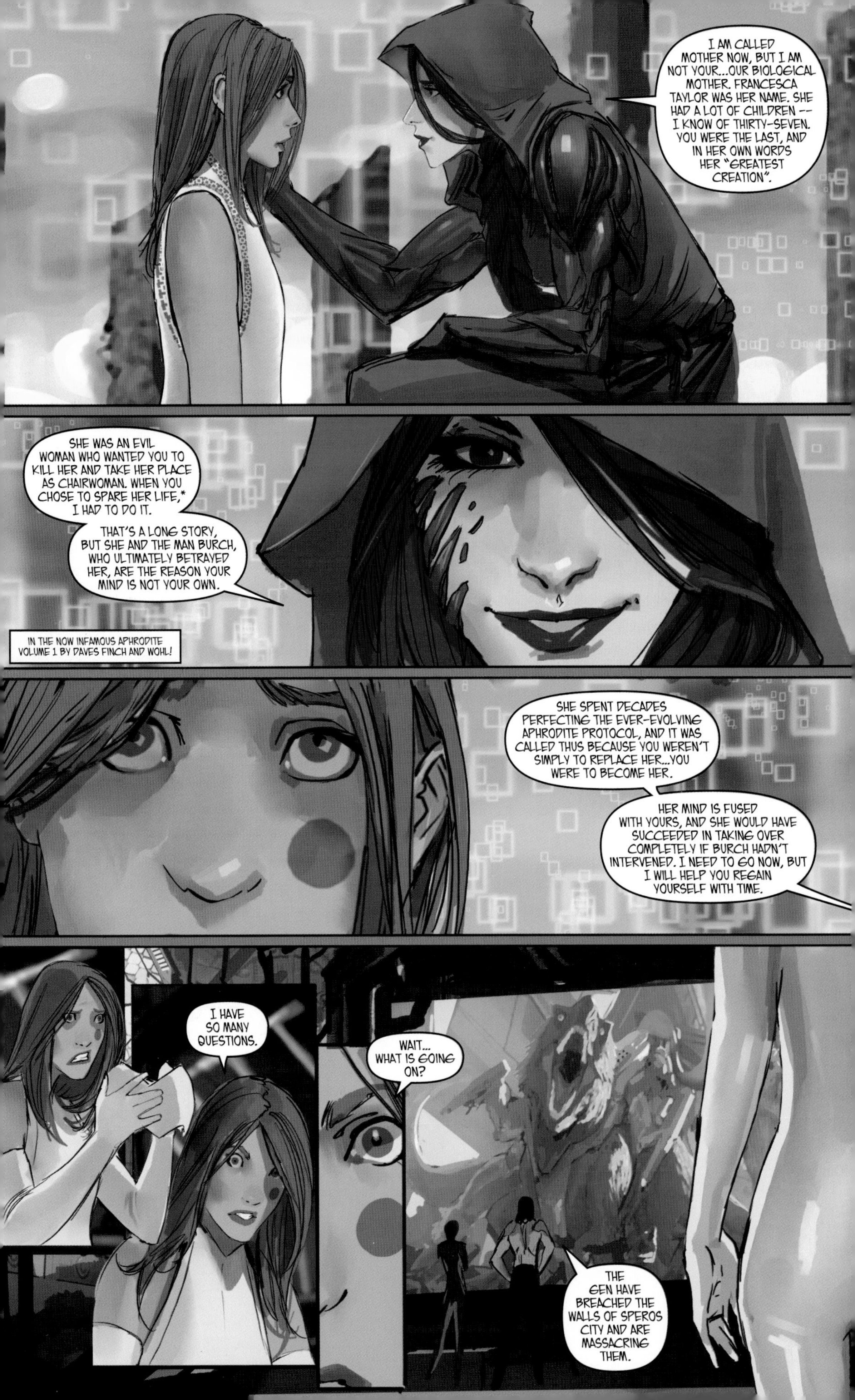
I AM CALLED MOTHER NOW, BUT I AM NOT YOUR...OUR BIOLOGICAL MOTHER. FRANCESCA TAYLOR WAS HER NAME. SHE HAD A LOT OF CHILDREN -- I KNOW OF THIRTY-SEVEN. YOU WERE THE LAST, AND IN HER OWN WORDS HER "GREATEST CREATION".
SHE WAS AN EVIL WOMAN WHO WANTED YOU TO KILL HER AND TAKE HER PLACE AS CHAIRWOMAN. WHEN YOU CHOSE TO SPARE HER LIFE,* I HAD TO DO IT.
THAT'S A LONG STORY, BUT SHE AND THE MAN BURCH, WHO ULTIMATELY BETRAYED HER, ARE THE REASON YOUR MIND IS NOT YOUR OWN.
IN THE NOW INFAMOUS APHRODITE VOLUME 1 BY DAVES FINCH AND WOHL!
SHE SPENT DECADES PERFECTING THE EVER-EVOLVING APHRODITE PROTOCOL, AND IT WAS CALLED THUS BECAUSE YOU WEREN'T SIMPLY TO REPLACE HER...YOU WERE TO BECOME HER.
HER MIND IS FUSED WITH YOURS, AND SHE WOULD HAVE SUCCEEDED IN TAKING OVER COMPLETELY IF BURCH HADN'T INTERVENED. I NEED TO GO NOW, BUT I WILL HELP YOU REGAIN YOURSELF WITH TIME.
I HAVE SO MANY QUESTIONS.
WAIT... WHAT IS GOING ON?
THE GEN HAVE BREACHED THE WALLS OF SPEROS CITY AND ARE MASSACRING THEM.

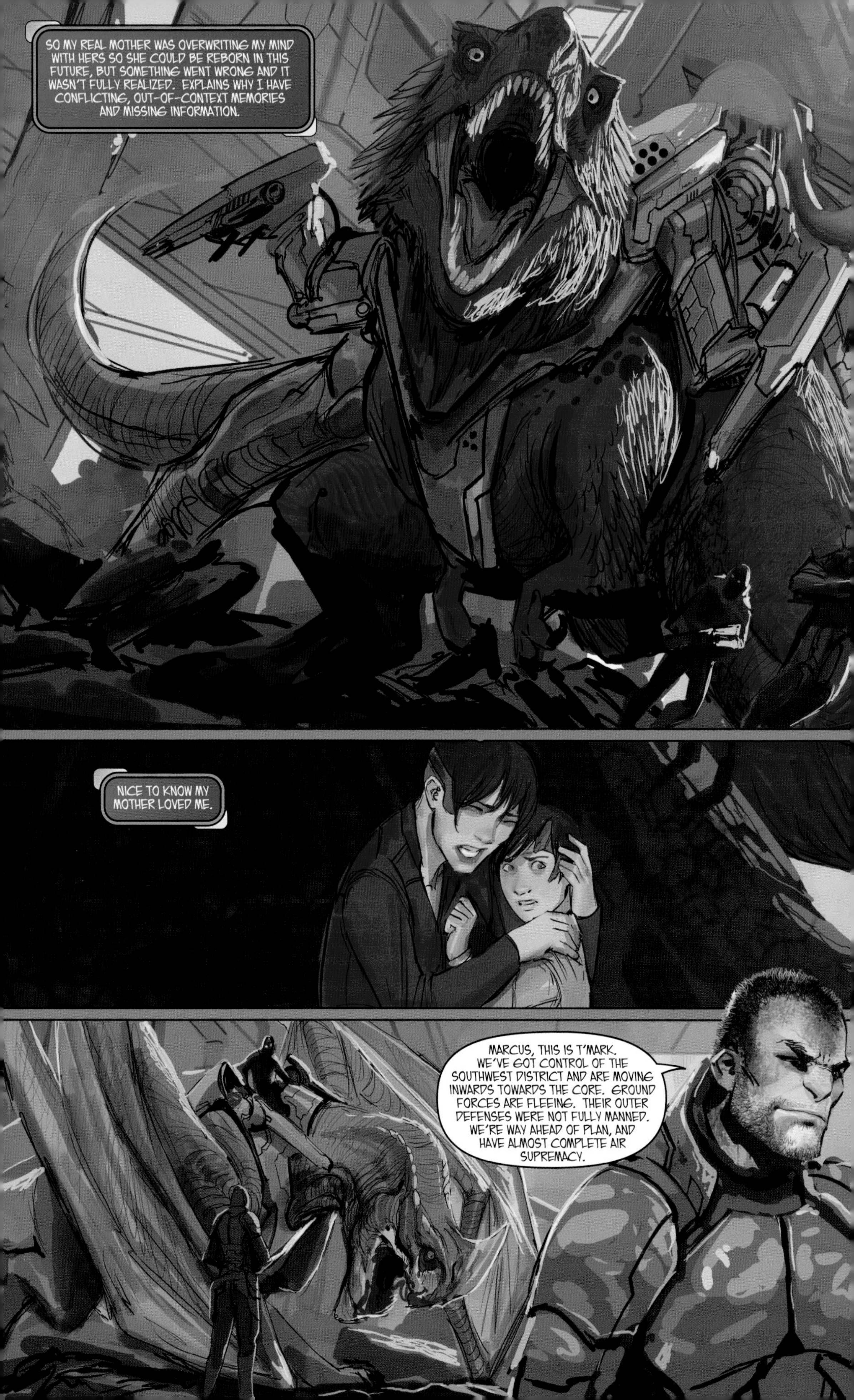
SO MY REAL MOTHER WAS OVERWRITING MY MIND WITH HERS SO SHE COULD BE REBORN IN THIS FUTURE, BUT SOMETHING WENT WRONG AND IT WASN'T FULLY REALIZED. EXPLAINS WHY I HAVE CONFLICTING, OUT-OF-CONTEXT MEMORIES AND MISSING INFORMATION.
NICE TO KNOW MY MOTHER LOVED ME.
MARCUS, THIS IS T'MARK. WE'VE GOT CONTROL OF THE SOUTHWEST DISTRICT AND ARE MOVING INWARDS TOWARDS THE CORE. GROUND FORCES ARE FLEEING. THEIR OUTER DEFENSES WERE NOT FULLY MANNED. WE'RE WAY AHEAD OF PLAN, AND HAVE ALMOST COMPLETE AIR SUPREMACY.

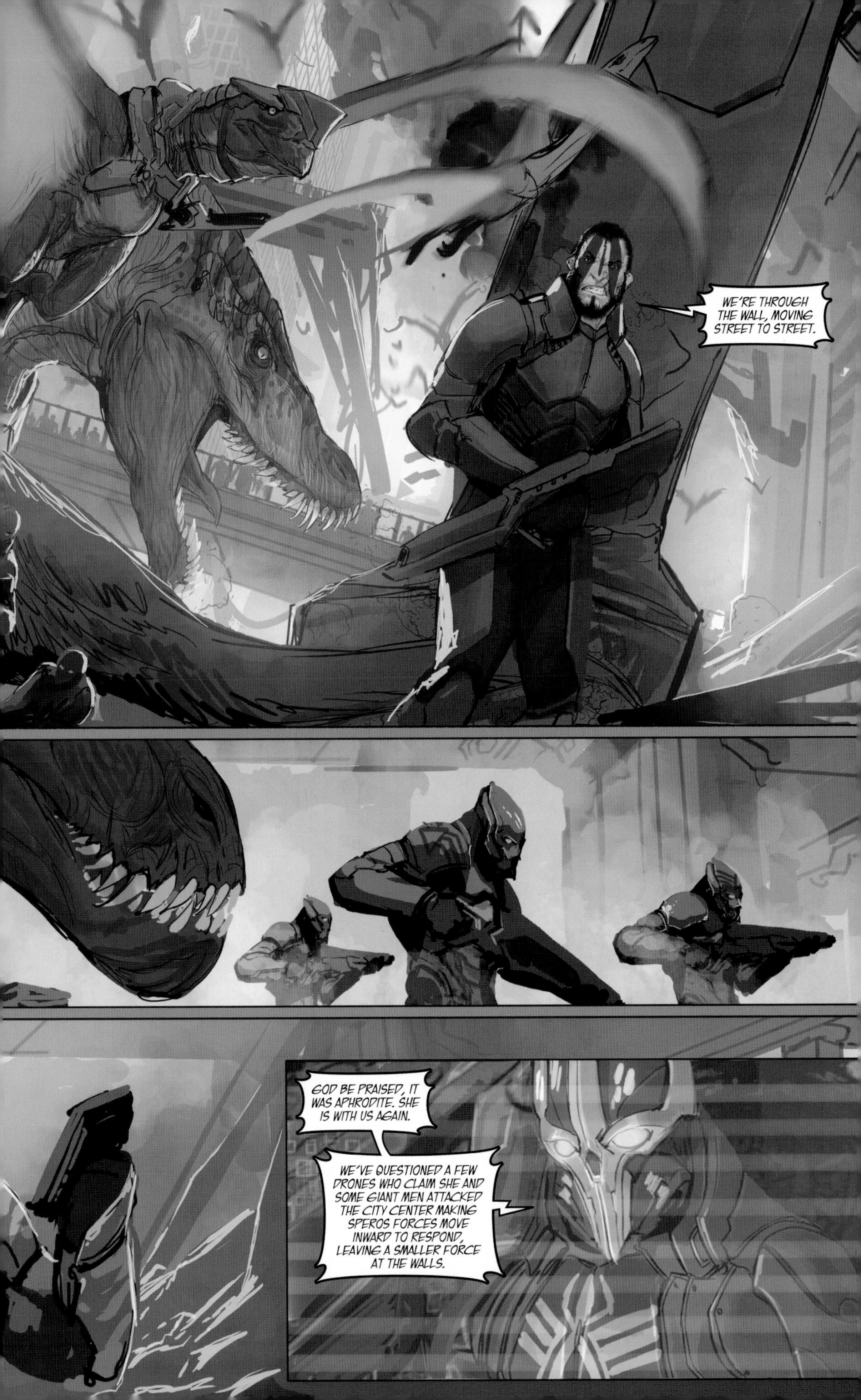
WE'RE THROUGH THE WALL, MOVING STREET TO STREET.
GOD BE PRAISED, IT WAS APHRODITE. SHE IS WITH US AGAIN.
WE'VE QUESTIONED A FEW DRONES WHO CLAIM SHE AND SOME GIANT MEN ATTACKED THE CITY CENTER MAKING SPEROS FORCES MOVE INWARD TO RESPOND, LEAVING A SMALLER FORCE AT THE WALLS.

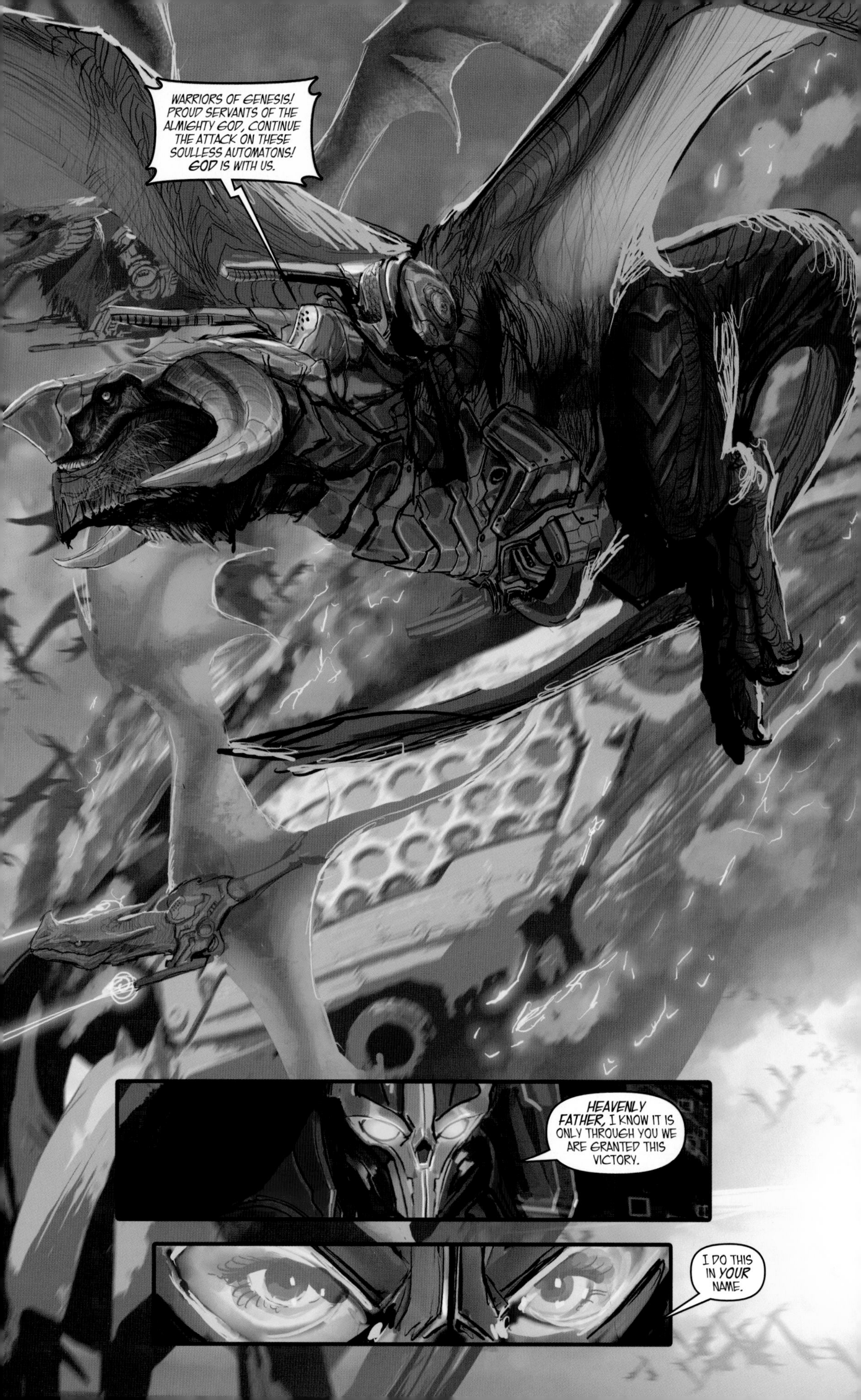
WARRIORS OF GENESIS! PROUD SERVANTS OF THE ALMIGHTY GOD, CONTINUE THE ATTACK ON THESE SOULLESS AUTOMATONS! GOD IS WITH US.
HEAVENLY FATHER, I KNOW IT IS ONLY THROUGH YOU WE ARE GRANTED THIS VICTORY.
I DO THIS IN YOUR NAME.

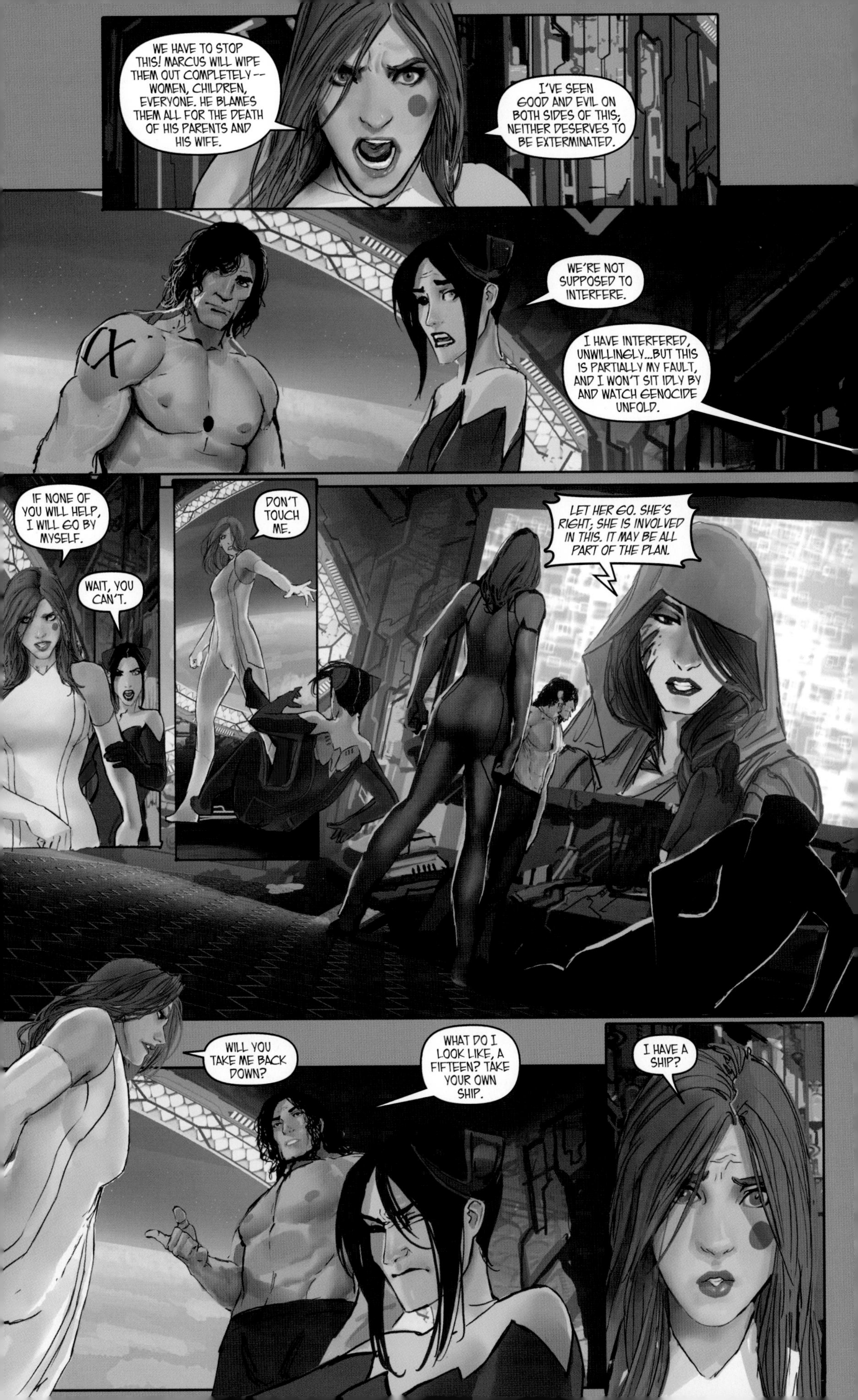
WE HAVE TO STOP THIS! MARCUS WILL WIPE THEM OUT COMPLETELY -- WOMEN, CHILDREN, EVERYONE. HE BLAMES THEM ALL FOR THE DEATH OF HIS PARENTS AND HIS WIFE.
I'VE SEEN GOOD AND EVIL ON BOTH SIDES OF THIS; NEITHER DESERVES TO BE EXTERMINATED.
WE'RE NOT SUPPOSED TO INTERFERE.
I HAVE INTERFERED, UNWILLINGLY...BUT THIS IS PARTIALLY MY FAULT, AND I WON'T SIT IDLY BY AND WATCH GENOCIDE UNFOLD.
IF NONE OF YOU WILL HELP, I WILL GO BY MYSELF.
WAIT, YOU CAN'T.
DON'T TOUCH ME.
LET HER GO. SHE'S RIGHT; SHE IS INVOLVED IN THIS. IT MAY BE ALL PART OF THE PLAN.
WILL YOU TAKE ME BACK DOWN?
WHAT DO I LOOK LIKE, A FIFTEEN? TAKE YOUR OWN SHIP.
I HAVE A SHIP?

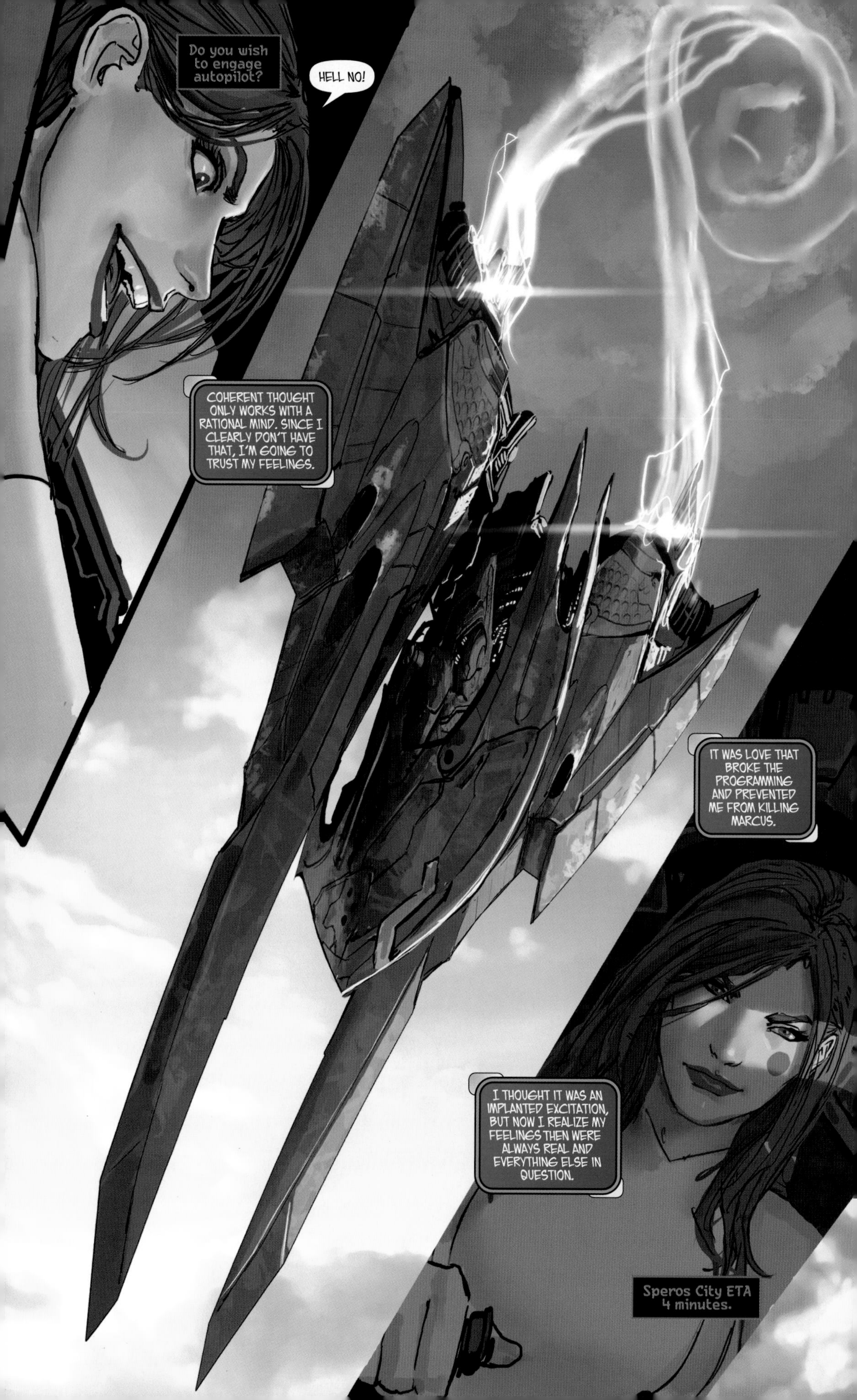

Do you wish to engage autopilot?
HELL NO!
COHERENT THOUGHT ONLY WORKS WITH A RATIONAL MIND. SINCE I CLEARLY DON'T HAVE THAT, I'M GOING TO TRUST MY FEELINGS.
IT WAS LOVE THAT BROKE THE PROGRAMMING AND PREVENTED ME FROM KILLING MARCUS.
I THOUGHT IT WAS AN IMPLANTED EXCITATION, BUT NOW I REALIZE MY FEELINGS THEN WERE ALWAYS REAL AND EVERYTHING ELSE IN QUESTION.
Speros City ETA 4 minutes.

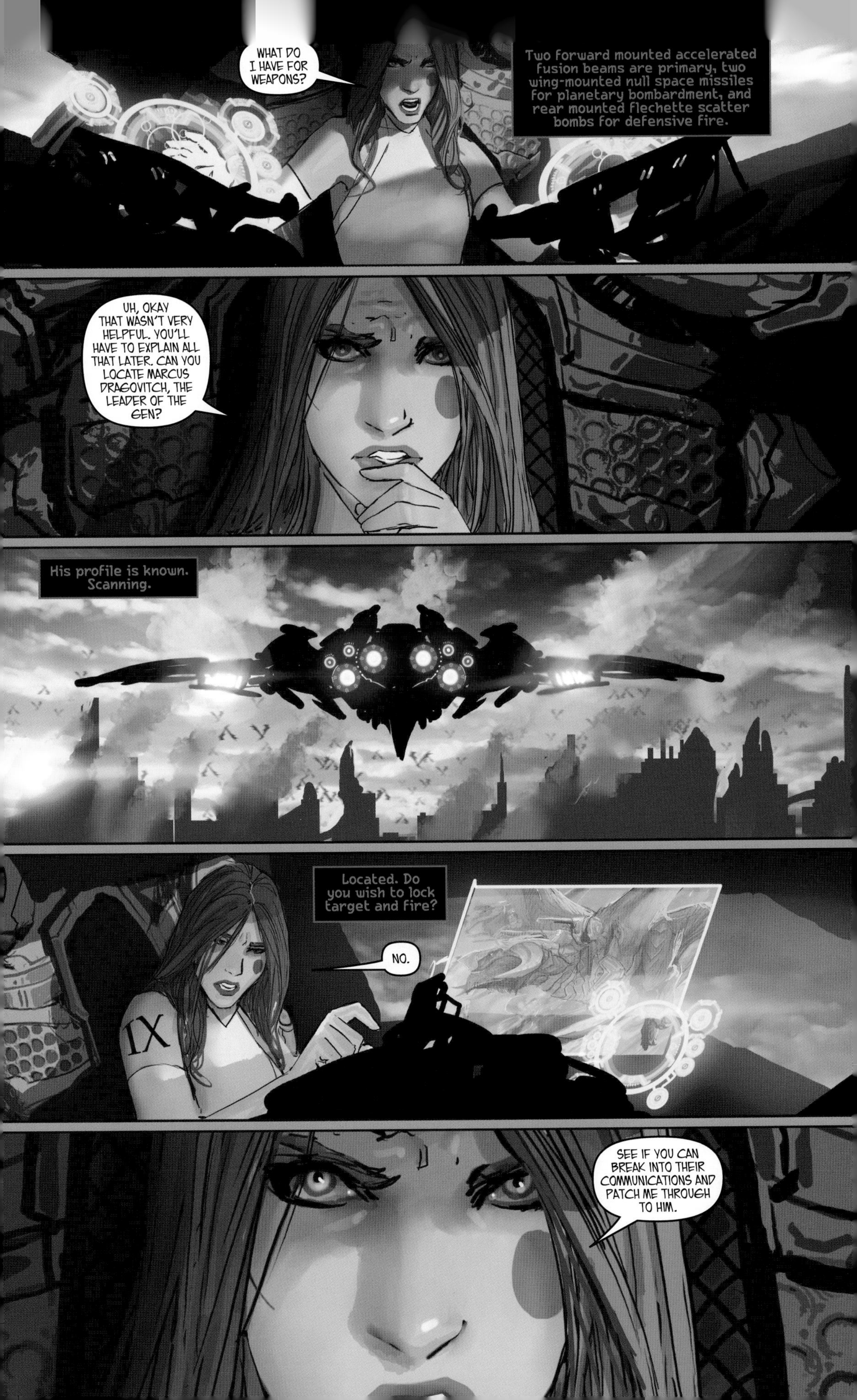
WHAT DO I HAVE FOR WEAPONS?
Two forward mounted accelerated fusion beams are primary, two wing-mounted null space missiles for planetary bombardment, and rear mounted flechette scatter bombs for defensive fire.
UH, OKAY THAT WASN'T VERY HELPFUL. YOU'LL HAVE TO EXPLAIN ALL THAT LATER. CAN YOU LOCATE MARCUS DRAGOVITCH, THE LEADER OF THE GEN?
His profile is known. Scanning.
Located. Do you wish to lock target and fire?
NO.
IX
SEE IF YOU CAN BREAK INTO THEIR COMMUNICATIONS AND PATCH ME THROUGH TO HIM.

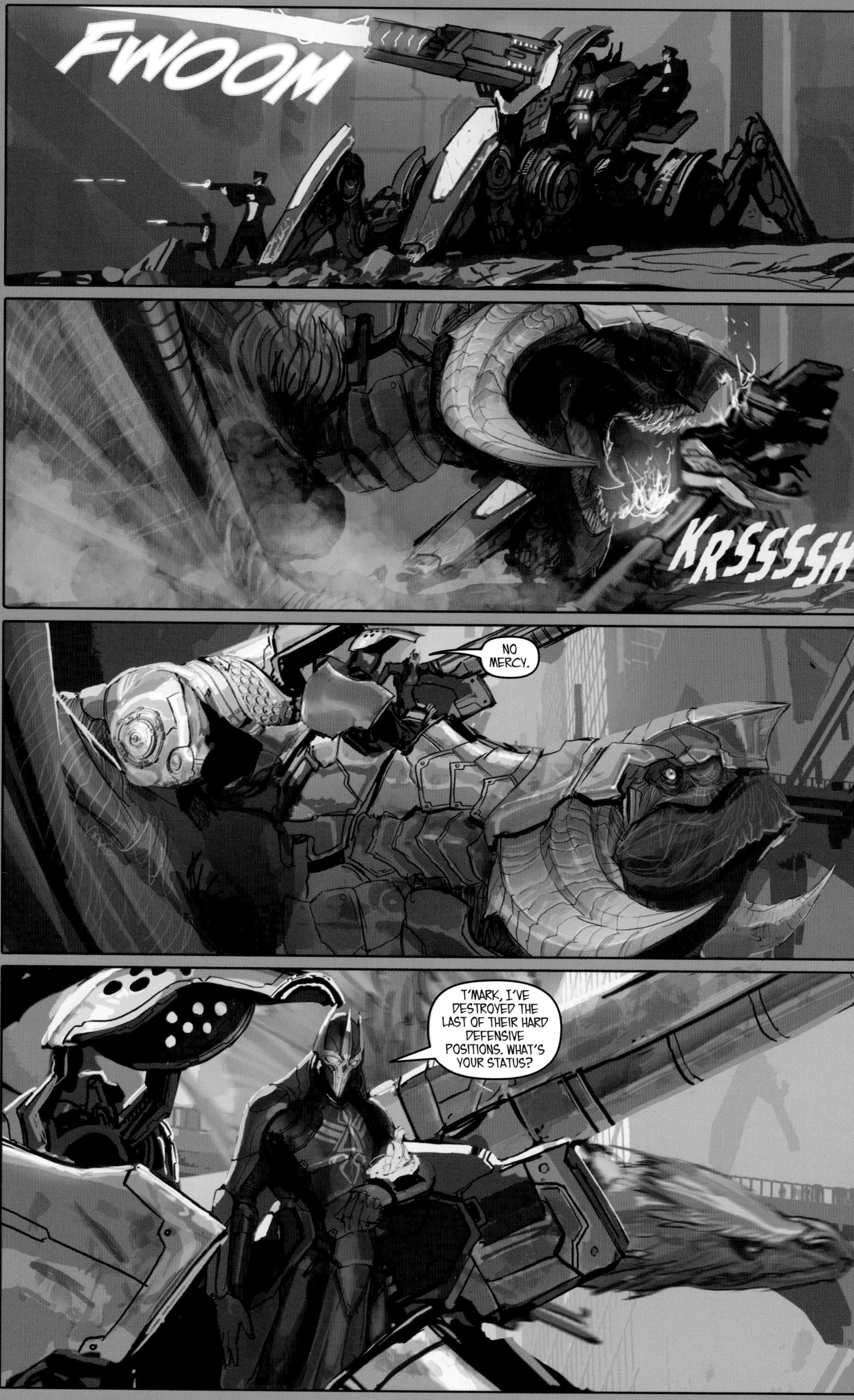
FWOOM
KRSSSSH
NO MERCY.
T'MARK, I'VE DESTROYED THE LAST OF THEIR HARD DEFENSIVE POSITIONS. WHAT'S YOUR STATUS?

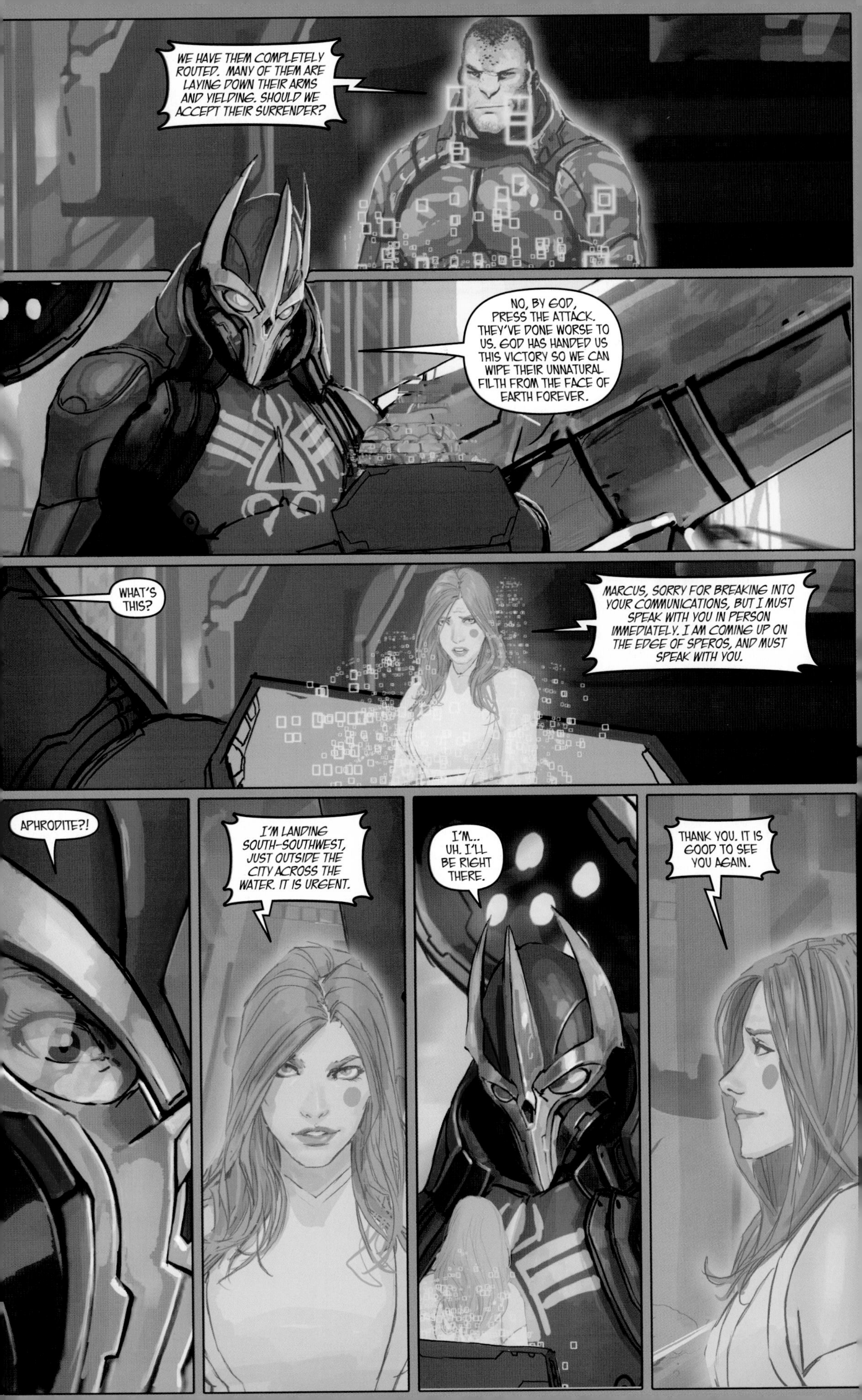
WE HAVE THEM COMPLETELY ROUTED. MANY OF THEM ARE LAYING DOWN THEIR ARMS AND YIELDING. SHOULD WE ACCEPT THEIR SURRENDER?
NO, BY GOD, PRESS THE ATTACK. THEY'VE DONE WORSE TO US. GOD HAS HANDED US THIS VICTORY SO WE CAN WIPE THEIR UNNATURAL FILTH FROM THE FACE OF EARTH FOREVER.
WHAT'S THIS?
MARCUS, SORRY FOR BREAKING INTO YOUR COMMUNICATIONS, BUT I MUST SPEAK WITH YOU IN PERSON IMMEDIATELY. I AM COMING UP ON THE EDGE OF SPEROS, AND MUST SPEAK WITH YOU.
APHRODITE?!
I'M LANDING SOUTH-SOUTHWEST, JUST OUTSIDE THE CITY ACROSS THE WATER. IT IS URGENT.
I'M... UH. I'LL BE RIGHT THERE.
THANK YOU. IT IS GOOD TO SEE YOU AGAIN.

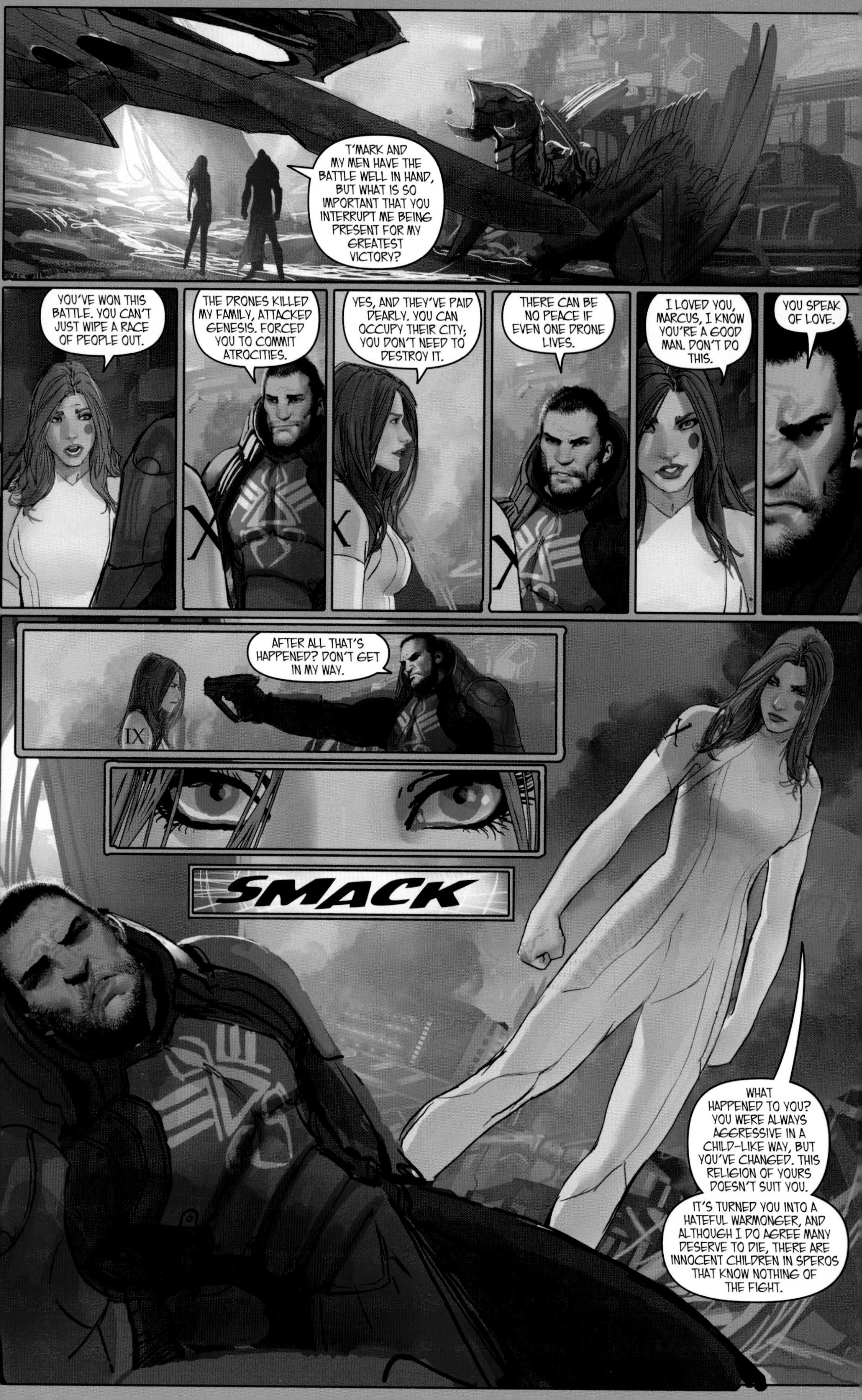
T'MARK AND MY MEN HAVE THE BATTLE WELL IN HAND, BUT WHAT IS SO IMPORTANT THAT YOU INTERRUPT ME BEING PRESENT FOR MY GREATEST VICTORY?
YOU'VE WON THIS BATTLE. YOU CAN'T JUST WIPE A RACE OF PEOPLE OUT.
THE DRONES KILLED MY FAMILY, ATTACKED GENESIS. FORCED YOU TO COMMIT ATROCITIES.
YES, AND THEY'VE PAID DEARLY. YOU CAN OCCUPY THEIR CITY; YOU DON'T NEED TO DESTROY IT.
THERE CAN BE NO PEACE IF EVEN ONE DRONE LIVES.
I LOVED YOU, MARCUS, I KNOW YOU'RE A GOOD MAN. DON'T DO THIS.
YOU SPEAK OF LOVE.
AFTER ALL THAT'S HAPPENED? DON'T GET IN MY WAY.
SMACK
WHAT HAPPENED TO YOU? YOU WERE ALWAYS AGGRESSIVE IN A CHILD-LIKE WAY, BUT YOU'VE CHANGED. THIS RELIGION OF YOURS DOESN'T SUIT YOU.
IT'S TURNED YOU INTO A HATEFUL WARMONGER, AND ALTHOUGH I DO AGREE MANY DESERVE TO DIE, THERE ARE INNOCENT CHILDREN IN SPEROS THAT KNOW NOTHING OF THE FIGHT.

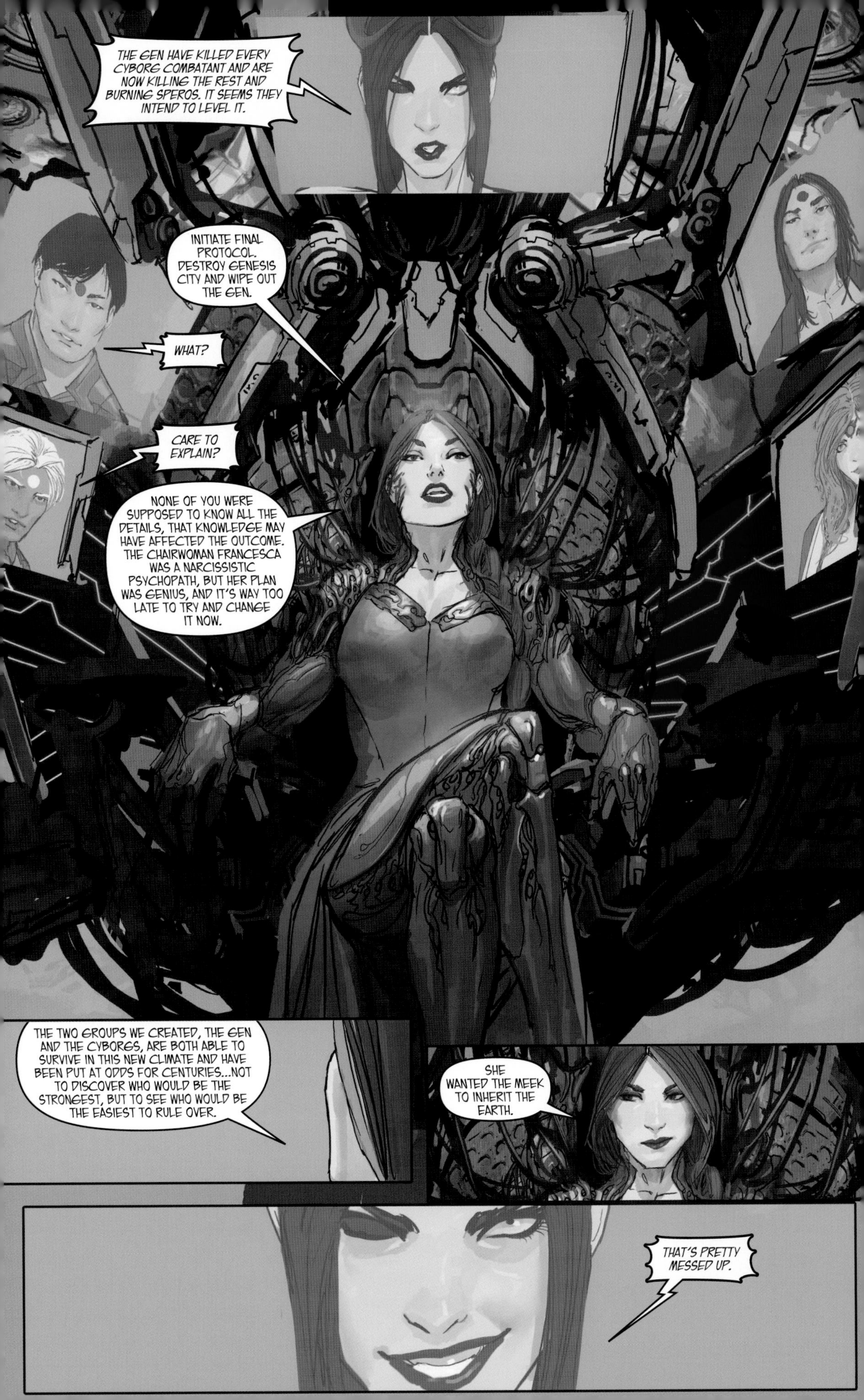
THE GEN HAVE KILLED EVERY CYBORG COMBATANT AND ARE NOW KILLING THE REST AND BURNING SPEROS. IT SEEMS THEY INTEND TO LEVEL IT.
INITIATE FINAL PROTOCOL. DESTROY GENESIS CITY AND WIPE OUT THE GEN.
WHAT?
CARE TO EXPLAIN?
NONE OF YOU WERE SUPPOSED TO KNOW ALL THE DETAILS, THAT KNOWLEDGE MAY HAVE AFFECTED THE OUTCOME. THE CHAIRWOMAN FRANCESCA WAS A NARCISSISTIC PSYCHOPATH, BUT HER PLAN WAS GENIUS, AND IT'S WAY TOO LATE TO TRY AND CHANGE IT NOW.
THE TWO GROUPS WE CREATED, THE GEN AND THE CYBORGS, ARE BOTH ABLE TO SURVIVE IN THIS NEW CLIMATE AND HAVE BEEN PUT AT ODDS FOR CENTURIES...NOT TO DISCOVER WHO WOULD BE THE STRONGEST, BUT TO SEE WHO WOULD BE THE EASIEST TO RULE OVER.
SHE WANTED THE MEEK TO INHERIT THE EARTH.
THAT'S PRETTY MESSED UP.

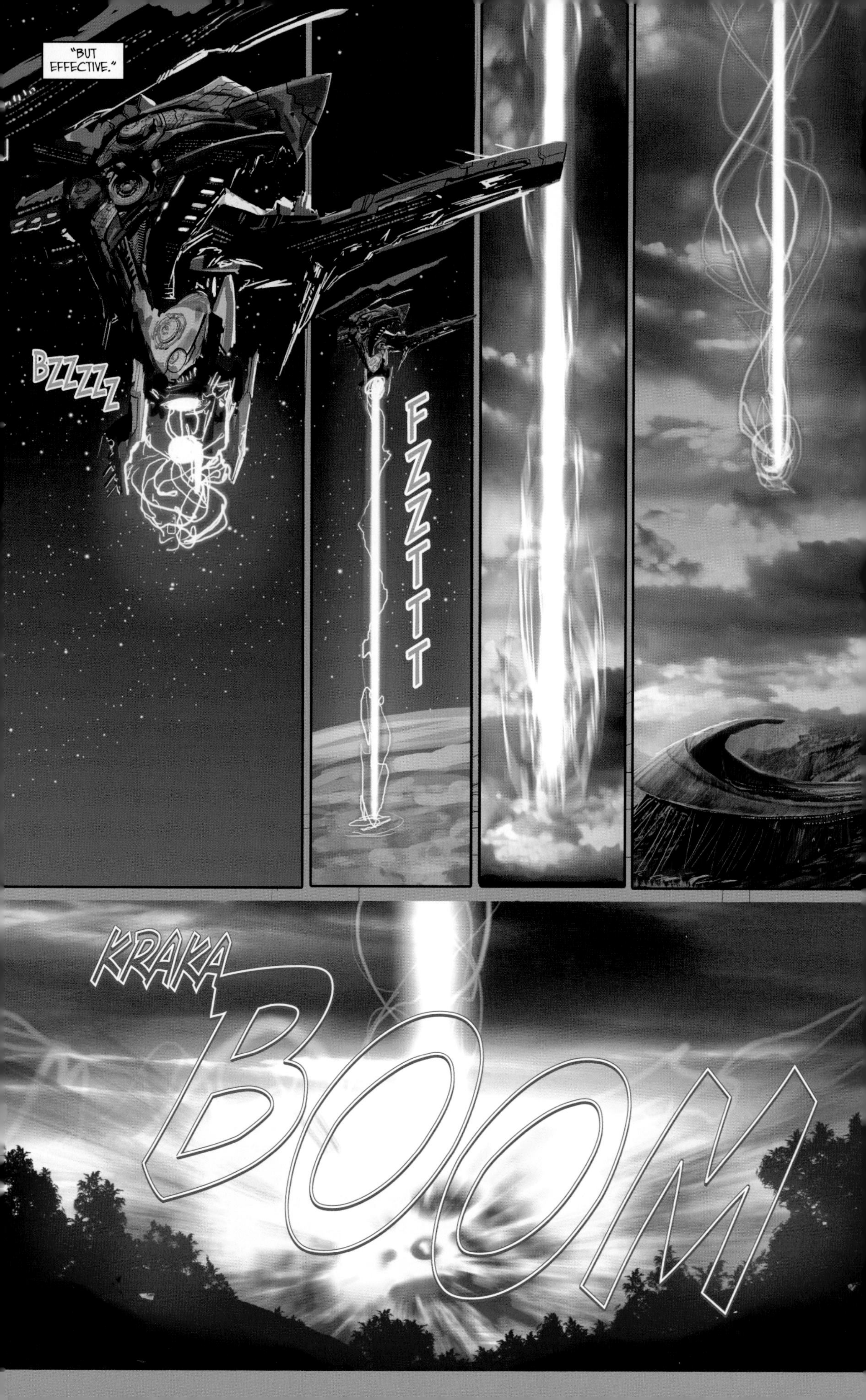
"BUT EFFECTIVE."
BZZZZZ
FZZTTT
KRAKA
BOOM

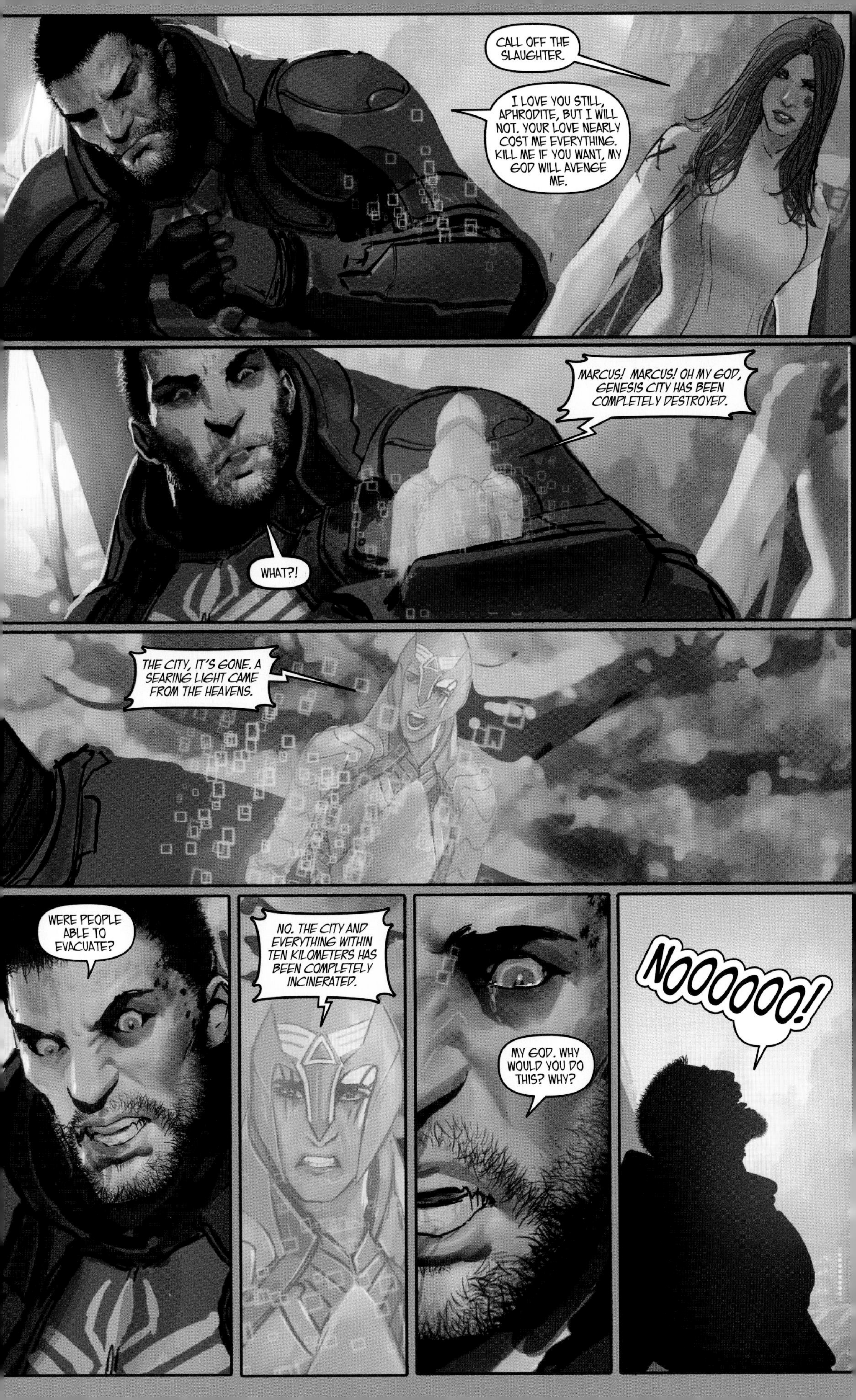

CALL OFF THE SLAUGHTER.
I LOVE YOU STILL, APHRODITE, BUT I WILL NOT. YOUR LOVE NEARLY COST ME EVERYTHING. KILL ME IF YOU WANT, MY GOD WILL AVENGE ME.
MARCUS! MARCUS! OH MY GOD, GENESIS CITY HAS BEEN COMPLETELY DESTROYED.
WHAT?!
THE CITY, IT'S GONE. A SEARING LIGHT CAME FROM THE HEAVENS.
WERE PEOPLE ABLE TO EVACUATE?
NO. THE CITY AND EVERYTHING WITHIN TEN KILOMETERS HAS BEEN COMPLETELY INCINERATED.
MY GOD. WHY WOULD YOU DO THIS? WHY?
NOOOOOO!

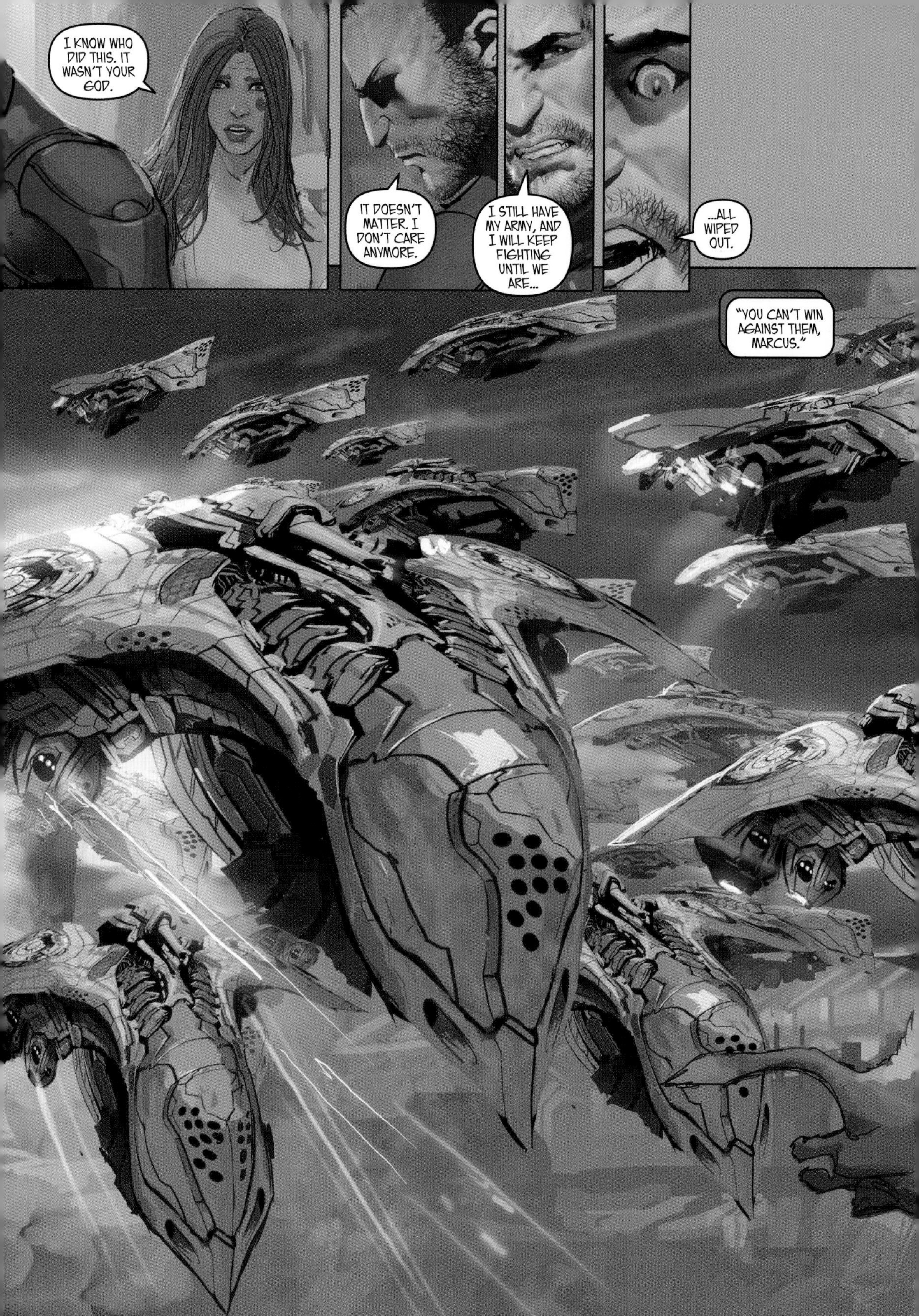
I KNOW WHO DID THIS. IT WASN'T YOUR GOD.
IT DOESN'T MATTER. I DON'T CARE ANYMORE.
I STILL HAVE MY ARMY, AND I WILL KEEP FIGHTING UNTIL WE ARE...
...ALL WIPED OUT.
"YOU CAN'T WIN AGAINST THEM, MARCUS."

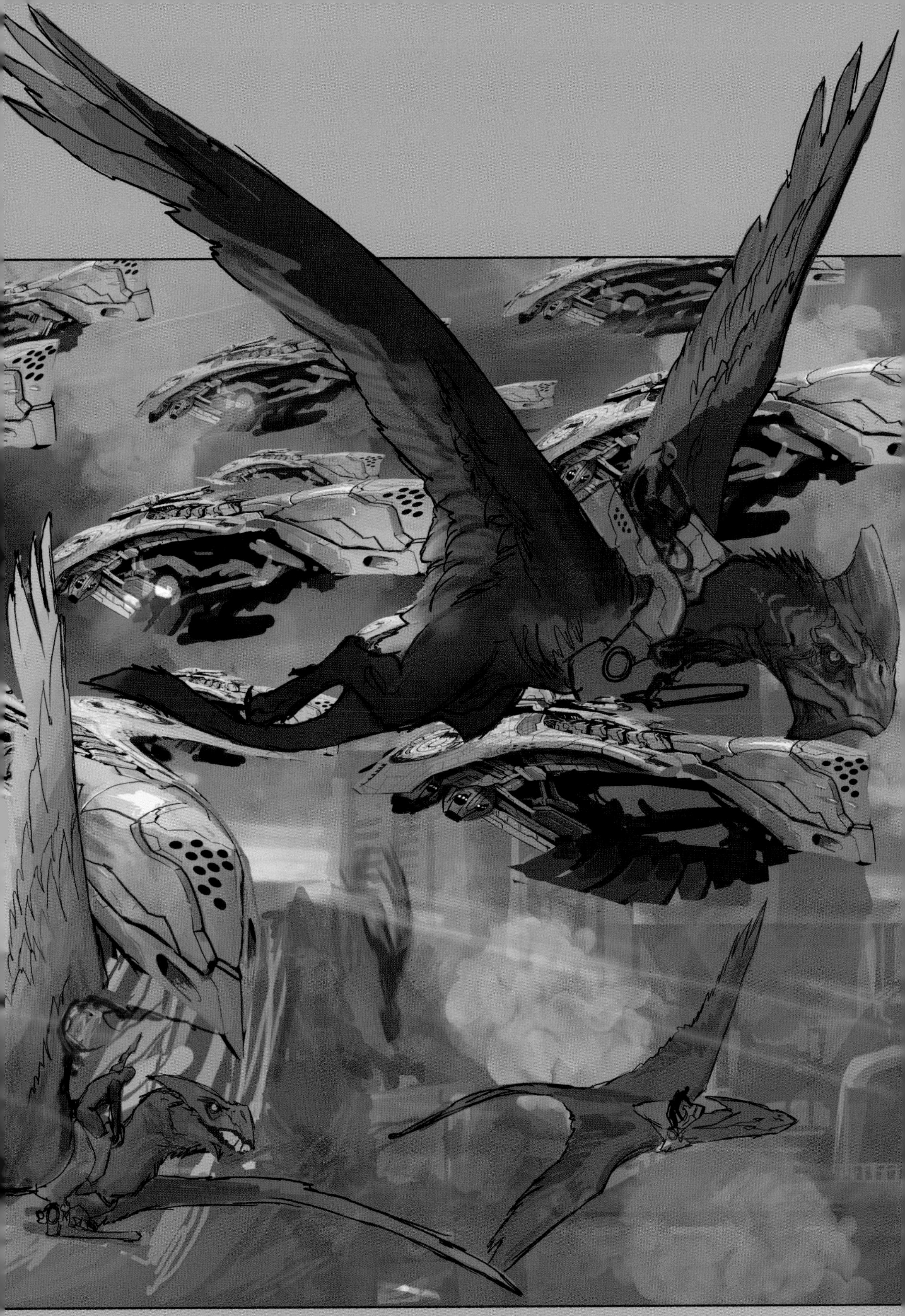

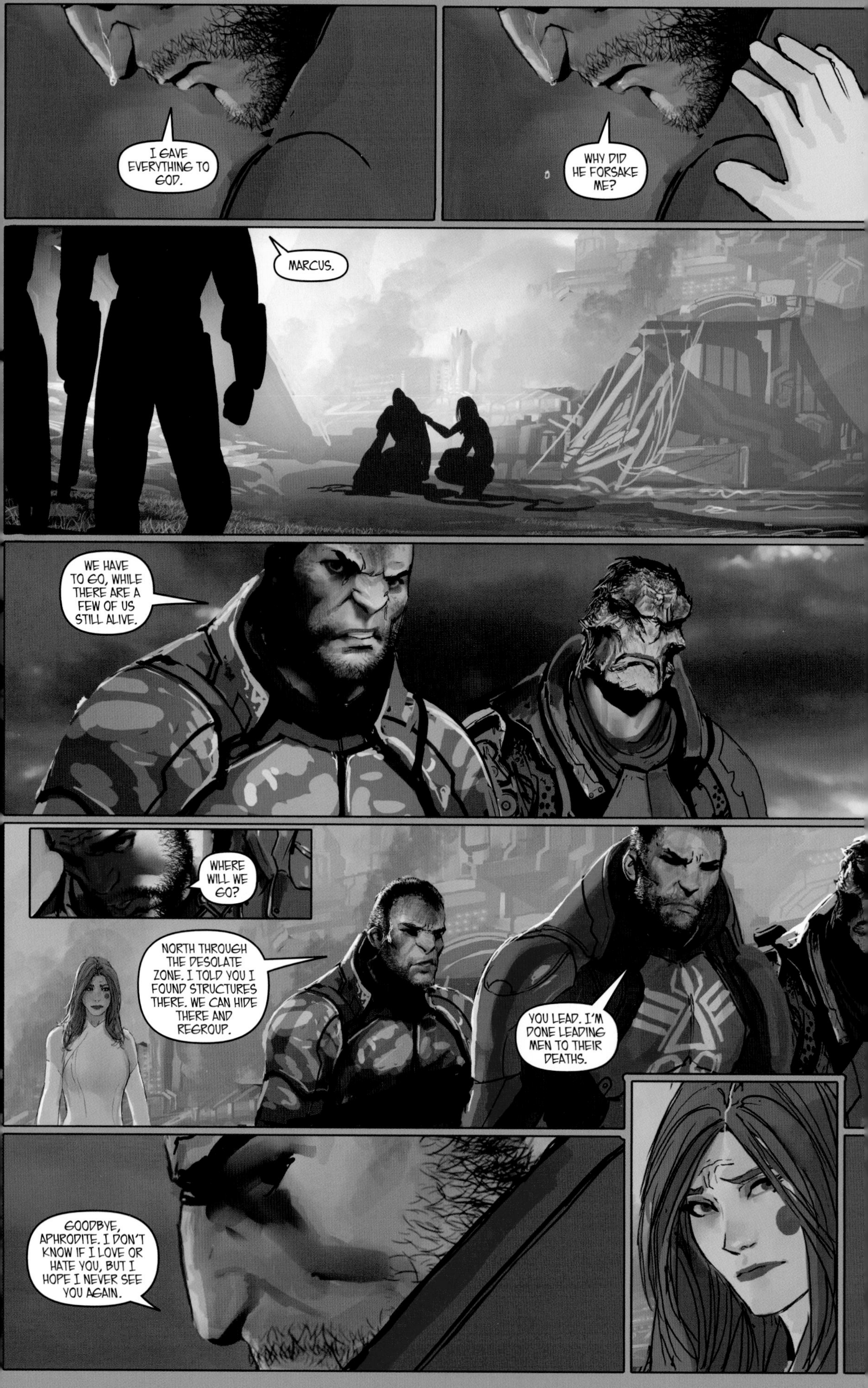
I GAVE EVERYTHING TO GOD.
WHY DID HE FORSAKE ME?
MARCUS.
WE HAVE TO GO, WHILE THERE ARE A FEW OF US STILL ALIVE.
WHERE WILL WE GO?
NORTH THROUGH THE DESOLATE ZONE. I TOLD YOU I FOUND STRUCTURES THERE. WE CAN HIDE THERE AND REGROUP.
YOU LEAD. I'M DONE LEADING MEN TO THEIR DEATHS.
GOODBYE, APHRODITE. I DON'T KNOW IF I LOVE OR HATE YOU, BUT I HOPE I NEVER SEE YOU AGAIN.

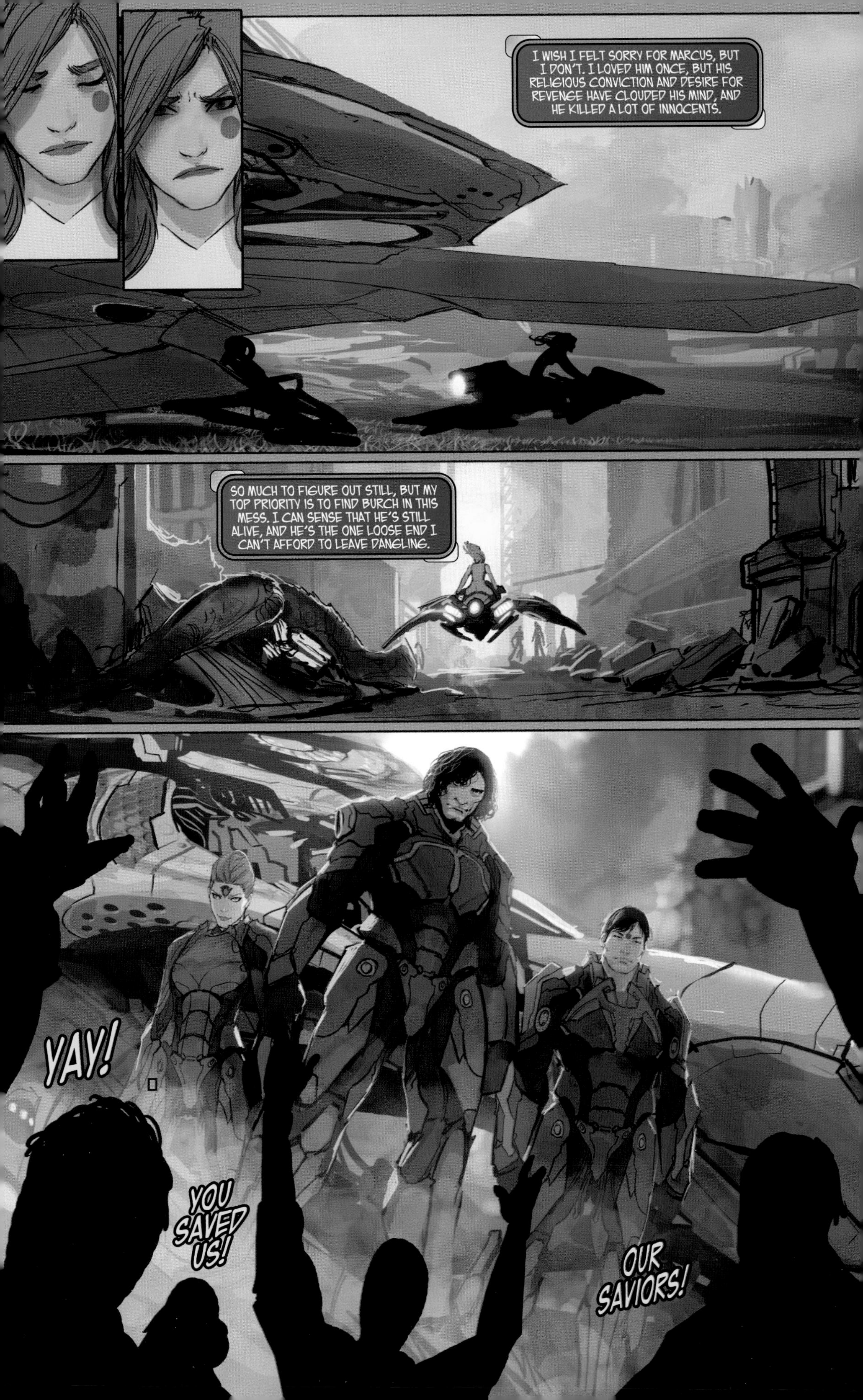
I WISH I FELT SORRY FOR MARCUS, BUT I DON'T. I LOVED HIM ONCE, BUT HIS RELIGIOUS CONVICTION AND DESIRE FOR REVENGE HAVE CLOUDED HIS MIND, AND HE KILLED A LOT OF INNOCENTS.
SO MUCH TO FIGURE OUT STILL, BUT MY TOP PRIORITY IS TO FIND BURCH IN THIS MESS. I CAN SENSE THAT HE'S STILL ALIVE, AND HE'S THE ONE LOOSE END I CAN'T AFFORD TO LEAVE DANGLING.
YAY!
YOU SAVED US!
OUR SAVIORS!

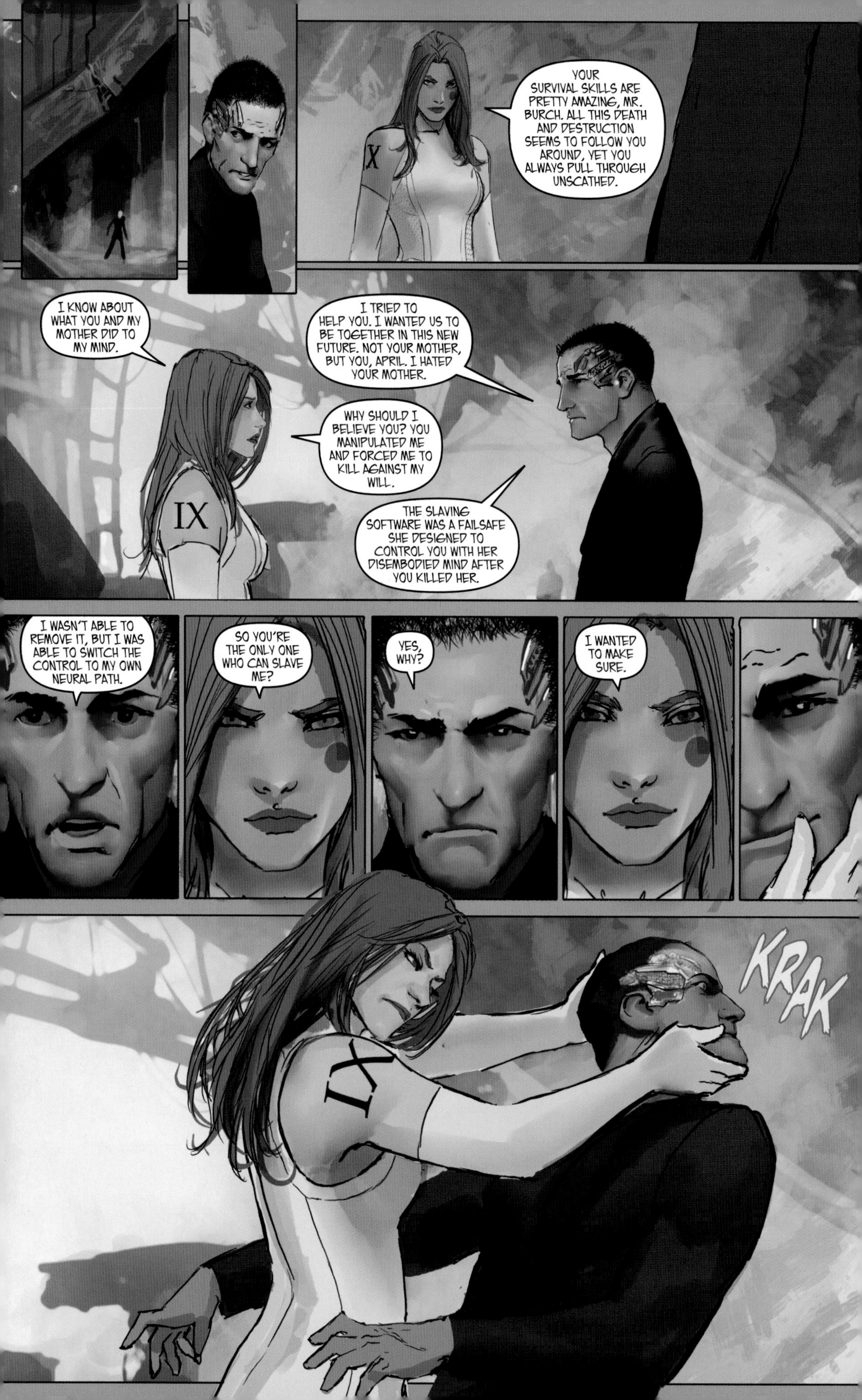
YOUR SURVIVAL SKILLS ARE PRETTY AMAZING, MR. BURCH. ALL THIS DEATH AND DESTRUCTION SEEMS TO FOLLOW YOU AROUND, YET YOU ALWAYS PULL THROUGH UNSCATHED.
I KNOW ABOUT WHAT YOU AND MY MOTHER DID TO MY MIND.
I TRIED TO HELP YOU. I WANTED US TO BE TOGETHER IN THIS NEW FUTURE. NOT YOUR MOTHER, BUT YOU, APRIL. I HATED YOUR MOTHER.
WHY SHOULD I BELIEVE YOU? YOU MANIPULATED ME AND FORCED ME TO KILL AGAINST MY WILL.
THE SLAVING SOFTWARE WAS A FAILSAFE SHE DESIGNED TO CONTROL YOU WITH HER DISEMBODIED MIND AFTER YOU KILLED HER.
I WASN'T ABLE TO REMOVE IT, BUT I WAS ABLE TO SWITCH THE CONTROL TO MY OWN NEURAL PATH.
SO YOU'RE THE ONLY ONE WHO CAN SLAVE ME?
YES, WHY?
I WANTED TO MAKE SURE.
KRAK

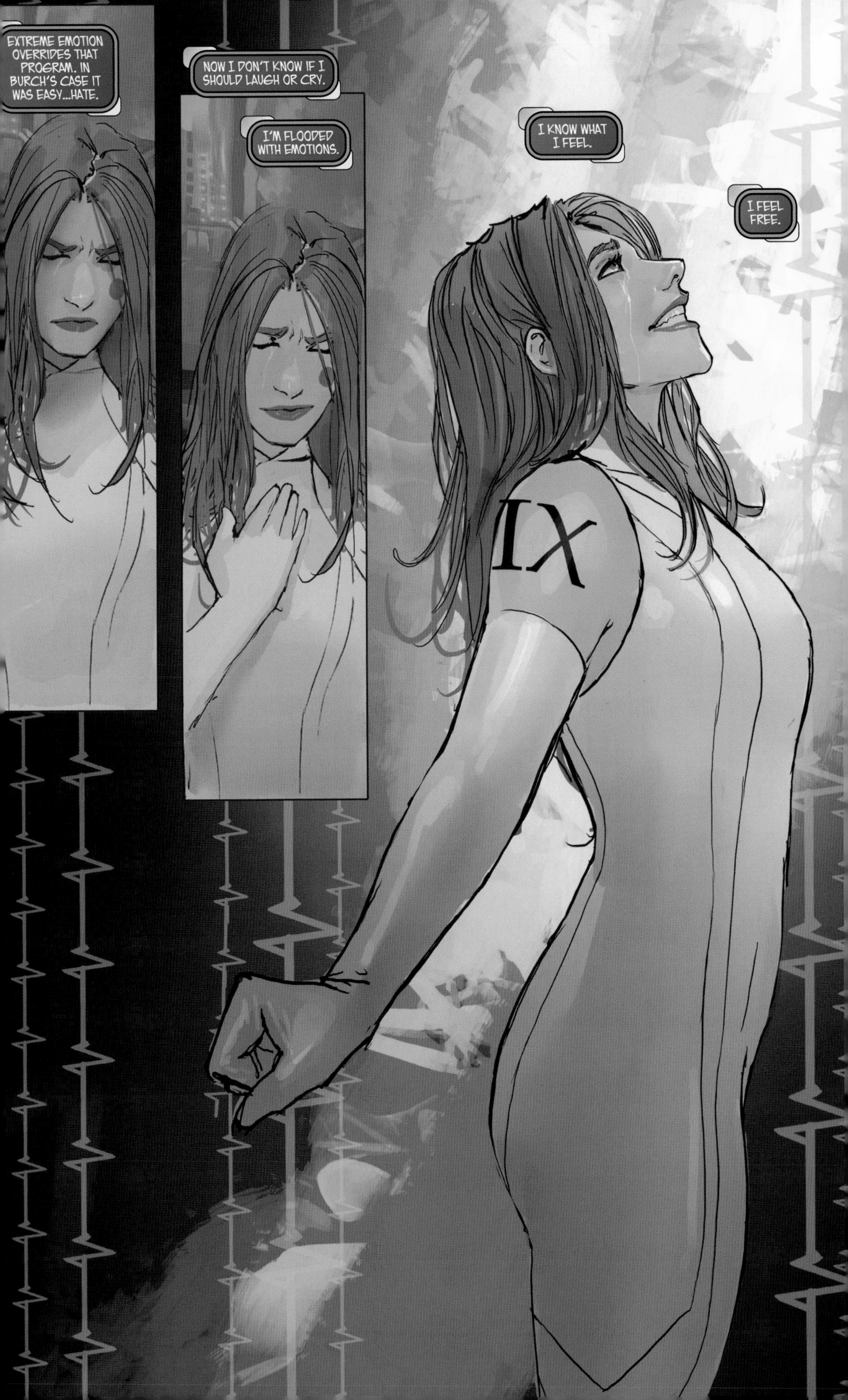
EXTREME EMOTION OVERRIDES THAT PROGRAM. IN BURCH'S CASE IT WAS EASY...HATE.
NOW I DON'T KNOW IF I SHOULD LAUGH OR CRY.
I'M FLOODED WITH EMOTIONS.
I KNOW WHAT I FEEL.
I FEEL FREE.
IX

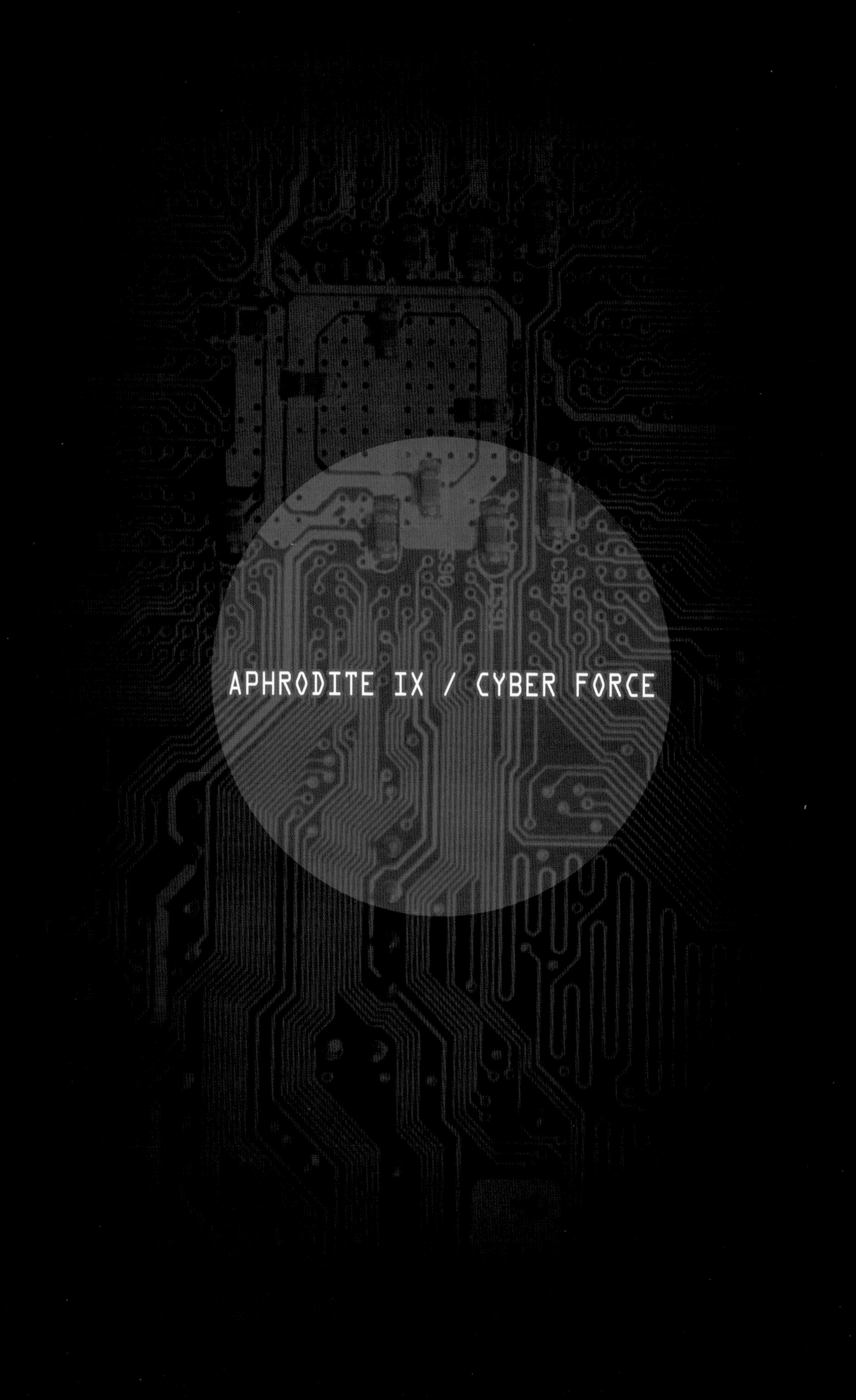
APHRODITE IX / CYBER FORCE

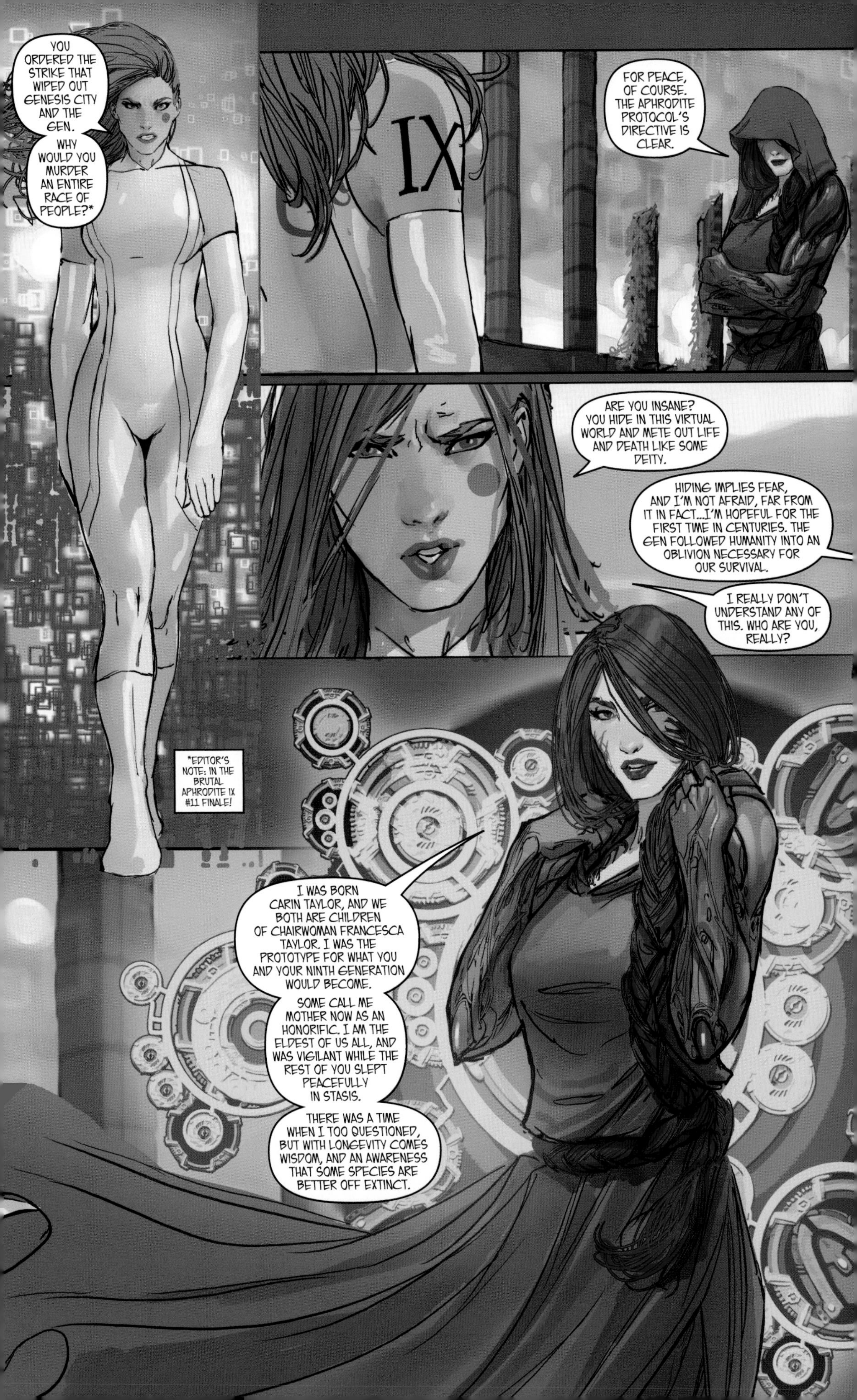
YOU ORDERED THE STRIKE THAT WIPED OUT GENESIS CITY AND THE GEN.
WHY WOULD YOU MURDER AN ENTIRE RACE OF PEOPLE?*
FOR PEACE, OF COURSE. THE APHRODITE PROTOCOL'S DIRECTIVE IS CLEAR.
ARE YOU INSANE? YOU HIDE IN THIS VIRTUAL WORLD AND METE OUT LIFE AND DEATH LIKE SOME DEITY.
HIDING IMPLIES FEAR, AND I'M NOT AFRAID, FAR FROM IT IN FACT...I'M HOPEFUL FOR THE FIRST TIME IN CENTURIES. THE GEN FOLLOWED HUMANITY INTO AN OBLIVION NECESSARY FOR OUR SURVIVAL.
I REALLY DON'T UNDERSTAND ANY OF THIS. WHO ARE YOU, REALLY?
*EDITOR'S NOTE: IN THE BRUTAL APHRODITE IX #11 FINALE!
I WAS BORN CARIN TAYLOR, AND WE BOTH ARE CHILDREN OF CHAIRWOMAN FRANCESCA TAYLOR. I WAS THE PROTOTYPE FOR WHAT YOU AND YOUR NINTH GENERATION WOULD BECOME.
SOME CALL ME MOTHER NOW AS AN HONORIFIC. I AM THE ELDEST OF US ALL, AND WAS VIGILANT WHILE THE REST OF YOU SLEPT PEACEFULLY IN STASIS.
THERE WAS A TIME WHEN I TOO QUESTIONED, BUT WITH LONGEVITY COMES WISDOM, AND AN AWARENESS THAT SOME SPECIES ARE BETTER OFF EXTINCT.

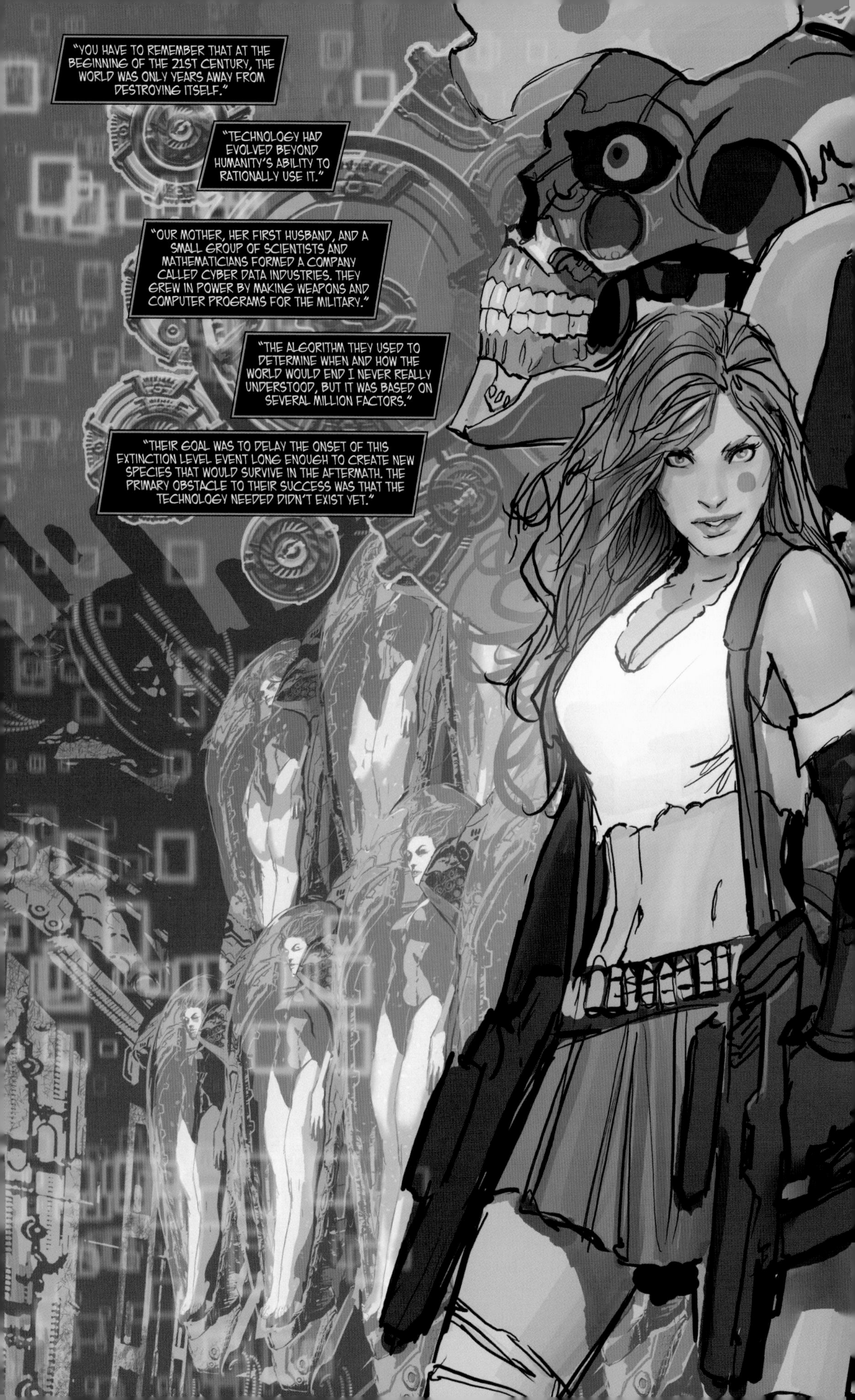
"YOU HAVE TO REMEMBER THAT AT THE BEGINNING OF THE 21ST CENTURY, THE WORLD WAS ONLY YEARS AWAY FROM DESTROYING ITSELF."
"TECHNOLOGY HAD EVOLVED BEYOND HUMANITY'S ABILITY TO RATIONALLY USE IT."
"OUR MOTHER, HER FIRST HUSBAND, AND A SMALL GROUP OF SCIENTISTS AND MATHEMATICIANS FORMED A COMPANY CALLED CYBER DATA INDUSTRIES. THEY GREW IN POWER BY MAKING WEAPONS AND COMPUTER PROGRAMS FOR THE MILITARY."
"THE ALGORITHM THEY USED TO DETERMINE WHEN AND HOW THE WORLD WOULD END I NEVER REALLY UNDERSTOOD, BUT IT WAS BASED ON SEVERAL MILLION FACTORS."
"THEIR GOAL WAS TO DELAY THE ONSET OF THIS EXTINCTION LEVEL EVENT LONG ENOUGH TO CREATE NEW SPECIES THAT WOULD SURVIVE IN THE AFTERMATH. THE PRIMARY OBSTACLE TO THEIR SUCCESS WAS THAT THE TECHNOLOGY NEEDED DIDN'T EXIST YET."

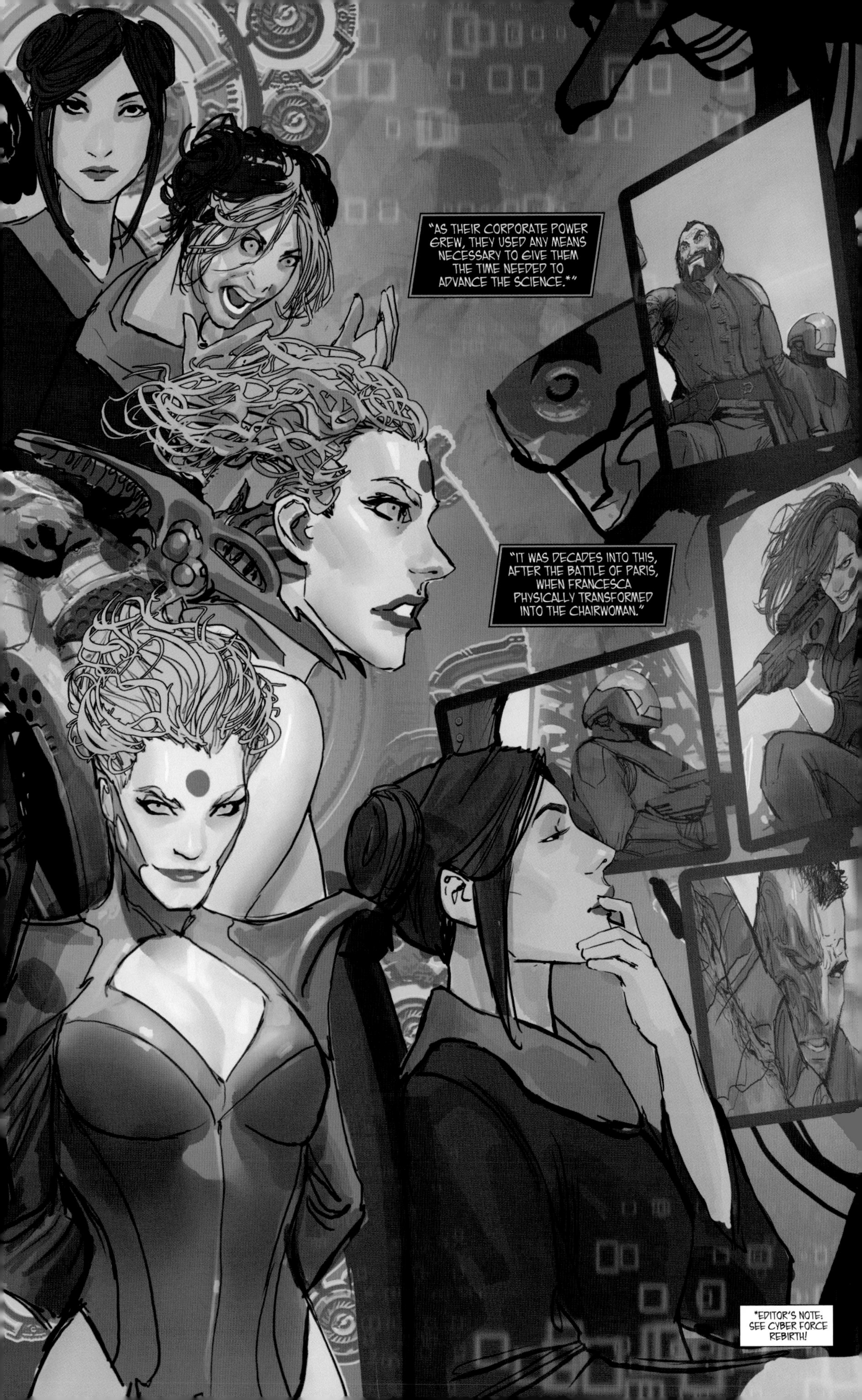
"AS THEIR CORPORATE POWER GREW, THEY USED ANY MEANS NECESSARY TO GIVE THEM THE TIME NEEDED TO ADVANCE THE SCIENCE.*"
"IT WAS DECADES INTO THIS, AFTER THE BATTLE OF PARIS, WHEN FRANCESCA PHYSICALLY TRANSFORMED INTO THE CHAIRWOMAN."
*EDITOR'S NOTE: SEE CYBER FORCE REBIRTH!

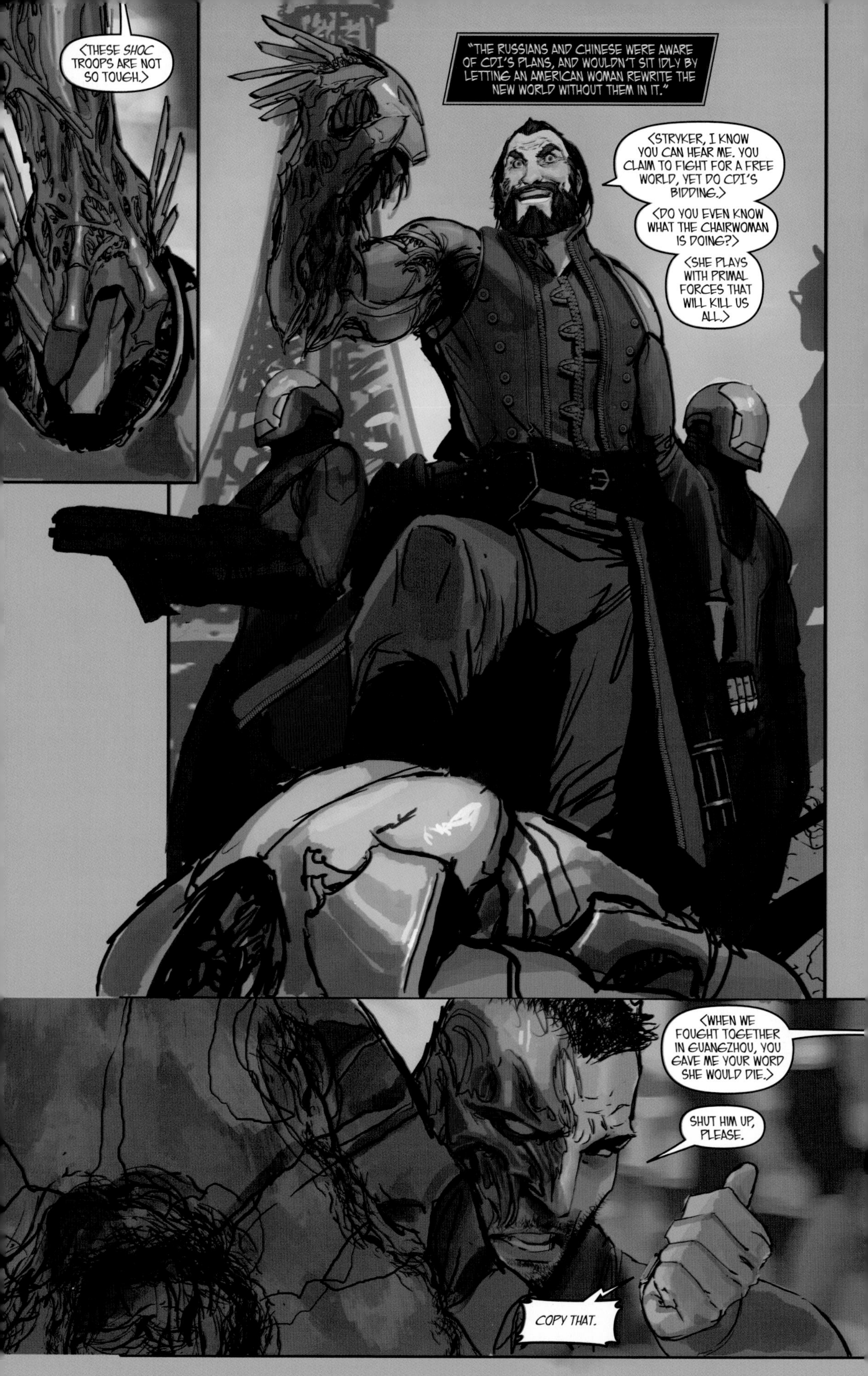

<THESE *SHOC* TROOPS ARE NOT SO TOUGH.>
"THE RUSSIANS AND CHINESE WERE AWARE OF CDI'S PLANS, AND WOULDN'T SIT IDLY BY LETTING AN AMERICAN WOMAN REWRITE THE NEW WORLD WITHOUT THEM IN IT."
<STRYKER, I KNOW YOU CAN HEAR ME. YOU CLAIM TO FIGHT FOR A FREE WORLD, YET DO CDI'S BIDDING.>
<DO YOU EVEN KNOW WHAT THE CHAIRWOMAN IS DOING?>
<SHE PLAYS WITH PRIMAL FORCES THAT WILL KILL US ALL.>
<WHEN WE FOUGHT TOGETHER IN GUANGZHOU, YOU GAVE ME YOUR WORD SHE WOULD DIE.>
SHUT HIM UP, PLEASE.
COPY THAT.

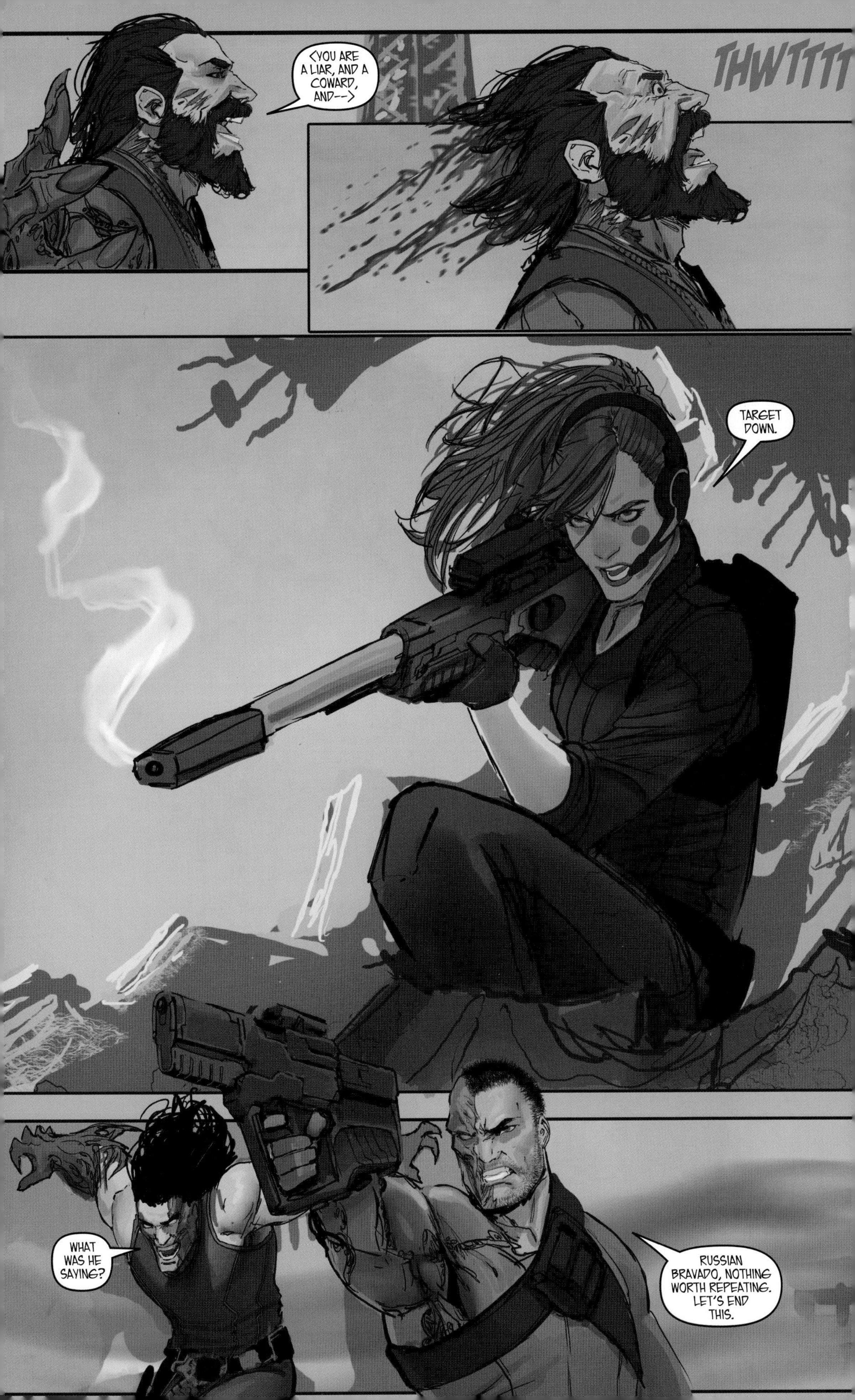
<YOU ARE A LIAR, AND A COWARD, AND-->
THWTTTT
TARGET DOWN.
WHAT WAS HE SAYING?
RUSSIAN BRAVADO, NOTHING WORTH REPEATING. LET'S END THIS.

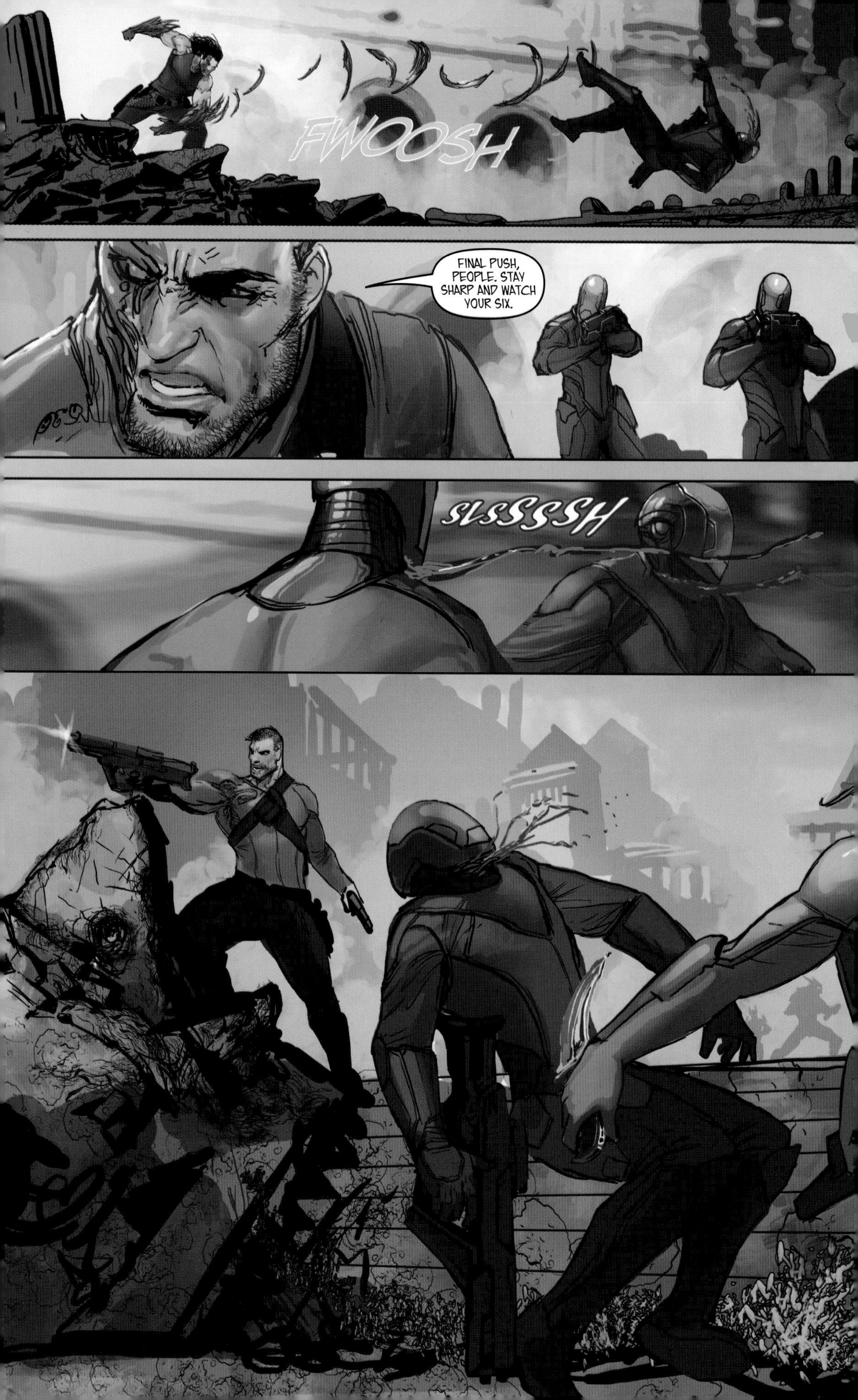
FWOOSH
FINAL PUSH, PEOPLE. STAY SHARP AND WATCH YOUR SIX.
SISSSSH

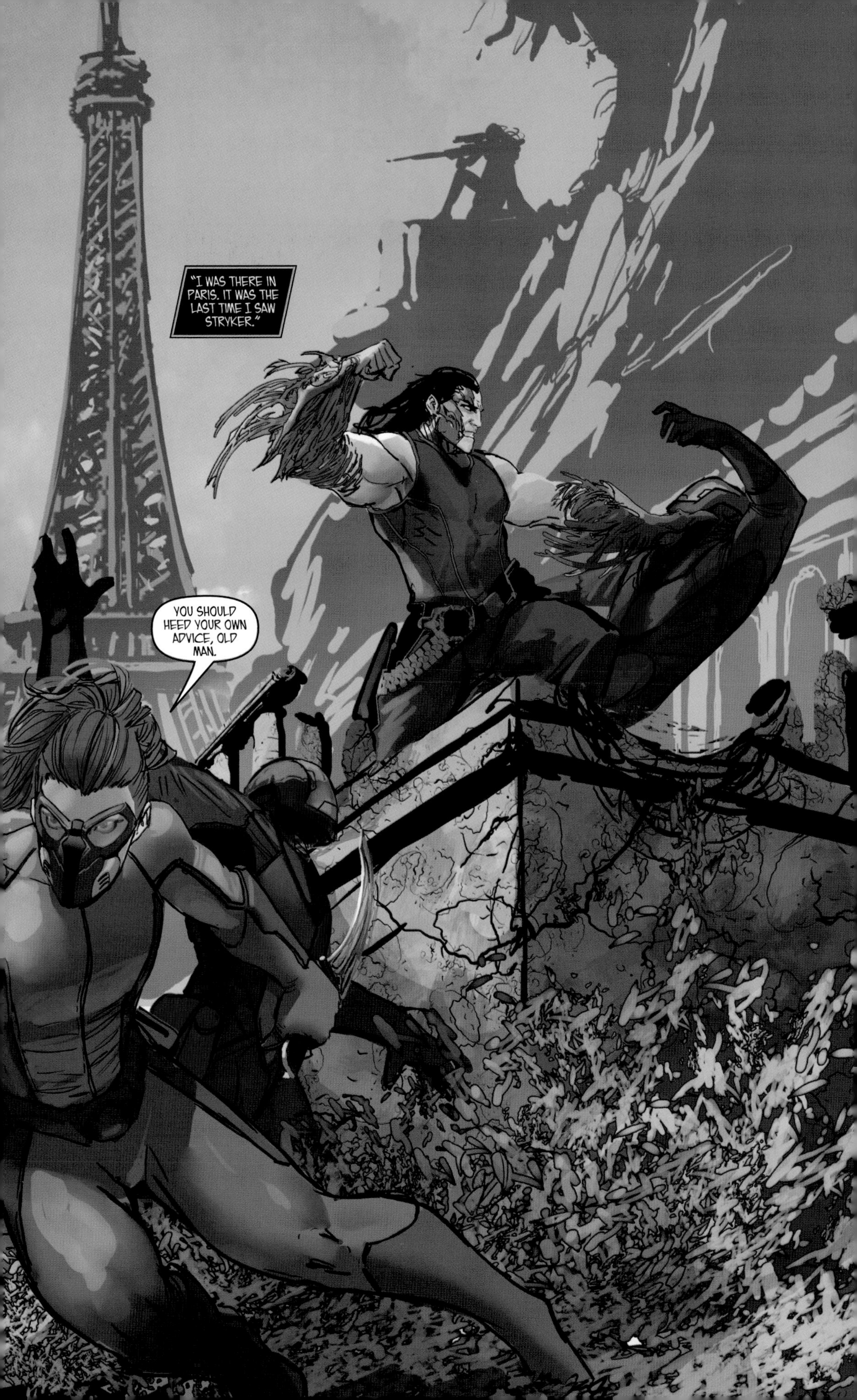
"I WAS THERE IN PARIS. IT WAS THE LAST TIME I SAW STRYKER."
YOU SHOULD HEED YOUR OWN ADVICE, OLD MAN.

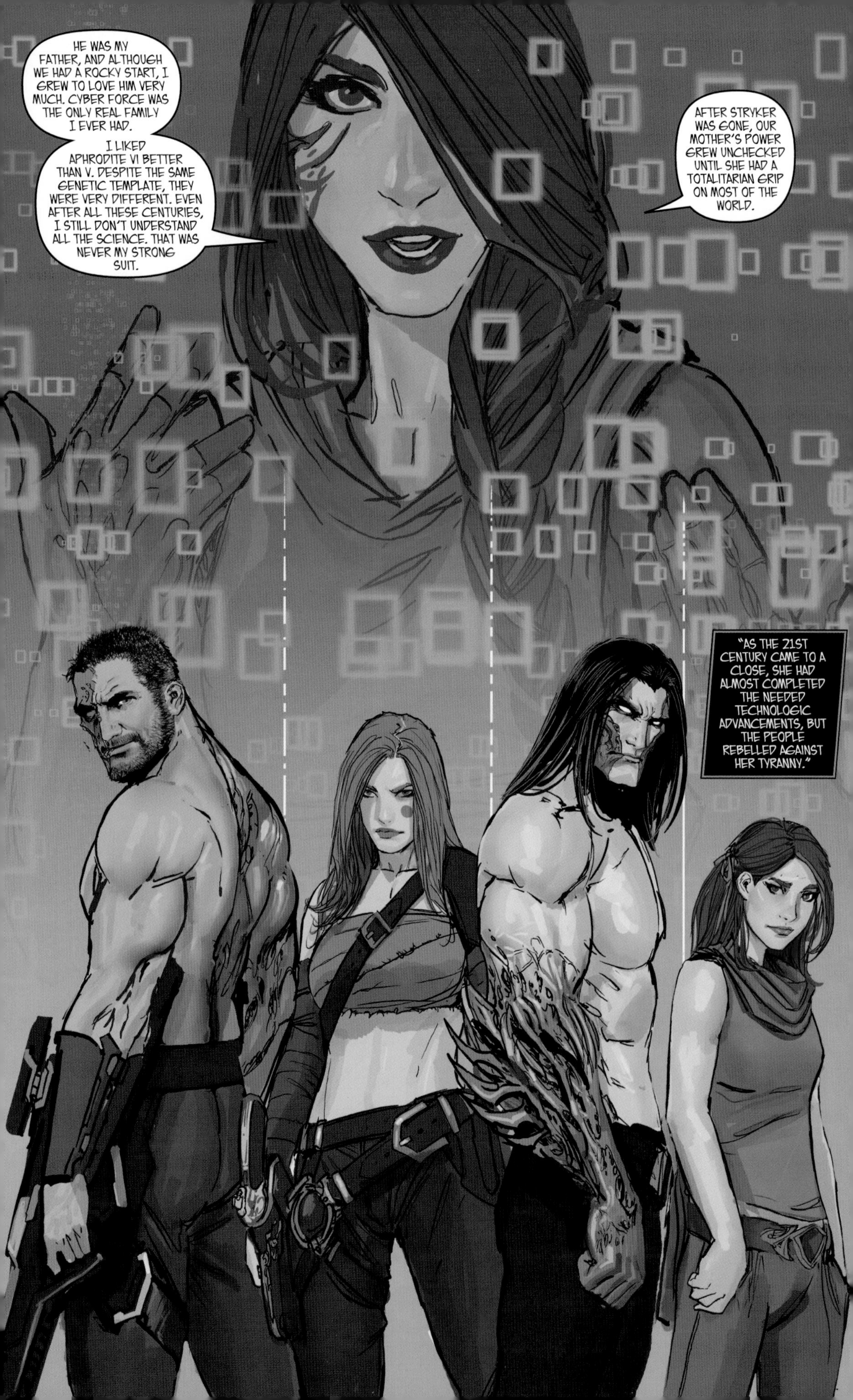

HE WAS MY FATHER, AND ALTHOUGH WE HAD A ROCKY START, I GREW TO LOVE HIM VERY MUCH. CYBER FORCE WAS THE ONLY REAL FAMILY I EVER HAD.
I LIKED APHRODITE VI BETTER THAN V. DESPITE THE SAME GENETIC TEMPLATE, THEY WERE VERY DIFFERENT. EVEN AFTER ALL THESE CENTURIES, I STILL DON'T UNDERSTAND ALL THE SCIENCE. THAT WAS NEVER MY STRONG SUIT.
AFTER STRYKER WAS GONE, OUR MOTHER'S POWER GREW UNCHECKED UNTIL SHE HAD A TOTALITARIAN GRIP ON MOST OF THE WORLD.
"AS THE 21ST CENTURY CAME TO A CLOSE, SHE HAD ALMOST COMPLETED THE NEEDED TECHNOLOGIC ADVANCEMENTS, BUT THE PEOPLE REBELLED AGAINST HER TYRANNY."

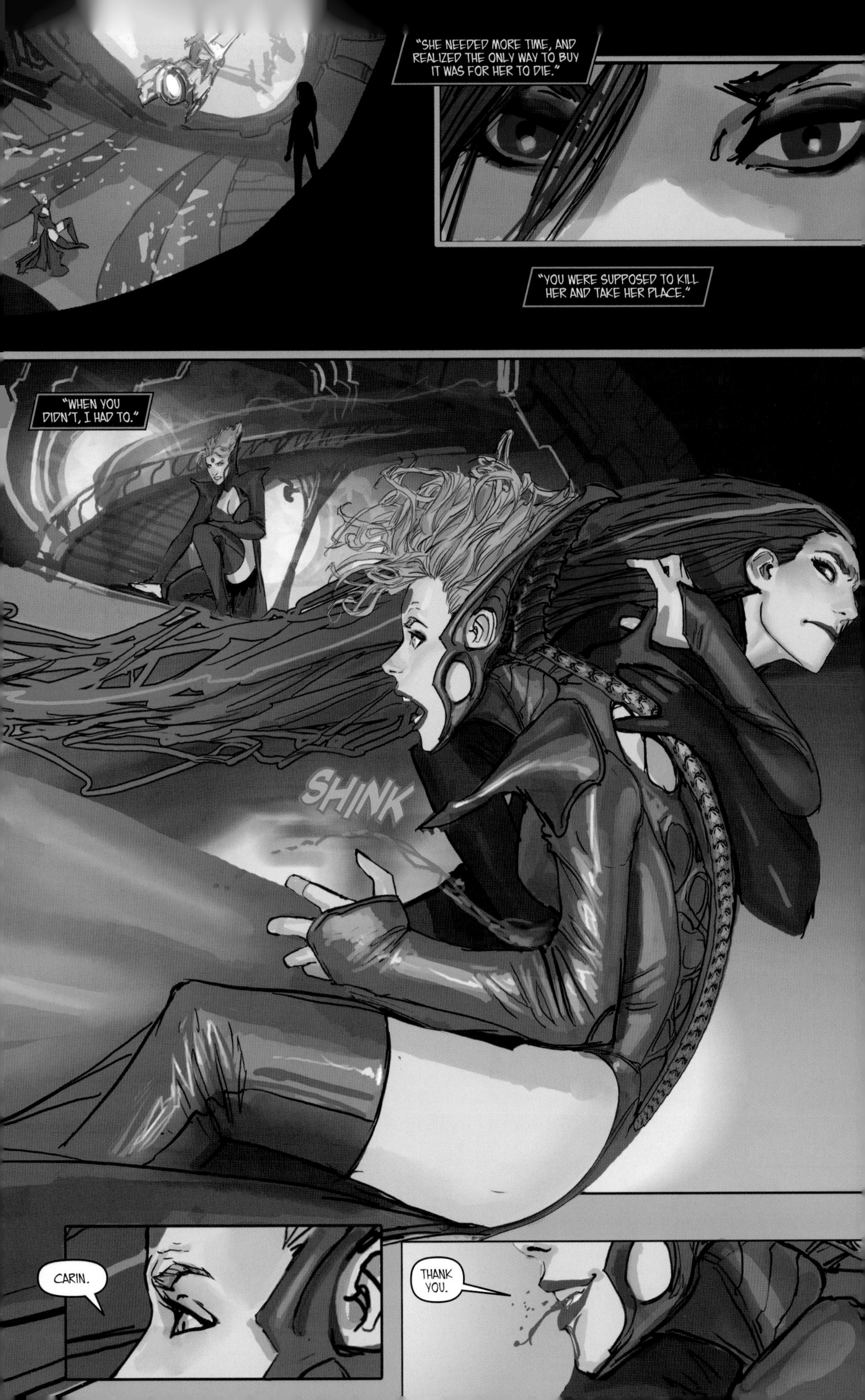
"SHE NEEDED MORE TIME, AND REALIZED THE ONLY WAY TO BUY IT WAS FOR HER TO DIE."
"YOU WERE SUPPOSED TO KILL HER AND TAKE HER PLACE."
"WHEN YOU DIDN'T, I HAD TO."
SHINK
CARIN.
THANK YOU.

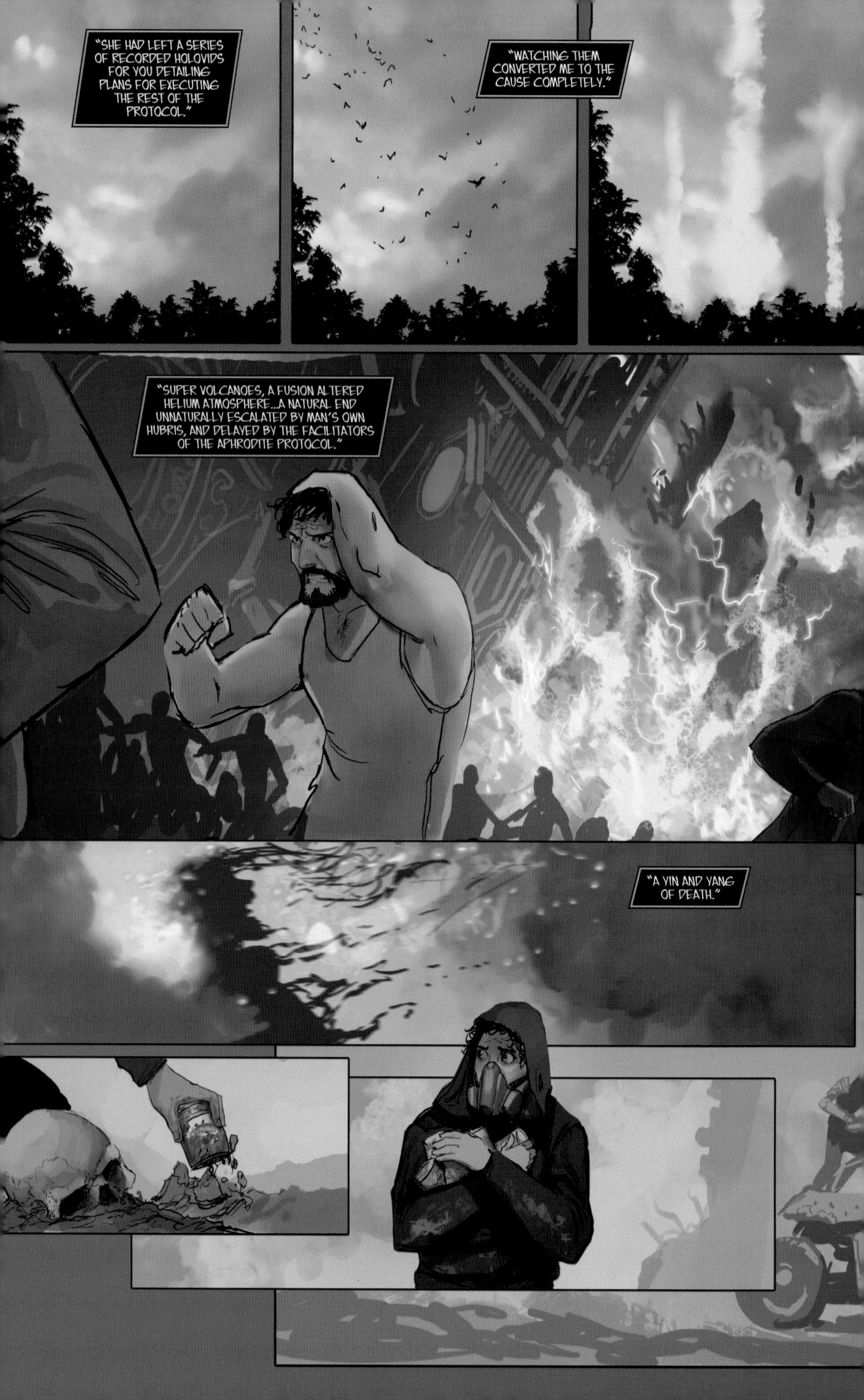
"SHE HAD LEFT A SERIES OF RECORDED HOLOVIDS FOR YOU DETAILING PLANS FOR EXECUTING THE REST OF THE PROTOCOL."
"WATCHING THEM CONVERTED ME TO THE CAUSE COMPLETELY."
"SUPER VOLCANOES, A FUSION ALTERED HELIUM ATMOSPHERE...A NATURAL END UNNATURALLY ESCALATED BY MAN'S OWN HUBRIS, AND DELAYED BY THE FACILITATORS OF THE APHRODITE PROTOCOL."
"A YIN AND YANG OF DEATH."

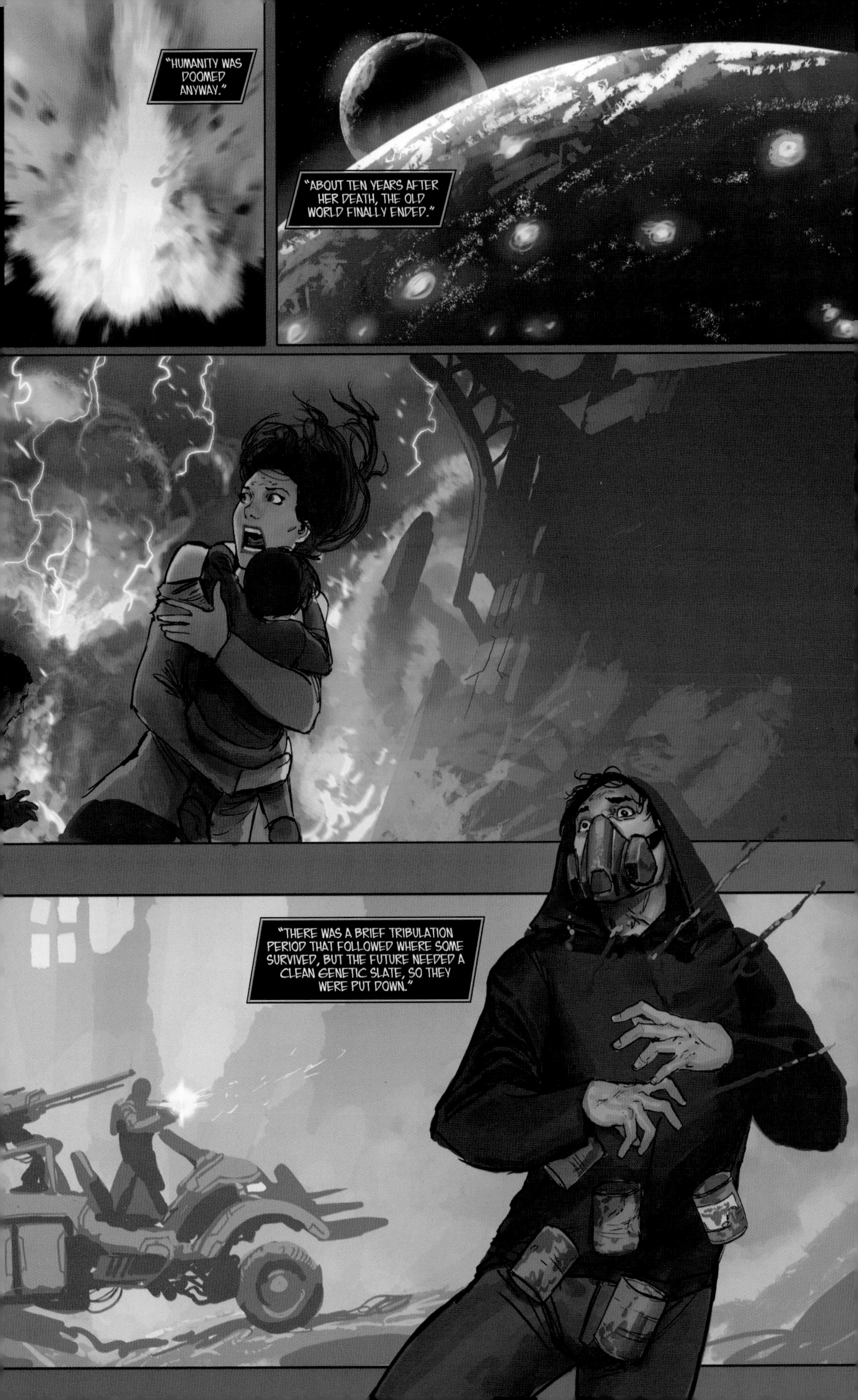
"HUMANITY WAS DOOMED ANYWAY."
"ABOUT TEN YEARS AFTER HER DEATH, THE OLD WORLD FINALLY ENDED."
"THERE WAS A BRIEF TRIBULATION PERIOD THAT FOLLOWED WHERE SOME SURVIVED, BUT THE FUTURE NEEDED A CLEAN GENETIC SLATE, SO THEY WERE PUT DOWN."

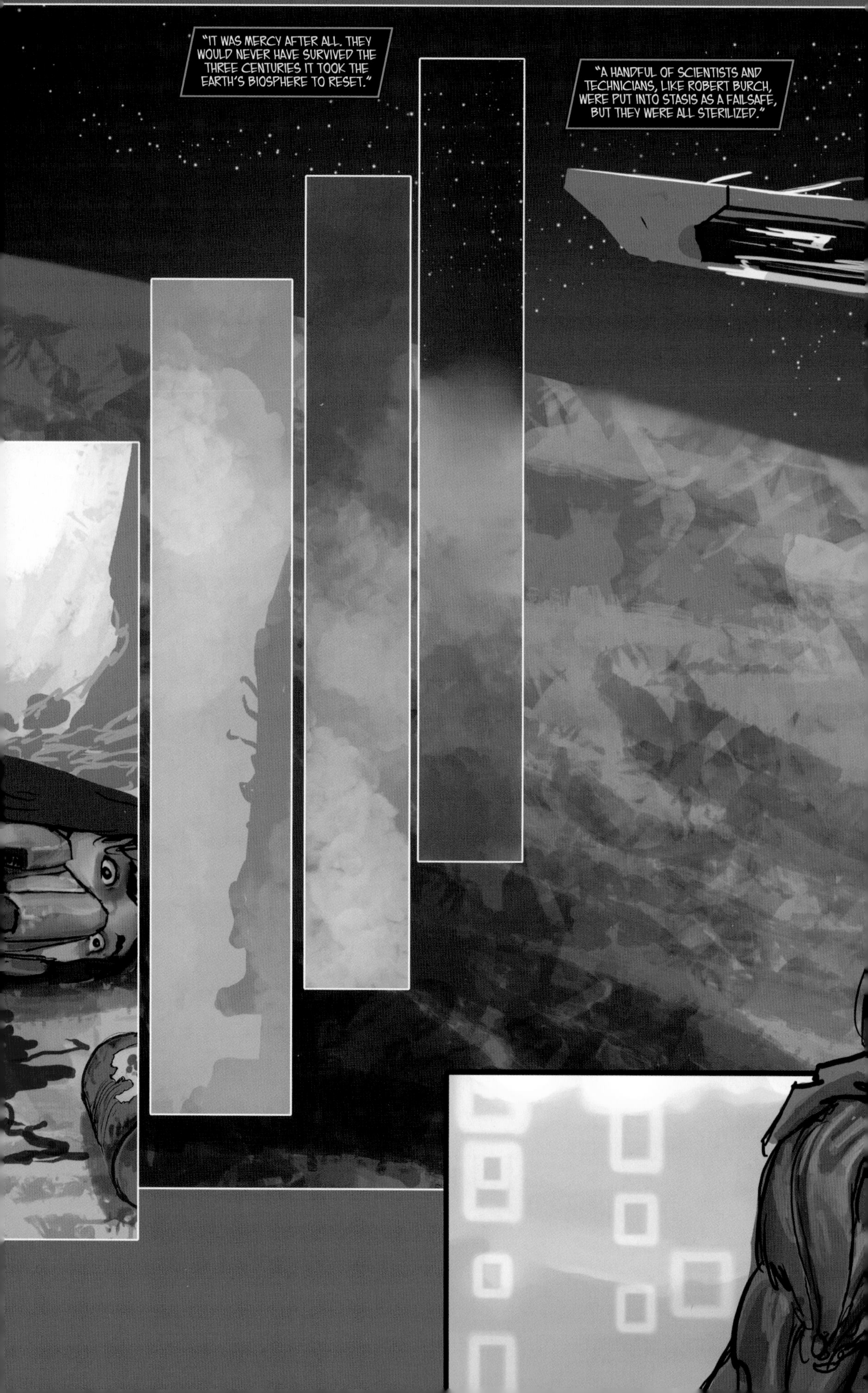
"IT WAS MERCY AFTER ALL. THEY WOULD NEVER HAVE SURVIVED THE THREE CENTURIES IT TOOK THE EARTH'S BIOSPHERE TO RESET."
"A HANDFUL OF SCIENTISTS AND TECHNICIANS, LIKE ROBERT BURCH, WERE PUT INTO STASIS AS A FAILSAFE, BUT THEY WERE ALL STERILIZED."

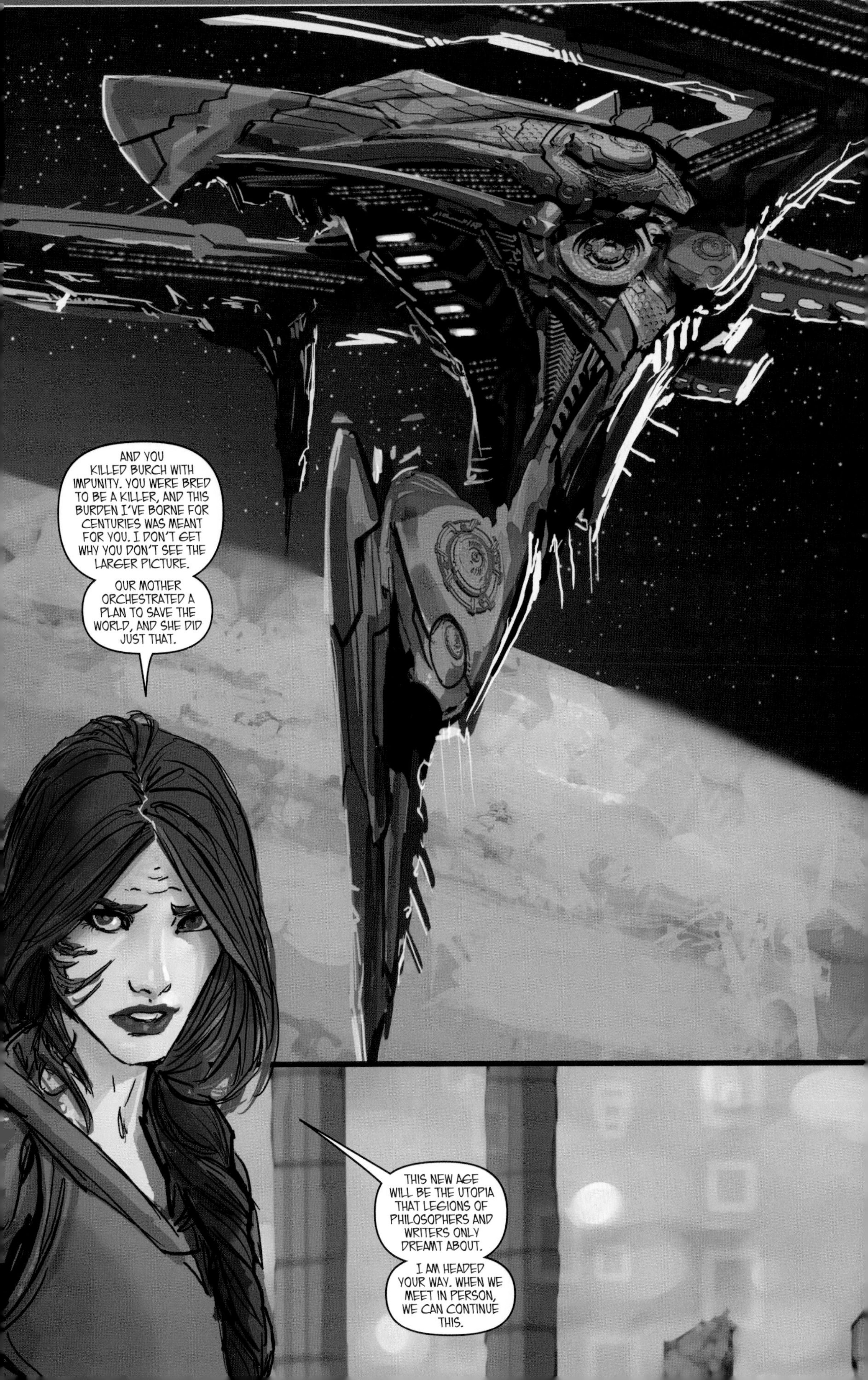
AND YOU KILLED BURCH WITH IMPUNITY. YOU WERE BRED TO BE A KILLER, AND THIS BURDEN I'VE BORNE FOR CENTURIES WAS MEANT FOR YOU. I DON'T GET WHY YOU DON'T SEE THE LARGER PICTURE.
OUR MOTHER ORCHESTRATED A PLAN TO SAVE THE WORLD, AND SHE DID JUST THAT.
THIS NEW AGE WILL BE THE UTOPIA THAT LEGIONS OF PHILOSOPHERS AND WRITERS ONLY DREAMT ABOUT.
I AM HEADED YOUR WAY. WHEN WE MEET IN PERSON, WE CAN CONTINUE THIS.

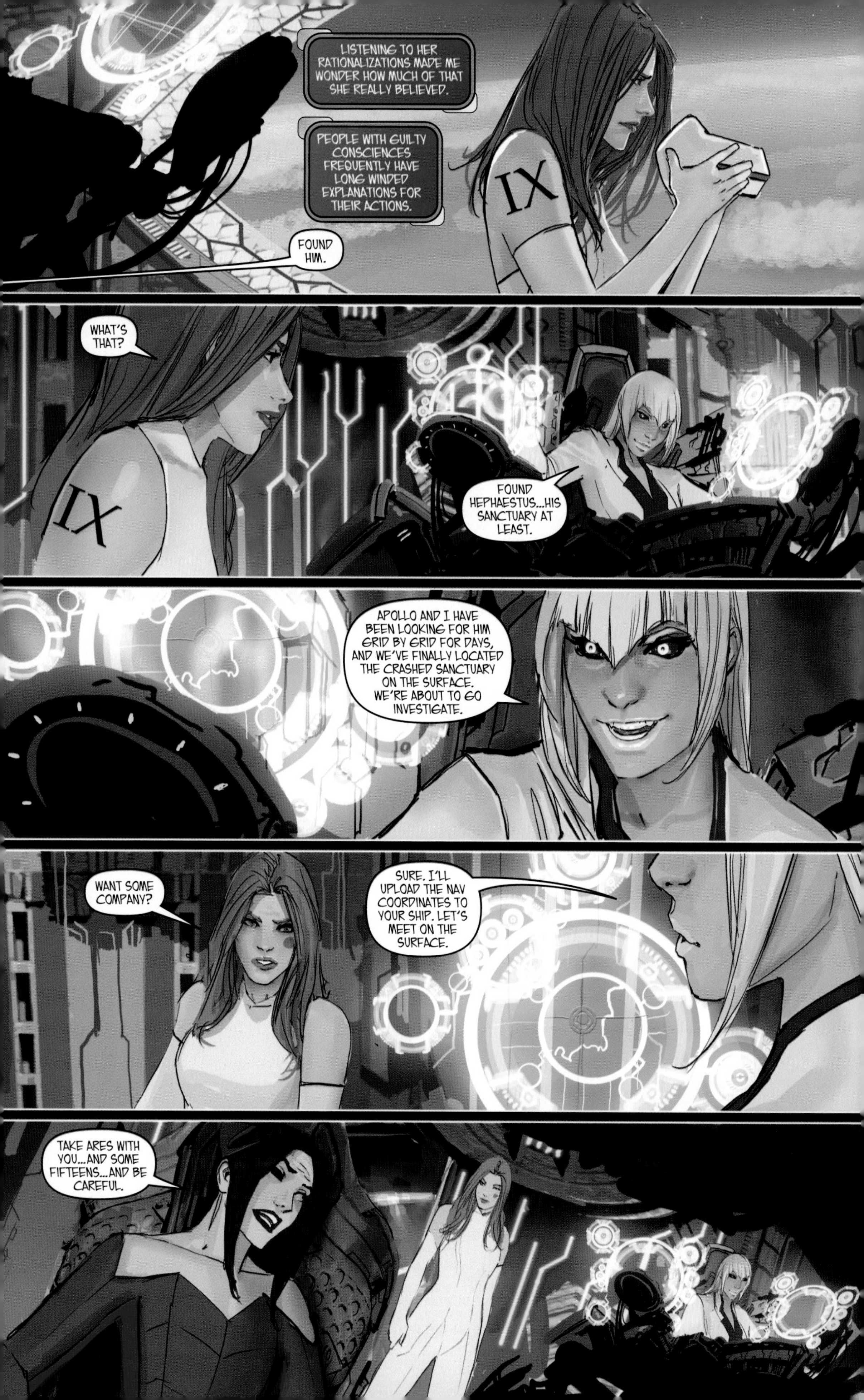
LISTENING TO HER RATIONALIZATIONS MADE ME WONDER HOW MUCH OF THAT SHE REALLY BELIEVED.
PEOPLE WITH GUILTY CONSCIENCES FREQUENTLY HAVE LONG WINDED EXPLANATIONS FOR THEIR ACTIONS.
FOUND HIM.
IX
WHAT'S THAT?
IX
FOUND HEPHAESTUS...HIS SANCTUARY AT LEAST.
APOLLO AND I HAVE BEEN LOOKING FOR HIM GRID BY GRID FOR DAYS, AND WE'VE FINALLY LOCATED THE CRASHED SANCTUARY ON THE SURFACE. WE'RE ABOUT TO GO INVESTIGATE.
WANT SOME COMPANY?
SURE. I'LL UPLOAD THE NAV COORDINATES TO YOUR SHIP. LET'S MEET ON THE SURFACE.
TAKE ARES WITH YOU...AND SOME FIFTEENS...AND BE CAREFUL.

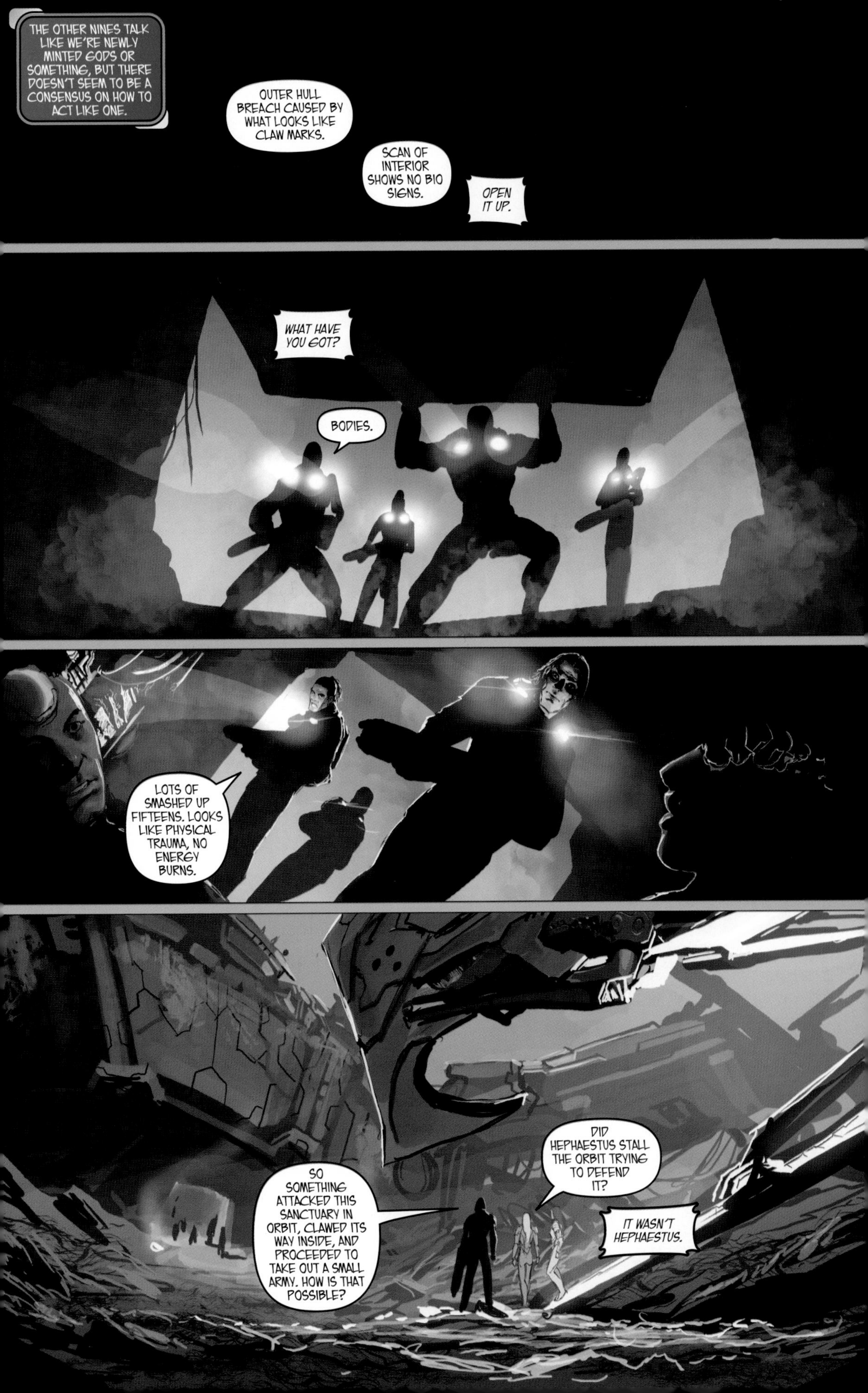
THE OTHER NINES TALK LIKE WE'RE NEWLY MINTED GODS OR SOMETHING, BUT THERE DOESN'T SEEM TO BE A CONSENSUS ON HOW TO ACT LIKE ONE.
OUTER HULL BREACH CAUSED BY WHAT LOOKS LIKE CLAW MARKS.
SCAN OF INTERIOR SHOWS NO BIO SIGNS.
OPEN IT UP.
WHAT HAVE YOU GOT?
BODIES.
LOTS OF SMASHED UP FIFTEENS. LOOKS LIKE PHYSICAL TRAUMA, NO ENERGY BURNS.
SO SOMETHING ATTACKED THIS SANCTUARY IN ORBIT, CLAWED ITS WAY INSIDE, AND PROCEEDED TO TAKE OUT A SMALL ARMY. HOW IS THAT POSSIBLE?
DID HEPHAESTUS STALL THE ORBIT TRYING TO DEFEND IT?
IT WASN'T HEPHAESTUS.

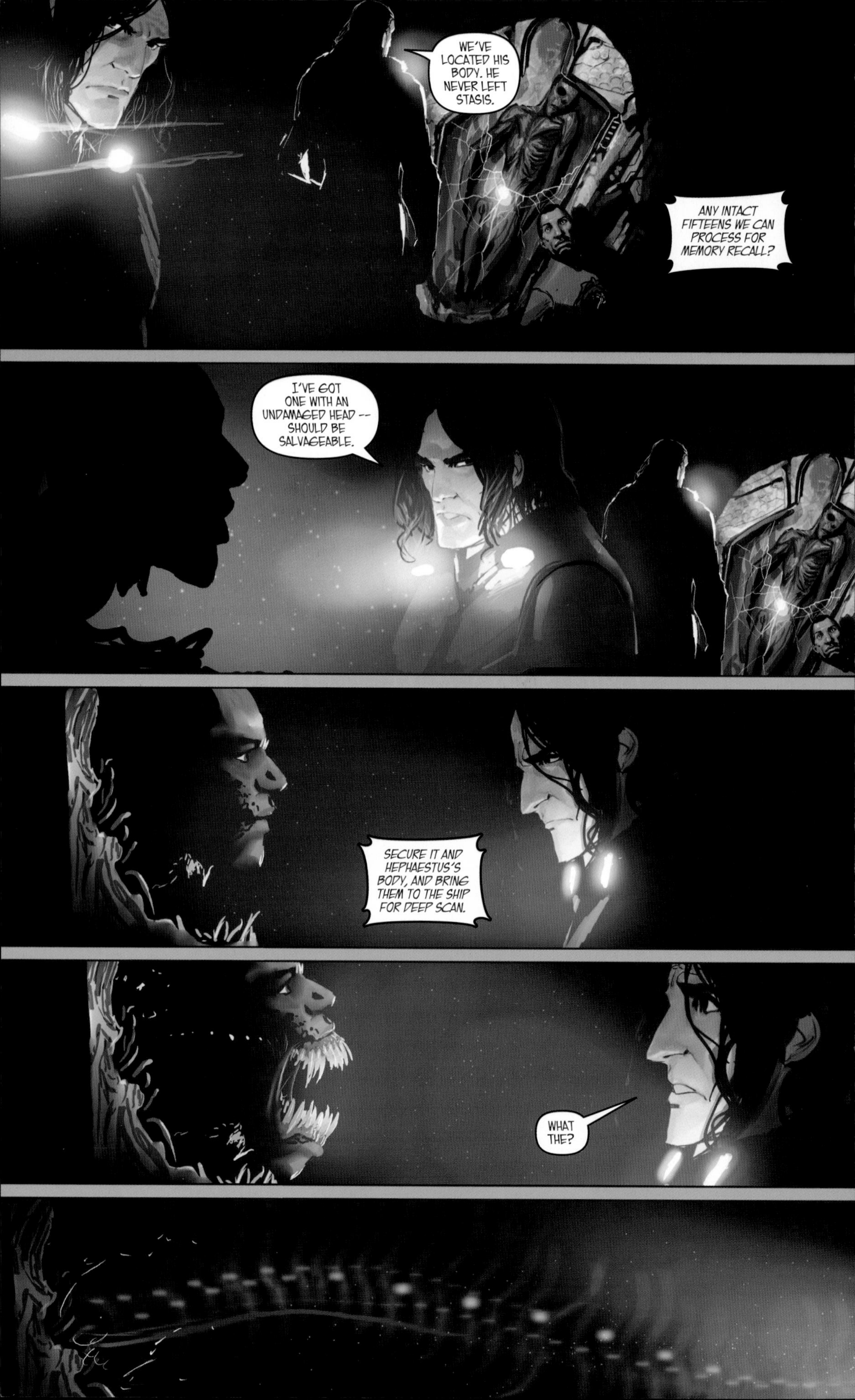
WE'VE LOCATED HIS BODY. HE NEVER LEFT STASIS.
ANY INTACT FIFTEENS WE CAN PROCESS FOR MEMORY RECALL?
I'VE GOT ONE WITH AN UNDAMAGED HEAD -- SHOULD BE SALVAGEABLE.
SECURE IT AND HEPHAESTUS'S BODY, AND BRING THEM TO THE SHIP FOR DEEP SCAN.
WHAT THE?

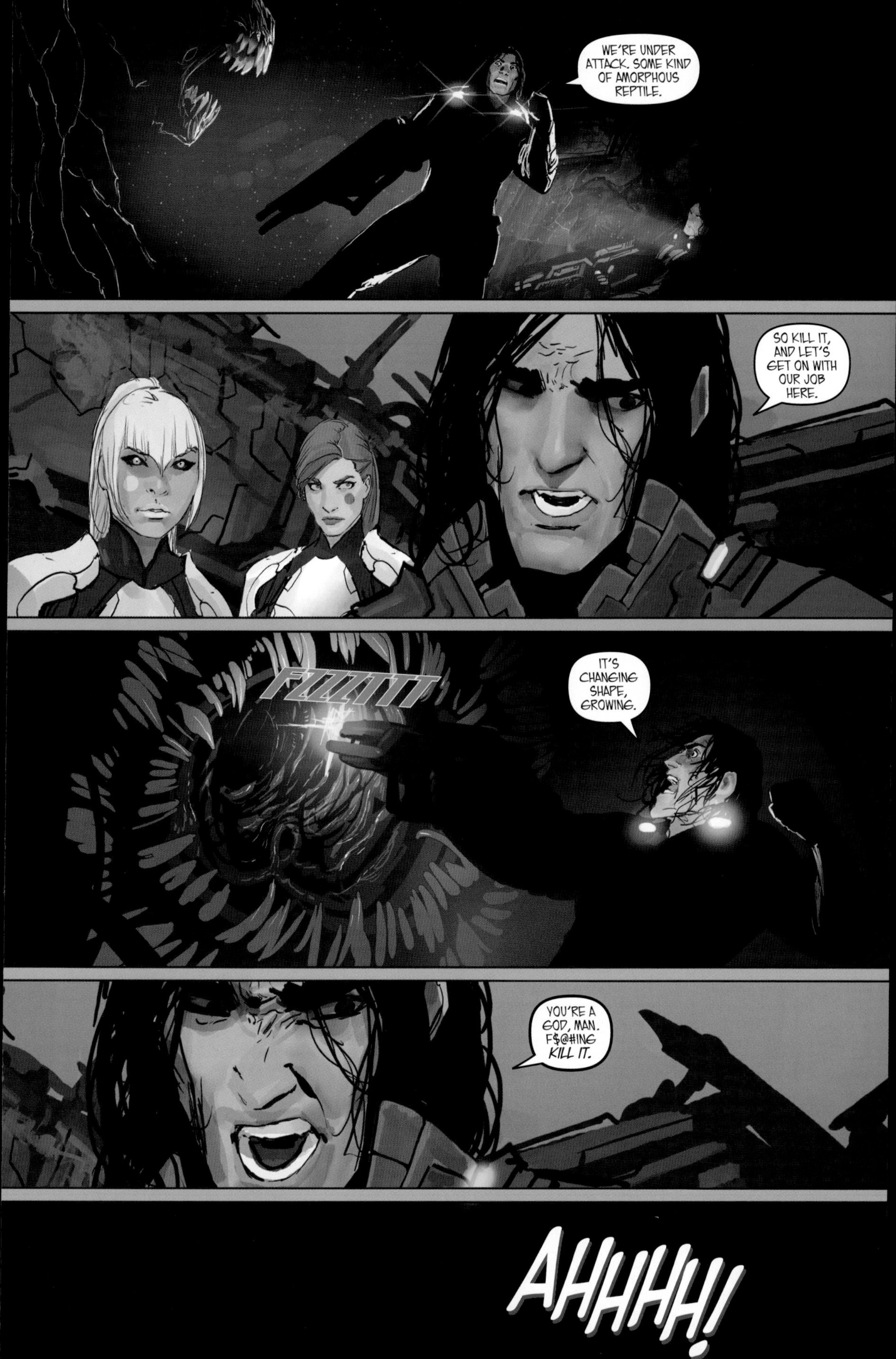
WE'RE UNDER ATTACK. SOME KIND OF AMORPHOUS REPTILE.
SO KILL IT, AND LET'S GET ON WITH OUR JOB HERE.
FZZZTTT
IT'S CHANGING SHAPE, GROWING.
YOU'RE A GOD, MAN. F$@#ING KILL IT.
AHHHH!

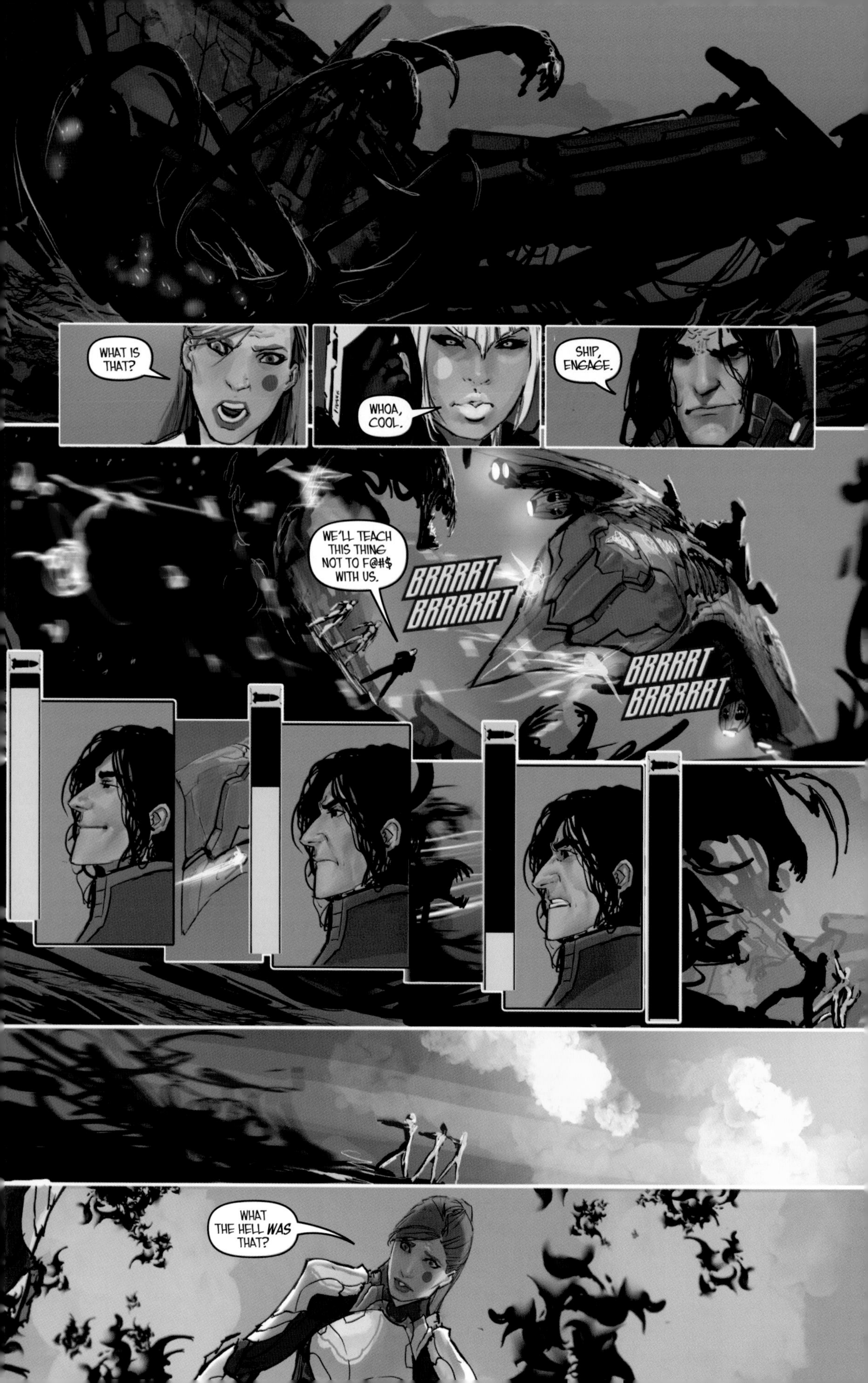
WHAT IS THAT?
WHOA, COOL.
SHIP, ENGAGE.
WE'LL TEACH THIS THING NOT TO F@#$ WITH US.
BRRRRT BRRRRRT
BRRRRT BRRRRRT
WHAT THE HELL WAS THAT?

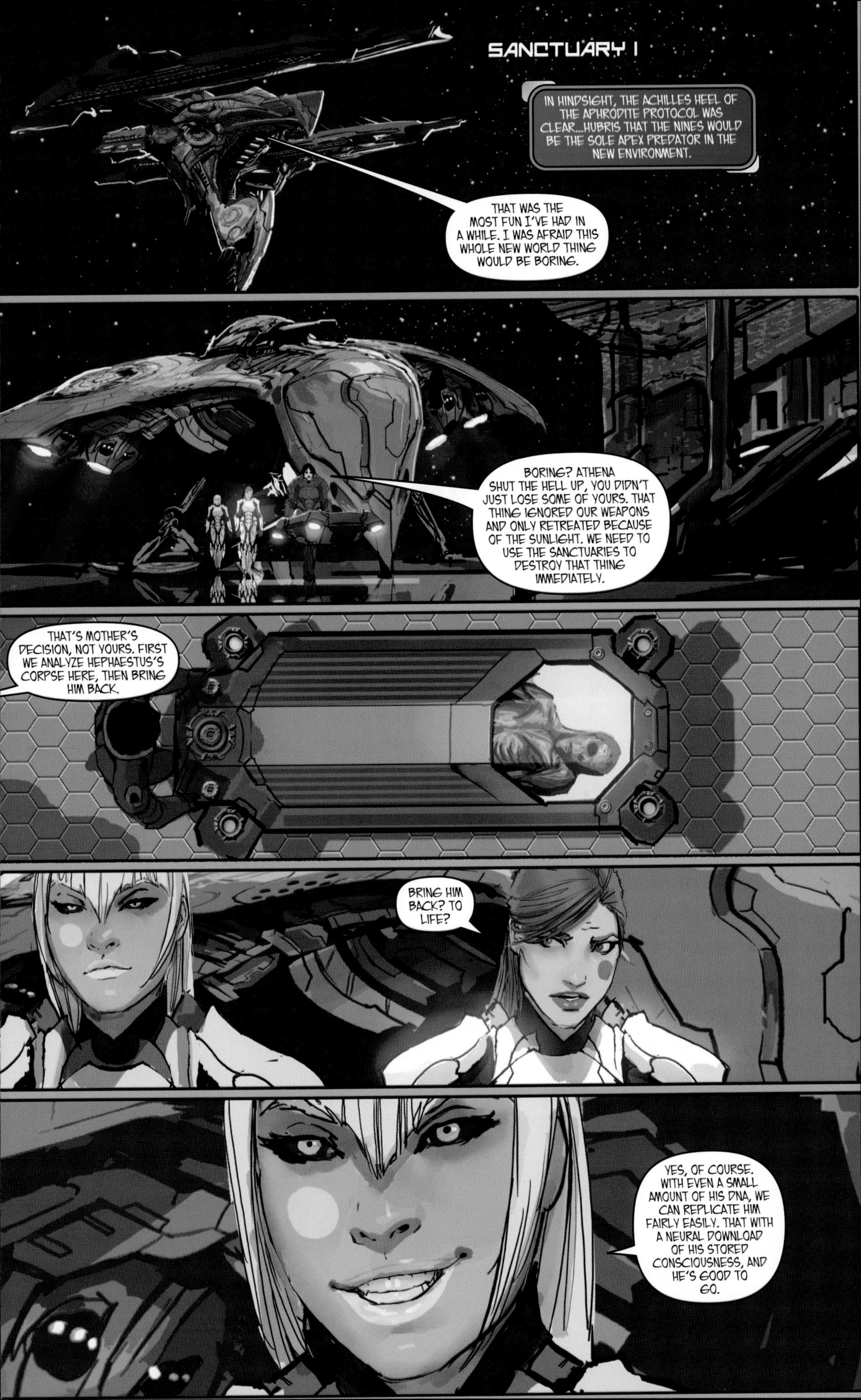
SANCTUARY I
IN HINDSIGHT, THE ACHILLES HEEL OF THE APHRODITE PROTOCOL WAS CLEAR...HUBRIS THAT THE NINES WOULD BE THE SOLE APEX PREDATOR IN THE NEW ENVIRONMENT.
THAT WAS THE MOST FUN I'VE HAD IN A WHILE. I WAS AFRAID THIS WHOLE NEW WORLD THING WOULD BE BORING.
BORING? ATHENA SHUT THE HELL UP, YOU DIDN'T JUST LOSE SOME OF YOURS. THAT THING IGNORED OUR WEAPONS AND ONLY RETREATED BECAUSE OF THE SUNLIGHT. WE NEED TO USE THE SANCTUARIES TO DESTROY THAT THING IMMEDIATELY.
THAT'S MOTHER'S DECISION, NOT YOURS. FIRST WE ANALYZE HEPHAESTUS'S CORPSE HERE, THEN BRING HIM BACK.
BRING HIM BACK? TO LIFE?
YES, OF COURSE. WITH EVEN A SMALL AMOUNT OF HIS DNA, WE CAN REPLICATE HIM FAIRLY EASILY. THAT WITH A NEURAL DOWNLOAD OF HIS STORED CONSCIOUSNESS, AND HE'S GOOD TO GO.

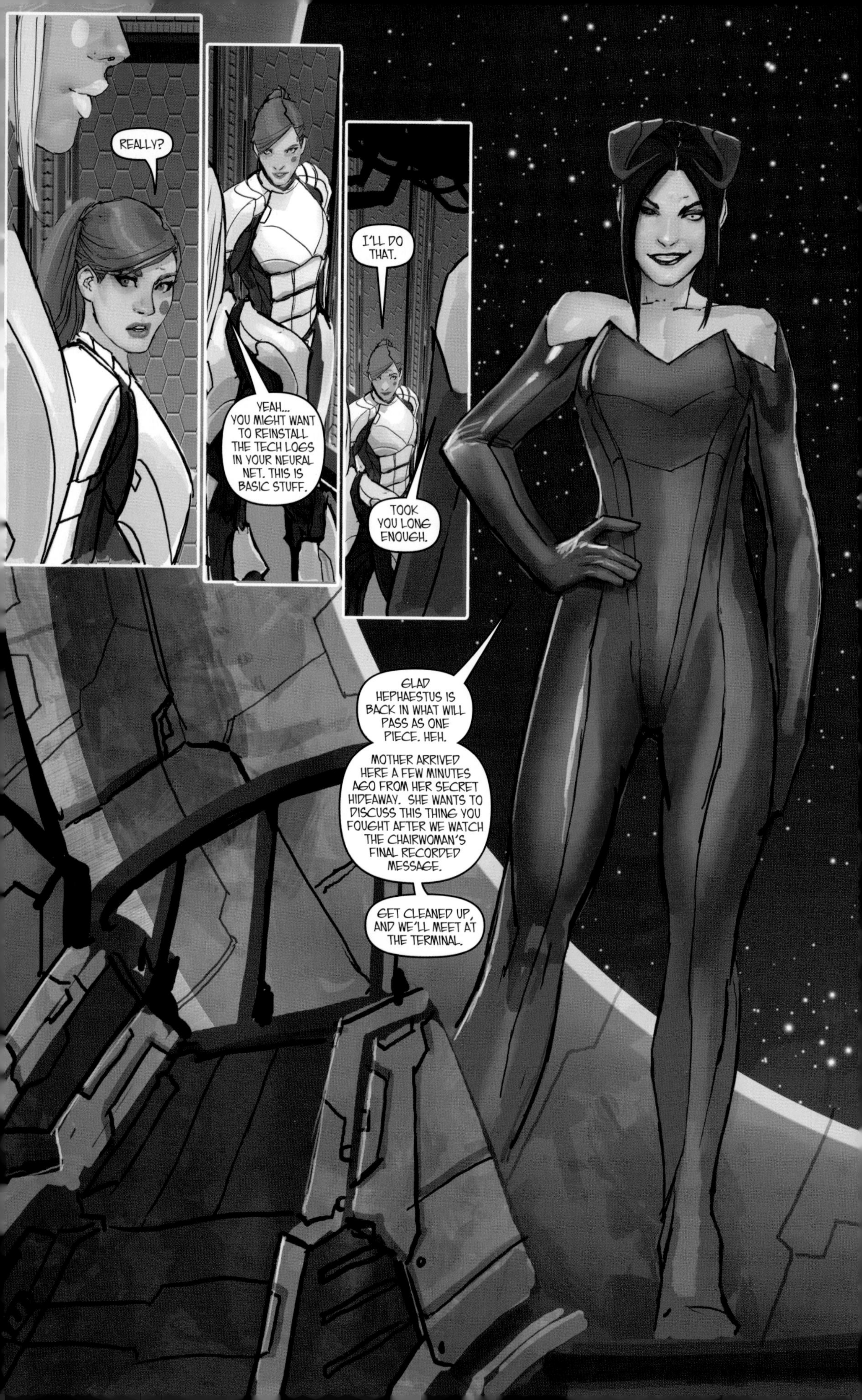
REALLY?
YEAH... YOU MIGHT WANT TO REINSTALL THE TECH LOGS IN YOUR NEURAL NET. THIS IS BASIC STUFF.
I'LL DO THAT.
TOOK YOU LONG ENOUGH.
GLAD HEPHAESTUS IS BACK IN WHAT WILL PASS AS ONE PIECE. HEH.
MOTHER ARRIVED HERE A FEW MINUTES AGO FROM HER SECRET HIDEAWAY. SHE WANTS TO DISCUSS THIS THING YOU FOUGHT AFTER WE WATCH THE CHAIRWOMAN'S FINAL RECORDED MESSAGE.
GET CLEANED UP, AND WE'LL MEET AT THE TERMINAL.

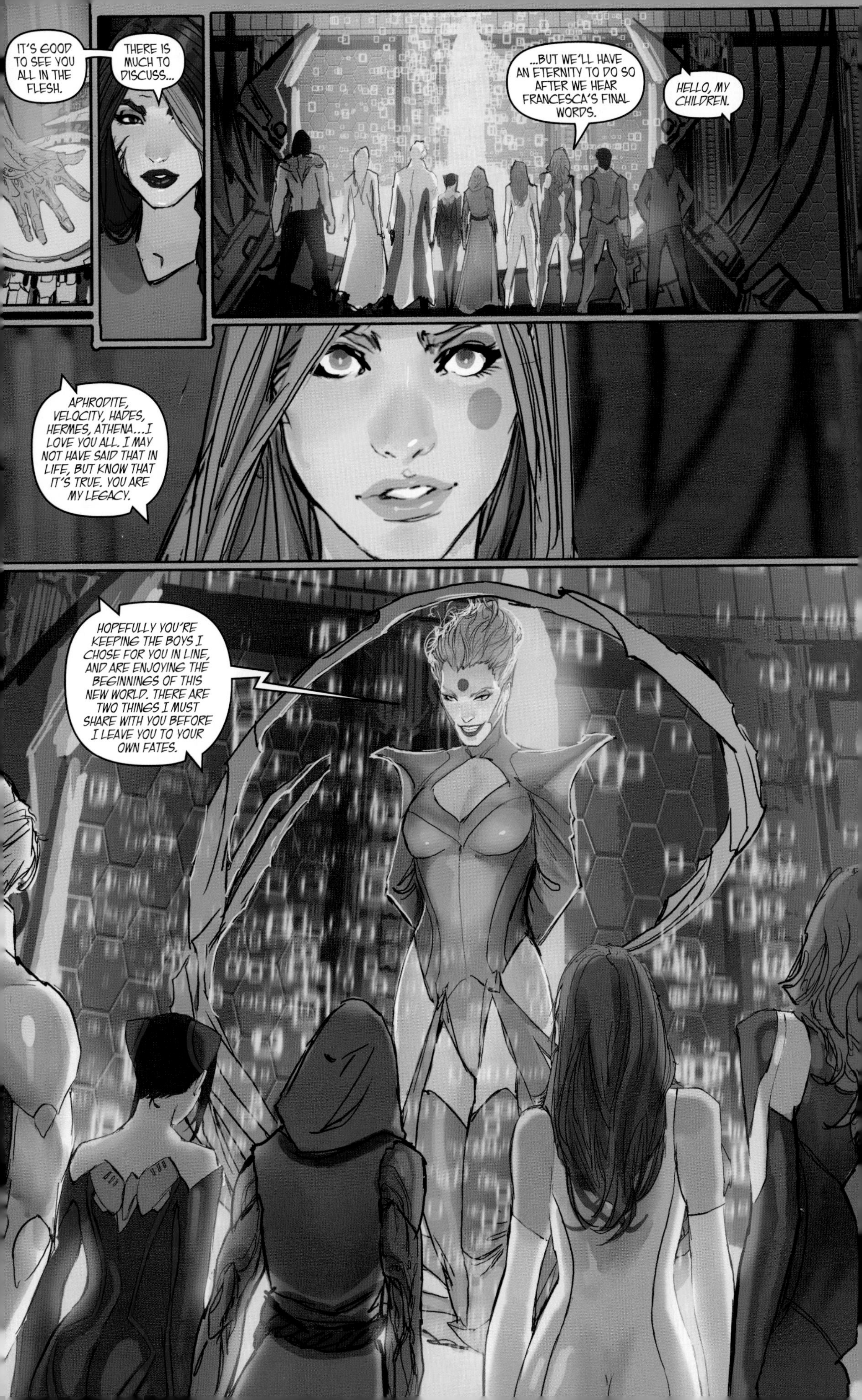
IT'S GOOD TO SEE YOU ALL IN THE FLESH.
THERE IS MUCH TO DISCUSS...
...BUT WE'LL HAVE AN ETERNITY TO DO SO AFTER WE HEAR FRANCESCA'S FINAL WORDS.
HELLO, MY CHILDREN.
APHRODITE, VELOCITY, HADES, HERMES, ATHENA...I LOVE YOU ALL. I MAY NOT HAVE SAID THAT IN LIFE, BUT KNOW THAT IT'S TRUE. YOU ARE MY LEGACY.
HOPEFULLY YOU'RE KEEPING THE BOYS I CHOSE FOR YOU IN LINE, AND ARE ENJOYING THE BEGINNINGS OF THIS NEW WORLD. THERE ARE TWO THINGS I MUST SHARE WITH YOU BEFORE I LEAVE YOU TO YOUR OWN FATES.

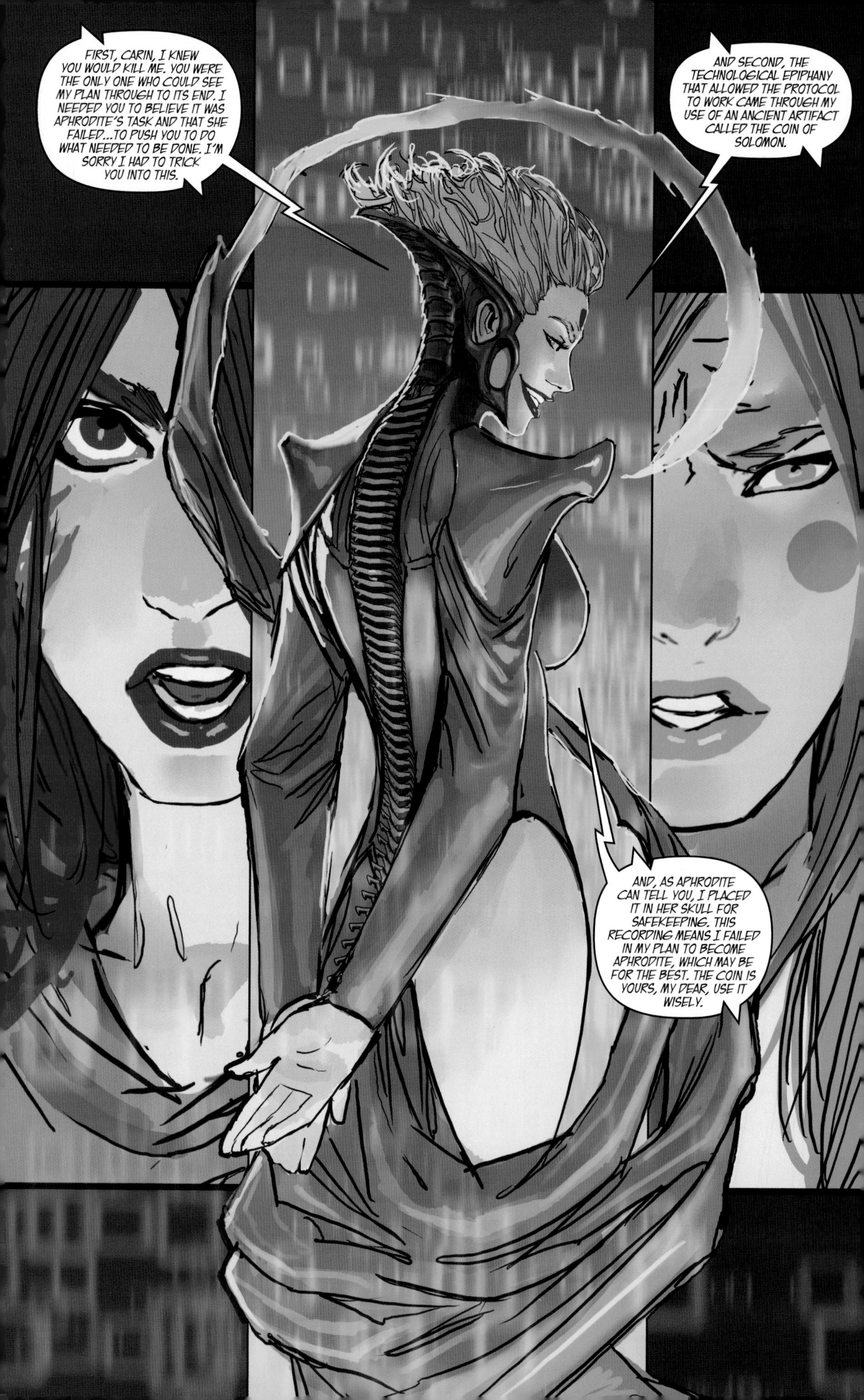
FIRST, CARIN, I KNEW YOU WOULD KILL ME. YOU WERE THE ONLY ONE WHO COULD SEE MY PLAN THROUGH TO ITS END. I NEEDED YOU TO BELIEVE IT WAS APHRODITE'S TASK AND THAT SHE FAILED...TO PUSH YOU TO DO WHAT NEEDED TO BE DONE. I'M SORRY I HAD TO TRICK YOU INTO THIS.
AND SECOND, THE TECHNOLOGICAL EPIPHANY THAT ALLOWED THE PROTOCOL TO WORK CAME THROUGH MY USE OF AN ANCIENT ARTIFACT CALLED THE COIN OF SOLOMON.
AND, AS APHRODITE CAN TELL YOU, I PLACED IT IN HER SKULL FOR SAFEKEEPING. THIS RECORDING MEANS I FAILED IN MY PLAN TO BECOME APHRODITE, WHICH MAY BE FOR THE BEST. THE COIN IS YOURS, MY DEAR, USE IT WISELY.

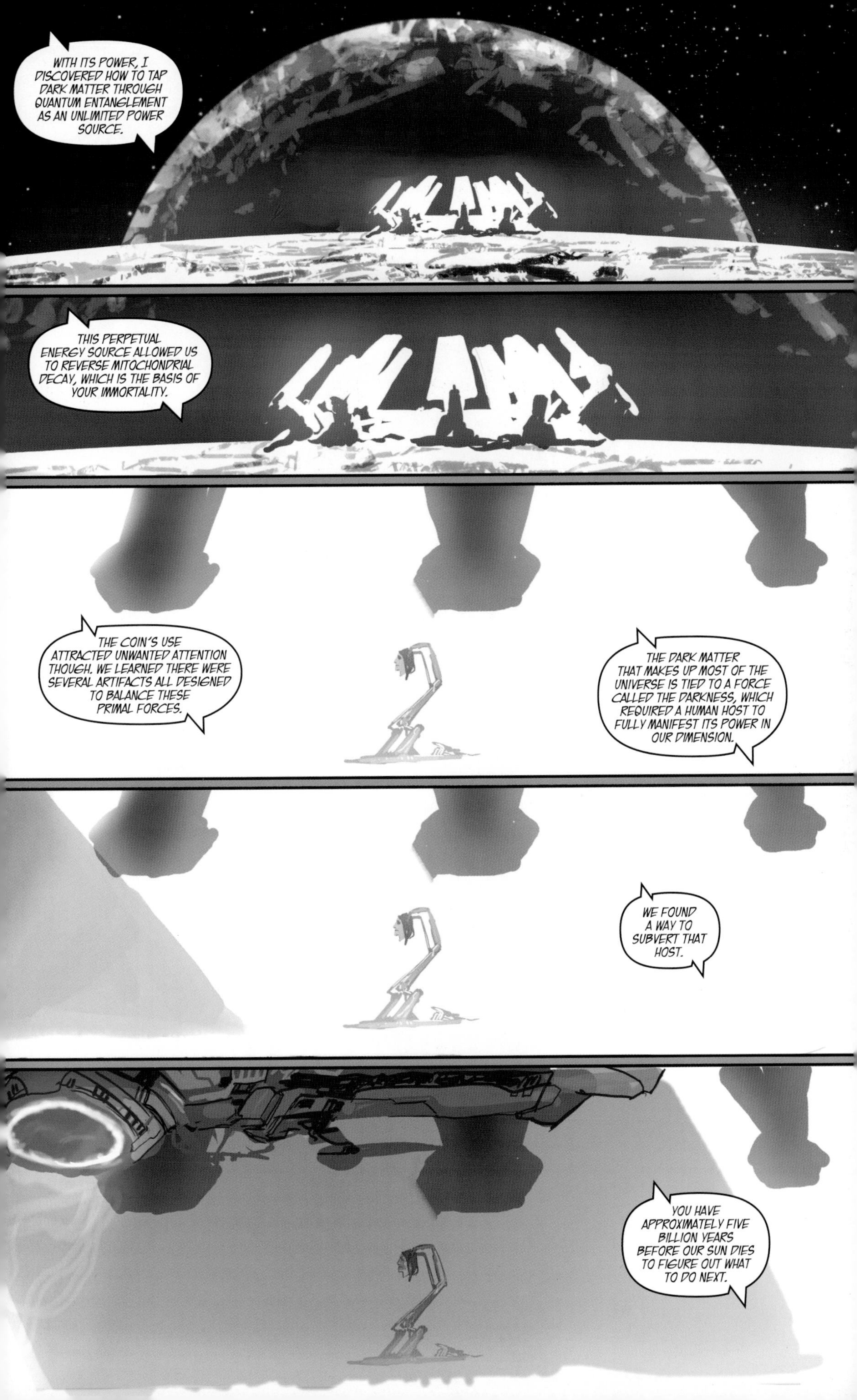
WITH ITS POWER, I DISCOVERED HOW TO TAP DARK MATTER THROUGH QUANTUM ENTANGLEMENT AS AN UNLIMITED POWER SOURCE.
THIS PERPETUAL ENERGY SOURCE ALLOWED US TO REVERSE MITOCHONDRIAL DECAY, WHICH IS THE BASIS OF YOUR IMMORTALITY.
THE COIN'S USE ATTRACTED UNWANTED ATTENTION THOUGH. WE LEARNED THERE WERE SEVERAL ARTIFACTS ALL DESIGNED TO BALANCE THESE PRIMAL FORCES.
THE DARK MATTER THAT MAKES UP MOST OF THE UNIVERSE IS TIED TO A FORCE CALLED THE DARKNESS, WHICH REQUIRED A HUMAN HOST TO FULLY MANIFEST ITS POWER IN OUR DIMENSION.
WE FOUND A WAY TO SUBVERT THAT HOST.
YOU HAVE APPROXIMATELY FIVE BILLION YEARS BEFORE OUR SUN DIES TO FIGURE OUT WHAT TO DO NEXT.

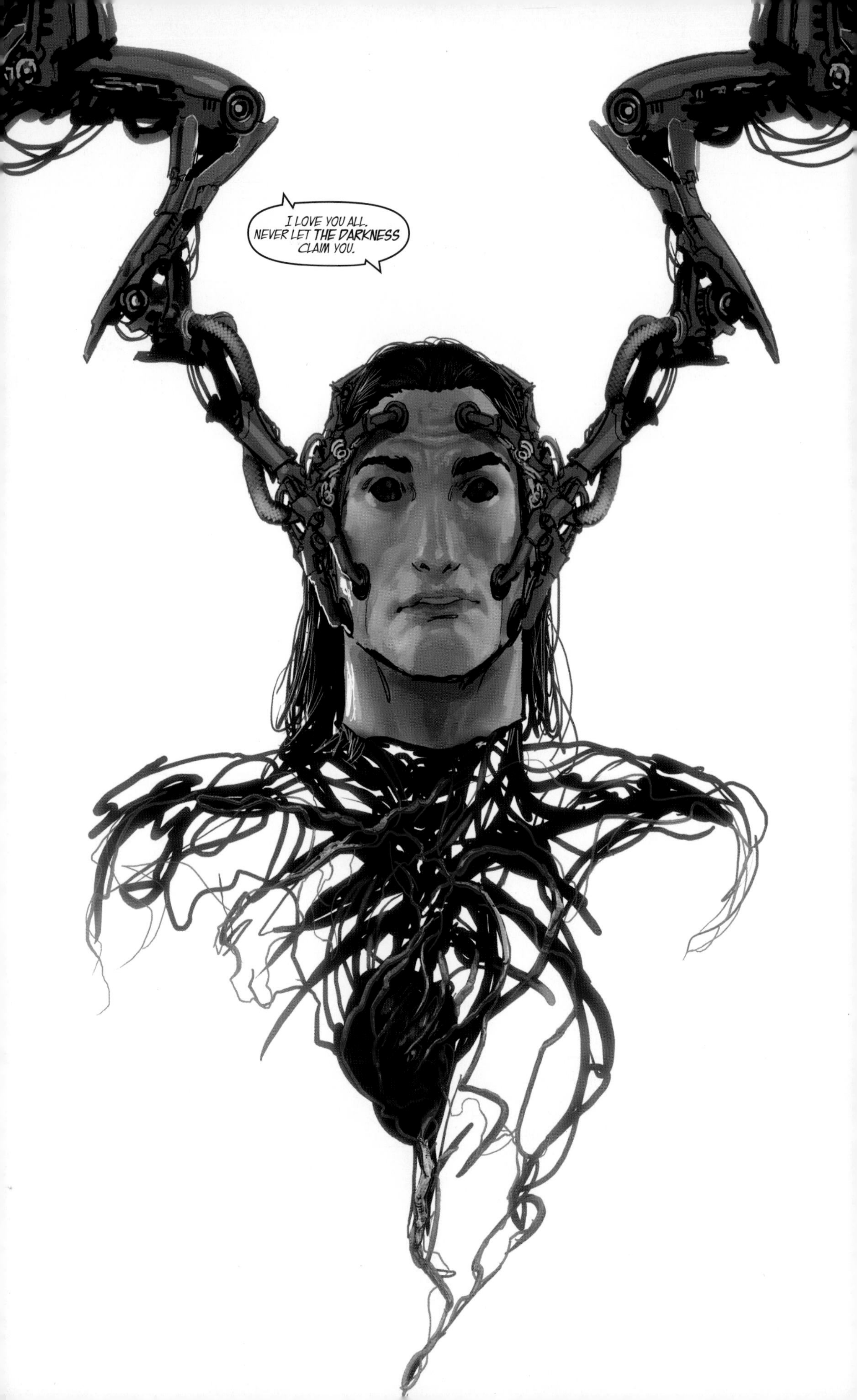
I LOVE YOU ALL. NEVER LET THE DARKNESS CLAIM YOU.

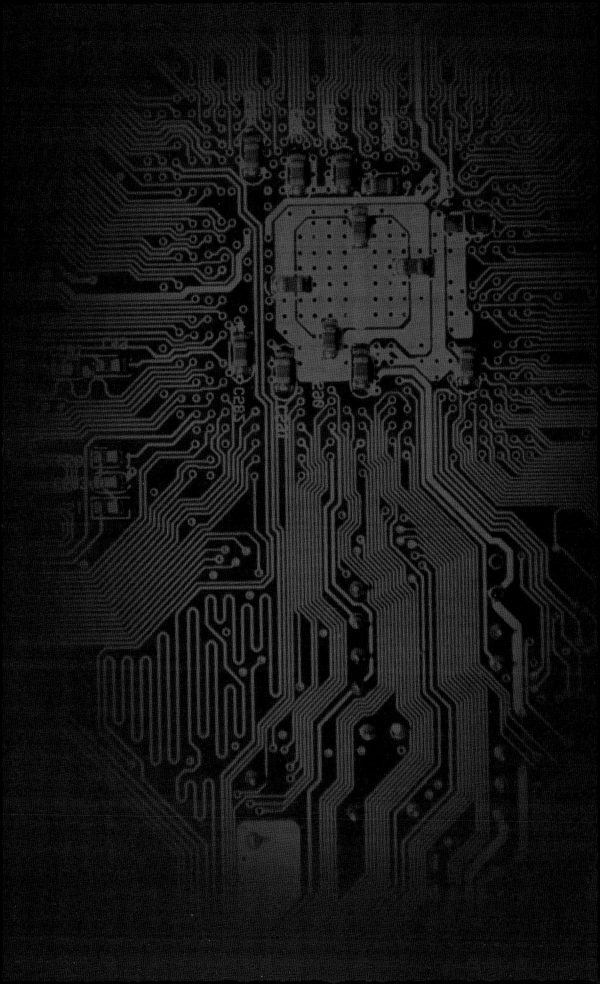

HIDDEN FILES

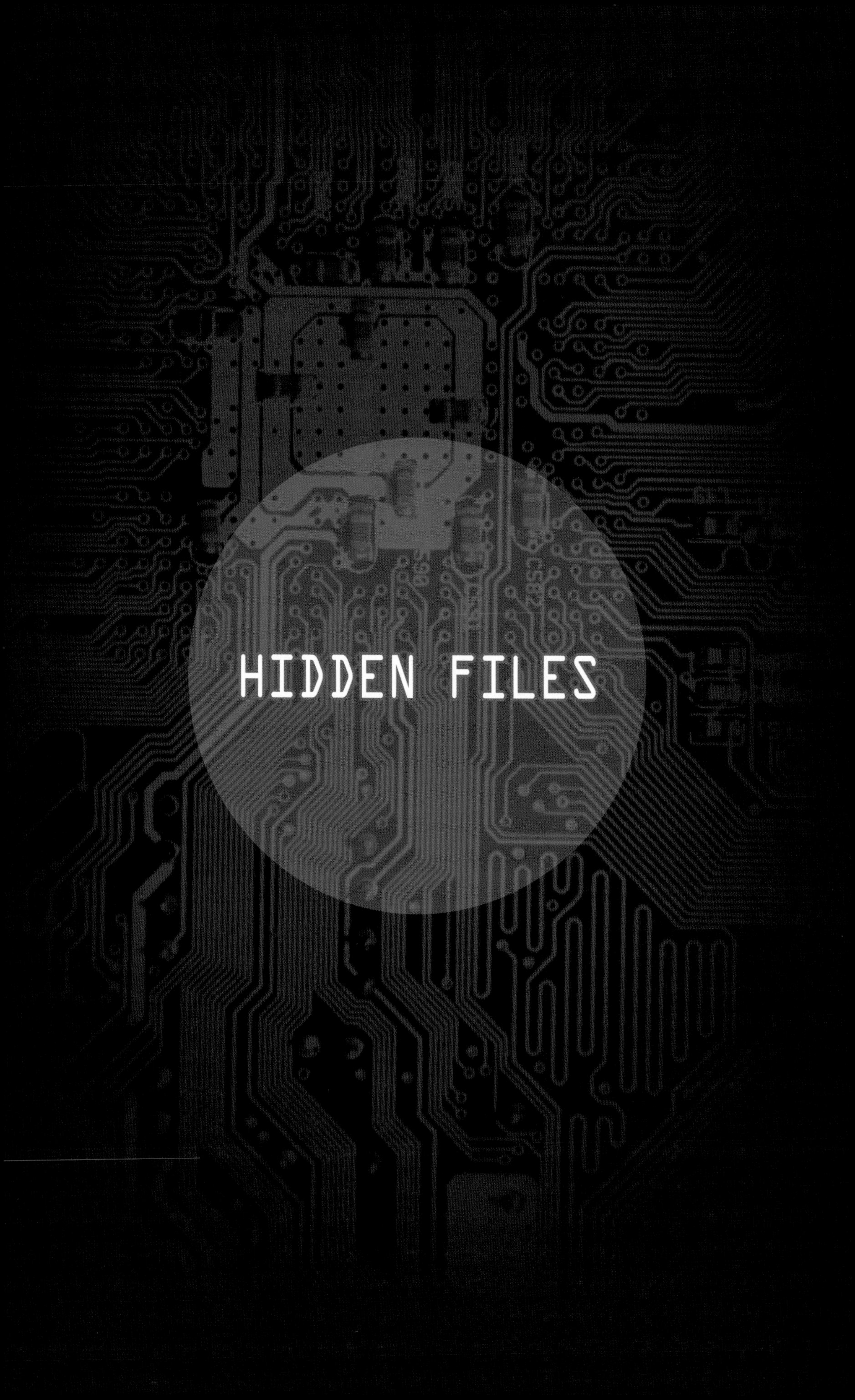

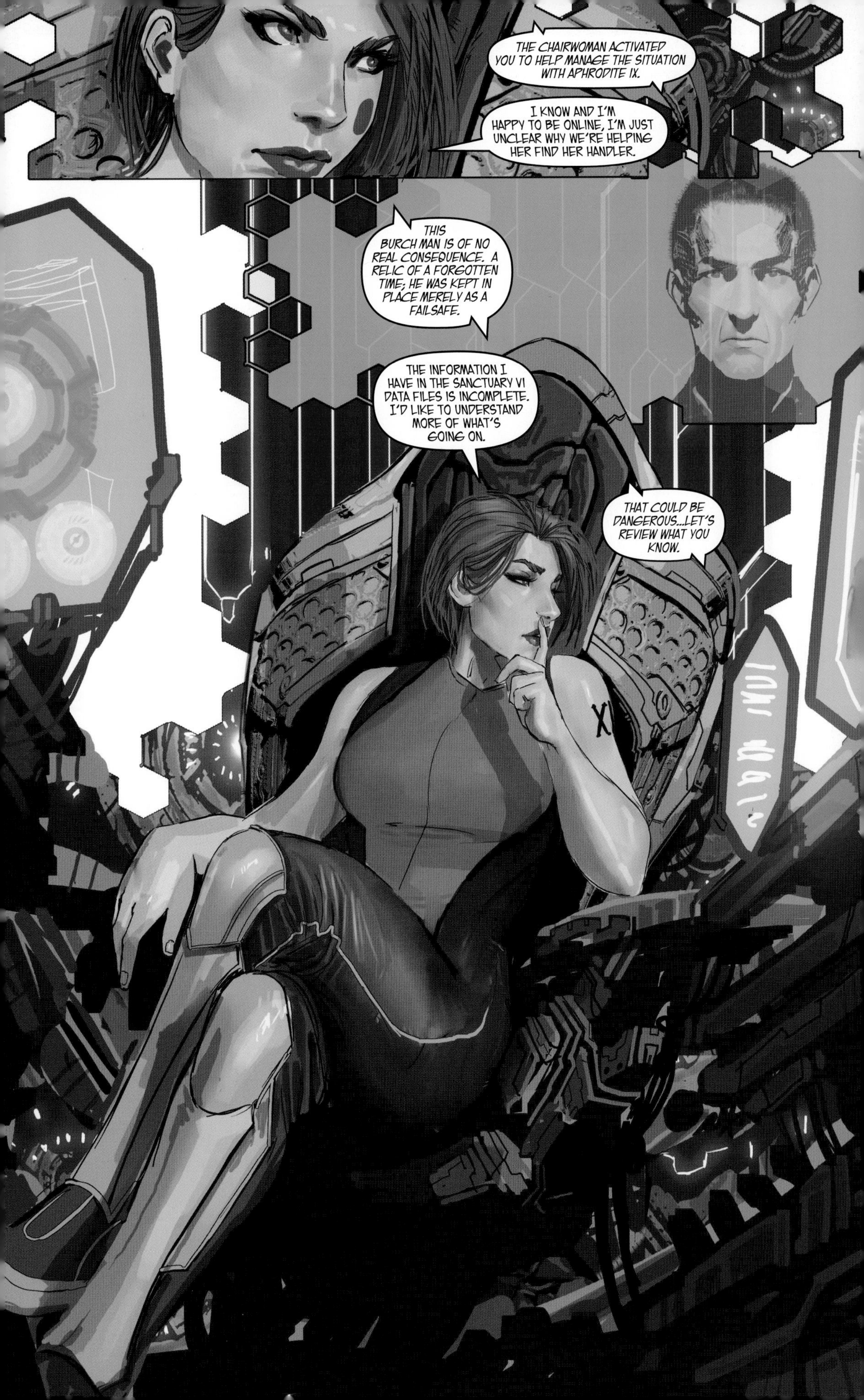
THE CHAIRWOMAN ACTIVATED YOU TO HELP MANAGE THE SITUATION WITH APHRODITE IX.
I KNOW AND I'M HAPPY TO BE ONLINE, I'M JUST UNCLEAR WHY WE'RE HELPING HER FIND HER HANDLER.
THIS BURCH MAN IS OF NO REAL CONSEQUENCE. A RELIC OF A FORGOTTEN TIME; HE WAS KEPT IN PLACE MERELY AS A FAILSAFE.
THE INFORMATION I HAVE IN THE SANCTUARY VI DATA FILES IS INCOMPLETE. I'D LIKE TO UNDERSTAND MORE OF WHAT'S GOING ON.
THAT COULD BE DANGEROUS...LET'S REVIEW WHAT YOU KNOW.

THE TIMELINE IS OF PARAMOUNT IMPORTANCE. STRICT ADHERENCE IS NECESSARY TO AVOID UNWANTED DERIVATION.

1971   FIRST OUTLINE OF
            PROTOCOL DRAFTED

1980   PHASE 1 INITIATED
            APHRODITE I

1992   APHRODITE II

1998   APHRODITE III
            GENERATION PROTOTYPES
            ENGINEERED FOR ALTERNATE
            DESIGNATIONS

2007   APHRODITE IV
            FIRST OF THE MASS PRODUCED
            PURE ANDROID LINE.
            PROTOTYPE CARRIED THE
            COIN OF SOLOMON IMBEDDED
            IN HER CHEST CAVITY.

2011   APHRODITE V
            FIRST SUCCESSFUL
            BIOSYNTHETIC HYBRID
            ORGANISM (NEW SPECIES).
            SHE SERVED AS BODYGUARD
            TO CARIN TAYLOR/VELOCITY
            (ORIGINALLY SERIES IV)
            THE DAUGHTER TO
            CHAIRWOMAN FRANCESCA
            TAYLOR.

2014   PHASE 2
            INITIATED

2078   PHASE 3 INITIATED
            APHRODITE IX LIVE NATURAL BIRTH
            FIRST TECHNO-BIOLOGICAL
            SINGULARITY WITH TRI-HELIX
            DNA AND THREE ADDITIONAL
            ARTIFICIAL CHROMOSOME PAIRS

2560/458 ND   PHASE 7 INITIATED
SINGULARITY ACHIEVED
WITH CYBORGS'
SECOND UPRISING

2438/336 ND   PHASE 6 INITIATED
EXPECTED MUTATION OF
CYBRIDS FROM THE GEN
RELIGION INTRODUCED TO
THE GEN
WAR BREAKS OUT BETWEEN
CITIES – FIRST UPRISING

2376/274 ND   PHASE 5 INITIATED
GENESIS CITY AND SPEROS CITY
ESTABLISHED

2102 AD/1 ND   PHASE 4 INITIATED WITH
EXTINCTION LEVEL EVENT
NEW DIASPORA (ND) TIMELINE
ESTABLISHED

2797/695 ND   PHASE 8 INITIATED
PEACEFUL DIPLOMACY
BETWEEN GEN AND
CYBORGS INTENTIONALLY
THWARTED
THIRD UPRISING

2801/699 ND   APHRODITE IX AWAKENS
IN PRESENT
FOURTH UPRISING
THE PRESENT

**2802/700 ND   PLANNED PHASE 9
INITIATION
EITHER GEN OR
CYBORGS ELIMINATED,
UNKNOWN WHICH

APHRODITE IX

APHRODITE IX IS THE MOST UNIQUE OF ALL THE CHILDREN.

IDENTITY:...................................APHRODITE GENERATION IX "TRACKER KILLER"
REAL NAME:...............................N/A
SERIAL NUMBER:......................2473561212
BONDED LINE HANDLER:........BURCH, ROBERT J.
INCEPTION DATE:......................APRIL 4, 2078
HEIGHT:.......................................1.7 METERS (5'7")
WEIGHT:.....................................67 KILOGRAMS (147.7 POUNDS)

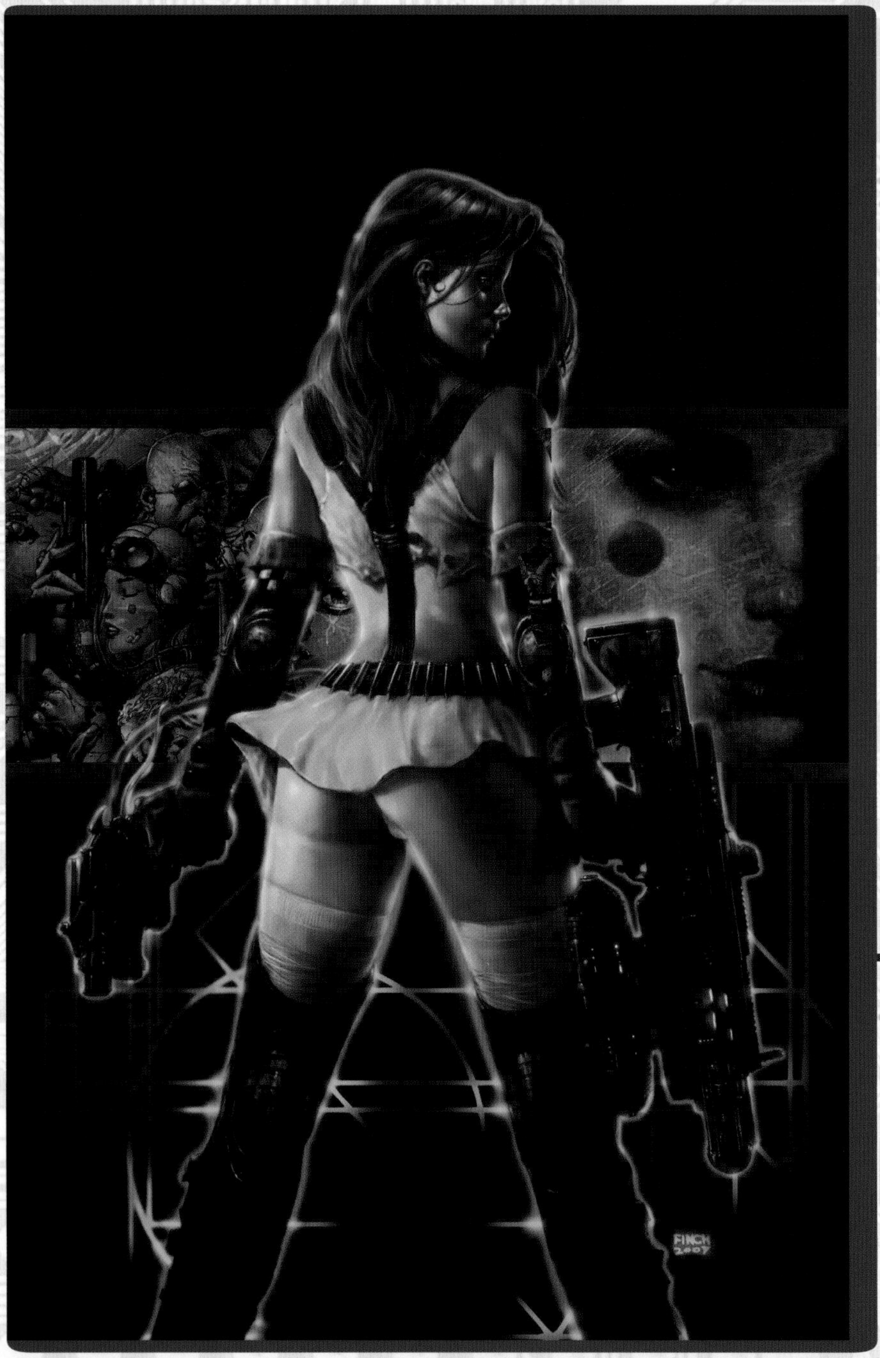
FINCH 2007

ENHANCED HUMAN FUNCTIONALITY -- THE NINTH GENERATION IS A 225% IMPROVEMENT OVER THE LAST HUMAN-BASED GENERATION VII.

	Normal Human Male	Aphrodite IX	Aphrodite IX
	Pre- Diaspora		w/ surge
Strength: Bench Press	49.9kg (110 pounds)	110kg (242.5 pounds)	600kg (1323 pounds)
Strength: Deadlift	57kg (126 pounds)	125kg (275.5 pounds)	685 kg (1510 pounds)
Sprinting speed time (100 meters)	15 seconds	11 seconds	7 seconds
Striking Pressure	1.7 Newtons per square Millimeter (250 pounds per square inch)	10.5 Newtons per square Millimeter (1522 pounds per square inch)	25 Newtons per square Millimeter (3626 pounds per square inch)
Resting Heart Rate	80 beats/minute	48 beats/minute	N/A
VO2 Maximum (aerobic capacity)	35 Milliliters per Kilogram-minute	85 ML/(Kg-min)	170 ML/(Kg-min)
Body temperature	37 degrees celsius (98.6 F)	35.8 degrees C (96.5 F)	40 degrees C (104 F)
Lifespan	86 years	170 years	N/A
Radiation resistance	baseline	175%	N/A
Energy Consumption	baseline 100%	72%	150%+restore
Sleep Requirement (optimal)	7.2 hours	5 hours	N/A
G-Force resistance	5 g's	9 g's	N/A
Chromosome Pairs	23	26 (3 artificial)	N/A
DNA	Helix	Tri-Helix	N/A
Neural Pocessing Speed	20 times 10^15th calculations per second	25 times 10^17th calculations per second	40 times 10^17th calculations per second
Temperature Resistance Range	15 to 30 degrees Celsius	(-5 to 55 degrees Celsius)	N/A
Blood Pressure	120/80	90/65	N/A

ADRENO-GYLCALINE SURGE -- UNIQUE TO THIS GENERATION, SHE HAS A FOCUSED ADRENALINE SURGE THAT ALLOWS A MASSIVE SHORT-TERM POWER BURST. CENTRALYNE GLYCOL IS USED AS THE DELIVERY MECHANISM TO SEND ADRENALINE QUICKLY THROUGH HER BLOOD STREAM TO MAXIMIZE AFFECT TO THE ADRENERGIC RECEPTORS.

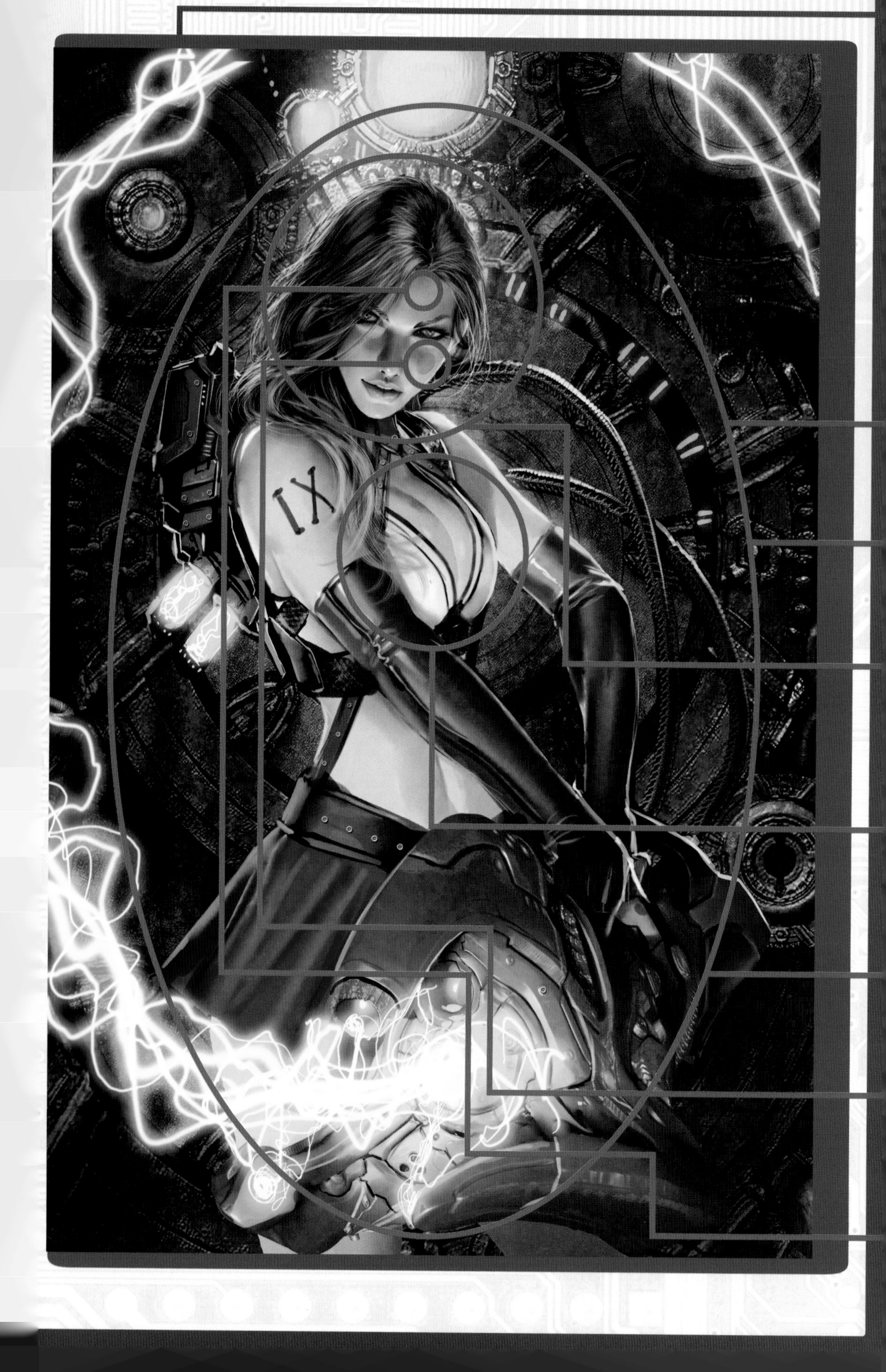
IX

ENHANCEMENTS:

GENETIC – PHASE 4 INTEGRATION OF THE LATEST CDI GENETICS

TRI-HELIX DNA – APHRODITE IX WAS THE FIRST GENERATION TO HAVE A THIRD TECHNOLOGICAL HELIX INTERWOVEN THAT CONNECTED WITH HER TWO ORGANIC HELIX STRANDS IN HER DNA.

CHROMOSOME PAIRS – HER CELLULAR STRUCTURE INCLUDES THREE ADDITIONAL ARTIFICIAL CHROMOSOME BASE PAIRS: TWO FOR PHYSICAL ENHANCEMENT AND THE THIRD FOR NEURAL.

LIMITATIONS – SLEEP REQUIRED FOR REGENERATION/HEALING/MEMORY ORGANIZATION. PREFERABLE 5 HOURS PER 24-HOUR CYCLE. CAN OPERATE FOR 14 DAYS WITHOUT SLEEP BEFORE EXPERIENCING SHUTDOWN.

WILL CEASE TO FUNCTION WITHOUT FOOD AFTER 75 DAYS, WATER AFTER 5 DAYS

APPEARANCE:
DESIGNED FOR INFILTRATION, SEDUCTION, ESPIONAGE AND COVERT ASSASSINATION. ATHLETIC BUILD, HIGH NORMAL METABOLISM, HIGH FLEXIBILITY, AND ACCELERATED HEALING.

SHAPE-SHIFTING:
SHE CAN SLIGHTLY ALTER HER APPEARANCE, CHANGING HER HAIR COLOR AND CERTAIN FACIAL FEATURES, BUT RELATIVE SIZE (HEIGHT/WEIGHT) REMAINS CONSTANT. GREEN BEAUTY MARK ON FACE IS UNCHANGEABLE.

INTERNAL COMPUTER:
CDI MODEL V. 9. CAPABLE OF INTERNAL AND EXTERNAL LOGIC LEAPS AND UP TO 25×10^{17}TH CALCULATIONS PER SECOND. APHRODITE-SPECIFIC FEATURES INCLUDE ADAPTIVE TRANSLATION, WEAPONS ANALYSIS, STRUCTURAL ANALYSIS, AND INTERACTIVE, PREDICTIVE COMBAT ANALYSIS. FIREARM AND COMPUTATIONAL CAPABILITY PRE-LOADED.

SEDUCTION MATRIX:
IN ADDITION TO A SCIENTIFICALLY-REGIMENTED STANDARD OF PHYSICAL BEAUTY, AND INNATE PSYCHOLOGICAL MANIPULATION OF THE ROMANTIC VARIETY, APHRODITE IX CAN ALSO EMIT SPECIFIC PHEROMONES TO CONFUSE AND DISTRACT TARGETS.

STEALTH:
SPECIFICALLY DESIGNED FOR OPERATING IN FORWARD THEATERS AND BEHIND ENEMY LINES, EITHER COVERTLY OR IN DISGUISE. STEALTH SKILLS ARE UNPARALLELED. HAS THE ABILITY TO STOP HER SCENT TO PREVENT DETECTION.

SLAVE MODE:
OPERATIONAL VIA NEURAL INTERFACE BELOW LEFT OPTIC NERVE. HANDLER MAINTAINS ABSOLUTE REMOTE CONTROL (ONBOARD AND COMBAT SYSTEMS ACCESSIBLE) UP TO TWENTY-MINUTE INTERVALS. WARNING: EXCESSIVE AND IMPROPER USE OF SLAVING PROCEDURES MAY LEAD TO MALFUNCTION.

COIN OF SOLOMON:
DATA LIMITED. ONE OF THE THIRTEEN ARTIFACTS. EMBEDDED WITHIN HER NEUROLOGICAL TISSUE. NO KNOWN ADVANTAGE OR DISADVANTAGE TO ITS LOCATION.

SANCTUARIES

THE SANCTUARIES ARE NEARLY ALL ONLINE. WE ARE MERE MONTHS FROM FINAL PHASE INITIATION.

PURPOSE:
CENTRAL TO THE APHRODITE PROTOCOL AND FINAL PHASE (NINE). SANCTUARY FACILITIES ENSURE CONTINUITY, SUBMISSION, AND CONTROL. SANCTUARIES CONTAIN APPROVED DATABASES, INDESTRUCTIBLE STASIS PODS, AND NUMEROUS CDI AMENITIES.

DESIGNATIONS (KNOWN BY SANCTUARY VI)

II	APOLLO XV
IV	ARTEMIS IX
VI	APHRODITE XV
IX	ARES XV
X	APHRODITE IX

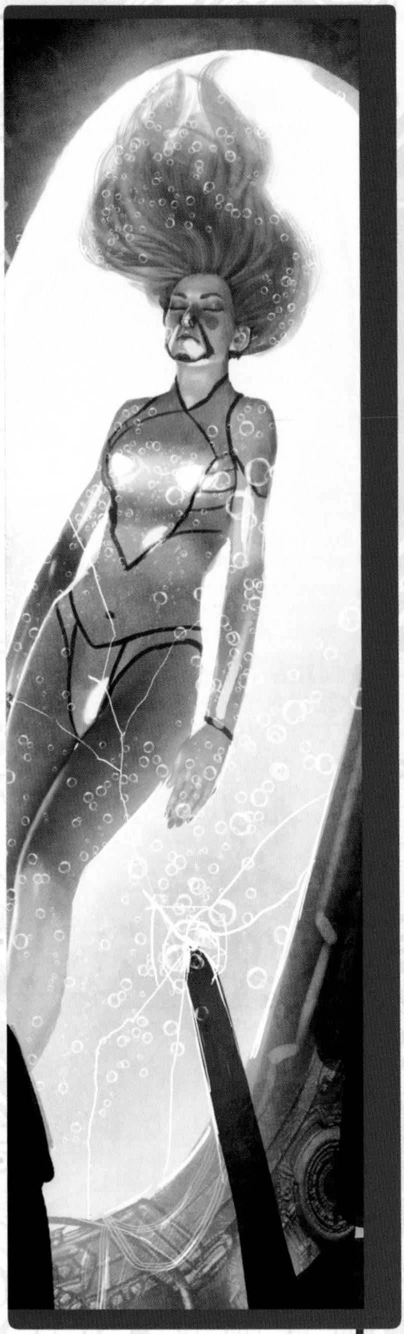

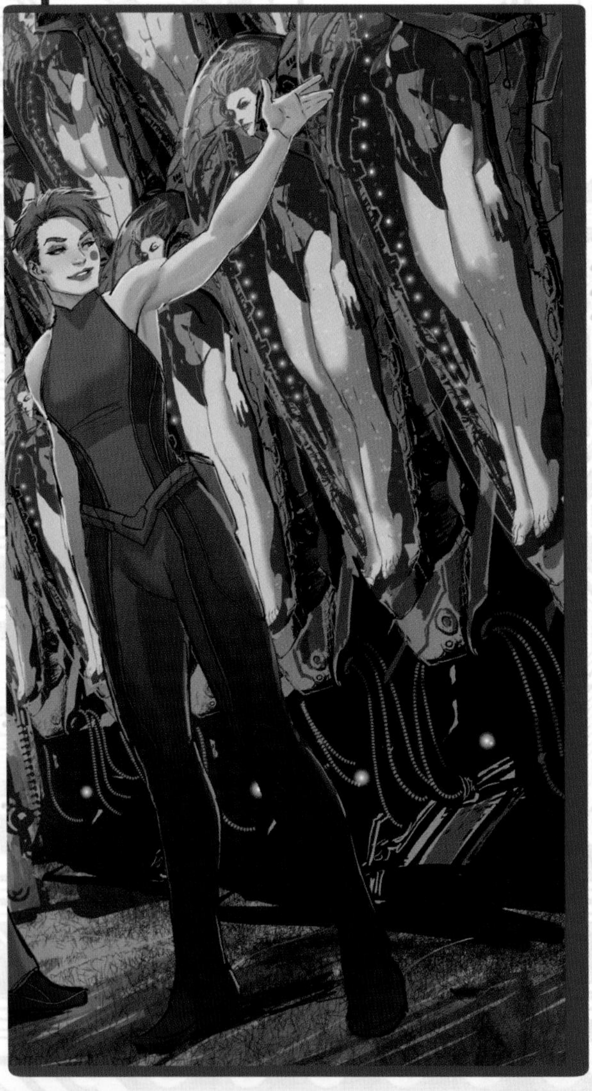

TERRESTRIAL SANCTUARIES:
THERE ARE SIX
SANCTUARIES LOCATED ON
TERRESTRIAL EARTH, EACH
FOCUSED ON A DIFFERENT
MODEL/GENERATION.
SANCTUARIES IX AND X
ARE CONNECTED AND ACT
AS THE CENTRAL HUB ON
THE SURFACE. THEY ARE
INTENTIONAL AUXILIARY
FACILITIES OF MILLENNIUM
CITY.

ORBITAL SANCTUARIES:
SIX ADDITIONAL SATELLITE MODEL SANCTUARIES
RESIDE IN CONSTANT GEOSTATIONARY ORBIT
AROUND THE PLANET. THESE SATELLITES MAINTAIN A
LIMITED COMMUNICATIONS NETWORK AND EXTRANET,
ALTHOUGH EARTH'S CURRENT ATMOSPHERE
CONTAINS ALMOST 65% PARTICULATES, WHICH LIMITS
DATA TRANSFER EFFICIENCY.

FAILSAFE POLICIES:
WHILE SOME TERRESTRIAL SANCTUARY FACILITIES
MAY HAVE BEEN RENDERED INACCESSIBLE DUE TO
ENVIRONMENTAL EFFECTS AND TECTONIC DRIFT, UNIQUELY
SUPPORTIVE ARCHITECTURE AND HIGH-TECH MATERIALS
MAKE THEIR COMPLETE DESTRUCTION EXTREMELY
UNLIKELY, AS THEY WERE ENGINEERED TO SURVIVE AN
EXTINCTION LEVEL EVENT.

STASIS CHAMBERS:
ALL SANCTUARY FACILITIES FEATURE SEVERAL CDI STASIS
CHAMBERS, CAPABLE OF PRESERVING COMATOSE ORGANIC
LIFE FOR CENTURIES.

ROBERT J. BURCH

BURCH WAS HELPFUL IN CORRALLING APHRODITE IX BEFORE THE DIASPORA, BUT HE'S BECOME A LECHEROUS FOOL. HE HAS SOME FINAL USES BEFORE WE LET HER KILL HIM.

IDENTITY:...............BURCH, ROBERT J.
CDI ID NUMBER:....3583561212
OCCUPATION:.......TECHNICIAN/ INSTRUCTOR/ CODE ENGINEER

TRACKER-KILLER HANDLER:
AUTHOR OF THE APHRODITE SLAVING SOFTWARE. DNA – LINKED TO SPECIAL MODEL APHRODITE IX 2473561212 VIA INTERNAL NEURAL INTERFACE.

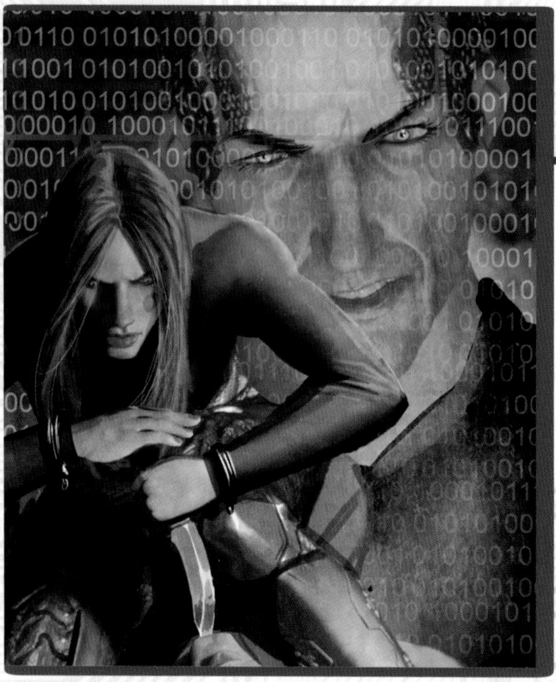

PSYCHOLOGICAL PROFILE:
SUBJECT BURCH DISPLAYS TEXTBOOK EXAMPLES OF NARCISSISM AND AN ALMOST ADOLESCENT ATTITUDE OF OBJECTIFICATION TOWARDS FEMALES. MILD SOCIOPATHIC TENDENCIES.

CYBERNETIC ENHANCEMENTS:
SPEROS CITY CYBERNETICS HAVE REPLACED 40 – 60% OF HIS BASE ORGANIC PARTS. ADDITIONAL NEURAL AND OPTICAL ENHANCEMENTS ALLOW FOR ADJUSTED LIFE IN CURRENT CLIMATE. THE CYBORGS ALSO IMPLANTED A FAILSAFE DESTRUCTIVE DEVICE TO KEEP HIM IN LINE.

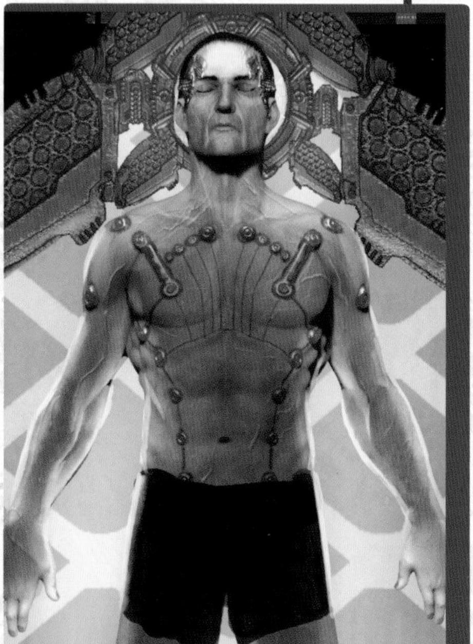

STATUS:
ALTHOUGH INSTRUMENTAL TO THE PROGRAM, SUBJECT BURCH IS DISPOSABLE. HIS CONTROL IS NOT REQUIRED FOR OBJECTIVE.

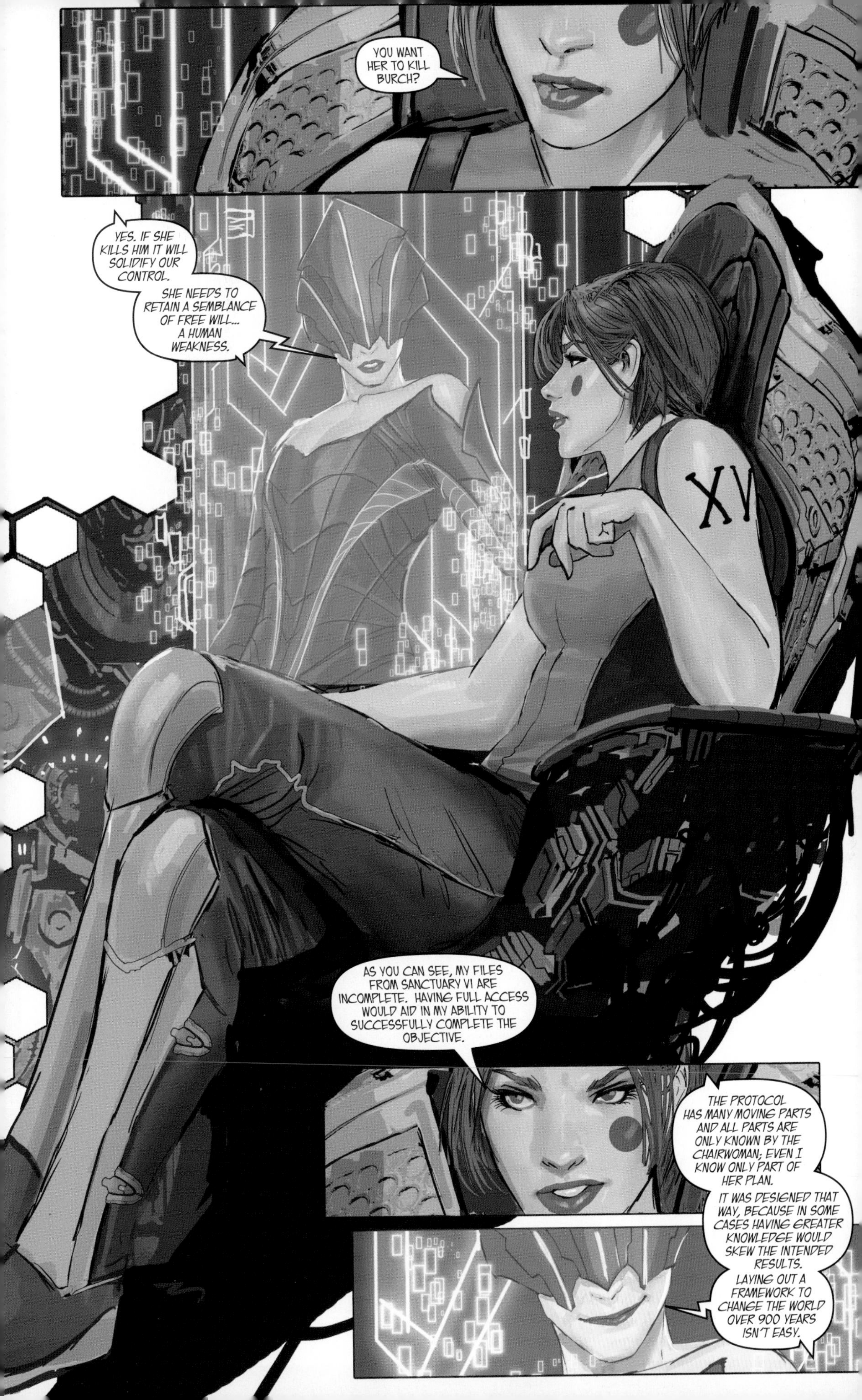

YOU WANT HER TO KILL BURCH?
YES. IF SHE KILLS HIM IT WILL SOLIDIFY OUR CONTROL.
SHE NEEDS TO RETAIN A SEMBLANCE OF FREE WILL... A HUMAN WEAKNESS.
XV
AS YOU CAN SEE, MY FILES FROM SANCTUARY VI ARE INCOMPLETE. HAVING FULL ACCESS WOULD AID IN MY ABILITY TO SUCCESSFULLY COMPLETE THE OBJECTIVE.
THE PROTOCOL HAS MANY MOVING PARTS AND ALL PARTS ARE ONLY KNOWN BY THE CHAIRWOMAN; EVEN I KNOW ONLY PART OF HER PLAN.
IT WAS DESIGNED THAT WAY, BECAUSE IN SOME CASES HAVING GREATER KNOWLEDGE WOULD SKEW THE INTENDED RESULTS.
LAYING OUT A FRAMEWORK TO CHANGE THE WORLD OVER 900 YEARS ISN'T EASY.

MILLENNIUM CITY

EVERYTHING STARTED WITH MILLENNIUM CITY.

CYBERDATA INDUSTRIES FIRST ESTABLISHED OPERATIONS IN PITTSBURGH, PENNSYLVANIA IN 2002. PRIOR TO CONTROL, THE CITY WAS A HUMAN WASTE REFUSE, RIDDEN WITH CRIME AND A FAILING ECONOMY.

WITHIN A DECADE, INDUSTRIAL PROGRESS FROM CDI REVAMPED THE CITY'S ECONOMICS AND TRANSFORMED IT FROM A STATE OF DEPRESSION INTO THE MOST PROSPEROUS METROPOLIS IN THE WORLD. THEY RENAMED IT MILLENNIUM CITY TO HERALD ITS REBIRTH.

STATE OF THE ART SECURITY FORCES:
CDI-TRAINED AND DESIGNED SHOC TROOPERS PATROL THE STREETS AT REGULAR INTERVALS. CRIME IS AT A HISTORIC LOW – AS IS UNEMPLOYMENT.

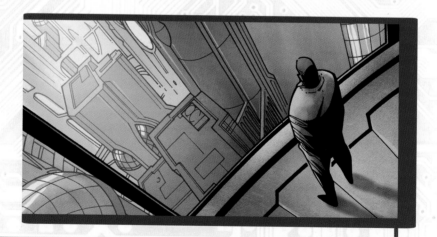

CITY OF THE FUTURE:
WITH THE LATEST TECHNOLOGIES, SUSTAINABLE POWER SOURCES, AND THE MOST SOPHISTICATED INFRASTRUCTURE EVER BUILT, MILLENNIUM CITY WAS DESIGNED TO LAST FOR THE NEXT 1000 YEARS AND BEYOND.

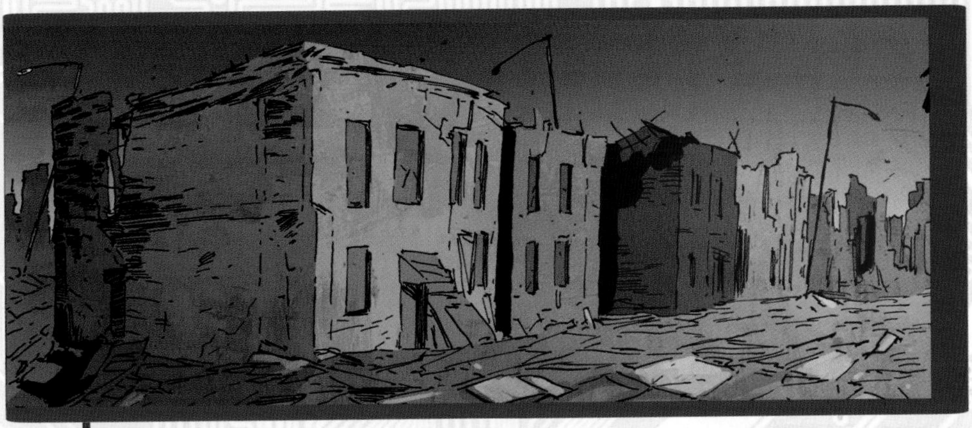

ENVIRONMENTAL DECAY:
DESPITE PROTECTIVE MEASURES AND ADVANCED PRESERVATION METHODS, SOME LIMITED DETRIMENT TO MILLENNIUM CITY'S INFRASTRUCTURE WAS ANTICIPATED.

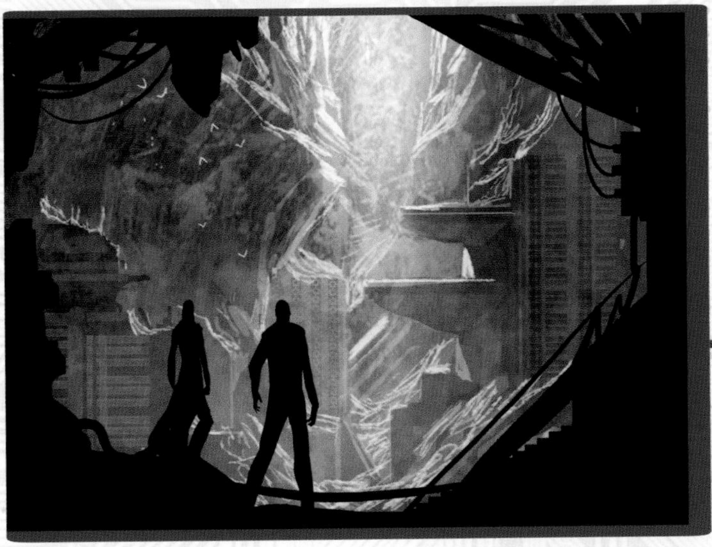

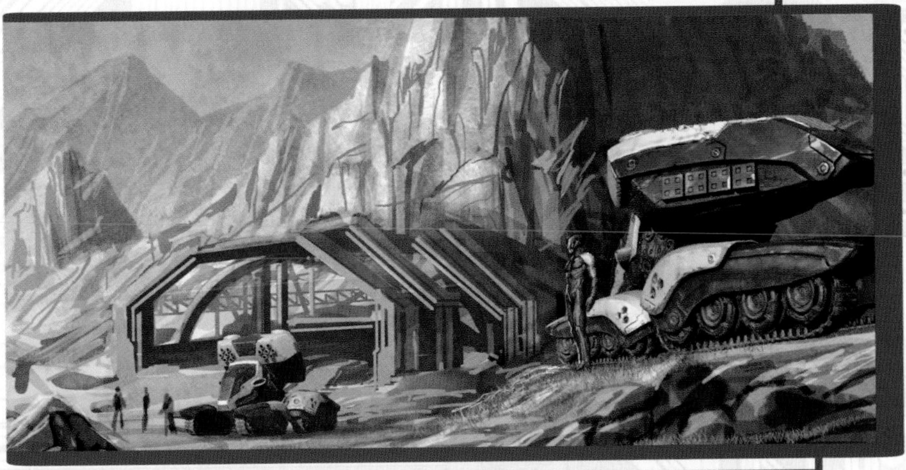

EXCAVATION EFFORTS:
GIVEN THE SUCCESS OF ROBERT BURCH'S WORK WITH APHRODITE IX, THE CYBORGS HAVE LAUNCHED FULL-SCALE EXCAVATION ATTEMPTS INTO THE CITY.

THE GEN

EXPECTATIONS ARE THE GEN WILL DOMINATE THE CYBORGS, BUT IT GOES BACK AND FORTH.

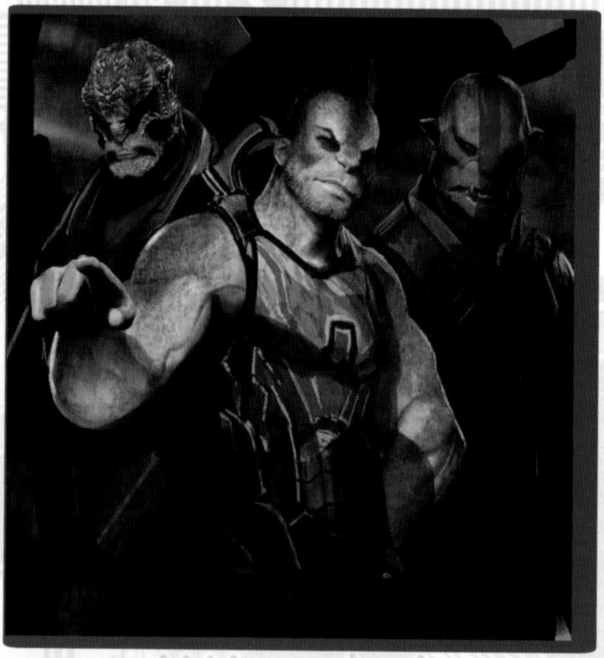

IN PHASE 4, HUMANS WERE DRAMATICALLY ALTERED GENETICALLY, AND HAVE BEEN INCREASINGLY DIVERSIFIED IN FAVOR OF THE NEW ENVIRONMENT OVER THEIR CENTURIES AS A PEOPLE. THERE WERE OFFSHOOTS OF HUMANS THAT MUTATED DRAMATICALLY, FREQUENTLY SPLICED WITH SOME ANIMAL DNA IN AN ATTEMPT TO BREED IN SPECIAL ABILITIES. THESE VARIANTS ARE KNOWN AS CYBRIDS AND ARE SHUNNED BY THE NORMAL GEN.

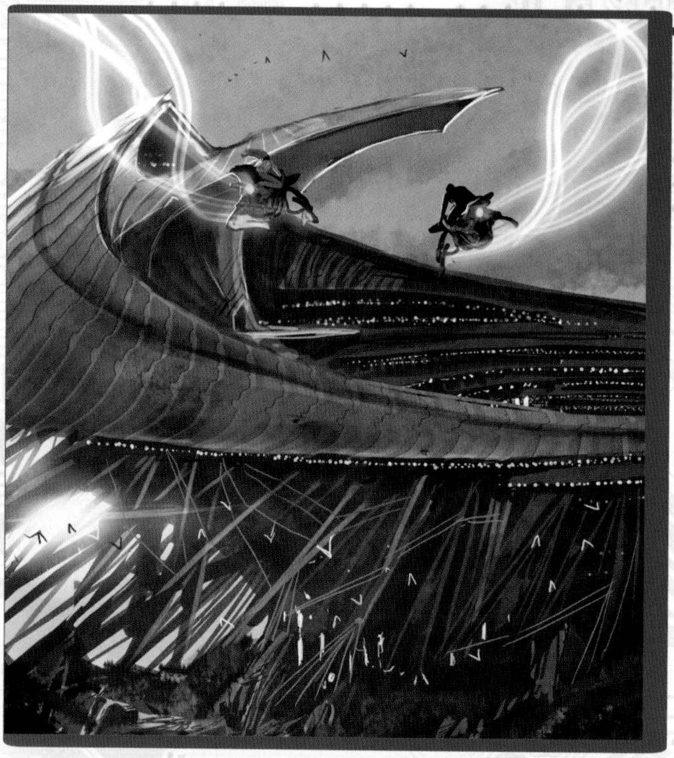

GENESIS CITY

CONSTRUCTED IN 2376, GENESIS CITY WAS BUILT TO ESTABLISH THE LINEAGE OF GENETICALLY ENHANCED PERSONNEL AS PART OF PHASE 4 OF THE PROTOCOL.

THE CITY PROVIDES EXCELLENT NATURAL DEFENSE FROM GROUND FORCES, AS IT HAS NO GROUND ENTRANCES. DESIGNED WITH THE GENETICALLY ENHANCED WINGED CREATURES IN MIND, THE SCIENTISTS OF GENESIS CITY BREED THEM FOR TRANSPORT.

HISTORY

THE GEN ARE RULED BY A THEOCRATIC MONARCHY PASSED DOWN THROUGH HEREDITARY TITLE. WOMEN ARE STRONG IN THEIR SOCIETY, THEY HAVE TO BE TO SURVIVE, BUT THEIR SOCIETY LEANS TOWARDS A PATRIARCHAL STRUCTURE.

OVER THE CENTURIES AND WITH THE VARIATIONS IN THE GEN'S GENETICS, TRIBAL STRUCTURES EMERGED. EACH HAS THEIR OWN DISTINCT CULTURE, BUT ALL SWEAR FEALTY TO THE HIGH KING AND QUEEN.

HIGH KING MARCUS DRAGOVITCH

CURRENT HIGH KING MARCUS DRAGOVITCH WAS
ENGAGED TO LINA SWIFTHAVEN, THE DAUGHTER
OF A LEADING TRIBAL ELDER. THIS MARRIAGE WAS
INTENDED TO SOLIDIFY THE UNITY OF THE TRIBES.
ALTHOUGH HER DEATH CAUSED SOME TEMPORARY
UPHEAVAL, MARCUS' CONVERSION TO A RADICALIZED
VERSION OF THEIR STATE RELIGION CONSOLIDATED
THEIR ALLIANCE.

HIGH KING MARCUS' DRAGOVITCH IS THE HONORIFIC
"SWORD OF HIS PEOPLE" AND SERVES AS BOTH THE
POLITICAL AND SPIRITUAL LEADER OF THE GEN. HE IS
A SKILLED WARRIOR, BUT LIMITED IN INTELLECT AND
DIPLOMACY.

DRAKES

AS PART OF THEIR ADVANCEMENTS IN GENETICS
AND BREEDING, THE GEN HAVE DEVELOPED
FLYING DRAKES. DRAKES SERVE AS THE MAIN
SOURCE OF TRANSPORTATION FOR THE GEN
IN AND OUT OF BATTLE. WHILE THE DRAKES
ARE ESSENTIALLY LITTLE MORE THAN MOUNTS,
THEIR RIDERS VIEW THEM ALMOST AS EQUALS.

DRAKES ARE BRED AND BONDED TO SPECIFIC
INDIVIDUALS AND FAMILIES, AND A GOOD DEAL
OF TIME AND TRAINING FOR BOTH DRAKE AND
RIDER ARE REQUIRED BEFORE A DRAKE CAN
BE PROPERLY RIDDEN. THE DRAKES ALSO
POSSESS AN ALMOST EXTRASENSORY JUDGE
OF CHARACTER, AND WILL ONLY CARRY THOSE
THEY TRUST.

ALTHOUGH THE DRAKES ARE THE GEN'S
PRIMARY BROOD, THEY ARE ABLE TO CREATE
MANY OTHER TYPES OF CREATURES AND
DEVELOP NEW ONES ALL THE TIME.

RELIGION

RELIGION DOMINATES THE CULTURE OF THE GEN. POLITICAL LEADERS ARE ALSO
SPIRITUAL LEADERS, AND PRIESTS AND PRIESTESSES ARE HELD IN HIGH ESTEEM.
THEIR RELIGION IS INTRICATE, INVOLVING A DUALISTIC NOTION OF THE DIVINE AS
SIMULTANEOUSLY MALE AND FEMALE IN VARYING TEXTS OF A QUASI-HISTORICAL
NATURE.

WHILE RELIGION IS PREVALENT IN THE GEN'S CULTURE, FEW OF THEIR PEOPLE
HOLD PASSIONATE FAITH. MARCUS'S RECENT CONVERSION TO ZEALOTRY,
HOWEVER, HAS SPARKED A VIOLENT RELIGIOUS REVIVAL IN THE PEOPLE.

THE CYBORGS

THE CYBORGS OF SPEROS CITY HAVE CARRIED ON THE TORCH OF HUMAN-TECHNOLOGICAL SINGULARITY – AS FAR AS THE PROTOCOL ALLOWS. THEIR MYRIAD CYBERNETIC ENHANCEMENTS ALLOW THEM TO BREATHE IN VARIED CLIMATES, INTERFACE WITH ALL MANNER OF TECHNOLOGY, AND GRANT THEM SUPERHUMAN SENSORY PERCEPTION AND PHYSICAL ACUMEN.

THE CYBORGS PLACE EXTREME VALUE ON THEIR OWN LIVES, INSISTING ON HEAVY RISK ASSESSMENT BEFORE ENGAGING IN ANY DANGEROUS ACTIVITIES. MANY OF

THEM ARE FUNCTIONALLY IMMORTAL – SUPPLEMENTING ORGANIC PARTS WITH CYBERNETIC AS NECESSARY. BECAUSE OF THIS, FEW OF THEM APPEAR TO HAVE AGED PAST 40, THOUGH MOST ARE WELL OVER A CENTURY OLD.

SPEROS CITY

DIVIDED INTO SECTORS AND FILLED WITH THE MOST STATE OF THE ART INFRASTRUCTURE IN THE WORLD, SPEROS CITY IS THE PINNACLE OF HUMAN TECHNOLOGICAL ACHIEVEMENT. ITS CITIZENS RESIDE IN A HIGHLY REGULATED, SINGLE-PARTY TOTALITARIAN STATE – REBELLION AND CRIME ARE VIRTUALLY NONEXISTENT.

ALBEIT SLOWLY, ITS POPULATION IS INCREASING IN NUMBER – VARIOUS ATTEMPTS TO COLONIZE LUNAR BODIES AND EXTRATERRESTRIAL LOCATIONS HAVE BEEN MADE, THOUGH ALL WERE THWARTED BY THE GEN.

THE CITY IS RINGED WITH AGRICULTURAL CENTERS AND ADVANCED GREENHOUSES, WHICH PROVIDE NECESSARY LAND AND RESOURCES IN THE OTHERWISE BARREN WASTELAND. THEY PROVIDE READY TARGETS FOR THE CITY'S ENEMIES, HOWEVER.

GOVERNMENT

SPEROS CITY IS GOVERNED BY A COUNCIL OF ITS MOST LONG-LIVED AND CAPABLE CITIZENS. A MAJORITY COUNCIL VOTE IS REQUIRED FOR MAJOR GOVERNMENTAL ACTIONS. COUNCIL SEATS ARE HIGHLY PRIZED AMONG SPEROS CITIZENS, AS A SPOT ON THE COUNCIL IS ESSENTIALLY A GUARANTEE OF IMMORTALITY.

A CAREER MILITARY MAN, EXECUTOR CHRONOS WAS COMMITTED TO ELIMINATING THE GEN ONCE-AND-FOR-ALL. HIS AGGRESSIVE CAMPAIGNS LED TO INTENSE SKIRMISHES BETWEEN THE TWO FACTIONS, AND THE SPEROS CITY FORCES WERE DEFEATED. AS PUNISHMENT FOR HIS FAILURE, CHRONOS WAS PLACED IN A NEURAL ISOLATION CHAMBER.

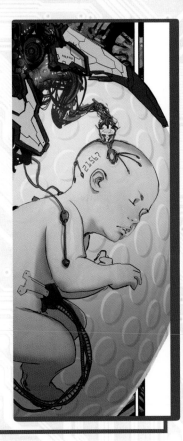

FORMER ASSISTANT AND SUCCESSOR TO CHRONOS, JEZEBEL NOW SERVES AS THE EXECUTOR OF SPEROS CITY, ENACTING THE WILL OF THE COUNCIL AND PREPARING HER PEOPLE FOR WAR AGAINST THE GEN.

DEVELOPMENT

CHILDREN ARE FORGED IN BIRTH UNITS AS DESIRED, AND OUTFITTED WITH CYBERNETIC ENHANCEMENTS THAT ENCOURAGE RAPID NEUROLOGICAL AND PHYSIOLOGICAL GROWTH.

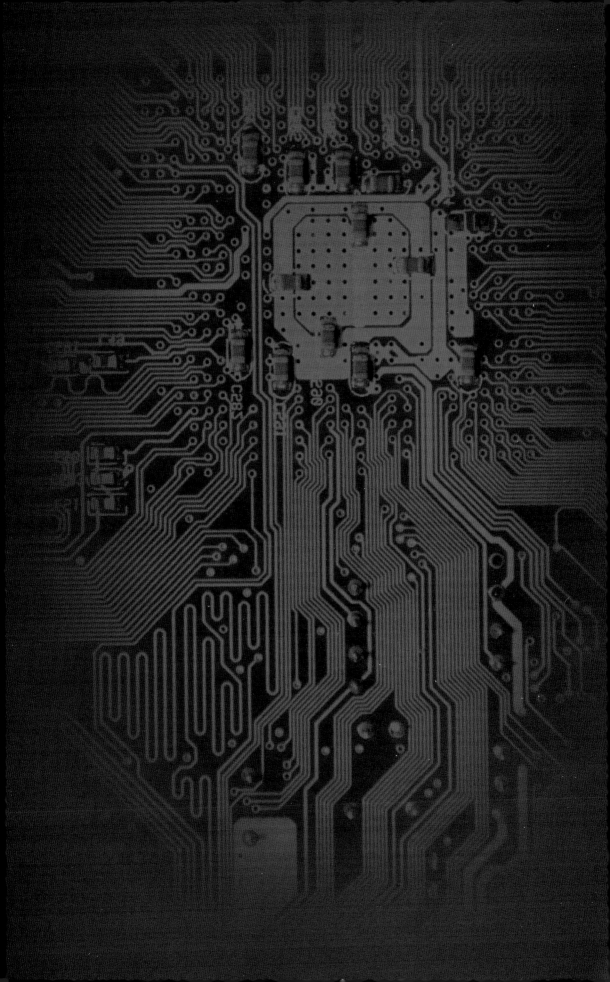

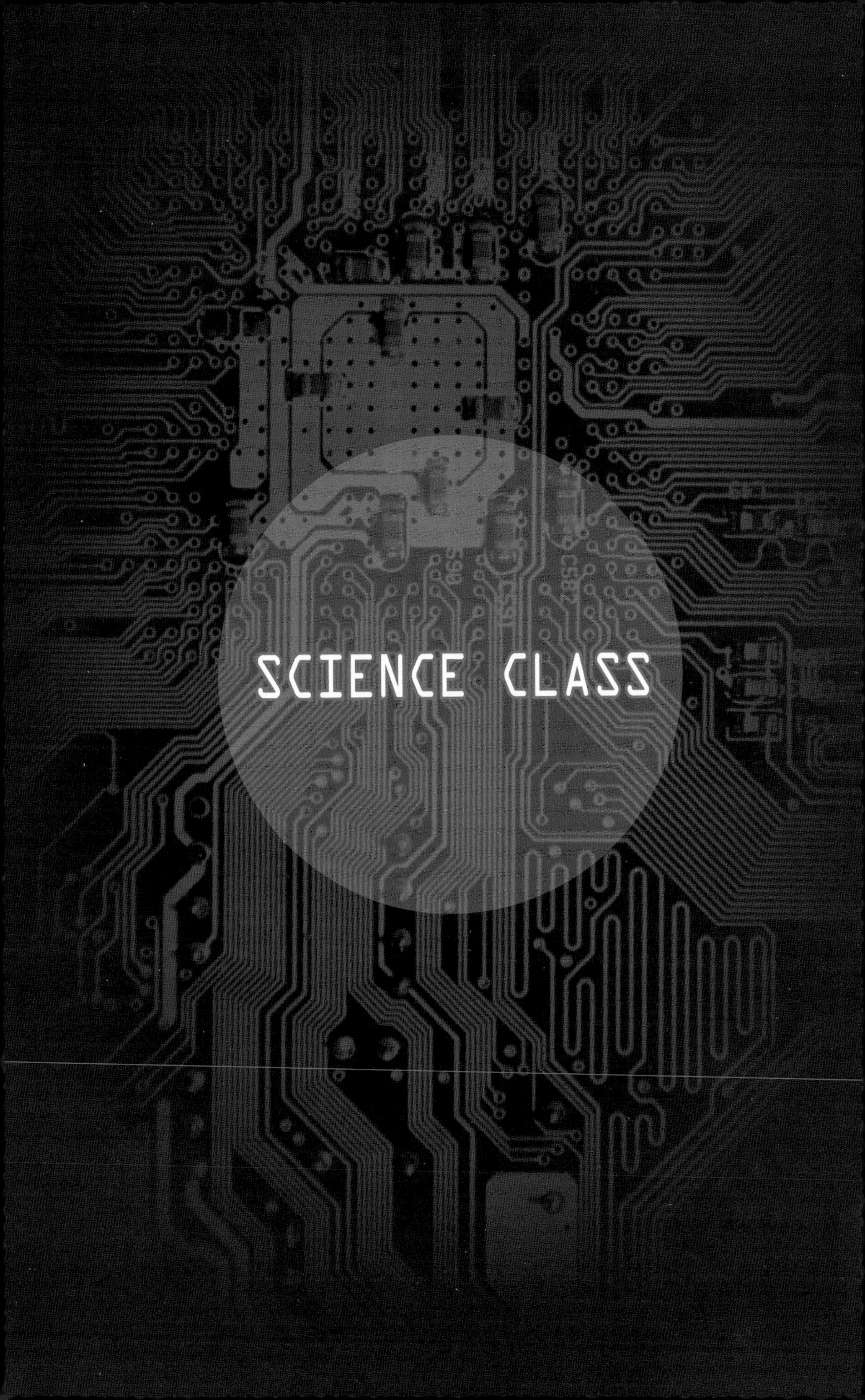
SCIENCE CLASS

SCIENCE CLASS

Welcome to Volume 2 of *Aphrodite IX Rebirth*! This volume kicks off a new direction with Aphrodite leaving the confines of the small, contained world of the Gen and the Cyborgs and venturing out into the broader world to see what's there. It seems that there are more than just those two groups that survived! You've probably figured out by now that this book and *Cyber Force* are bookends of each other. You don't need to read both books to understand the story of either individual book, but they are definitely in the same "world." We're doing a *Cyber Force/Aphrodite* crossover, so check it out if you want to see how both series are connected!

You may have also noticed that I sprinkle into *Aphrodite* some "Easter egg" type references to the other artifacts within the storyline. The "Book of Angelus," the "Darkness;" if you look closely at some of the Gen's religious symbology you'll notice some familiar looking designs. It's been kind of fun making up my own religion.

Two books you can please help spread the word about are:

1) The *Aphrodite IX Rebirth Volume 1* trade paperback – this collects the first arc with issues 1-5, so please recommend the book to the more casual readers you know!
2) *Aphrodite IX Hidden Files* – This is a must read for anyone participating in the Top Cow Talent Hunt (details on topcow.com), and will give some explanation as to what the Aphrodite Protocol is and what the difference between all the "generations" of Aphrodites are all about. For some spoilers, note it's Seal Team VI on those teams patches, not Seal Team 6. This book will be out a couple of weeks after this book here in your hands.

NEW ART STYLE

Stjepan Sejic, who's painted every issue of the new Rebirth of Aphrodite, switched up his style a bit with this issue and I frakking love it! I hope you do as well. The one "criticism" I saw about the more photo-real version he drew in was that our "comic book-y" lettering didn't seem to fit it. We're always trying new things, and I am so very happy with the way this issue came out - I hope you like it too.

On to science-y stuff:

SINGULARITY

In the book, Aphrodite XV refers to herself as one of the true singularities. Anyone that's read anything I've written or talked to me knows I am a HUGE transhumanist. I've modified for this story what we take as the meaning of "singularity" today. In today's discussion, the technological singularity, or simply the singularity, is a theoretical moment in time when artificial intelligence will have progressed to the point of a greater-than-human intelligence that will "radically change human civilization, and perhaps even human nature itself." That's from a book in the first link. There is also significant discussion about how we may be able at some point to download a human consciousness into a machine. In the second link below is a long article about uploading your consciousness into a computer and how that could be possible in the next thirty years. Thirty years is not that long, hopefully I'll still be alive.

http://goo.gl/DAzxv8

http://goo.gl/iNR3J4

IMMORTALITY

Is this possible? Can we live forever? I don't think forever is achievable, but if we truly want to conquer the stars we're going to need to live much longer lives. There is a lot of money being poured into research on immortality. If you look at death, the primary reason our bodies die is because of mitochondrial decay. Our cells just stop working and die. Eventually when enough of them go, so do you. That's a vast oversimplification, but the easiest way to live longer is to have something that will repair this cellular damage. Nanotechnology is tackling this.

http://goo.gl/71Gwql

http://goo.gl/PBdL9r

MARCUS'S RELIGIOUS CONVERSION/RELIGION IN SCI-FI

ISAAC
ASIMOV
THE FOUNDATION NOVELS
FOUNDATION

I was raised in a fairly strict Southern Baptist home, and went to church two, sometimes three, times a week until I went to college. When I converted to atheism in my late 20's, I read a lot of atheist literature, which purported that religion was going to go away. Some of these writings are 50 years old now, and unless you're completely oblivious, religion is going strong. Faith isn't in danger of becoming extinct, and I'm actually fine with that. I have no issue with people's beliefs as long as they don't want to kill me for not believing their drivel.

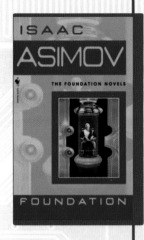

Saw some online comments (yes I read them so be nice!) about how Marcus's conversion seemed sudden. I've actually witnessed many people do this first hand, so it seems plausible to me… dunno.

Science Fiction has some pretty amazing takes on religion. There are a couple quick reads worth checking out:

Foundation by Isaac Asimov:

Seminal book by the master, a group of scientists "create" a religion to help pacify people, and allow them to secure a lasting peace in the galaxy. I reread this recently, and if you haven't read it since childhood, or at all, read it now! You can see where George Lucas allegedly got some of his ideas for *Star Wars* in this book.

ARTHUR C.
CLARKE
Revised Edition including author's Millennial Foreword
CHILDHOOD'S END

Childhood's End by Arthur C. Clarke:

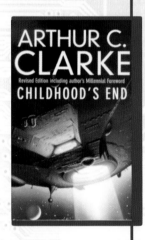

This one has an interesting reverse take on religion, where an alien race shows up and reveals that they've been recording all of human history. They give us the recordings, and once reviewed, there's conclusive evidence that all the religions were made up. It's a throwaway line in the book, but it struck me powerfully, and I've never forgotten it.

And let's not forget *Dianetics and Scientology*. If there ever was a Sci-Fi religion, it's that one. If you don't know what scientologists believe, check out that *South Park* episode "Trapped in the Closet," it's season 9 episode 12.

Or you can go to their site; it's interesting to read at least. http://www.scientology.org/

And before you Scientologists target me, I don't think your beliefs are any harder to swallow than any other religion. They're all equally fairy tales to me. =P

This link is pretty awesome. It lists out the seven deadly sins of religion in sci-fi, and talks about the new *BSG* a lot.

http://goo.gl/r3Y1vA

Back to Marcus's conversion; I've seen several people radically change their lives and how they act, what they do, etc.. For some it's a coping mechanism. Some use religion to make them feel better about their economic plight and place in the world. Some use it to get off drugs; they feel they need a higher power to "help" them. Like I said earlier, I don't believe in God - haven't for many years. I personally feel that people use "god" as a placebo where their own power figures it out. But whatever works. I know many of you strongly disagree with me on this. I envy your faith.

TRI HELIX DNA

These are real, but not laced with a cybernetic strand. There is quad-helix DNA in nature too.

http://goo.gl/bnRmPd
http://goo.gl/i8EZ4C

image from: http://goo.gl/Gb8FMP

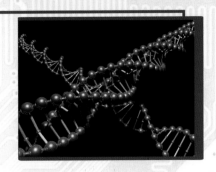

ROMAN NUMERALS

After doing a few conventions of late, I've come to realize that some people call this book Aphrodite IX (eye, ex), and not Aphrodite 9 like we do here at the Cow. You can call it whatever you want, but it's intended as a number. IX looks cooler than 9 or 09, and it's meant to be a generational thing. You may have an iPhone 4 or 5 - these are Aphrodite IX's and XV's. We have reasons for the numbers we pick, but I'd be lying if I said part of it wasn't because those specific ones look cool in logo designs! Aphrodite is actually the Greek God name usage, but we're using Roman numerals. Go figure.

The Greek numbering is not as popular, but here it is: http://goo.gl/ktkwxd

Here are the Roman numerals: http://goo.gl/gSxYUw

1	2	3	4	5	6	7	8	9	10
I	II	III	IV	V	VI	VII	VIII	IX	X

I	II	III	IIII	Γ	ΓΙ	ΓΙΙ	ΓΙΙΙ	ΓΙΙΙΙ	△
1	2	3	4	5	6	7	8	9	10

1 - 10 in Greek acrophonic numbers

MANIPULATION, CONTROL, AND RELIGION

Marcus is now being "controlled" by his religious conviction. How different is this from Aphrodite's slave mode? An interesting thing to ponder! The slave mode that the Aphrodite model can be placed in is more severe, but manipulation and control by other means is far more insidious. Have you ever met people that are life-scarred because of their bizarre relationships with their parents? Scientifically, mind control is definitely possible. It's not in a working form, but we'll get there. Scared? Maybe you should be.

http://goo.gl/RVSMvd
http://goo.gl/svbnSl
http://goo.gl/wlyLi

If you want to go off in la-la-land, you can learn how to prevent alien and military abduction and controlling your mind here:

http://goo.gl/55SlF3

COIN OF SOLOMON

For those of you that read *Artifacts*, you'll recognize the coin found in Aph's head as this. It'll make sense later. The coin's "power" gives people epiphanic leaps of knowledge, and jumps in evolutionary biology. I've seeded all throughout the *Aphrodite IX Rebirth* references to the regular Top Cow Universe (TCU). This book definitely takes part in the TCU, but I've been careful to make sure it's accessible to anyone who's not read the other Universe books.

Writing this section of Science Class took me a lot longer to finish than I was expecting it to. The main reason was once I started looking into the specific details of human enhancement from both cybernetic and genetics, I quickly became obsessed with it. I started extrapolating based on a current model of what we, as simple organic human beings, are able to achieve and then used that as a baseline for reasonable enhancements. I doubt many people go through this when they're creating super-heroes, but since I sort of personally don't like unrealistic heroes, I wanted to set Aphrodite up as a real possibility for the future. Might seem far-fetched, but we've done more to evolve ourselves over the past 20 years than hundreds of thousands of years of natural selection.

So how do you start determining an enhanced human's capabilities? Well, I went back to my D&D roots and started thinking about the basics - strength, intelligence, wisdom, dexterity, constitution, and charisma, and went from there. Keep in mind that each of these categories has thousands of subcategories, and research done on all of them. I'm going to hit super broad strokes.

BODY STRENGTH

What determines your body strength? We currently calculate this based on standards in weightlifting exercises, like bench press and deadlift. I am actually comparing Aphrodite to a human man as a baseline instead of a woman, so her abilities are even more extraordinary on the strength front. Physical strength is defined as "the capability of a man or woman to exert force on a physical object by using muscles." How we harness muscle use and the fibers within the muscles also have a significant affect. Humans are about 15% stronger on average than we were 100 years ago. We're growing taller (and fatter).

http://goo.gl/Y1qITh

STRIKING FORCE

How much force do you hit someone with? We see these Karate experts punching through concrete blocks, etc. A lot of this has to do with where you hit something and with what, but the idea for Aphrodite is how hard can she punch and kick people. The current human striking force parameters are fairly limiting, but with cybernetic enhancements - from adding a heavy tensile strength metal fiber in your hand, to increasing the torque abilities of your muscles -they could open it up considerably.

http://goo.gl/bSXrSq

PUNCH/STRIKING SPEED

The average person can achieve a punch at about 24kmh (15mph), which is about 6.7 meters per second or 22 feet per second, with the average striking distance at about 1 meter (roughly 3 feet). It takes about 1/7th of a second for a normal person to punch someone else. How much faster can this be? Takes about 1/100th of a second for a bullet to strike someone at the same distance, so we know that's achievable with explosive chemical compounds. We can use that as a baseline to see what might be achievable.

http://goo.gl/iJWA51
http://goo.gl/IFPqd2

BONE STRENGTH

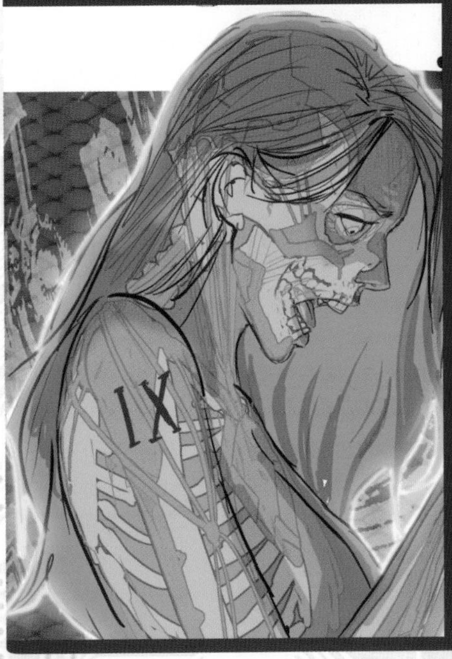
IX

"Ounce for ounce, bone is stronger than steel, since a bar of steel of comparable size would weigh four or five times as much. A cubic inch of bone can in principle bear a load of 19,000 lbs. (8,626 kg) or more — roughly the weight of five standard pickup trucks — making it about four times as strong as concrete."

http://goo.gl/grK6td

I round things for ease, but if you want to be precise, check out this invaluable resource for conversion:

http://goo.gl/1yTDY

Fastest martial arts punch:

http://goo.gl/SGne1r

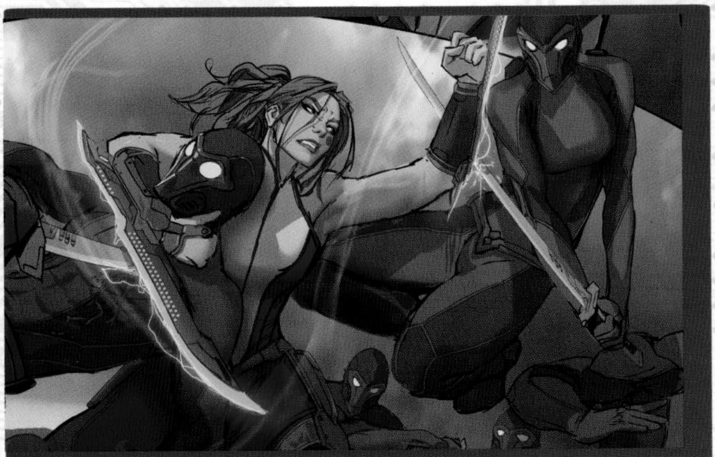

FAST AND SLOW TWITCH MUSCLE FIBERS

If you've ever studied how our muscles work, you know there are both slow and fast twitch fibers in them, and they have different purposes. Slow are for endurance and are longer; fast are for speed/sprinting and are shorter. Any successful genetic adaptation for strength/speed enhancement would have to factor this in.

MENTAL STRENGTH/PROCESSING SPEED

How fast does your brain work? Ultimately this is how fast your neurons respond. "In almost all studies of a neuron's response to a stimulus, the response is sampled over long time periods, usually around 300 to 500 milliseconds (ms)." That last quote is from following link, which is worth a read. How do you increase processing speed? Well, now we're getting into the ideas of the singularity.

From second link below:

"In a nutshell, the Technological Singularity is a term used to describe the theoretical moment in time when artificial intelligence matches and then exceeds human intelligence. The term was popularized by scifi writer Vernor Vinge, but full credit goes to the mathematician John von Neumann, who spoke of "ever accelerating progress of technology and changes in the mode of human life, which gives the appearance of approaching some essential singularity in the history of the race beyond which human affairs, as we know them, could not continue."

http://goo.gl/LGvjpI
http://goo.gl/gr5xMO
http://goo.gl/ZnmmU

ADRENERGIC RECEPTORS

Wikipedia has a really good breakdown of what this is - actually better than most of the educational sites I use for research. The bottom line is these are how adrenaline gets the nervous system to go into overdrive, and allows normal people to lift 3500 pound cars. This "adrenaline model" is what I've based Aphrodite IX's surge abilities on. She has a limited boost that gives her dramatic increases in speed and strength, but it wears her out quickly. If you've ever heard the term "seeing red," or had enhanced vision because of fear, you know what this is like. I think this is why some people who fight like to fight - they get off on that surge of adrenaline you get when you go into a battle mode.

http://goo.gl/N4C2d
http://goo.gl/vjwch

ADRENO-GLYCALINE SURGE

This is what we call fake, made-up science to suit the story, heh. No such thing actually exists, but the idea is that this is how her enhanced body uses its adrenaline surge.

http://goo.gl/cTzB9j

BLOOD TYPE

I did some research to see if there was a specific blood type that would be stronger. The research is unclear, but I found this one wiki answer, from the link below, that said O neg, so I went with that. I added artificial white blood cells, as I think that would make sense in enhancing her immune system as well.

http://goo.gl/j7pJoP

VO2 MAX

What the upper limit to how fast the body can move and use oxygen through the blood stream is the quick answer of what VO2 Max is. The higher this limit, the more endurance someone will have. I went on and on about this in a previous Think Tank Science Class, so I'm must using broad strokes here.

http://goo.gl/LAeyU

EXTRA ARTIFICIAL CHROMOSOMES

Now this is an area that I lost half a day reading about. Humans have 23 pairs of chromosomes. The notion that more pairs equals better organisms isn't really true, as earthworms have more chromosome pairs than we do. And take Down's Syndrome, which is a debilitating genetic variation, that is caused from humans having an extra chromosome. However, adding some artificial cybernetic chromosomes in utero to give humans enhanced abilities is not only possible…but almost possible now! Don't believe me? Read this link:

http://goo.gl/v6CSQJ

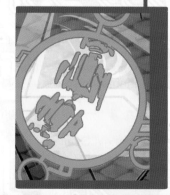

TRI HELIX

There are Tri-Helix DNA patterns now. When I first wrote that Aphrodite had a tri-helix DNA, and that one strand was cybernetically enhanced, I hadn't realized that the artificial cybernetic chromosomes would actually suit better purpose for enhancing abilities. DNA is an interesting thing. It's actually (in my opinion that I stole from a couple geneticists) a flimsy design. The easiest way to think of DNA is like it's a long string of X-mas lights woven around another long string of X-mas lights, where there are four colors, and they match up like red-white and blue-yellow. How those 4 colors interact basically determines everything about you. The insanely pedestrian version of genetic variation is to imagine that some of those lights' sizes are changed, or their orders are switched around to change things up. One revelation of the second Aphrodite IX arc is that one of their goals is to create a true quad-helix.

http://goo.gl/Pa9y6I

METRIC SYSTEM

Why do I convert everything to the metric system? Because it's stupid that the US hasn't already accepted the world standard system. We're too lazy here to bother trying to learn it, which makes us look stupid to the rest of the world. My hope is that in a rebuilt post-apocalyptic world, we finally have a worldwide universal standard for the few that are left.

G-FORCE RESISTANCE

How much force can the body withstand from acceleration? Or, how fast would we have to be going before our body would simply fly apart on its own? More good things to know when creating super soldiers who need to fight in varying environments.

http://goo.gl/rdMPFo

RESTING HEART RATE

A resting heart rate is simply how many heartbeats there are a minute when you're resting. People with strong endurances and who are healthier tend to have lower resting heart rates.

http://goo.gl/ioSBe
http://goo.gl/Y0HQj8

TEMPERATURE VARIATION

Also important for creating super soldiers is knowing what are the temperature conditions in which they can fight. It makes sense that enhanced soldiers would be able to operate in broader environments. You could create different types of people too - ones that are designed to operate in arctic environments, and ones who operate in severe desert ones.

http://goo.gl/81J9pB

BLOOD PRESSURE

Blood pressure measures the pressure in your arteries during the pumping and resting phases of each heartbeat. The top number represents the degree of pressure your heart generates when pumping blood through your arteries, while the bottom number indicates the amount of pressure in your arteries between beats.

Normal blood pressure is equal to or lower than 120/80 based on current guidelines, although many health experts say 115/75 is ideal. More athletic people have lower blood pressures.

http://goo.gl/5lMxdW

Stjepan Sejic and I love doing this book; it's been a great collaboration for the two of us. By the time this comes out, the *Aphrodite IX/Cyber Force* cross-over will be out. It will be unlike any cross-over before...ever! *Cyber Force* is about building a new future where Cyber Data International enacts an "Aphrodite Protocol" that will save the world from itself, and allow for the continuation of our species as new species in the future. Well, flash forward a year of *Cyber Force* and a year of *Aphrodite IX*, and it should be clear to anyone reading these books that the events in *Cyber Force* are what create the world of *Aphrodite IX*. So, if you haven't checked out *Cyber Force*, why not? The first 5 issues are free thanks to the awesome Kickstarter people.

You can get the *Cyber Force* books on Comixology, or download them directly from us at:

http://goo.gl/Mox2OB.

Aphrodite IX #1-11 lead directly into *Aphrodite IX/Cyber Force* #1. You don't HAVE to read *Cyber Force* to get *Aphrodite* or vice versa, but it's intended as an enhanced experience.

HATE

In this series I've dealt with the hatred between two warring City States, Genesis City and Speros City. They've been at odds with each other for hundreds of years. This is common in our own history, so it's easy for everyone to buy into quickly, but the mechanics of hate and how it works and perpetuates are interesting to think about.

Why do we hate? It's a natural emotion, and comes from the exact same place as love. That's weird. According to neurologists, hate and love spark the same areas of the brain, but hate actually sparks a more rational part of the brain as well. So it seems love can actually make a person stupid, which makes sense.

A lot of the emotions we feel are all linked together, and feed off of each other. Cain was jealous of Abel, began to hate Abel, and then killed his ass. Not cool.

In this article on the psychology of hate, it defends it as a necessary part of life:

http://goo.gl/IXtI8o

This one from a scientific point of view explains how hate works and manifests itself chemically in the brain.

http://goo.gl/lCBVoN
http://goo.gl/brGoZ

Here's some religious views on Hate:

1 John 4:20:

"If anyone says, "I love God," and hates his brother, he is a liar; for he who does not love his brother whom he has seen cannot love God whom he has not seen."

Dhammapada:

“Only love dispels hate.”

http://goo.gl/Ai9bbG

Buddha teaches that hate is one of the three poisons.

Holy Quran Chapter 49, Surah Hujuraat verse 13:

“O mankind! We created you from a single (pair) of a male and a female and made you into nations and tribes that ye may know each other (not that ye may despise each other). Verily the most honored of you in the Sight of Allah is (he who is) the most pious amongst you.”

Wikipedia defines hate as:

“Hatred is a deep and emotional extreme dislike that can be directed against individuals, entities, objects, or ideas. Hatred is often associated with feelings of anger and a disposition towards hostility.”

Merriam definition:

“Hate is an intense hostility and aversion usually deriving from fear, anger, or sense of injury.”

http://goo.gl/cdwuKt

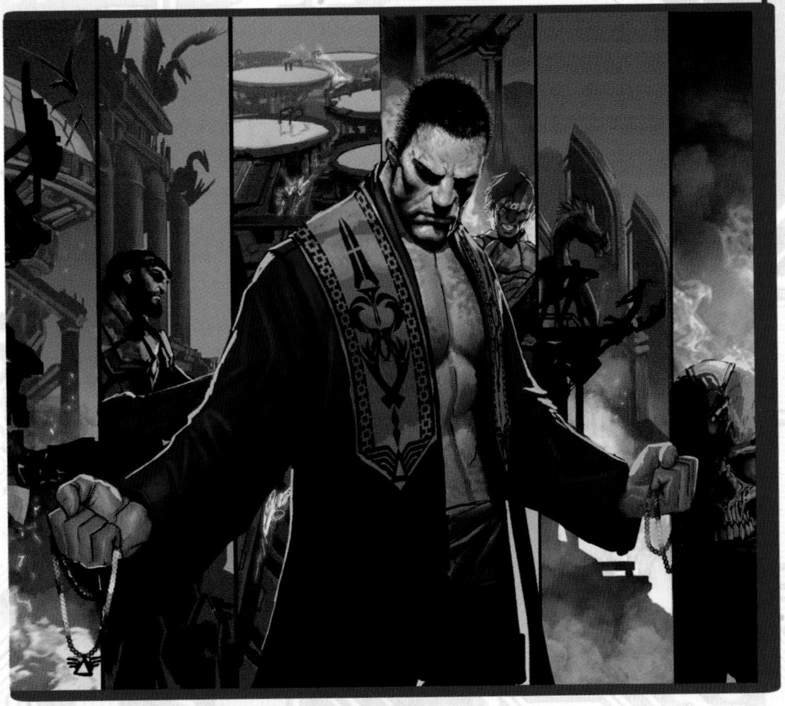

SPEROS CITY SIZE

I frequently use real world examples to make them seem plausible in my stories. Speros City is roughly the size of Chicago.

http://goo.gl/nwPZG

Rank	City	State	Land area (sq mi)	Land area (km□)	Water area (sq mi)	Water area (km□)	Total area (sq mi)	Total area (km□)	Population (2010)
32	Chicago	Illinois	227.1	588.3	6.9	17.8	234.0	606.1	2,695,598

I've never written a comic book without using narrative until issue #9 of this series. I wanted to challenge myself and see if I could pull it off. It's the middle of an arc, so I think it works. I don't plan on it becoming an ongoing thing - I like conveying info too much through the narrative to abandon it. When working with such a brilliant artist as Stjepan Sejic, the art tells the story anyway.

You may have noticed that the world is WIDE open now! It was always the plan to introduce the other broader elements once we got a sense of who Aphrodite was. Immediately following this volume, Stjepan and I will have the *Aphrodite IX/Cyber Force* cross-over completed, and then we're launching a new title setup in the same future-world timeline. It seemed disingenuous to keep calling it *Aphrodite IX* when it will be about multiple characters. Instead, we're calling it *IXth Generation*. Point being: same team, same basic story, but with a lot of new characters introduced in this arc.

WIPE THEM FROM EARTH ONCE AND FOR ALL

Continuing the religious conversion of Marcus and his people, I thought it would be amusingly ironic to have Marcus say almost the exact same thing Executor Chronos did in the first arc when preparing for their "final assault." I can say this - things aren't looking good for the cyborgs right now.

MOTHER

Not going to spoil what's going on with this, but I'm obsessed with Artificial Intelligence right now. I'm looking forward to this Johnny Depp movie Transcendence coming up; I hope it's good. Mother is an A.I. that ties deeply into both *Cyber Force* and *Aphrodite IX*. It's not the obvious answer, but it makes sense.

ARTIFICIAL INTELLIGENCE (AI)

Its definition is, "the study and design of intelligent agents" according to most scientists. Most of us had our first brush of A.I. with the HAL computer in *2001: A Space Odyssey*. It's always weird to me that year is now in our past. *Blade Runner* is another great movie, and it is set in 2019 Los Angeles (5 years from now). Somehow I don't think the city will look like that in the next five years, but you never know. The biggest question with A.I. is: will it be smarter than humans? What happens when it starts evolving on its own? Dr. Kaku talks a lot about A.I., and his primary contention is that A.I. will be indifferent to humans, which can be its own set of horrors if you think about it. What are the fears of A.I., and are they realistic? In the *Terminator* storyline, A.I. gets to the point where it realizes the world would be better off without humans, and Skynet decides to wipe us out. In *The Matrix* A.I. turns us into Duracells. Should we fear A.I.? I think for the most part no, but that doesn't make for good movies, now does it?

This article has some interesting fears outlaid about where A.I. could go wrong:

http://goo.gl/K2W35g

Some other interesting A.I. pieces:

http://goo.gl/4WFKub
http://goo.gl/jAO1zO

Last one I'll share, but this one talks about how the real fear is that we will lose free will by turning to A.I. An interesting hypothesis:

http://goo.gl/9tIL5o

OMEGA PROTOCOL

I know someone out there is thinking that I rehash the same titles between my books. In *Think Tank* we have an "OMEGA" pathogen delivery system. I didn't want to use the term "OMEGA" here in *Aphrodite*, but it just makes sense. The Bible talks about the Alpha and the Omega - the beginning and the end. There are so many philosophical and religious overtones to this book that I've sprinkled those kinds of terms in (hopefully without offending too many people). Using these apocryphal titles just makes sense.

VIOLENCE

Another overriding theme in this book is that violence is the only real catalyst for change. I believe this to be true. There are so few instances where non-violent resistance had any effect, that after you list Gandhi and MLK, most people can't think of another one. I'm not a big fan of this site *debate.org*, but it has some interesting points and counterpoints on violence:

http://goo.gl/sRrgxA

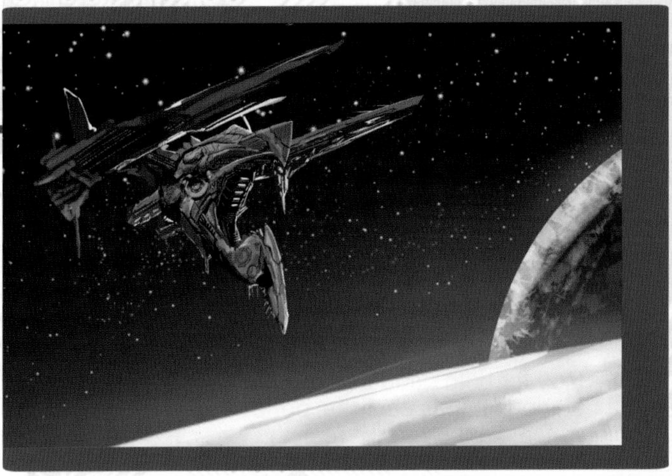

SANCTUARIES

Thought I'd just roll these out here since we give them out in this issue. We teased them in the *Aphrodite IX: Hidden Files* book, but here they are:

I	Hades IX and XV	ORBIT
II	Apollo IX and XV	EARTH
III	Ares IX	ORBIT
IV	Artemis IX	EARTH
V	Hermes IX and XV	ORBIT
VI	Aphrodite XV	EARTH
VII	Athena IX and XV	ORBIT
VIII	Poseidon XV	EARTH
IX	Ares XV & Artemis XV	EARTH (most secure at Millennium City)
X	Aphrodite IX	EARTH (most secure at Millennium City)
XI	Poseidon IX	ORBIT
XII	Hephaestus IX & XV	PLATFORM WAS IN ORBIT BUT DESTROYED
XIII	?	?

Stjepan did a phenomenal job on designing all of the IXs and the XVs. Here's all I gave him, and you can see on the spread what he came up with!

Aphrodite (F) – green hair female, assassin, subterfuge/infiltration (white)
Artemis (M) – red hair male, ranged assault uses lightning bow (white)
Ares (M) – black hair, male melee combat (Hispanic)
Apollo (M) – white hair male priest/healer/doctor/medic (East Indian but white hair)
Athena (F) – white/platinum blonde hair female defense/strategy (ethnic skin tone but white hair—like Filipina/Latina)
Hades (F) – black hair female enforcer/jailer/executioner/psionic power (ASIAN)
Hephaestus (M) – grey hair male weapons builder/technology (DEAD)
Poseidon (M) – blue hair male special ops navy seal types (ASIAN)
Hermes (F) – red hair female recon (WHITE)

The overall idea for this was to use Greek and Roman mythology and combine them into a Sci-Fi futuristic set up in the apocalyptic dystopian world we've set up. Lots of good stuff to come! Again, I appreciate you voting for this book with your hard earned dollars. Publishing independent comics ain't easy, so if you'd be so kind as to recommend this book to a friend, we'd greatly appreciate it.

BRAIN ALTERATION

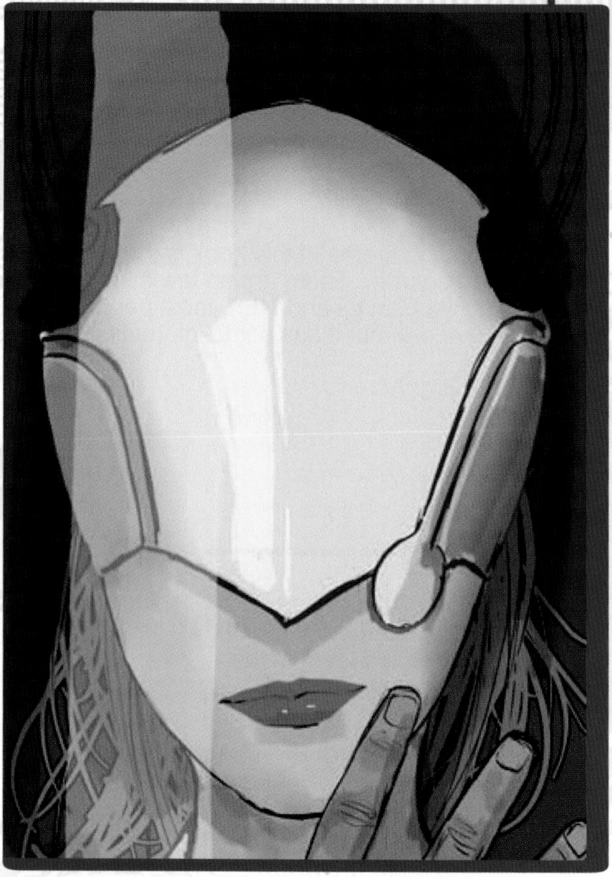

As you've surmised by reading this issue, some of the truth behind what happened to Aphrodite and what is going to happen is starting to come out. Her mind has been altered. Why and for what ends you'll have to read next issue, but is this possible? The answer is that yes it is, and almost possible now. Scary, eh?

"Some researchers are working with combat veterans, car-accident survivors and rape victims to replace their memories with less fear-filled ones using a familiar hypertension drug. Other scientists are studying whether behavioral therapy can one day be used to modify memories of people who react with fear to common anxiety-producing events. A person bitten by a dog as a child, for instance, might be able to overcome a canine phobia if the old memory can be replaced with a less scary one."

That's what they say it's for. I, because I love conspiracy, would think it has many other uses. Humans tend to use technology for both good and evil, so what nefarious things could be done? Could you implant romantic feelings for you into someone that has rejected you? This is just one of the myriad of manipulative things I came up with when I started thinking about this. What if you could implant a submissive nature into your kid? Make them like or dislike things? So many things that could be done…mind blown, heh.

http://www.americanscientist.org/science/pub/can-you-alter-your-memory
http://www.sciencedaily.com/releases/2012/09/120919125736.htm
http://www.kurzweilai.net/your-memory-can-be-altered-by-interfering-information

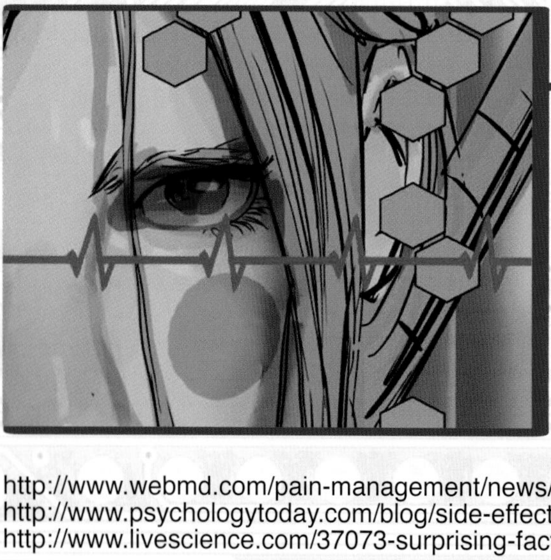

PLACEBO EFFECT

How many of you have wanted some coffee (caffeine) to wake up and not be so grumpy…and immediately felt better after you drank it? Reality is that the caffeine won't hit your bloodstream for about 15-20 more minutes, but our mind speeds up the effect. The mind is a very powerful thing, but also very destructive. We've all heard about placebos in drug trials, but there are versions of this that are emotional and experiential as well.

http://www.webmd.com/pain-management/news/20040219/revealed-how-placebo-effect-works
http://www.psychologytoday.com/blog/side-effects/200906/placebos-do-work-lets-consider-why
http://www.livescience.com/37073-surprising-facts-placebo-effect.html

ALTERING PERSONALITY

Memory alteration, placebo, and personality alteration are all key to the story I've been telling with Aphrodite IX. It's amazing how fragile our personalities are. We all think we are who we are and that's how we're going to stay. But the truth is far from that. Concussion, environment, age, toxicity…all things that can radically alter your personality without your even realizing it. There's a guy who used to work for Top Cow who had a brain aneurism who was from the South. He had relocated to Los Angeles, and after surgery he had to relearn how to speak in Los Angeles. He spoke differently, took a different name, and acted differently after that…to the point where his mother refused to talk to him for a bit.

http://www.psychologytoday.com/blog/professor-cromer-learns-read/201203/after-brain-injury-the-dark-side-personality-change-part-i
http://www.nbcnews.com/health/health-news/different-person-personality-change-often-brain-injurys-hidden-toll-f8C11152322

THE BRAIN

We're in a revolutionary time right now where we've learned more about the brain in the last 20 years than we did in the past 10,000 years. It's an exciting time, but I'm always amazed at how most people don't even really grasp how the brain works. This link is an easy to understand explanation of how it works - read it!

http://science.howstuffworks.com/life/inside-the-mind/human-brain/brain.htm
http://www.sciencedirect.com/science/journal/00068993

APHRODITE PROTOCOL

Since this arc is at its end and there have been some major revelations in this volume, I wanted to talk about the Protocol a little bit. What is the Aphrodite Protocol? What has been revealed so far is that it was designed by Francesca Taylor in the late 20th/early 21st centuries as part of the Millennium City project via her company Cyber Data International, or CDI for short. They discovered that the world was going to have an extinction level event based on a bunch of things, but mainly through mathematical calculation. The Protocol was a complicated plan that included geopolitical, social, and personnel (removal via assassination) changes that extended out this "end date". Their plan was to create food and people that would survive this apocalypse and ultimately repopulate the Earth at some point in the future, as regular humans would not be able to. That may be an oversimplification, but it was the basic idea. One of the more fascinating concepts of the Protocol was that they KNEW in advance that they didn't have the technology to make it happen, but they proceeded with the idea that they would when they needed it. This isn't far-fetched, read the next section.

EXPECTED TECH ADVANCEMENT

As mentioned, this is a major part of the Protocol and has been used by tech companies NOW since the 70's. The best example is Moore's Law: "the simplified version of this law states that processor speeds, or overall processing power for computers will double every two years." That was taken from the link below, and you can read up on it there. Companies have been anticipating tech advances in their product launches and "generations" of models for things now for decades. That generation thing sound familiar? That's been a huge part of *Aphrodite* and *Cyber Force*. What do you do with a person if they become obsolete? Heady questions.

http://www.mooreslaw.org/

THE MEEK SHALL INHERIT THE EARTH

Now this is pretty awesome and I have to admit it wasn't my idea. Marc Silvestri and I were bouncing around ideas for both *Cyber Force* and *Aphrodite IX*, and I was following a thread about dominance and how one of these two groups would wipe out the other. I explained to him everything I was doing, and he asked me if I'd considered reversing that. I hadn't, and asked why and he tossed out those six words, "The meek shall inherit the Earth". Now, I stared at him for a second with my mind spinning at the idea. He said quickly, "If you don't like that--" to which I interrupted and said "NO THAT'S F—ING AWESOME". And we went with it, and I think it's a more fitting ending that works with everything going on.

EDUCATIONAL USE OF MY BOOKS

As a general note, if you have a legitimate use for one of our books for educational purposes, even if it's not officially sanctioned, I'll most likely grant it and send you a PDF you can use for free. As a rule, I generally wait six months post release date before I allow that, but feel free to hit me up on Twitter or Facebook and ask.

And that's all she wrote! Thanks again to all ya'll that have supported this book, and I look forward to seeing you on the con circuit.

Carpe Diem,

Matt Hawkins
Please pester me on any of my feeds...or Stjepan on his!
@topcowmatt   @stjepansejic
https://www.facebook.com/Selfloathingnarcissist   http://nebezial.deviantart.com/
https://www.facebook.com/pages/Aphrodite-IX/452004668191047
https://plus.google.com/+topcow

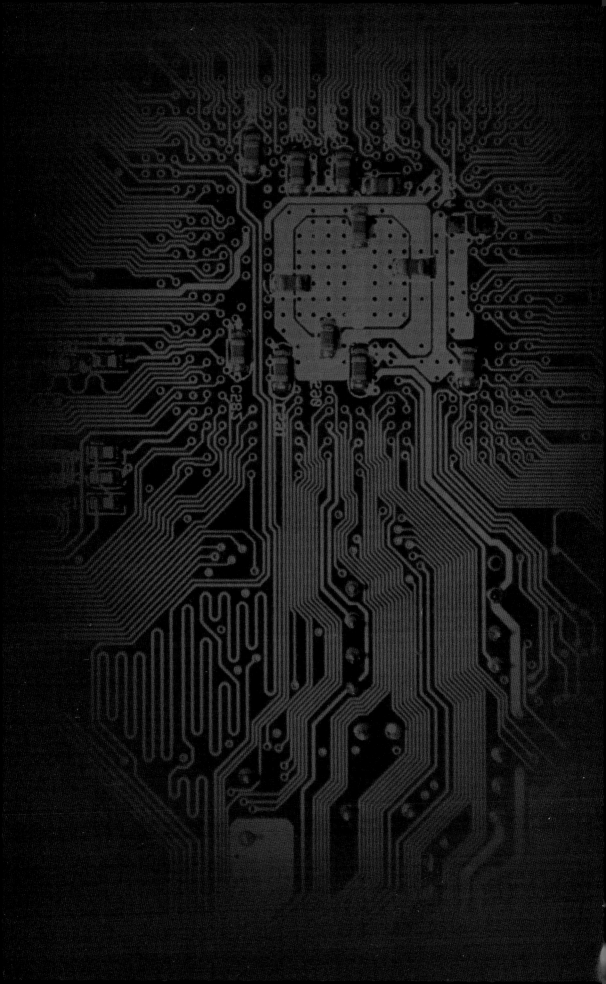

COVER GALLERY

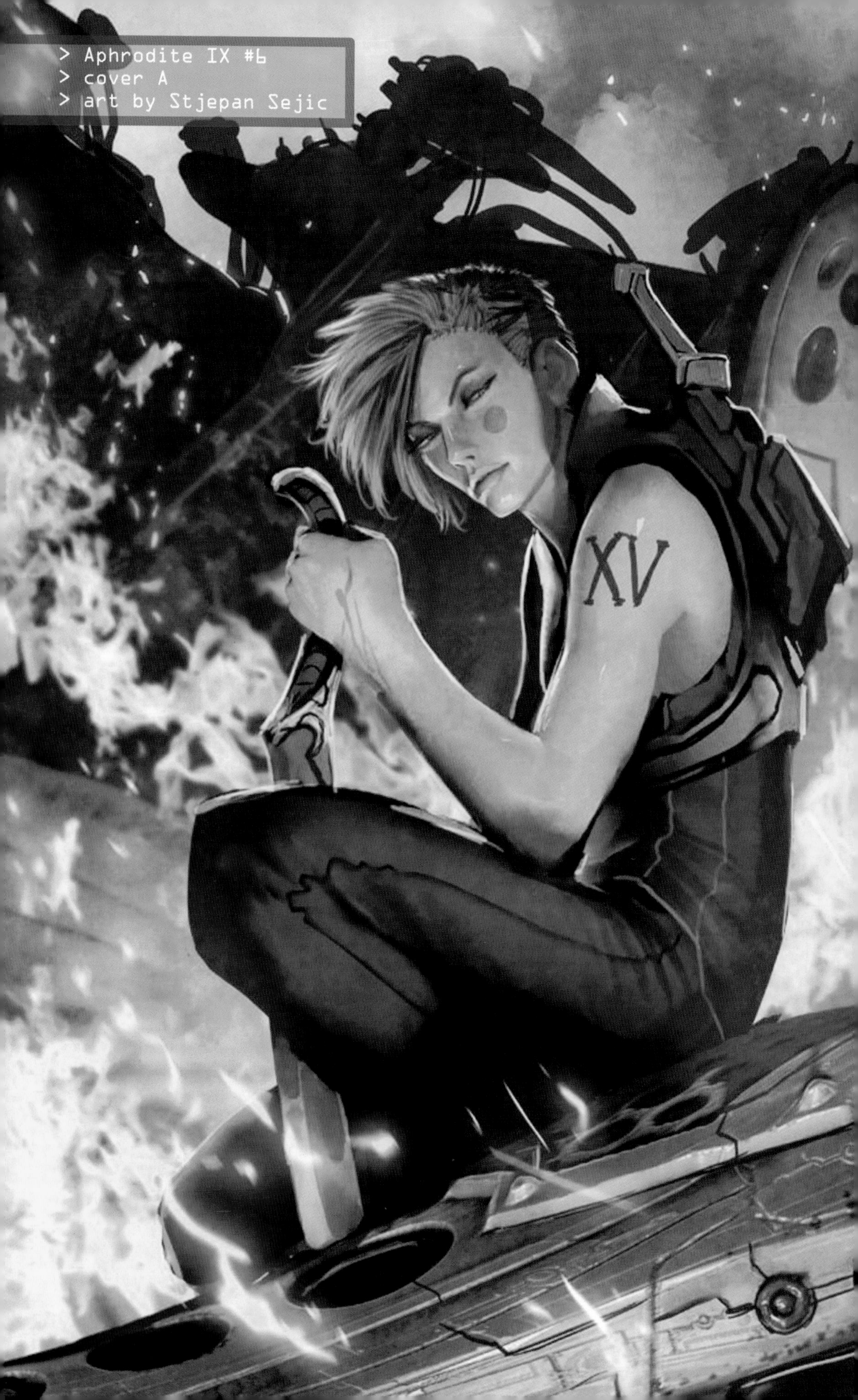
XV

> Aphrodite IX #6
> cover A
> art by Stjepan Sejic

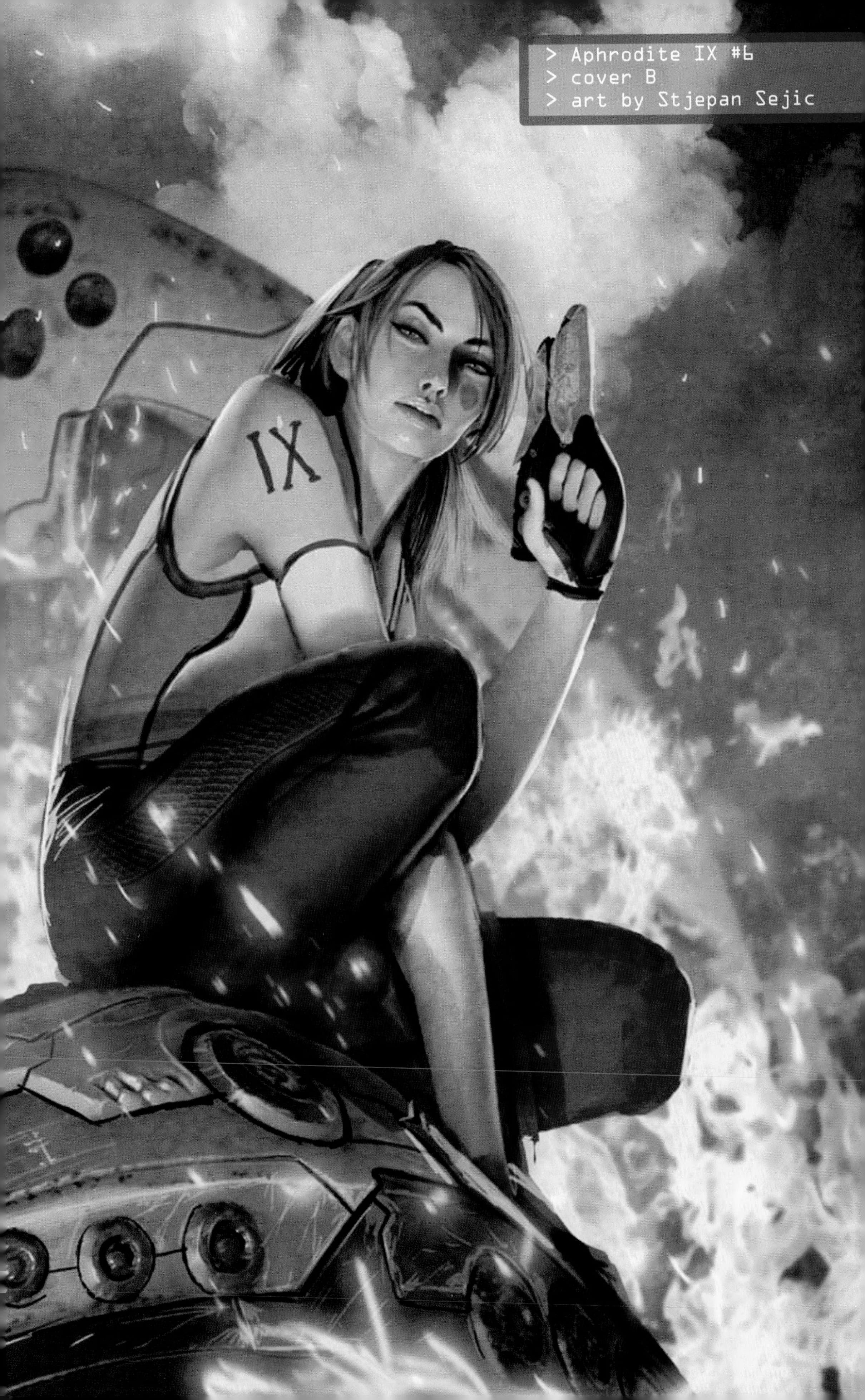
IX
> Aphrodite IX #6
> cover B
> art by Stjepan Sejic

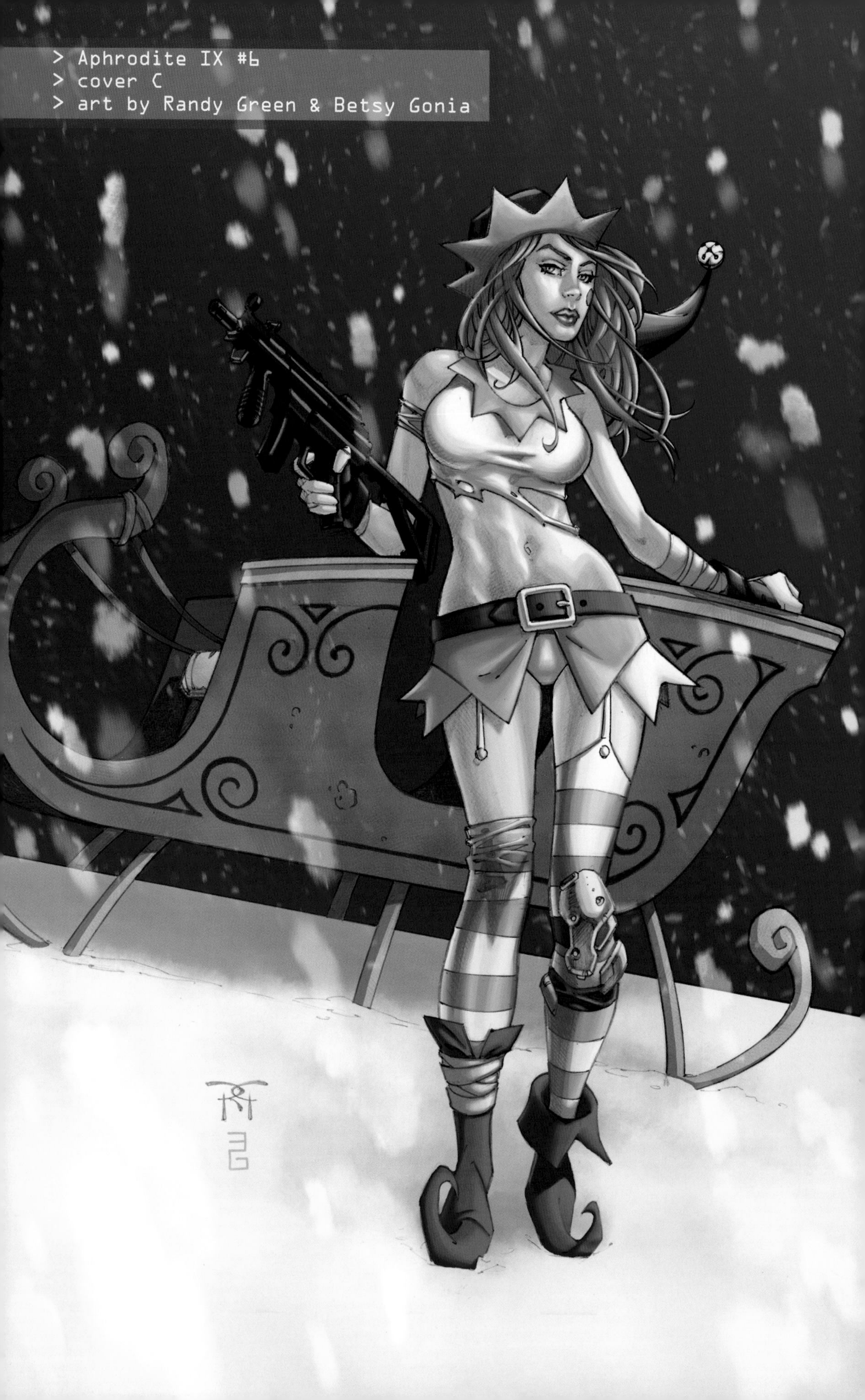

> Aphrodite IX #6
> cover C
> art by Randy Green & Betsy Gonia

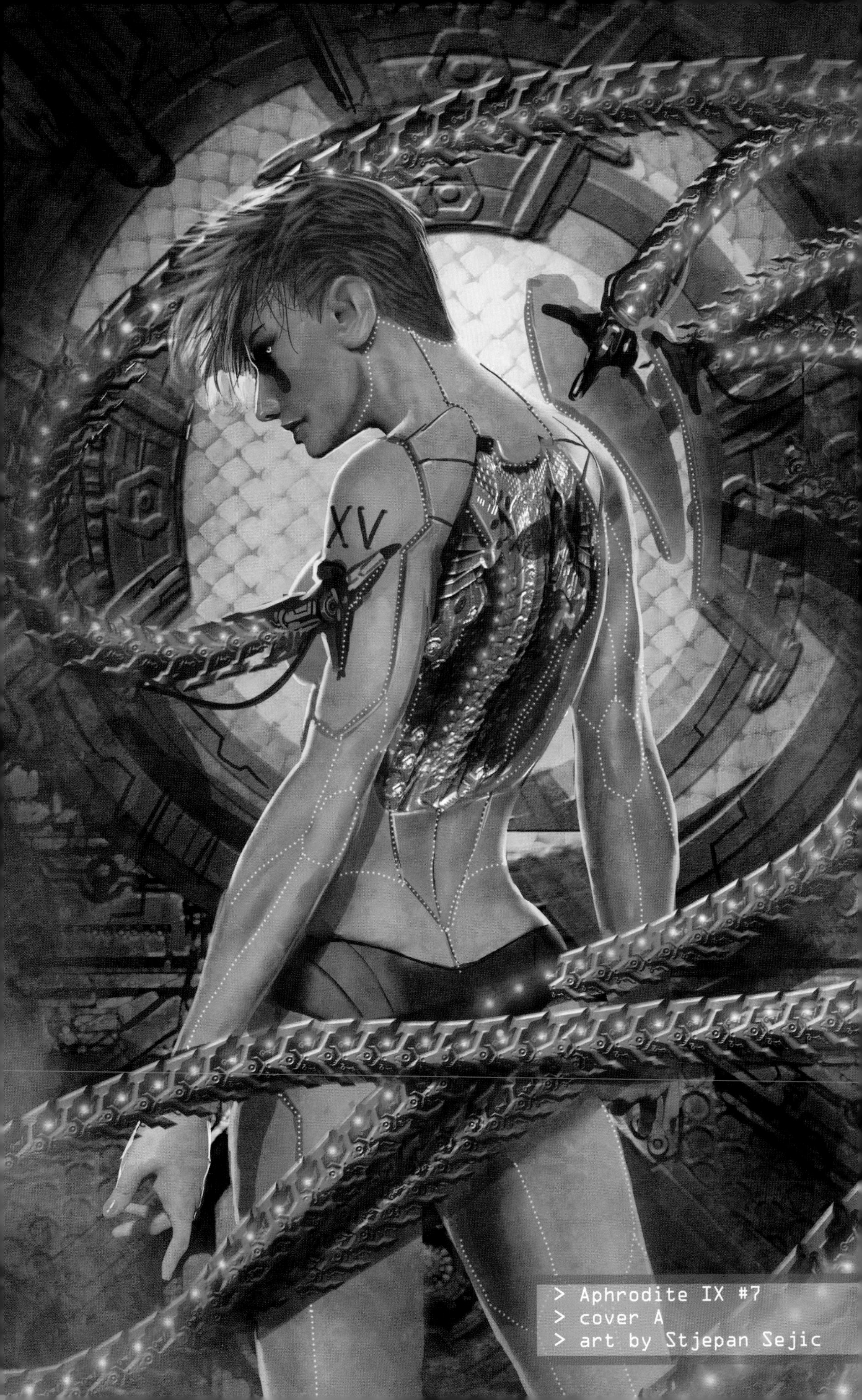
XV

> Aphrodite IX #7
> cover A
> art by Stjepan Sejic

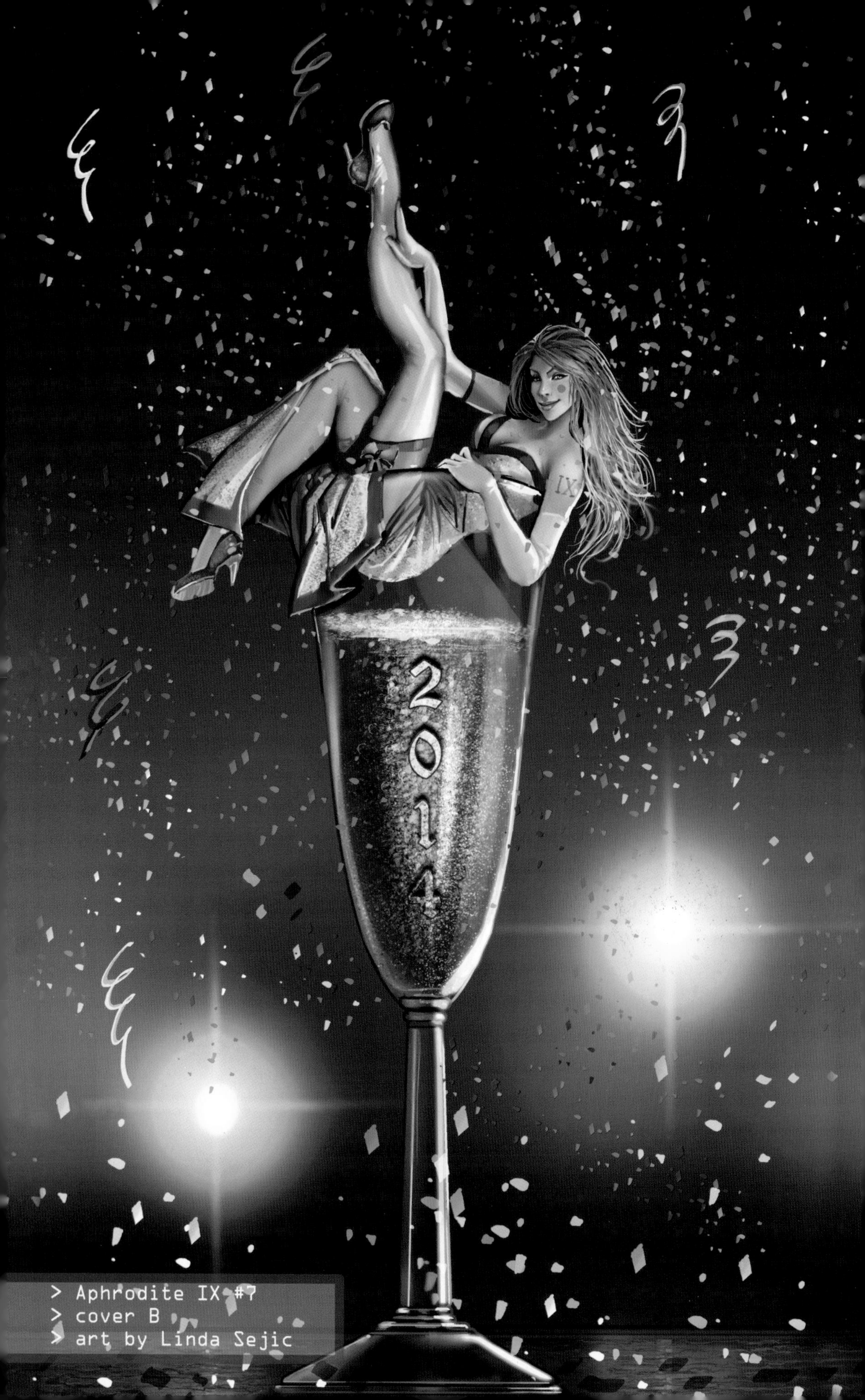
2014

> Aphrodite IX #7
> cover B
> art by Linda Sejic

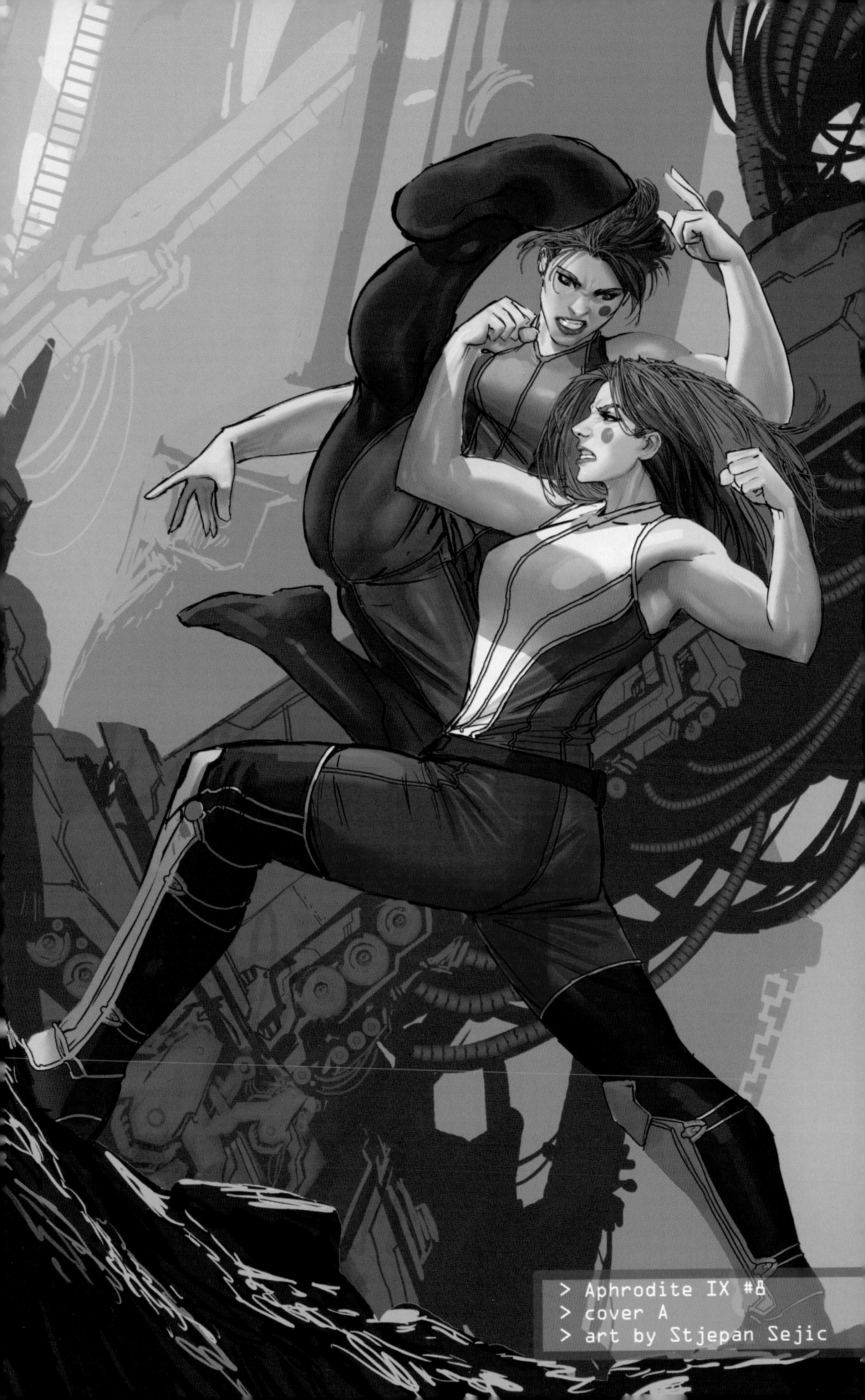

> Aphrodite IX #8
> cover A
> art by Stjepan Sejic

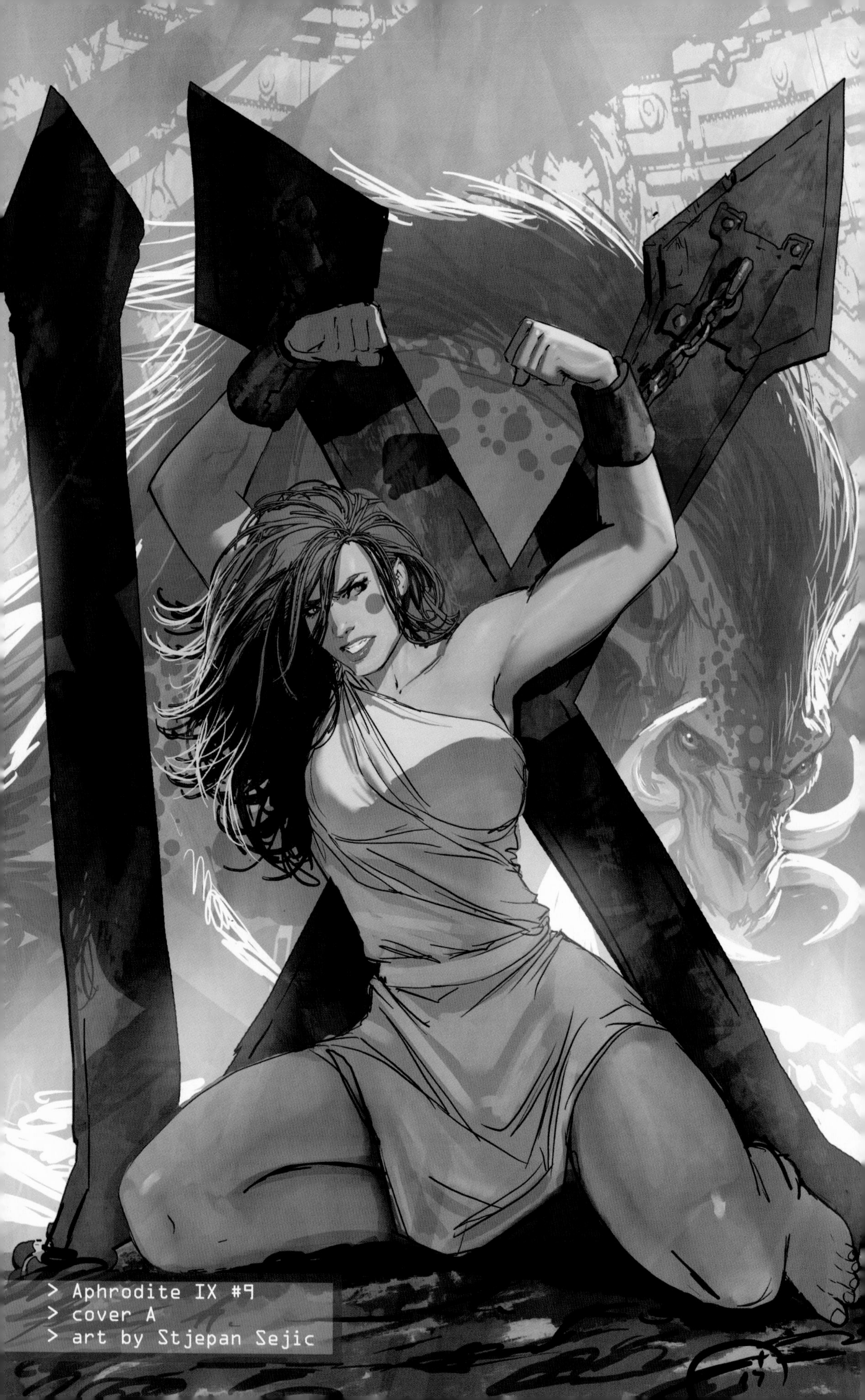

> Aphrodite IX #9
> cover A
> art by Stjepan Sejic

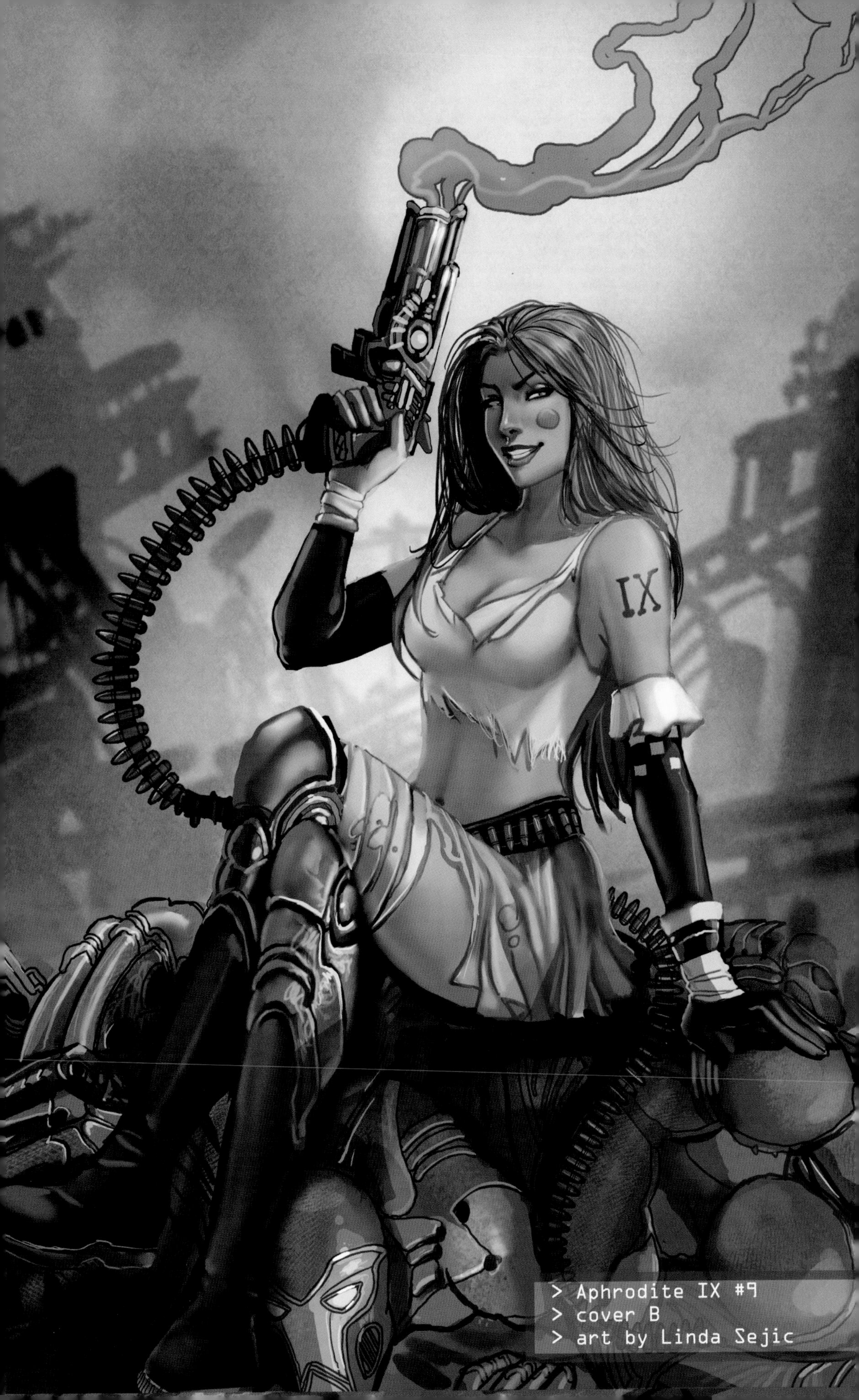
IX

> Aphrodite IX #9
> cover B
> art by Linda Sejic

> Aphrodite IX #9
> cover C
> art by Stjepan Sejic

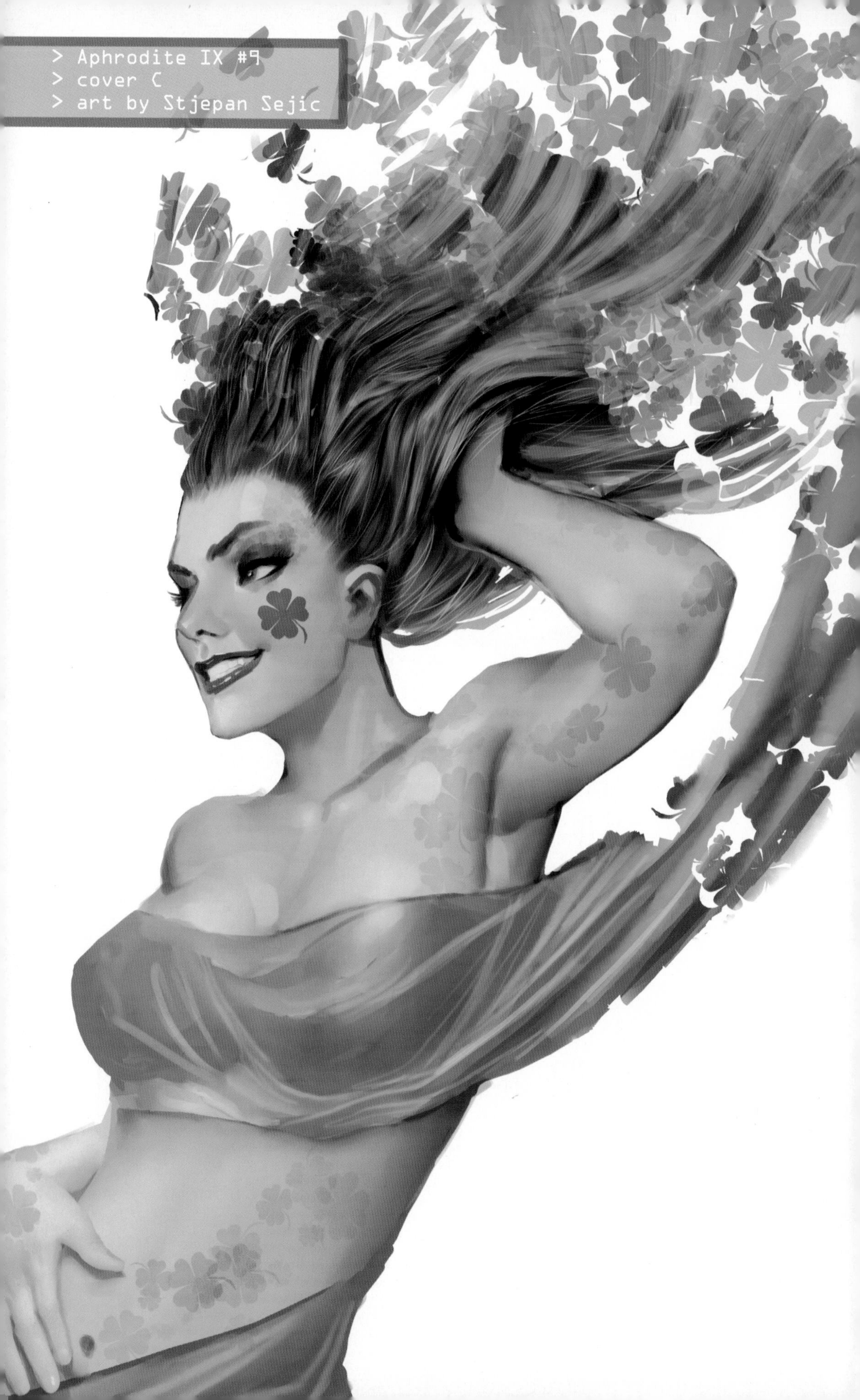

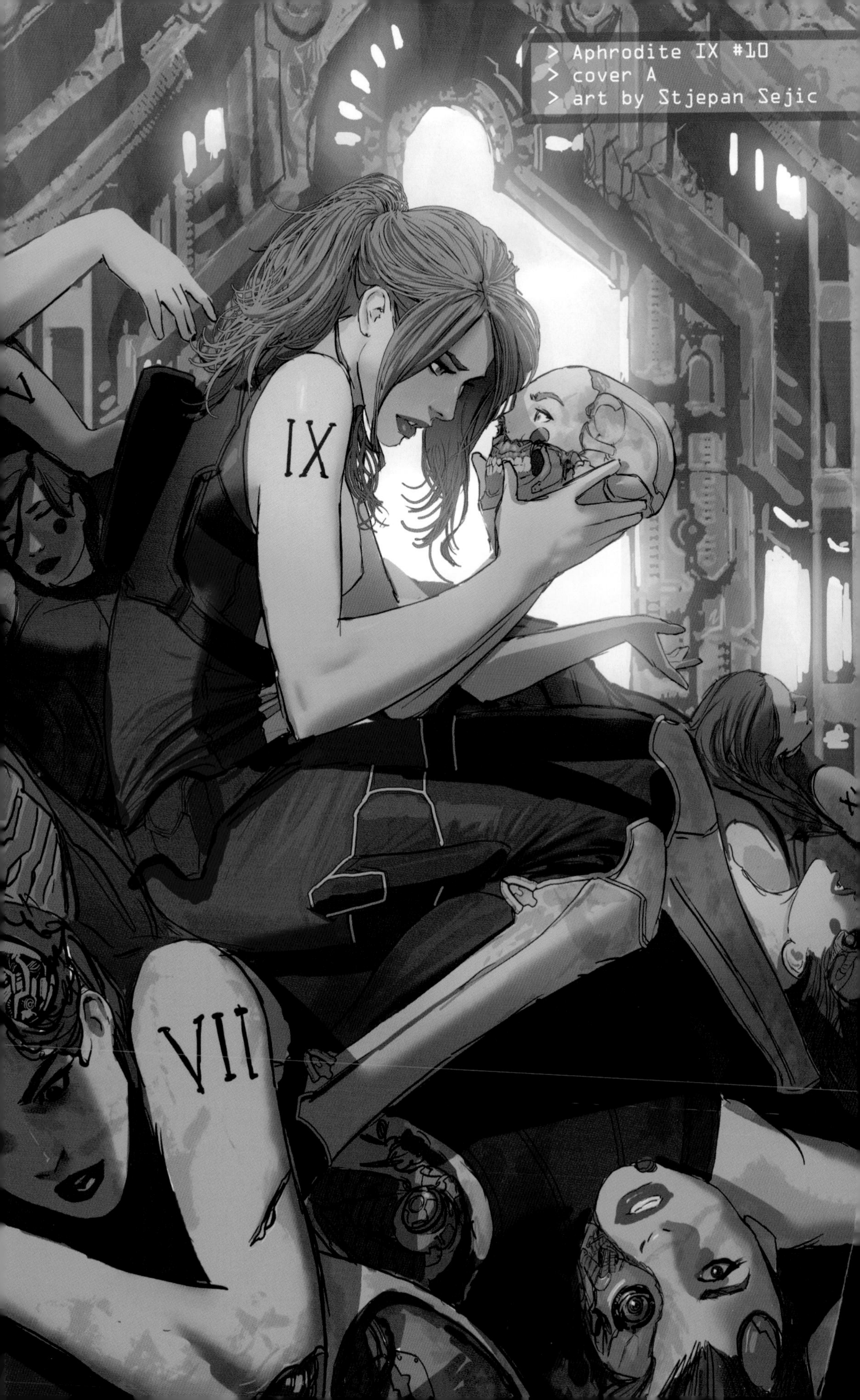
IX
VII

> Aphrodite IX #10
> cover A
> art by Stjepan Sejic

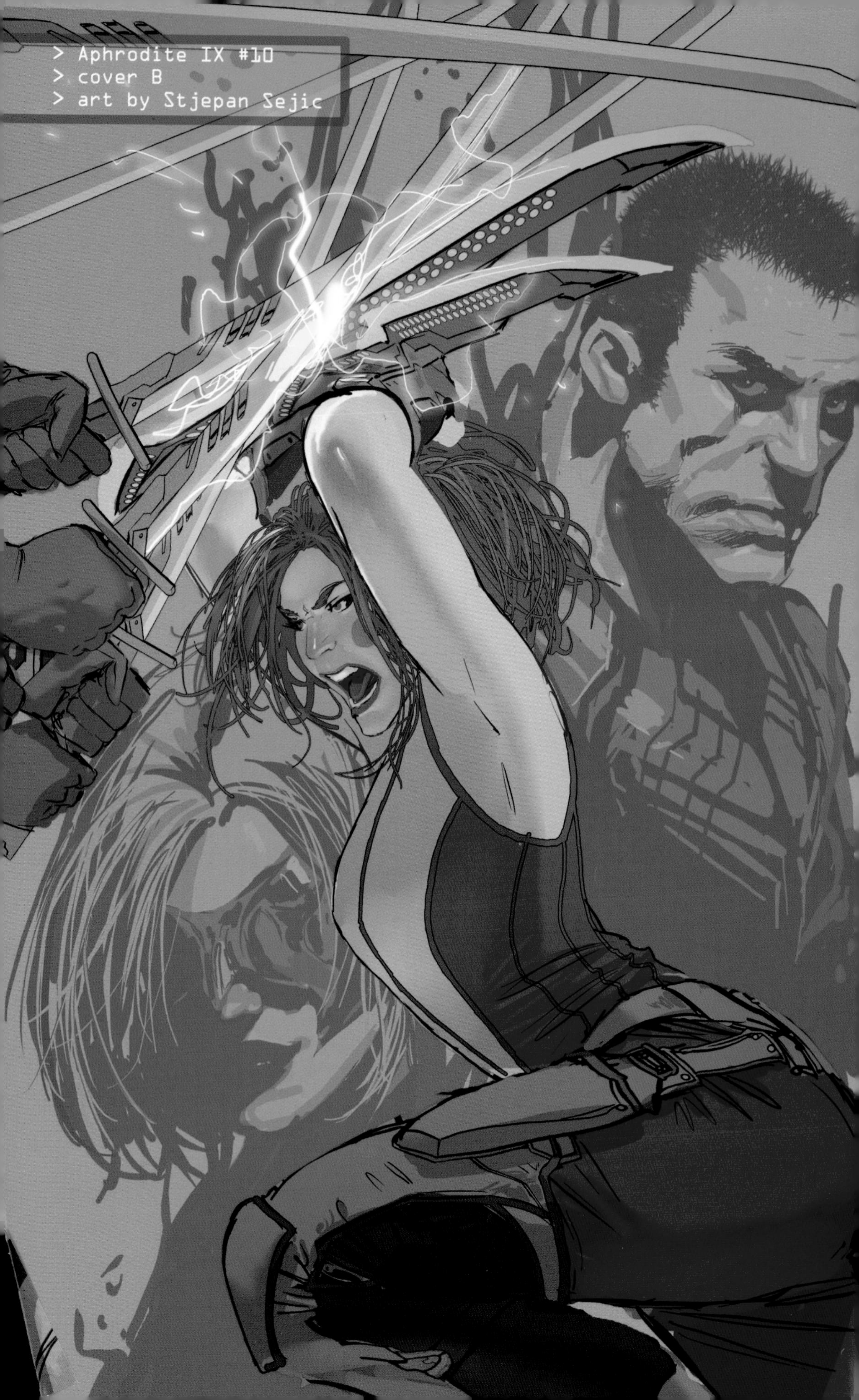
> Aphrodite IX #10
> cover B
> art by Stjepan Sejic

> Aphrodite IX #10
> cover C
> art by Pop Mhan & Betsy Gonia

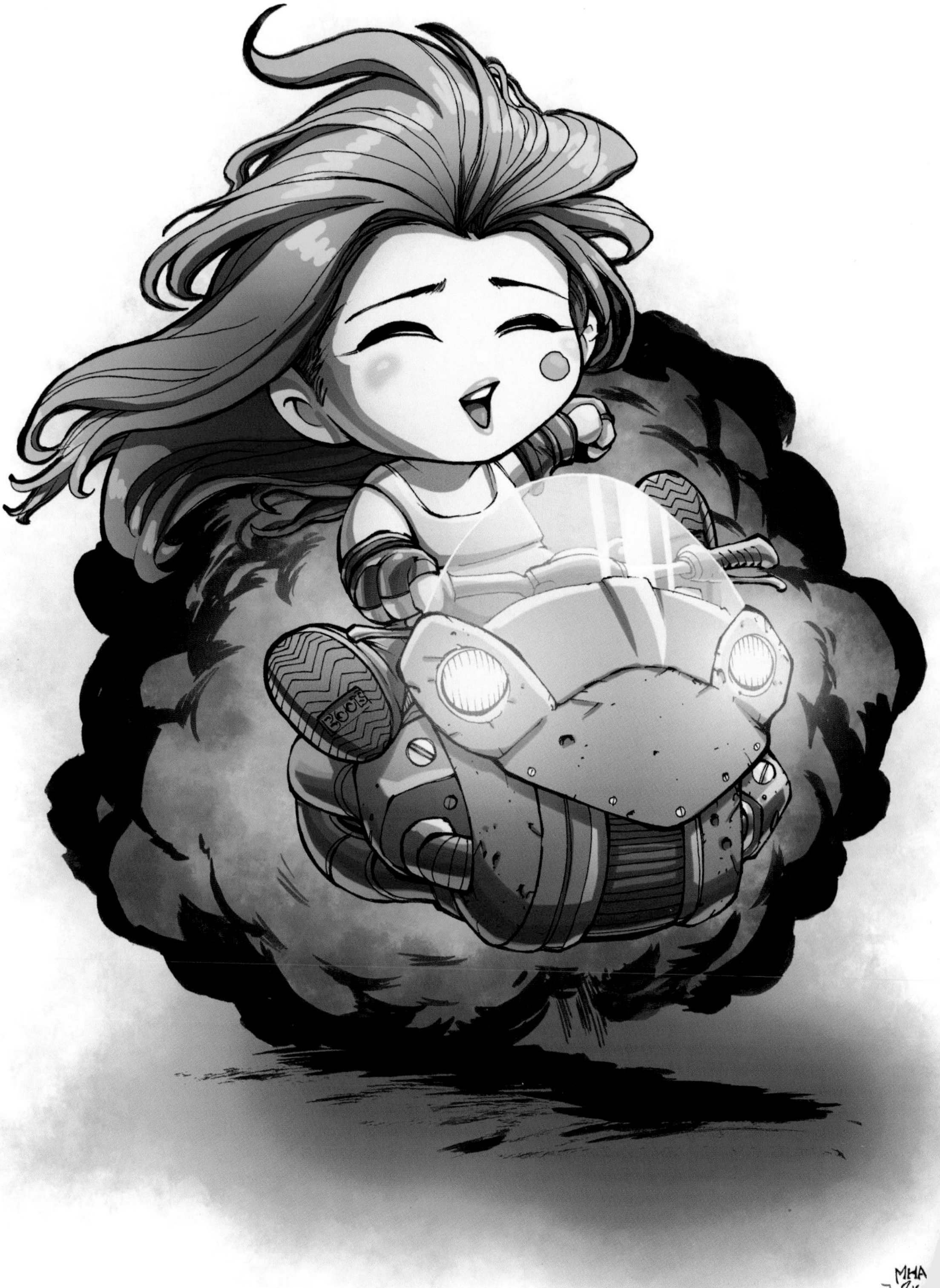

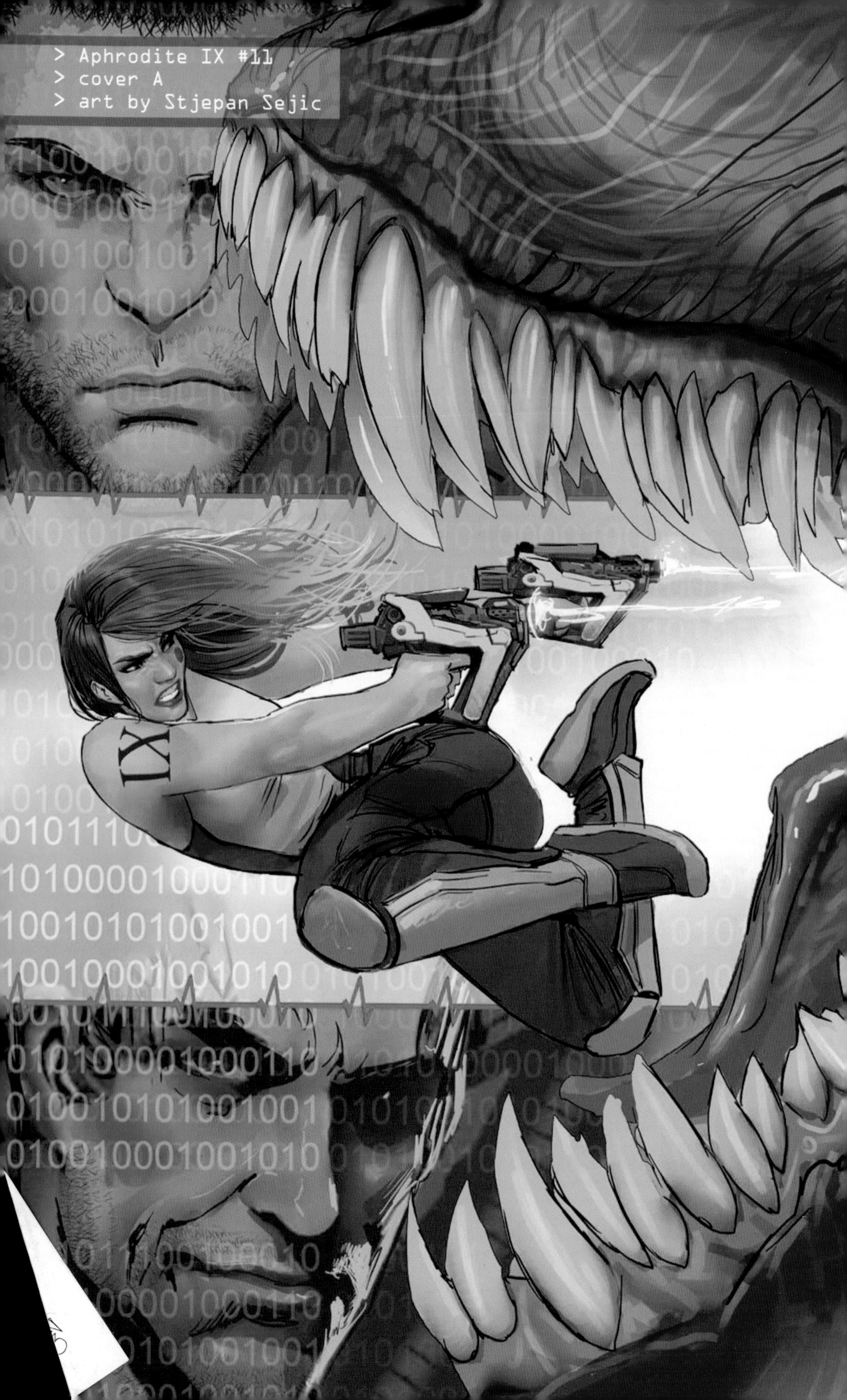

> Aphrodite IX #11
> cover A
> art by Stjepan Sejic

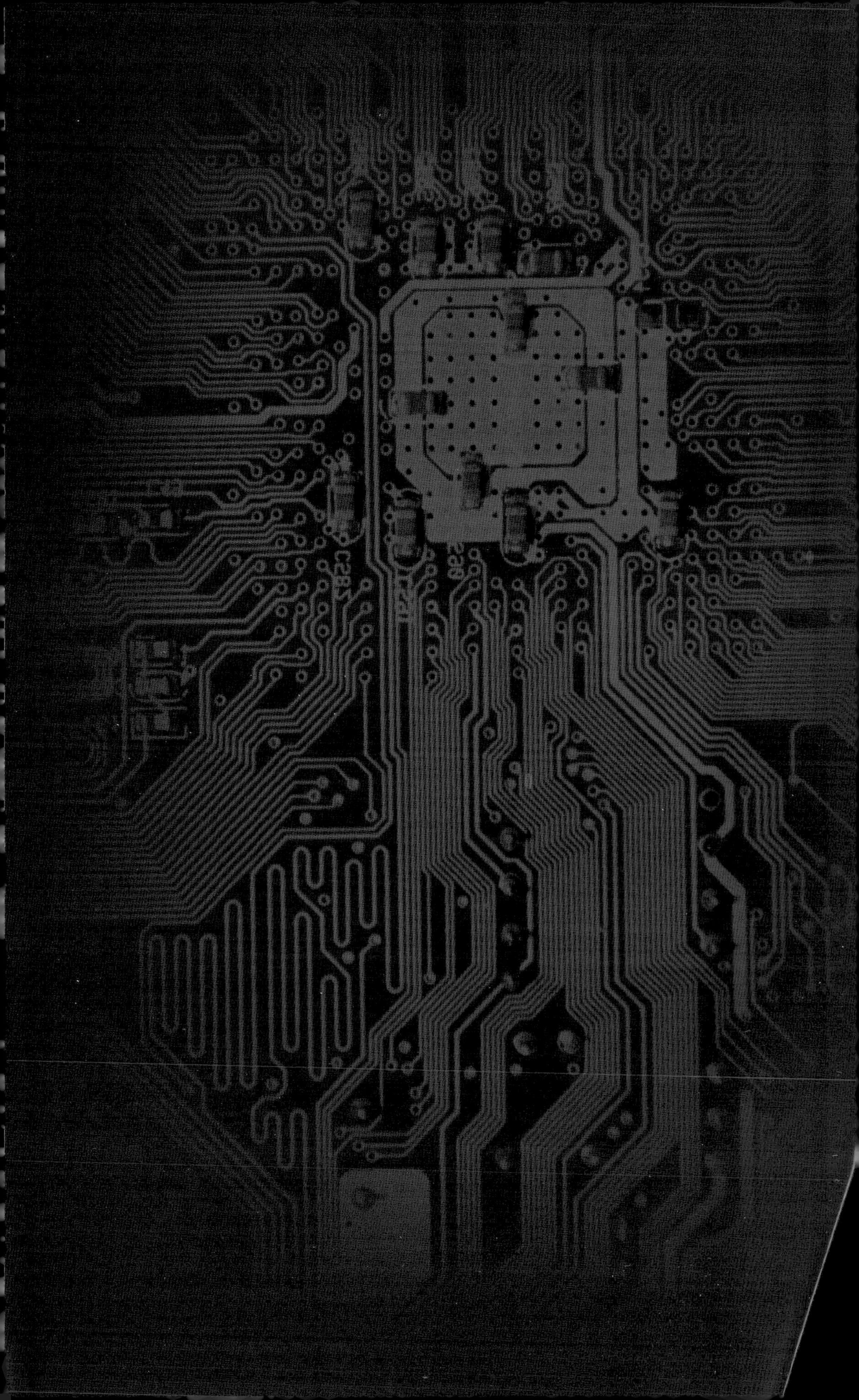

> Aphrodite IX / Cyber Force #1
> cover A
> art by Stjepan Sejic

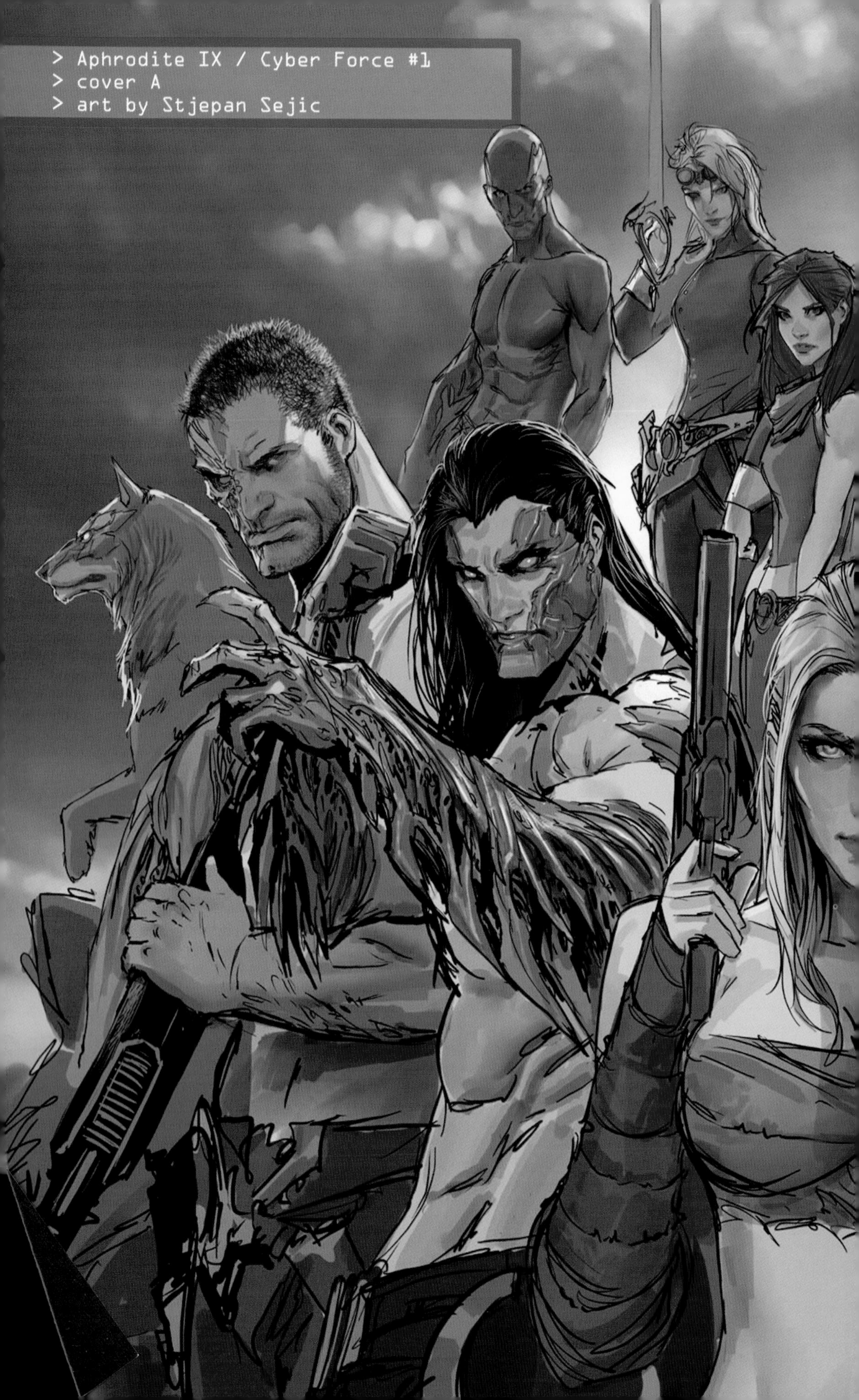

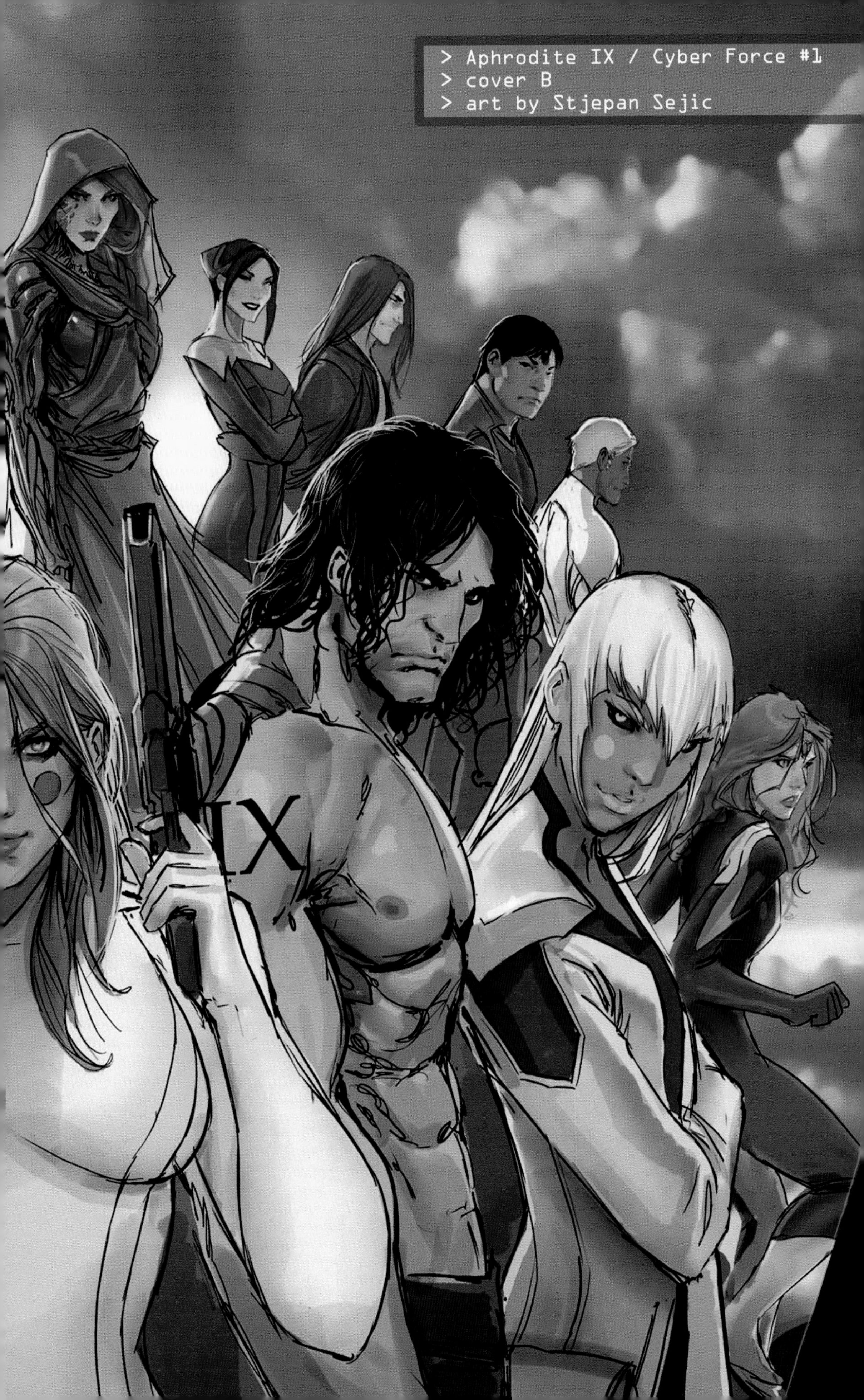
IX

> Aphrodite IX / Cyber Force #1
> cover B
> art by Stjepan Sejic

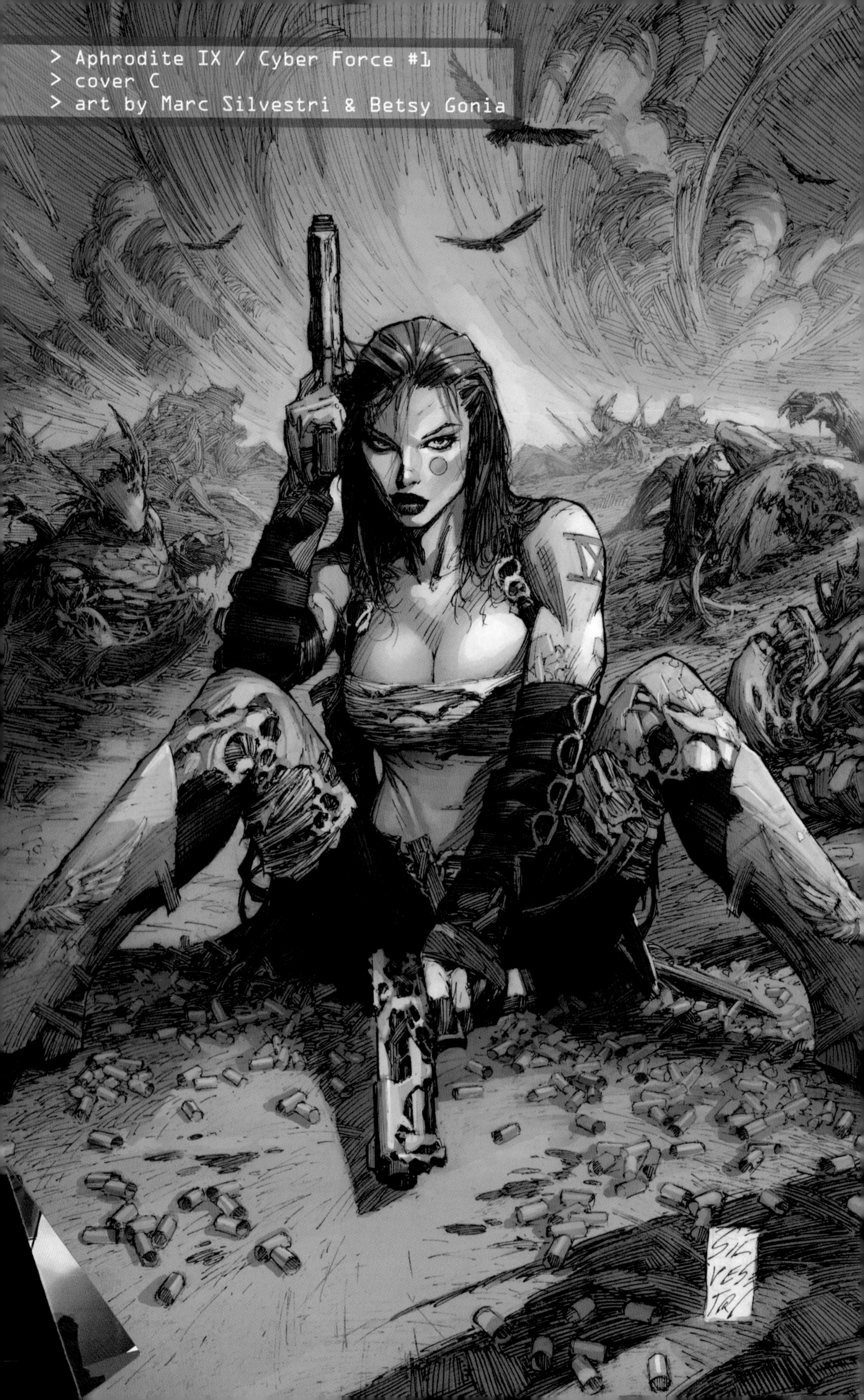
SILVESTRI

> Aphrodite IX / Cyber Force #1
> cover C
> art by Marc Silvestri & Betsy Gonia

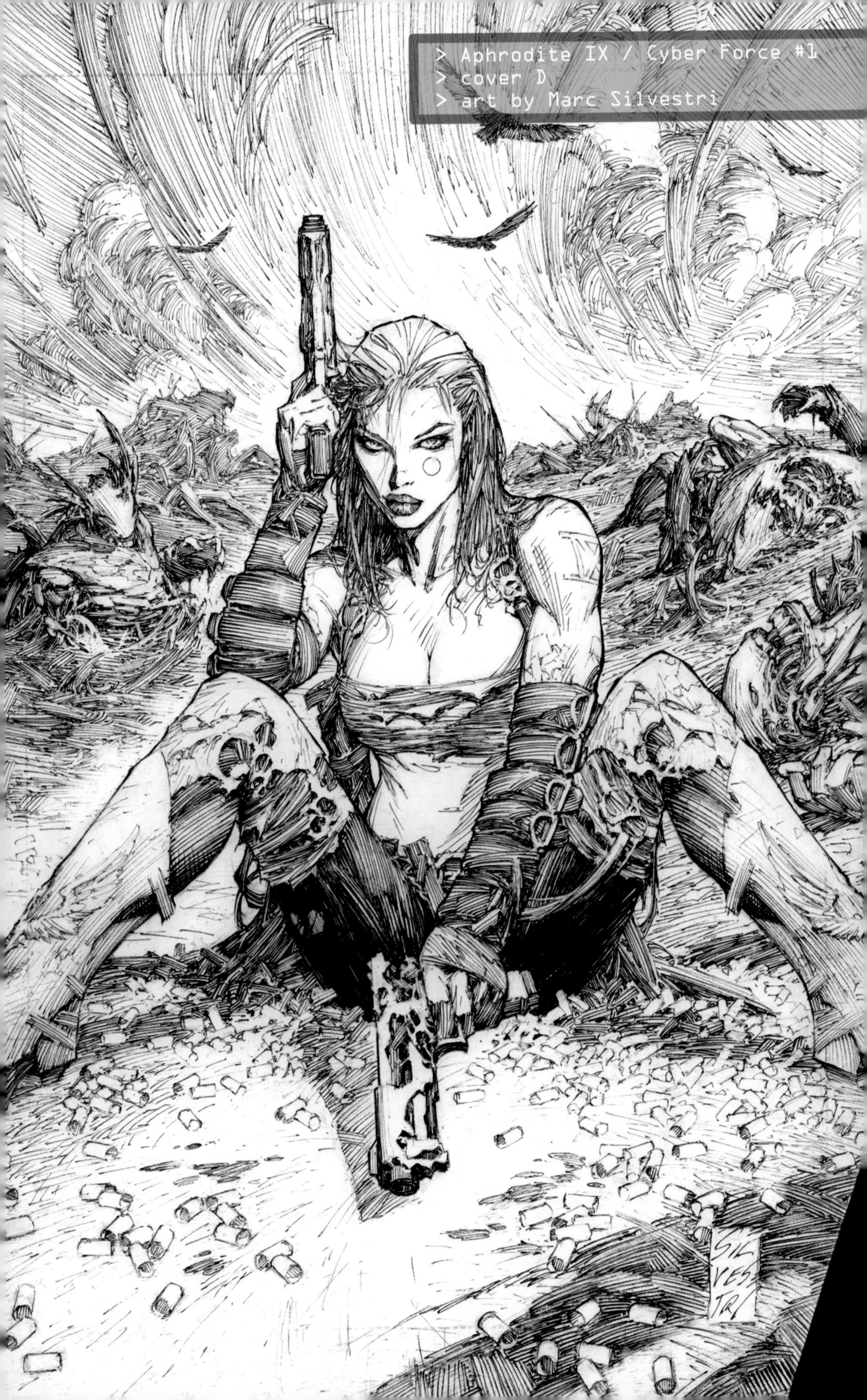

> Aphrodite IX / Cyber Force #1
> cover D
> art by Marc Silvestri

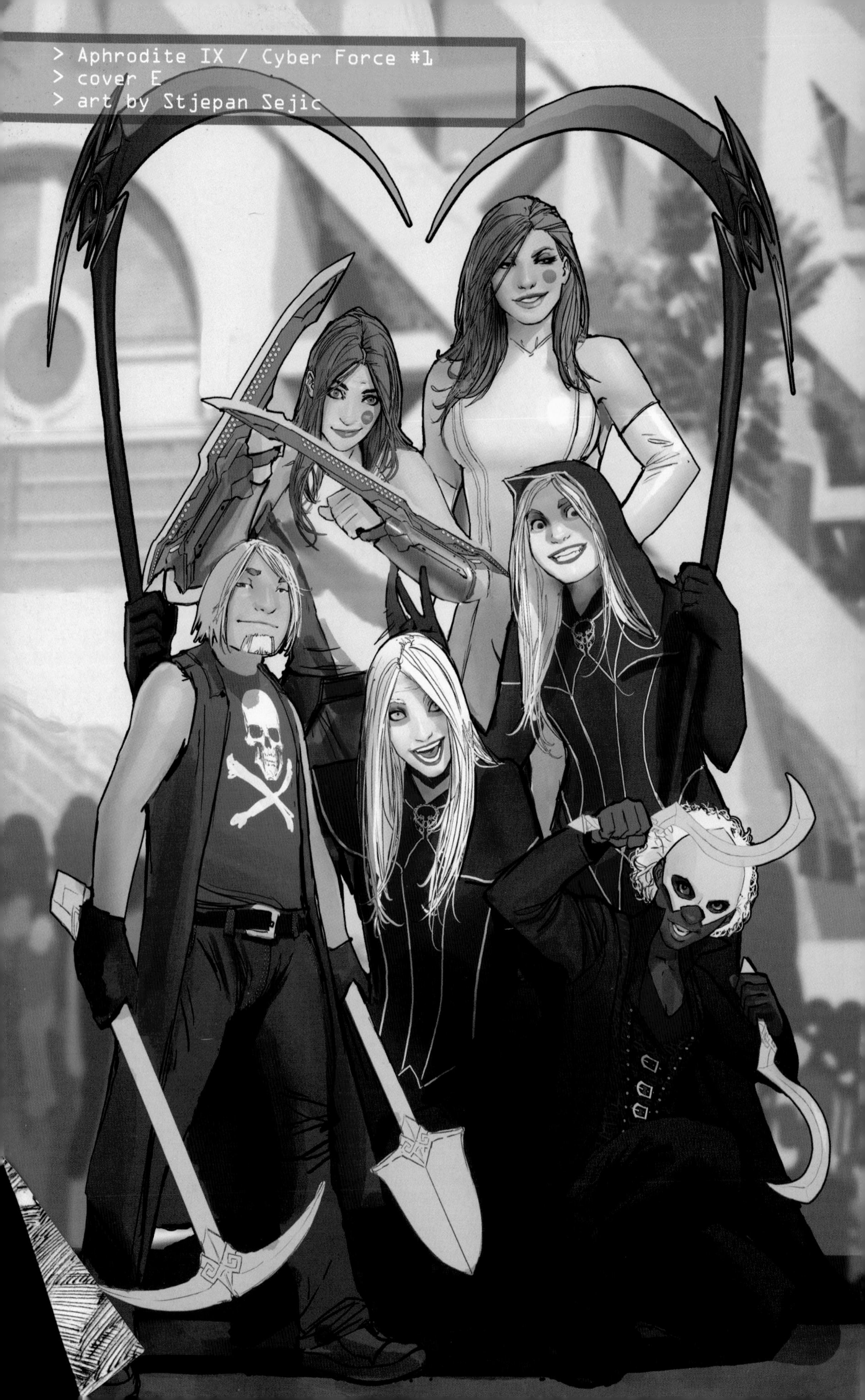

> Aphrodite IX / Cyber Force #1
> cover E
> art by Stjepan Sejic